BOOKS BY TIM FRANKOVICH

Heart of Fire
Until All Curses Are Lifted
Until All Bonds Are Broken
Until All the Gods Return
Until All the Stars Fall

Dragontek Lore
Viridia
Incarnadine
Auric
Onyx
Amaranth
Atramentous
Chroma

The Certainty of Blood
Wolf Chosen

TIM FRANKOVICH

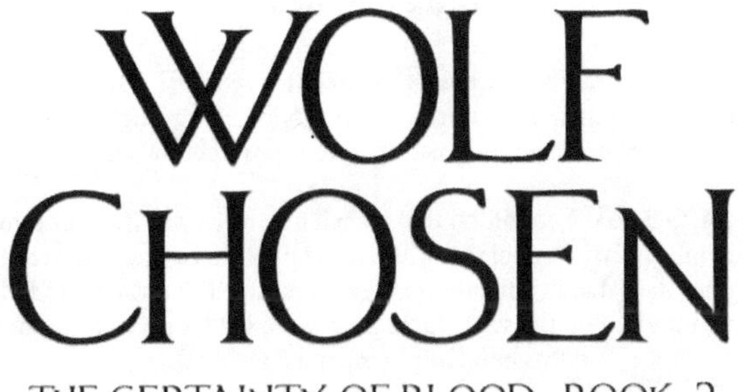

WOLF CHOSEN

THE CERTAINTY OF BLOOD, BOOK 2

*Dedicated to Carl Barks,
who taught me all about
hidden civilizations*

Table of Contents

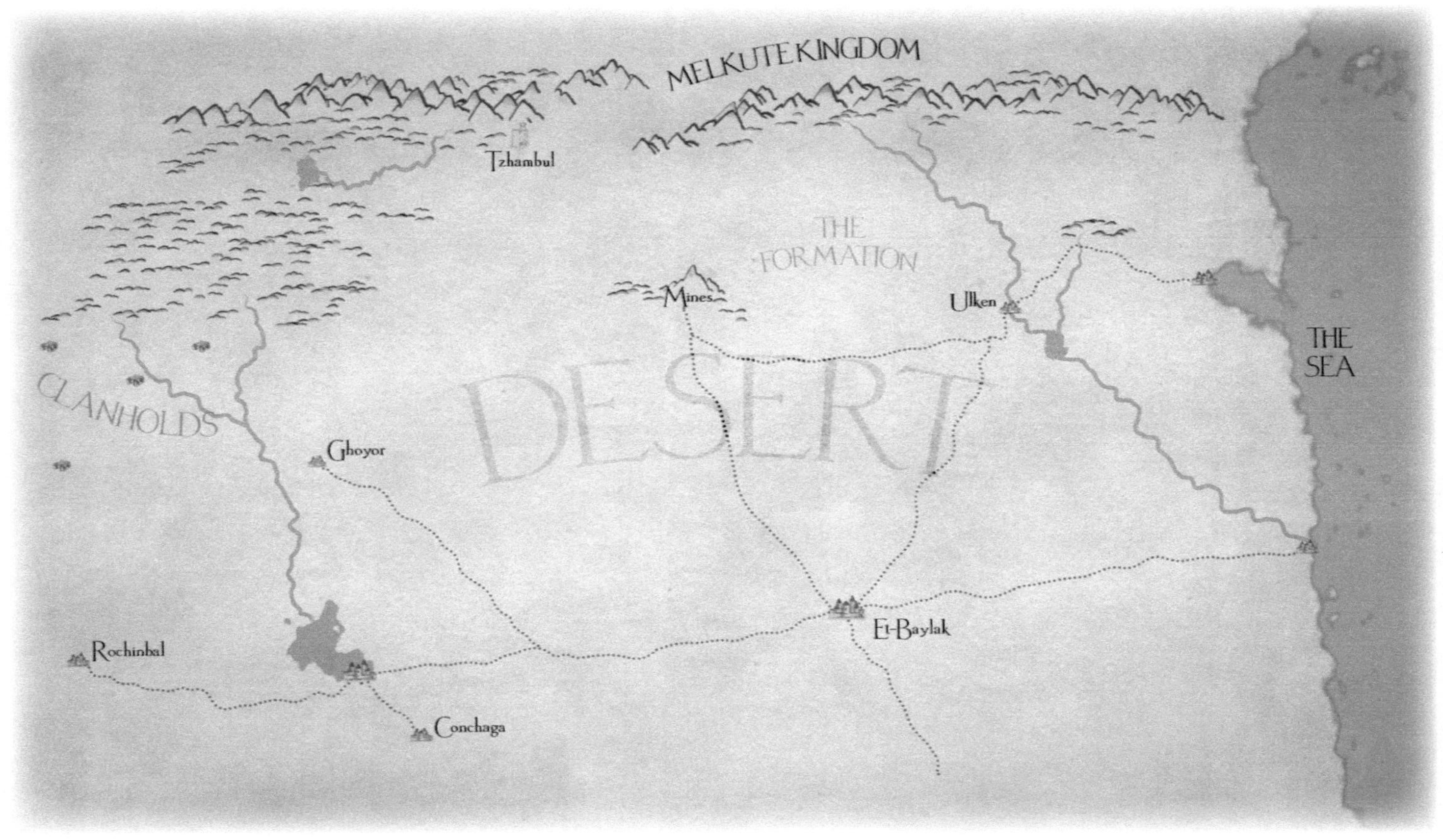

MELKUTE KINGDOM
Tzhambul
THE SEA
THE FORMATION
Mines
Ulken
CLANHOLDS
DESERT
Ghoyor
Et-Baylak
Rochinbal
Conchaga

Part One

GHOUK

DAY THREE

Then

"What kind of magic is this one using?" Clanless asked as he adjusted his bracers.

Badaar hesitated before answering. "It's speed. The blood-magic makes him move faster."

"How much faster?" Clanless looked out into the arena where Zaluu had just won his fight for the day.

"It depends on how much he's used," Badaar said. He picked up the moonblade and held it out. "It may be enough to just make him move a little faster than you. Or he may have gone crazy and used too much. Then he'll be running circles around you."

"Crazy?"

"It may help him win a fight, but it takes a toll. The human body isn't meant to go that fast. I guess it depends on how desperate he is to beat you."

Zaluu returned from the sand in time to hear the last bit. "Desperate to beat Clanless? Everyone is! He's the best ever seen here!"

"Tore another cape, I see." Clanless chuckled and took the moonblade from Badaar.

Zaluu held up the tattered edge of his cape. "Alas, Geku will be beside himself. This one was brand new for this fight." He shrugged. "The price of being magnificent."

"No doubt." Hearing the presenter use his name, Clanless trotted out onto the sand. The crowd roared at his appearance, and he acknowledged them by raising the moonblade. The roar grew louder.

His eyes darted to the opposite door, watching for his opponent. He almost didn't notice when a blur shot out. For a split second, his mind couldn't accept the idea of someone moving that fast. Then he saw the sand flying in a trail headed straight for him. He couldn't see the enemy's actual movements, but his rapid steps kicked up the dry sand, giving away his position.

Even so, Clanless wasn't prepared. He braced himself, watching the sand flurries approach, but it only revealed the enemy's rough position… not the reach of his weapon. Before Clanless could try to swing his own blade, something hard connected with his left rib cage. He caught a brief glimpse of the delight on his opponent's face before he sped past.

Exclamations from the crowd followed Clanless as he stumbled to one knee. The blow must have broken several ribs. A couple more shots like that, and he would be out of this fight.

The dust trail made a wide circle in returning toward him. Either the speed-enhanced fighter was slowing, or Clanless's eyes were getting better at tracking him: he could make out a blurred figure now leading the cloud of sand.

He prepared himself, squinting to keep the other man in view. The blur approached on the left. Clanless shifted his grip, ready to swing in that direction. He judged the distance, waited until the proper time, and swung.

But at the last moment, the runner shifted his direction, faster than Clanless would have believed possible. The moonblade missed. And the enemy mace slammed into his right shin, shattering the bone. Clanless screamed and collapsed to his knee.

The crowd roared as the enemy circled around. This could easily be the blow that finished Clanless for good. He pushed the pain of his leg aside and focused. He could see more of a blurred shape of the runner now; maybe the blood-magic was diminishing.

Clanless leaned on the moonblade to pull himself up. He staggered, trying to balance on one leg. It left him in an even more vulnerable position, but he had to risk it. Somehow, he had to spill blood on this opponent. The Taint would slow him down.

The runner came to a stop thirty feet away and lifted his arms toward the crowd with a huge grin. He turned back toward Clanless. Though he stood still, the opponent's whole body trembled, the magic still operating within him.

"Not so powerful now, are you?" the enemy taunted.

In Clanless's experience, those who took time out of battle to taunt were the most unsure of their own prowess. Knowing this, he took taunts in the opposite way of which they were intended.

"Time to end the Clanless reign." The enemy spun and almost vanished again as he ran, circling to the left this time.

Clanless could think of only one thing to do. He waited a few precious seconds as his opponent raced closer. He wanted to move at the last possible moment, but the disparity in speed made it impossible to judge. He threw all his weight on his left leg and raised the moonblade in an upward arc. Using the blade's momentum, he spun completely in a circle—more than a full circle, in fact. At some point, the moonblade struck something and keep moving.

The crowd exploded in cheers. As he fell, Clanless activated the Taint. He hit the ground, rolled, and twisted his head to see his opponent. Only then did he realize he hadn't needed the Taint after all.

Some thirty feet away, the enemy lay face-down, unmoving. At first, it confused Clanless. And then motion drew his eyes to the left.

The enemy's head rolled to a stop five or six feet away. Clanless stared at the empty eyes looking toward him. The frozen expression showed shock, as if the man couldn't believe his fate. Blood flowed from what remained of the neck.

He'd beheaded a man. He hadn't meant to. The shock of it removed his own pain momentarily. He'd killed before, but… not like this.

Clanless tore his view from those staring, dead eyes. He needed blood. That's all that mattered. He fumbled for the Siphon at his belt and began to crawl toward the body before he remembered he'd used the Taint. The blood was worthless. He rolled onto his back and let himself relax. At least the priests would be unhappy.

Now

Clanless jerked awake, sitting up with an abrupt motion. He stifled a cry from the pain his movement agitated in his gut. He couldn't remember the last time he'd had to wait so long for an injury to heal. Even if more healing blood could be obtained now, it wouldn't be as effective on an injury already in the healing process. He shook his head, beads of sweat raining from the locks of his hair. The sheets were drenched in his perspiration.

Every time he slept, new memories returned. Unlike the flood of details that had assaulted him when Zektel first left, these memories came one at a time. His overwhelmed brain had somehow readjusted and found a way to integrate the old memories bit by bit. His mind appeared to recognize the changes while he slept, reminding him of things long forgotten and suppressed.

Many were like the one he'd just experienced, moments of violence he didn't like to recall. He disliked the reminders of his own brutality. At least that beheading had been unintentional. Others... hadn't been.

The worst memories were of Uncle Sejikdi. He tried to repress those again. Some things did not need remembering.

Clanless pulled loose the damp sheet and tried to wipe more of the sweat from his face and hair. He had no idea of the time... but he made certain of the day. Three days since the Hawk King fell. Today was his third day as a free man. For so many years, he'd spent his time counting and re-counting what he needed to become free: the blood and the battles. But that was all over. From now on, he would count only his days of freedom.

Kekeen had been by his side for so much of these three days, yet he'd slept for far too long. She must have gone to get some sleep of her own right now. Good for her. Clanless closed his eyes and took a deep breath. He didn't deserve that girl.

A knock came at the door, and he smiled. She was back. "Come in," he called.

To his surprise, Qara entered his room instead of Kekeen. Her eyes wandered over him before looking down at the floor. "Clanless. It's good to see you sitting up. Are you able to walk?"

In answer, he got to his feet, wincing a little. Qara sounded odd, not her usual ebullient self. But he supposed it made sense: Daviland planned to shut down the arenas. She would be out of a job. Except... hadn't she been a slave as well? He was ashamed that he couldn't remember.

Qara nodded. "We are assembling the Dohor in the dining hall. Your presence is requested." She glanced at the moonblade in its place on the wall. "Bring your weapon as well."

"What's this all about?" Clanless ran a hand through his damp hair.

"It is an assembly," she reiterated. "Probably the last time we are all together." She turned toward the door. "Will you come?"

"Sure." He didn't see any reason to refuse. And she was probably right. Hagh and the others would all be going their separate ways soon. Unlike

Clanless, they didn't need to wait for full healing. They could leave at any time.

Qara nodded and left the room. He'd never seen her so subdued. Clanless pushed his hair back with both hands and looked around the room. He should put on fresh clothes at least. If this was to be the last gathering of the Dohor, he didn't want to show up a complete mess. No time for a visit to the baths, unfortunately.

Dressing turned out to be more difficult than he'd anticipated, but he struggled through. He'd never once considered how much he had to bend over while dressing and undressing. The injury to his gut protested throughout the process. At last, he put the beastman necklace over his head and fastened the wolf pelt into place. At least he would look his best for this assembly.

Once clothed, he took the moonblade from the wall. Would he ever wield it in battle again? It had become such a part of his life over the past few years. He ran his fingers over the smooth terebinth handle. He knew every inch of this weapon, more than he knew anything else in his life. Curious. He'd never thought about it in that way.

He left his room and looked up and down the hallway. Kekeen would have no trouble finding him if she returned during this assembly thing. There weren't many places he could go right now. His injuries wouldn't let him go for a long walk, even if the weather permitted it. The dining hall wasn't far, but he ached by the time he reached it. How did other people deal with healing without magic?

"Clanless! You're on your feet!" Sugh boomed as he entered. The huge warrior stood up and approached him, arms spread as if to embrace him.

Clanless held up a hand. "Still hurting." He set the moonblade on a table beside Sugh's axe.

Hagh, sitting at the next table with Hawking, coughed. "Let the lad be, Sugh," he said. "Without the blood, it takes time, ya know."

Sugh folded his arms and sniffed. "In my day, we healed without the blood-magic. We fought on, heal or not."

"In your day?" Hawking erupted. "You're not any older than the rest of us!"

Sugh shook his head. "Young people of this generation. They have no respect."

Clanless didn't hear Hawking's retort. He eased himself into a chair, but his eyes turned toward Qara. She stood at the side of the room where she had often addressed them before Arena Night. She didn't meet his gaze. In fact, she kept glancing at the door, while wringing her hands in front of her. Her nervousness was contagious. He grasped the moon-blade's handle.

Bain entered last of all, slipping into a chair beside Clanless. "What's this all about?"

Clanless shrugged. "Qara said we were having an assembly."

"Now that the laziest one is here, we can begin, yes?" Sugh looked toward the hostess. "What is our purpose here, lovely Qara?"

"One moment, please." She glanced at the door again.

"You summoned us," Hawking complained. "We're here. Let's get this over with."

"One moment," she repeated.

Clanless heard an odd noise from the doorway before he turned to see. It sounded like metal tapping against metal…

"You." Sugh's hand closed on his axe's handle.

In the door stood a young man. His clothes were bedraggled, but their high quality gave him away, even if Clanless hadn't recognized his face: Ghouk, the Hawk King's son. The tapping sound came from a stack of metal plates in his hands. With a chill, Clanless recognized them. "The bloodbonds!"

"Ridiculous." Sugh picked up the axe. "The Hawk King could not possibly have transferred them before he died."

Ghouk, for his part, chuckled. "Would you like to put that to the test, Dohor?" He made a point of looking through the metal plates and selecting one.

"I would." Sugh took a step toward Ghouk.

Ghouk put a fingertip onto the metal plate and twisted it. Even though he'd seen it before, Clanless winced as Sugh's whole body jerked as if yanked upward. He stood frozen in mid-stride, his precarious pose looking as though he might fall at any moment.

Hagh and Hawking both shouted curses. A blackness swirled in Clanless's mind. He'd thought himself free for only a couple of days… yet it felt as if half his life had been yanked away from him. Everything he'd hoped. It couldn't be over so easily, could it? His throat constricted. He couldn't speak.

Bain leaned back in his chair and crossed his arms. "Interesting. How did you accomplish this, King's Son?"

Ghouk moved around the room to stand beside Qara. He patted her on the shoulder. "You may go finish the preparations." She nodded, eyes downcast, and hurried back out. Ghouk turned to look at the assembled warriors. "That fool Daviland was so excited about winning the fight, he didn't make sure my father was completely dead." He chuckled again. "I crawled across your bloody sands to his body, pretending to be weeping over my murdered father. Instead, I took these"—he held up the blood-bonds—"and smeared his blood on them, just before he breathed his last. That's all it takes, really."

Ghouk motioned with his finger on the metal plate again. Sugh stumbled forward, recovered his balance, and glared at the king's son. "Bastard!"

"Now, now." Ghouk shook his head. "You know that isn't true. My mother is the Hawk King's one and only, despite what some others would have you believe." His eyes darted to Hawking.

"What do you want from us?" Hagh demanded.

Ghouk raised his eyebrows. "The Empire is in chaos. A mob has taken control of our beloved capital and killed our king. Why wouldn't I want to secure the best bodyguards available?"

"You want more than that," Bain said. "You sent Qara to prepare something. What's happening?"

Clanless frowned at him. How could Bain be so calm and relaxed? Nausea gathered around the edges of his mouth. The darkness continued to swirl, threatening to steal his consciousness.

"We're all going on a trip," Ghouk said. "By rights, the Sar Empire belongs to me. I will be taking it back."

Hagh pointed toward the door. "Are you moonbent? High Winter's begun! And not just any High Winter, but a chaos moon High Winter!"

"It is inconvenient, I'll admit." Ghouk moved toward the door. "But necessary all the same. You will all be coming with me. Come. We should leave before anyone else shows up."

Kekeen. Clanless trembled. What if Kekeen showed up in the middle of this? He desperately wanted to see her, but if she did… who knows what Ghouk would do, and they'd all be powerless to stop him. He got to his feet. "As you command," he said quietly.

Hagh gave him a searching stare before nodding and also standing. Sugh looked ready to tear Ghouk apart, but he didn't say anything else. Bain continued to look thoughtful.

Hawking, however, wasn't ready to give up. "This is insane! The Hawk King is dead! We're all free men now!"

Bain got to his feet. "The magic says otherwise, it appears. And the magic doesn't care who sits on the throne."

"We'll never get out of the city," Hawking argued. "We only have to tell one person what's happening, and the citizens will swarm you. They won't let you escape."

Ghouk narrowed his eyes. In that moment, Clanless thought he looked most like his father. He'd never forget the look the Hawk King had given him while murdering Silence, one of the previous members of the Dohor. Clanless lifted his hand toward Hawking, but before he could say anything, Ghouk spoke: "No one will see us. And even if they do, it won't matter. As your master, slaves, I am ordering all of you not to speak another word until we are past the city walls."

The words died in Clanless's throat. He looked to the others, one at a time. No one made a sound. Technically, they could disobey, but the consequences would be dire. None of them were willing to experience it.

"Now that that's settled, follow me," Ghouk ordered. "It's a long trip, and we need to get moving."

With silent glares, the five arena fighters followed Ghouk into the hall. He led the way past their rooms and toward the exit. Clanless glanced at his own door as they passed. His mind raced, but he couldn't think of any way to leave a message for Kekeen. Ghouk would certainly not allow him to write anything, even if he had the materials. He could only hope that, despite Ghouk's words, someone would see them leaving and inform Daviland or one of the other rebel leaders.

When Ghouk opened the exterior door, a blast of frigid air struck them all. If they'd been allowed to speak, all would have protested or at least suggested gathering warmer clothes. None of them had expected to venture outside.

A carriage waited a few feet from the door. Clanless recognized it as one of the Hawk King's own, a special conveyance for traveling during High Winter. Completely enclosed, the carriage's thick walls would protect its occupants from the worst of the weather. It would also conceal them from outside viewing. No one would know who rode inside. With the Hawk King already dead, were the rebels even concerned about any of his retinue? Had Daviland considered Ghouk a threat of any kind?

Ghouk opened the carriage door to reveal Qara sitting within, holding the reins to the six oxen harnessed to the carriage. A narrow window allowed the driver to see just enough to direct the beasts. "Sugh, I want you to drive for now," Ghouk commanded. "The rest of you find a seat." He paused. "But I sit next to Qara."

This time, Clanless narrowed his eyes. He could endure Ghouk's orders, at least until an alternative presented itself, but he would not tolerate mistreatment of a woman. If Ghouk stepped over the line with Qara, he would intervene, regardless of consequences.

"Snow comin'," Hagh muttered with a glance at the sky.

As he stepped up to the carriage door, Clanless took one last look up and down the street and back at the arena. No one watched them. No one saw. He ducked his head and entered the carriage. His days as a free man ended at three.

COMPANY

"I'm staying."

Clanless's eyes shot open, and his head spasmed. What was that? It seemed like one of his forgotten memories returning, but… he had only heard a voice speaking two words.

"You all right?" Bain asked beside him.

"Yeah." Clanless unfolded his arms and blinked. He'd fallen asleep in the carriage after only a few minutes. Despite the desperation of their circumstances, his body was still exhausted and healing from the fight with Daviland.

Bain shifted, and Clanless winced. The two of them were packed into one side of the carriage with Sugh and Hagh. A tight fit, made even more awkward by the presence of their large weapons. Ghouk, Qara, and Hawking faced them on the other side. Ghouk wore an arrogant smile, but everyone else looked miserable. Clanless didn't know how long they'd been traveling. But if he could speak, they must be outside of the city of Et-Baylak, at the least.

His mind returned to the odd memory, if memory it had been. He felt like he should know the voice, but he couldn't place it. It had been masculine, so not Zektel. Regardless, why suppress a two-word memory? What did it signify? How could it be important enough for the blood-wraith to want him to forget it?

Ghouk put his arm around Qara. "At least I'll have you to keep me warm tonight, fair Qara."

Clanless clenched his fist. "Hagh."

The older warrior coughed. "Yah?"

"What exactly are the consequences if a slave kills his master?"

"I've heard several tales. Not sure which is true."

Hawking stirred. "I heard the blood boils in your body."

Hagh nodded. "That's one of 'em. Whatever the details, it's always fatal."

"Very well." Clanless picked up his moonblade and pointed it at Ghouk.

"What are you doing, you fool?" the Hawk King's son snarled.

"Hear me, Ghouk, and hear me well. I will do your bidding. I will follow you on this journey as you require." He pulled himself to his feet. "But you will remove your hand from that woman. If you harm her in any way, I will kill you, regardless of what happens to me."

Qara's eyes widened. Ghouk pulled his arm away from her and pulled out the metal plates. "I could freeze you in place and make you watch!"

"And then I would kill you," Bain said in a calm voice without moving.

"Aye," Hagh agreed. "So say we all."

Ghouk stared at them. "You would sacrifice your lives for this… this whore?"

The carriage swayed. Clanless put one hand against the wall, but kept the moonblade at ready. "If you want our service, you will treat her with respect." He had no idea if any of this were true. Would he be able to strike at Ghouk at all, or would the magic of the bloodbond prevent even that?

Ghouk, if he knew any better, did not say so. He eyed Clanless for a moment before returning the bloodbonds within his coat. "Very well. But only if there is to be total obedience from this point on!"

"You leave her alone, and it will be so." Clanless squeezed back into his seat.

"It's too crowded in here," Hawking griped.

Clanless kept his eyes on Ghouk. The prince reached for the blood-bonds several times, but didn't bring them back out. His eyes darted from one of the Dohor to the next. They'd pushed him over Qara. It wouldn't work again. Clanless knew not to underestimate the prince. If he'd inherited any of his father's intelligence—and most of their interactions indicated he had—then he was a foe to be reckoned with.

He glanced away and found Qara staring at him. She smiled and mouthed "thank you." He tried to smile in return. But the whole thing made him think of Kekeen.

What was she thinking right now? She'd have returned to his room to discover him missing, along with all of the other arena fighters. She'd probably searched on her own a few minutes, then gone to find her father, who would have told Daviland… Was the whole city searching for them now? Would anyone think to search outside the city? As if to remind him of the dangers outside, the carriage shook from another heavy gust of wind. No one would travel in this, not unless they had to. There would be no pursuit, no rescue.

"I need to piss," Sugh complained. "What should we do about that, oh master?"

Qara pointed at Hawking. "There's a door behind him with an alcove. You'll find a covered hole you can open and… use."

Hawking twisted. "I never even noticed."

"Take the reins." Sugh got up and handed them to the other fighter. They squeezed around each other in the narrow space.

"What's behind us, then?" Bain asked, rapping the panel at his back.

"Storage," Qara said. "Some food and water. Winter clothing. Blankets for sleeping. And keeping warm."

"We'll be needing those," Hagh said. "Suirel is unleashing his wrath out there."

Ghouk snorted. "It's High Winter, fool. It's always this way."

Hagh shook his head. "Not like this."

"What will we do when it gets dark?" Bain asked. "You can't keep driving the animals all night."

"Tell them, Qara." Ghouk closed his eyes and folded his arms across his chest.

Qara tapped the wall beside her. "The sides can extend when we're not moving. It allows for more room. The Hawk King would sleep in here himself."

Hawking raised his eyebrows. "Is there room for seven?"

"Not… comfortably." Qara glanced at Ghouk. "But I think we can manage."

"And the animals?" Clanless asked.

"They'll be fine," Ghouk said without opening his eyes. "Any more foolish questions? Or do I need to order silence again?"

"Only one," Bain said. "Where are we going?"

Ghouk popped one eye open to look at Bain. "You'll find out when we get there."

"You said you were going to take back the Empire," Bain pressed. "How will leaving the city help that? More importantly, how will going north help that?"

Ghouk studied him with both eyes. "You're the clever one, aren't you? How'd you know which direction we were going?"

Bain didn't answer.

Ghouk snorted. "As I said, you'll find out when we get there."

Sugh returned and traded places with Hawking again.

A few moments later, Clanless cocked his head toward Bain. "What is to the north of Et-Baylak?"

"Nothing," Bain answered. "Nothing but the desert."

The desert. What little Clanless heard of the northern wastelands never sounded pleasant. He'd grown up in the wilderness around the clanhold, of course, but it didn't compare. Stories abounded of the strange creatures and other dangers that filled the desert. Clanless glanced down at his right foot and its four toes. The creature who'd taken his other toe came from the desert, or so they'd said.

In the stories, brave (or foolhardy) adventurers entered the desert seeking fame or new challenges. Yet in all the stories he'd heard, Clanless couldn't recall any that told of traveling the desert during High Winter. In fact, the stories were quite adamant about leaving before High Winter could arrive. Not even Okteral the Wild would attempt that.

"The animals won't be fine," Hagh grumbled. "They're built for cold, true, but not as cold as it's gonna get."

The Melkute Kingdom, sometimes enemy and sometimes ally to the Sar Empire, also lay to the north, Clanless recalled. But he'd never understood how far north. It must be beyond the desert.

"The almaz mines!" Bain exclaimed.

"The what?"

"The crystal." Bain managed to turn himself sideways and fumble at a pouch on his belt. At last, he withdrew a blood vial. "This crystal. It's only found in some mines to the north!" He looked at Ghouk. "That's where we're going, isn't it?"

"My father was right about you," Ghouk said quietly.

"It is, isn't it?" Bain leaned forward. "But why would the mines give you back the Empire?"

"Everything is built on blood," Qara said. "And the blood requires crystal."

"But Daviland is getting rid of the blood…" Clanless trailed off when Ghouk started to laugh.

"Why are you laughing?" Hagh demanded.

"Your naïveté is so amusing." Ghouk pretended to wipe a tear from his eye. "Daviland can't get rid of the blood sacrifices or the blood economy or anything. Nothing is going to change, you idiots!"

Qara and the fighters all stared at him.

"You cannot remove an empire's currency. Everything would fall into chaos." Ghouk shook his head again. "I suppose I shouldn't expect slaves to understand such things."

"But… the sacrifices," Clanless said. "They don't need them. Not really."

"The sacrifices give the vials their value," Ghouk said. "And we need them for the magic."

"Which gives strength to our army," Qara suggested.

"And for the goddess," Hagh added.

Ghouk snorted yet again.

Clanless hadn't told anyone about his encounter with the goddess. The first time he'd thought the goddess spoke to him, it had turned out to be Zektel. This latest vision seemed… authentic, but who would believe him? The answer popped into his head immediately: Kekeen. She'd believe him without question. For that matter, Hagh probably would as well.

The occupants of the carriage fell silent for a while. Bain shifted multiple times, a frown on his face. Something about Ghouk's claims clearly bothered him. Clanless replayed the conversation in his own mind. Ghouk had never answered Bain's question. Why would these mines help him control the Empire?

"You're bleeding." Ghouk's voice broke the silence.

Clanless looked down. A small dark spot colored his shirt over his gut. "It's nothing," he said. "My wound opened up a little."

"The blood of the clanless one." Ghouk shook his head. "You don't even know. How many times did my father ask you for samples of your blood?"

"I don't remember."

"Because you didn't notice unless I asked," Qara broke in. "Usually, I took the samples just before you were healed from an arena fight."

Clanless wrinkled his brow. "I don't understand."

"Of course you don't. Idiot."

They said little more through the rest of the day. Ghouk no longer seemed inclined to talk, and the fighters didn't press him. Between the despair of the bloodbonds, and the general discomfort of the crowded carriage, Clanless didn't feel much like talking, and he assumed the others felt the same.

When at last Ghouk allowed the oxen to stop for the day, he forced Sugh and Hawking to get out and feed the animals. Qara instructed the others on extending the walls. As promised, it created enough room for then to lie down. Qara curled up on one set of seats, while Ghouk took the other. The winter winds outside sounded as though they grew stronger as darkness fell.

Clanless tried to stay awake, to be sure Ghouk kept his word about Qara. But his body insisted on seizing what rest it could find. His eyes closed, leading him back into the realm of memory.

COMPANY

Then

"Clanless! Help me!"

"Zaluu!"

Clanless used the moonblade as a plow, shoving barbarians aside. He couldn't stop, couldn't let them deter him.

Zaluu fell. Four barbarians surrounded the spot where he'd been. Their weapons rose and fell.

Clanless spun, swinging the moonblade in a complete circle. The bloodrush pounding in his ears drowned out the cries of pain and anger from the barbarians. He swung again and again in vast arcs of liquid spray. He thought he screamed, but he couldn't hear that either.

The barbarians gave back for a moment, only a moment. But it was enough. He could see.

Zaluu's body. What was left of it. The remains of the purple cape—barely recognizable as that color with all of the blood—obscured his friend's head.

The barbarians closed in again. Clanless screamed and heard it this time.

Now

"Shut him up!" Ghouk shouted.

Clanless's eyes flew open to see Hagh's face staring down at him. It took him a moment more to realize Hagh was shaking him. "What-what happened?"

"You were screamin' yer head off," Hagh said. "Woke us all up." He sat back. "Scared the blood half out of me."

Clanless jerked his head around, eyes darting everywhere. They were all watching him: Qara, Bain, Sugh, Hawking. Drenched in sweat, he couldn't slow his breathing. The memory had been so real, so horrible…

"Wake me again, and you'll be riding an ox the rest of the way," Ghouk growled.

"Are you all right?" Hagh asked, trying to get Clanless to focus on him.

"I… I will be."

The memory had been more vivid than ever that time. As the others settled back to sleep, Clanless tried to calm himself. He lay awake, staring at the carriage's ceiling, his breath slowly coming under control.

He'd wondered how he'd missed Zaluu's death. Turns out he hadn't. Zektel had suppressed the memory almost right after it happened. Why? Had it been out of compassion, to spare him from the despair? She couldn't know how much he'd agonized over missing it… could she? She'd never shown the capability of reading his thoughts if he didn't speak them out loud.

But returning the memory to him was nothing less than pure cruelty, especially the glimpses she'd shown him during his fight with Daviland. Even if Zektel had been protecting him back then, she'd shown her true nature at the end.

Even so… he missed her. He would never say it out loud to anyone. But Zektel had been a part of his life since the day he'd been taken from his family. Her absence left a hole inside.

So many thoughts fought for dominance in his mind: the departure of Zektel, the suppressed memories, his encounter with the goddess, separation from Kekeen, the current situation. His brain refused to abandon any of these threads, bouncing from one to the other, preventing him from sleeping.

Just as well. He didn't want to sleep any more, not with the kind of memories he'd been recovering.

The pain from his injuries didn't help. He shifted to his left side to seek some relief. He blinked. Qara lay awake also, staring at him. Her lips moved. At first he didn't get it, but she repeated the words: "Are you all right?"

He nodded and tried to smile. She raised her eyebrows in return, clearly not convinced. He widened his smile a bit and nodded. Qara rolled her eyes, but she also rolled away.

Left to his own thoughts once more, Clanless lay awake for the rest of the night. He wrestled with each of the subjects troubling him, but found no answers for any of them.

((((●))))

Ghouk woke them all up in the morning in a foul mood. "I hate this. I hate all of you," he grumbled, stepping on Sugh as he pushed into the alcove to relieve himself.

"We return the sentiment," Bain said.

Clanless pulled himself up into a crouch, leaning on the moonblade. "Is there any way out of this?" he whispered to Bain.

"Out of a bloodbond? I don't know of any. As long as he holds those, we're his property. You know that."

Clanless scowled. Lack of sleep didn't put him in a good mood either. "You're supposed to be clever, remember? Surely you can think of something."

"Maybe I already have." Bain scratched his scalp. "I'm missing the baths," he grumbled. He cast a quick glance at the alcove, then leaned back to Clanless. "Let's just keep trying to make him talk. If he tells us his plans, it may provide some options."

"Why would he tell us?"

"Because he's arrogant, and it'll give him a chance to show off." Bain grinned. "That's something I understand." He leaned closer. "What about your special friend? Does she have any advice?"

Clanless hesitated. But if he was going to tell anyone, it would be Bain. "Zektel left me during the fight with Daviland."

Bain's eyebrows rose as he cocked his head. "Really? That's... interesting." He turned away and watched for Ghouk's return.

Clanless settled into his seat as Qara helped Sugh retract the carriage walls. Hawking and Bain were sent to check on the oxen. Soon after, Ghouk gave the order to continue the journey.

"I've been thinking," Bain announced a few minutes later.

"Oh, glorious," Ghouk said. "What now?"

Bain pointed ahead. "Let's say you take control of the crystal mines, using us as your… enforcers. I still don't see how that gives you the Empire. I would think there's enough crystal in use as it is. Surely they don't need much more on a regular basis."

"You'll understand when we get there."

"But I'd rather understand now." Bain leaned forward. "You've forced us into this position. But if you can give me—us—a good reason for these actions, we'll be more… cooperative in your work."

"I don't need your cooperation." Ghouk almost laughed. "You're slaves. You do what I say, no matter what."

"Slaves will follow your orders, true," Bain countered. "But without some kind of reciprocation or enticement, they will not cooperate as readily. Your father understood this, which is why he sent us to Pasque House all the time."

"He also killed one of you for poor associations," Ghouk said, eyes narrowed.

Bain nodded. "Consider it this way: assume I'm your slave, and you tell me to go kill a man. I obey at once, heading in that direction. But if I think there's no good reason for this order, I might not move as fast as I could. I might allow this man to escape from me. I'll *try* to kill him, thus obeying your order, but it's not a problem to me if he happens to get away."

"I suppose I'll have to be very specific in my orders then."

Bain held both palms out. "You could do that… or you could persuade us you have good reason for what you're doing. Then maybe we'd be good little slaves and work harder to help you."

Ghouk shook his head. "You Dohor make me laugh. You're the most pampered slaves in the Empire. You have everything you could want, while all you have to do is put on a show of killing someone once a week. And now… when someone reminds you of your true status, you can't accept it."

"Pampered, are we?" Bain pulled his shirt open. "Do you know where these scars came from?"

Clanless frowned. He'd seen Bain's scars, of course; they all had scars. Sometimes the healing didn't come fast enough or didn't work as well.

"They are not from the arena!" Bain said before Ghouk could answer. "Before I came to Et-Baylak, I was the most successful arena fighter in Mantukhai. The arena's owner, Chenkhiz, enjoyed the power he possessed over slaves."

"Bain…" Clanless whispered, putting a hand on his shoulder.

Bain shrugged it off. "Chenkhiz would freeze us with the bloodbonds and then cut us himself. He would watch us bleed, unable to do anything about it. He wanted us to have scars. He claimed the people needed to see scars to believe in the arena fights."

Ghouk's expression did not change. "Then it's a good thing my father rescued you from that place, isn't it?"

"Yes." Bain closed his shirt. "Which is why I was his most loyal servant. Let me be that for you, as well. The Hawk King never condescended to me. He treated me like a man. Do the same, and I will serve you the same."

Most loyal servant? What did Bain mean by that? He'd never shown any love for the Hawk King, at least as far as Clanless knew.

Ghouk sat silent for a few moments. "Then consider this, most loyal slave," he said at last, emphasizing the final word, "where does the blood go?"

"The blood?" Hagh interjected. "From the sacrifices?"

"From everything. Where does it go?" Ghouk fumbled in a pouch and pulled out a blood vial. "Here's a single drop. Small amounts are kept for magic use. But what about the rest?"

Bain wrinkled his brow. "Are you saying it goes where we're going?"

"Consider it, I said." Ghouk folded his arms and said no more.

Clanless repositioned himself to avoid pressure on his wounds. He glanced around the tight space at the others. Bain settled back beside him, muttering to himself. The other three fighters appeared angry, but trying to hold it in. Qara stared aimlessly at the ceiling. Clanless wondered what she was thinking now. She hadn't said anything since the carriage began moving.

His thoughts turned to Kekeen. What would she be doing by now? What must she be thinking? He couldn't imagine. His eyelids grew heavy. The slow jostling of the carriage combined with the warmth of the interior drained his awareness. Against his own desire, he slid into sleep again. And the dreams returned… but not at all what he expected.

WEASELS

Then

"Okteral the Wild… are you sure you want another story of Okteral the Wild?" Father rubbed his mustache, his hand concealing part of his grin.

"Yes! Yes!" Aldan bounced on his little bed.

"Nothing too violent tonight, please," Mother's voice called from the living space.

Father winked at Aldan. "Perhaps then… the story of the giant weasel."

"Weasels are tiny!" Aldan protested.

"Ah, but not this one." Father sat beside Aldan's bed and waved his hand. "In days past, when Okteral the Wild roamed the northern desert, he had many strange adventures. He wandered far in the warmth of High Spring, alone and—"

"Okteral the Wild wasn't alone!" Aldan interrupted. "He had friends! And a wolfhound!"

"This time, he was alone," Father repeated. "And haven't you ever wondered where he found the wolfhound?"

Aldan's eyes widened.

"Okteral had heard stories of this land, stories of animals that had grown far beyond their normal size. He wanted to see such wonders for himself and so he wandered far and wide. Until one day…" Father leaned in close. "He saw one! At first, he thought it must be a bear, since it was large and furry. He drew his magic sword."

Father made a motion of drawing a sword from his belt. Aldan imitated it.

"For though it is evil to spill the blood of another man outside the temple, the goddess makes no such law for the blood of animals." Father's eyes darted upward toward the moon. "Imagine how shocked Okteral was when the creature turned toward him, and he saw… not a bear, but—"

"A weasel?"

"A weasel it was. A giant weasel with red hair on top."

"Like the one Borde saw outside the clanhold!"

"The very same."

Aldan glanced at his mother as she appeared at the doorway to his little bedroom. Her lips held a gentle smile as she watched Father spin his tale. Her hands held her stomach, which had grown so large in the past few months.

"When the weasel saw Okteral the Wild with his shining sword, it rose up on its hind legs, revealing its white fur underneath," Father went on. "It stood two feet above Okteral's head and stared down at him with its beady eyes."

Aldan held back the questions that leaped into his mind. If he asked too many, Father might get annoyed and not finish the story. It had happened once.

"Okteral was startled, but not afraid. He held forth his sword, preparing for battle. And then the weasel opened its mouth… and spoke."

"Weasels don't talk!" Aldan couldn't help himself.

"Oh, are you the expert on giant weasels?" Father's eyes twinkled. "This was no ordinary weasel, you know. 'Please don't kill me, oh mighty warrior,' it said.

"'How are you so… big?' Okteral asked. 'And how do you speak? What sorcery is this?'

"The weasel bowed its head in deference to the hero. 'I have bathed in the blood of your ancestors, and this is what became of me,' it said."

"What does that mean?" Aldan wrinkled his nose.

"I'm just telling you what it said," Father answered. "Okteral didn't know what it meant any more than you do. While he thought about it, still holding out his sword, he heard a sound. What do you think it was?"

"I don't know."

Father leaned in close again. "He heard… a whimper. A tiny, little whimper. Like a dog."

"Like a wolfhound!"

"Exactly. Okteral stepped to the side and looked past the weasel. He saw where the weasel had been digging: the remains of a wolf den. And huddled in the last bit of the den was a cub, a very young wolfhound."

"I knew it!"

"'Please, oh please let me live,' the weasel begged. Okteral thought carefully. He believed he could kill the weasel, though it might be a hard fight. The weasel possessed sharp claws and teeth of a very unusual size, after all. Also, he was loath to kill such an amazing creature. If it could speak, what else could it do?

"'I will let you live on one condition,' Okteral said. 'You must leave this spot right now, and leave that wolf cub behind.'

"Now the weasel hesitated. Its eyes darted back and forth as it considered the offer. Maybe it was thinking about whether it could defeat Okteral after all. Understanding its hesitation, Okteral the Wild stepped forward, eyes narrowed and ready for battle.

"At this, the weasel backed away. He was smart enough to recognize the danger of challenging Okteral the Wild."

"He'd better be!" Aldan punched the air, pretending he wielded a sword.

"Stories are supposed to calm him down, not rile him up," Mother observed in a tone Aldan didn't understand.

"The weasel spun around and raced away," Father continued. "Okteral watched it run, making sure it didn't turn back around and sneak up on him. Weasels can be tricky, as everyone knows. Once he knew it was gone, Okteral approached the wolf den. The cub tried to push its way deeper into the torn earth. Okteral put away his sword and spoke soothingly to it."

"And that's where he met his wolfhound?" Aldan asked.

"It is. And they were best friends from that day forward." Father stood up, signaling an end to the story for the night.

"But what about the giant weasel? Did he ever find it again? Or, or a giant bird? Or—"

"If there is such a story, you will have to wait for some other night." Father picked up the lantern and moved to the door where Mother waited.

Aldan yawned as he stretched out. "But what about…"

Now

Clanless jolted awake. As his mind returned to the present, he swallowed and stretched as best he could. He shook his head. So strange.

"More dreams?" Bain asked.

"Yeah."

"Not so horrible this time, I assume. You weren't screaming."

Clanless smiled. "No, it was… I remembered a story my father told me."

"So tell us."

"It's a children's story, Bain."

"So? We could use a good story." Bain gestured at everyone else. "How else should we pass the time?"

Clanless glanced around. Ghouk didn't offer any objections, and the others appeared curious or encouraging. He took a deep breath and winced from the pain. "All right. So, my father used to tell me stories of a great hero named Okteral the Wild."

Ghouk snorted.

"Let him talk," Qara said. "We need something to, to take our minds off things."

Bain nodded, and Clanless resumed. His words stumbled from his mouth; he hadn't told a story like this since… since he and Bain were in their training under Kan. As he told the story, he wondered what could have motivated Zektel to suppress this memory… or if she had. Perhaps he'd simply forgotten it, and it came to remembrance because of all the other strange things happening in his head.

"Bathed in the blood," Bain murmured when he'd finished.

"Kind of silly," Hawking said.

"It's just a story." Clanless shrugged.

"I liked it," Hagh offered.

Ghouk muttered something unintelligible.

"You told several of these stories to us during training, didn't you?" Bain asked.

"And you told stories of the blood-wraiths." Clanless smiled.

Bain half-smiled back. "Should have listened to me. All stories have something important about them."

Clanless nodded. Koland would have agreed with that sentiment. Could it be something important about this particular Okteral story that caused it to be suppressed? But what? Could there actually be a giant weasel? If so, what connection could it possibly have to blood-wraiths?

"Blood-wraiths," Ghouk echoed. "Now there's something you should pay attention to."

"What do you mean?" Bain asked.

"How much do you know of such creatures?"

"Enough." Bain glanced at Clanless.

"Have you spoken with one?" Ghouk's eyes stared past them. Clanless looked up at the carriage wall behind him to be sure nothing was there.

"I've… heard many stories," Bain said.

"Stories." Ghouk snorted, and his eyes regained their focus. "Who can say what is true and what isn't about… those creatures."

"You've spoken to one, haven't you?" Clanless asked. "Was there one inside your father?"

Ghouk's head jerked toward him. "Why would you ask such a thing?"

"It's… a… common belief among… certain populations," he stammered.

"Not surprising." Ghouk shook his head. "But the priests. Do you know what they say? They say the wraiths don't exist! They don't believe! They won't believe. And do you know why?"

Clanless shook his head, fascinated.

"Because it would challenge their beliefs?" Bain suggested.

"Because it's their fault!" Ghouk jabbed a finger toward Bain. "They created the wraiths themselves!"

"Blasphemy," Hagh muttered.

A memory nagged at the edge of Clanless's consciousness. Something related to this… but he couldn't bring it up.

"How did they do that?" Bain wanted to know.

"Through the blood-magic!" Ghouk was almost ranting now. "Every time they use the magic to a great extent, another of the wraiths are created. They don't even know they're doing it! It's a side effect."

Bain steepled his fingers and sat back. "Curious. I've never heard that theory before."

"It's not a theory. It's—" Ghouk cut himself off, apparently realizing how he appeared to this group of slaves. "Bah. I'm wasting my time with you lot." He folded his arms, sat back, and closed his eyes.

Clanless considered his words. The Ghamba Lam had been very interested in whether he kept hearing a voice after his childhood. Was he searching for information about the blood-wraiths? Maybe he'd known more than he let on, as well.

The winds howled even louder outside. The carriage rolled on, making slow but steady progress toward their mysterious destination.

$$\text{((((●))))}$$

"This is… audacious."

Kekeen took a few steps into the throne room and stopped. Even the splendor of the rest of the Hawk King's palace had not prepared her for this. The ceiling rose to an enormous height, at least equal to a four-story building. A series of ornate lanterns hung on long chains, but Kekeen couldn't imagine how someone could light them even at that height. The ceiling rose to a peak above them, but an enormous round window made of a dozen radial panes filled the center, revealing the moon. One of the panes vibrated from the high winds outside.

Vivid tapestries decorated the walls, depicting scenes from the Sar Empire's history (most of which appeared to involve the Hawk King in some way). Gold tassels lined the sides of each tapestry.

The floor consisted of huge marble tiles, at least a man's height in width. The coolness of the tiles seeped up through Kekeen's soft shoes. No doubt the Hawk King and his courtiers could afford thicker footwear.

"He's over there," her father said, pulling her attention away. She looked in the direction Koland pointed and saw Daviland, their leader, the man who overthrew the Hawk King, the "chosen one" of the goddess.

He stood staring at the Hawk King's throne as if entranced. Kekeen almost didn't blame him. The throne matched the room's audaciousness and exceeded it. A gold-covered hexagonal platform, fully ten feet across, formed the base of the structure. Six more platforms stacked on top of the base, each one foot smaller than the last, formed stairs on all sides leading up to the actual throne. On each corner of each hexagon perched a golden hawk in a variety of poses. The throne itself sported a huge pair of outstretched wings, also gold.

"It doesn't appear very comfortable," Koland said aloud.

Daviland turned, a smile on his face. "The seat needs a cushion, at least." The rebel leader's curly brown hair and beard had been trimmed since Kekeen last saw him, and his clothes were finer. "What can I do for you, my friends?"

"The fighters are still missing," Koland reported.

"It's been two days!" Kekeen added.

Daviland's smile faded. "And no one's seen anything yet?"

"No sign of them." Koland folded his arms. "One guard reported a royal carriage left the city, but couldn't tell who was inside."

"If they've left the city, there's nothing we can do," Daviland said. "The full force of this chaotic High Winter is upon us."

"This doesn't concern you?" Koland asked. "The five mightiest warriors of the Empire disappear after we overthrow the Hawk King. Something is going on."

Daviland shrugged. "I think you're making too much of it. They were mighty warriors, yes, but they were slaves. And now they're free."

"Aldan wouldn't leave like this!" Kekeen burst out.

"And all five of them at once?" her father added. "Along with the girl who managed them?"

Daviland shook his head. "I'm sorry. I didn't mean it that way." He ran a hand through his hair. "There have been so many things to think about here. We've taken Et-Baylak, but the bulk of the military is still out there. We have to think about them. Kekeen, I know Aldan matters to you. I'm not questioning that. But in the big picture of how we're transforming the Sar Empire… it's not weighing on my mind all that much." He stepped closer and put his hand on Kekeen's shoulder. "As soon as possible, we will do whatever we can to find him. I haven't forgotten the help you two gave me to get here."

"Thank you," Kekeen whispered.

"And here we are." Daviland gestured at the throne. "We made it. Our dreams are coming true."

Koland grunted, but didn't say anything.

"I know you expected faster change." Daviland chuckled. "Give it time, storyteller. We just got here, and we have this winter to survive." He looked at Kekeen. "You know, you should sing for me sometime."

She wrinkled her brow. "You've… heard me sing many times."

"Of course, of course." He spread both arms. "But not in here. Imagine your voice filling this space!"

"Maybe." She didn't much feel like singing right now.

Daviland's eyes darted past them. Kekeen turned to see three men entering the throne room. "What are they doing here?" she exclaimed.

She knew the three men—Lords Ulakan, Ezen, and Ghayaktal—well enough. They'd been in the Hawk King's booth when she'd been forced to sing during Aldan's battle with Daviland.

"These men have run the city of Et-Baylak for many years," Daviland said. "It is only right that I turn to them for advice as we… transition."

"What about your usual advisors?" Koland asked. Kekeen was surprised at the calmness in his voice. Her father was one of those advisors!

"I will need them as well." Daviland patted them both on the back. "We will all meet together later. But first, let me speak with these three. If you'll excuse me…"

Koland made a stiff nod and headed for the door. Kekeen followed, glancing at the three men as she passed. Did the other two know about the one who'd helped protect her from the Hawk King's wrath in the chaotic moments before Daviland attacked? She decided not to say anything at the moment, but her eyes locked with his for a brief second.

Daviland's behavior confused her. His reactions, his behavior—even his words—all seemed different than the man she'd gotten to know over the past few years. As she left the throne room, Kekeen had one immediate goal: find Borde.

WEASELS

"The Hawk King is… concerned about your apparent lack of killer instinct."

Clanless looked up in alarm, almost dropping his moonblade. "Is he displeased?"

Qara shook her head, knowing exactly what that word meant. "No, not yet. But he's told me to tell you…" She hesitated. "I'm trying to get this exactly right. He says he's noticed that you often will do only what is necessary to defeat an opponent. You'll do just enough, and no more."

Clanless frowned. "I'm not sure I understand."

Qara licked her lips. "As I understand it, he's saying that's not enough for the audience. You need to be more… brutal."

"Brutal," he repeated. He glanced toward the open arena doors and listened to the crowd cheering for Hagh. "All right. I can be brutal."

"Can you? I mean, you—"

"I'll handle it, Qara," he cut her off.

She bit her lip, also glanced toward the arena, and then hurried away.

Bain approached, wiping sweat from his head. "What was that all about?"

"More expectations from the Hawk King."

The roar of the crowd indicated the end of Hagh's fight. Clanless moved past Bain and waited at the entrance. The older fighter jogged back, breathing hard. "Hot out there today. Haven't seen it this bad in years."

"Seasons come and seasons go," Bain said. "The only constant is the moon above our heads."

"And blood," Clanless added. Without waiting for the presenter, he stepped out into the sun.

Hagh was right. The sun's heat radiated from the sand in a way he hadn't experienced in some time. Sweat broke out on his bare skin before he reached the center of the arena.

From the earlier briefing, he knew what to expect. Three men entered from the opposite door. Two he knew to be former soldiers searching for a way to gain fame and fortune. They rightly feared him and spread to either side, depending on their third companion to take the lead. An enormous man, he towered head and shoulders above the others. He swung a huge maul and shouted something to the crowd who responded in like fashion.

Three warriors would never be a challenge for Clanless, and everyone in the arena knew it. Everyone also knew the third warrior was using Clan Berge blood-magic to enhance his strength. He slammed the maul into the sand with such impact the entire arena floor trembled.

Clanless narrowed his eyes against the sand kicked up into the air. A dozen possible tactical situations played out in his head. He'd faced similar odds any number of times over the past few years. But the Hawk King didn't want his usual methods. He wanted brutal.

"Clanless doesn't seem too eager to bring the fight to these challengers," the presenter's voice echoed. "Is he intimidated, citizens?"

The crowd roared its own answer to the question. At the same time, Clanless shifted to his left and took a few side-steps. As expected, the soldier to his left stopped and even took a step backward. The soldier to the right advanced further, following Clanless's lead. Already, they did what he wanted, and not a single blow had been exchanged yet.

It didn't take long to change that. The enhanced warrior snarled an order and charged toward Clanless, his heavy footsteps slamming into the sand like a pounding drum. The other two hurried forward as well, encouraged by their leader.

Clanless waited until they had almost reached him. He side-stepped to the right four or five paces as fast as he could, lifting the moonblade just a little. The soldier on that side, assuming he was about to be attacked, stumbled and stepped backward, raising his mace and buckler.

Instead, Clanless spun back to his left and stepped in close to the main threat. The enhanced warrior swung his maul in an angled arc. Clanless leaped back to dodge it, let his shoulder hit the ground and rolled to the left. In a fluid motion, he came back to his feet almost on top of the third man, who'd naturally assumed he was too far away from the immediate fight. He lifted his buckler too late. The moonblade cut a gash across his chest and left bicep, leaving that arm almost useless. The crowd roared.

Instinct made Clanless dive forward and somersault away, just in time to avoid another smash from the maul. Ordinarily, he'd consider using the Taint at this point to eliminate the wounded man from the fight. But that wouldn't be brutal enough, would it?

The first man advanced slower now, eyes narrowed. He wouldn't be fooled a second time. The big man stepped to his left, trying to flank Clanless. The wounded man dropped his buckler, screaming in pain, but he also advanced behind his comrades, determined to stay in the fight.

Clanless charged the first man again, but this time he kept going. He feinted a stroke toward the soldier's head, drawing his buckler up. Then he shifted and brought the moonblade in low. It was a simple trick, something the soldier should have expected. But men like him were always shocked to discover how fast a veteran arena fighter could move. Clanless didn't use any blood-magic to enhance his speed, but his opponents—those who lived—often accused him of doing so.

The moonblade smashed into the soldier's right knee, almost severing the entire leg. The soldier dropped to the sand, screaming. Clanless raced on, intent on the remaining two opponents. He dodged another blow from the enhanced warrior.

Ones who used Clan Berge blood-magic were almost always idiots. Their extra strength only mattered if they could hit him, and Clanless wasn't about to let that happen. If the man had been smart, he would have opted for two lighter weapons, so he could strike faster. But like others before him, he couldn't resist the idea of wielding a huge weapon. He no doubt imagined himself taking the famous Clanless apart in one solid blow… and he would, if he ever hit.

Instead of waiting for him, Clanless circled and charged the wounded man. The enhanced warrior shifted toward them both. Clanless deflected the wounded man's weak mace strike, then tossed his moonblade into the sand. He seized hold of the soldier by his good arm and swung him into the path of the enhanced warrior's mace. The roar of the crowd barely drowned out the ensuing crunch.

Clanless sprinted back to the moonblade, pursued by the final enraged opponent. He rolled again, seizing the moonblade's handle as he passed, a maneuver he'd practiced a thousand times. He came to a stop, but remained on his back. Once again, he counted on the idiot factor. A smart opponent would bring the maul in a stroke from the side. But an idiot couldn't resist a downed opponent and the opportunity to smash him into the sand. The enhanced warrior lifted the maul sky-high, preparing to bring it straight down. And to be fair, if it struck, Clanless would be dead. No question.

He lifted the moonblade as if he meant to try to block the descending blow. But at the last moment, he rolled to the right. The maul smashed into the sand. Clanless released his left hand from the moonblade. As his left elbow helped him continue his roll, he swung the moonblade with his right hand, extended to its furthest reach. The heavy blade sliced through the warrior's wrist. His right hand fell into the sand, spewing blood. The Hawk King might be enjoying this, but the blood-priests would be appalled at the waste.

The fight was effectively over. Though he could still swing the maul one-handed, the warrior wasn't used to fighting with his left hand. Clanless toyed with him a while longer to please the crowd. With his final maneuver, he kicked the swinging maul into the sand, throwing the warrior off-balance. The moonblade removed his head.

While the crowd cheered, Clanless walked over to the first soldier, who still tried to hold his leg together. His cries for mercy were cut off with a second beheading.

Clanless acknowledged the Hawk King's box with a salute and a muttered "Brutal enough?" He removed his Siphon and got to work.

Now

"I've had enough of this," Ghouk announced the next morning.

"We agree then!" Sugh grinned and slapped a fist into his palm.

Ghouk scowled at him and pointed at the door. "Get out. All of you."

Clanless pulled himself upright. More violent dream-memories put him on edge. "Outside?"

"You heard me! Everyone. Outside!" He paused. "Not you, Qara. You can work on getting the carriage ready to leave."

Clanless shivered even before stepping outside. High Winter, boosted by the chaos moon's appearance, had arrived with a vengeance. The ever-present wind cut through even his new, warmer clothes with ease, chilling him to the bone.

He stared around in surprise. The landscape wasn't what he had expected. All his life, Clanless had heard about the northern "desert." The wilderness near his clanhold consisted of rocky outcroppings and sparse foliage. He'd assumed the desert would be something like that. Instead, he saw snow blanketing a mostly flat land, devoid of trees. Tufts of brown grass extended from the snow here and there. The wind picked up swirls of snow, tossing it around and adding a haze to the view. In the distance, a range of mountains loomed white against the pale blue sky. The moon appeared full and clear in its usual spot, its glowing shield facing the sun… while Suirel lingered above it.

Hagh kicked some of the snow aside and coughed. "Hard to b'lieve there's sand under all this." He pointed at it.

"Why are we out here?" Sugh demanded, hugging himself against the wind.

"The carriage is too crowded," Ghouk said.

"We said that from the beginning." Hawking rubbed his hands together and blew on them.

"I thought I needed all of you, but after careful consideration…" Ghouk paused. He pointed at Hawking. "You are not wanted."

Hawking blinked. "What?"

"Go away." Ghouk waved dismissively. "Head back to the city."

"It's two days' travel!" Clanless exclaimed. "He can't walk that far in this!"

"That's not my problem." Ghouk grasped the carriage door and pulled himself up. "The rest of you, get back aboard. We need to keep moving."

"You can't do this!" Hagh protested.

Ghouk glared at him. "I am the master here. You will obey me, slaves!" He looked at each of them in turn. "It's time you all were reminded of this." He pointed at Hawking again. "Start walking!"

Hawking gritted his teeth, turned, and trudged back in the direction they'd come.

"No!" Clanless cried. "You're sentencing him to death!"

"The Hawk King had only one son," Ghouk said with a coldness rivaling the wind. "And I am he." He ducked into the carriage. "Everyone else aboard. It's time to go."

Clanless wavered, staring at Hawking's back as he plodded through the snow. "We can't…"

"We have no choice." Sugh pounded a fist against his chest and held it up. "Farewell, brother of the Dohor! We will avenge you!"

Hawking turned and raised his own arm in a return salute. He pulled his cloak tighter and kept walking.

One by one, the other fighters climbed into the carriage. Clanless stood alone. He couldn't allow this. But he had no power over Ghouk. He could defy the prince, but… would it work? Did he have a chance? The others seemed to have accepted the travesty. They'd defied Ghouk when it came to Qara. Why not now?

Bain paused at the carriage door and turned back. "Listen, Clanless." He looked over his shoulder at the carriage. "We pushed our luck to save Qara, but we can't do it again. He can stop us, and he knows it… sort of. If we try to stop him now and fail—"

"Who says we fail?" Clanless interrupted.

"He's had two days to think about it," Bain replied. "He had the blood-bonds in his hand, ready to use. If we failed to stop him now, we would also lose our victory to protect Qara."

Clanless gritted his teeth but said nothing.

Bain gestured at the disappearing figure of Hawking. "At least Hawking has a chance."

"Not much of one."

"But a chance. And Qara doesn't." Bain put a hand on his shoulder. "Stay the course."

"Move it, you two!" Ghouk called.

Bain climbed in. Clanless grasped the door handle and hesitated once more. With a last glance down the road, he pulled himself inside. His teeth were clenched so tight, he feared his jaw would snap.

☾ ☾ ☾ ☾ ● ☽ ☽ ☽ ☽

Borde proved impossible to visit. A servant girl would only tell Kekeen, "The lady has requested no visitors today. She is not feeling well."

"Is she ill? Does she need anything?" Kekeen glanced around the ornate hallway. Daviland and Borde had moved right into the palace, at least for now.

"She has requested no visitors," the girl repeated.

"I'm one of her best friends."

"She has requested no visitors."

Kekeen sighed. "All right. I'll come back tomorrow." She turned to go but stopped herself. "How long have you worked here in the palace?"

The girl lowered her eyes. "Most of my life, my lady. I was a slave until the Hawk King's death."

"Then… why are you still here? You're free now!"

She looked up with a sad smile. "Where would I go?" She gestured in the direction of the doors. "It's High Winter. If I have any family left, they're in Mantukhai, many miles from here. At least for now, I'm safe and warm." She lowered her head again. "It's more than I had a few days ago."

"You weren't safe before?"

The girl's eyes widened. "Here? None of us girls were safe, if you take my meaning, my lady."

Kekeen shuddered. "From the Hawk King?"

"No." She shook her head. "His son." She glanced around, as if he might appear. "Ghouk."

Kekeen took a deep breath. She understood completely. In her brief encounters with the Hawk King's son, she'd been terrified. The King himself had been the most frightening man she ever met, but Ghouk scared her in a different way. His eyes never stopped roving her body.

She forced herself to smile at the girl. "Well, you shouldn't have to worry now. Daviland won't treat you that way. And once High Winter passes, maybe you can find your family." She paused. "What happened to Ghouk, anyway?" She didn't remember seeing him in the chaos after the Hawk King's fall.

The girl shrugged. "No one knows. And no one wants to think about it." She almost bowed. "Pardon me, my lady."

Kekeen let her go and followed the hall herself, making her way back toward the exit that led to the arena. Maybe if she searched all of the arena fighters' rooms again, she'd find something to indicate where they'd gone.

Before she reached the door, she spotted the three Lords again, emerging from the throne room. They spoke together for a few moments before one split off from the other two and hurried down a different hall. Kekeen watched for a moment, then followed after him. She wasn't sure why, but any activity within the palace might provide a clue to Daviland's odd behavior.

From this distance, it looked like Lord Ulakan, if she had the name right. Kekeen had always been good with names. It came in handy in the entertainment business.

Ulakan moved with a sure and quick gait, evidence of someone who knew his way around and confidence in what he was doing. Kekeen hurried along to keep up, worried he would turn and see her, but more worried that she would lose sight of him. If so, she'd never find him again. She was already lost in this enormous building.

She almost got too close when Ulakan made an abrupt stop in front of a door. Kekeen ducked back around a corner before the Lord could glance in her direction. Hearing him knock, she peeked out to see who answered.

The door opened and a pair of blood-priests emerged. Kekeen's shoulders drooped. Nothing suspicious at all; Lord Ulakan was only seeking spiritual guidance… and then she remembered: the palace had a dedicated temple of its own, and they were nowhere near it. Why were these priests in here?

Kekeen held her breath, straining to hear anything of the conversation. After a few minutes, the men nodded to one another and went their separate ways. Kekeen hurried around another corner to avoid Lord Ulakan's return. She waited a full two minutes before emerging and seeking her way back to the exit.

Throughout the conversation, she'd only heard one word clearly and repeatedly: Suirel.

꙾ ꙾ ꙾ ꙾ ● ꙾ ꙾ ꙾ ꙾

When Clanless woke on the morning of the fourth day, something was different. Bain figured it out before he did. "The wind has died down!"

Indeed. When they stepped out of the carriage, one by one, in curiosity, they found a calm and pleasant day, nothing like the previous three. A gentle breeze stirred the snow, some of which had already begun to melt.

"Told you," Hagh grumbled. "Suirel makes the weather crazy. This won't last."

"Maybe not," Ghouk said. "But we'll enjoy it while it does. I'm riding outside today. You can each take turns out here with me, driving this thing."

Hagh took the first shift, and the rest piled back inside. They looked around at each other as the carriage began moving.

"Not so bad in here with just four," Sugh observed.

"And downright pleasant without Ghouk," Bain said.

They sat in silence for a few moments. Qara burst out laughing. "This is so ridiculous. All of it."

Clanless nodded, but no one else said anything.

Qara slapped both palms down on the seat on either side of her. "Look at us! You have the most powerful warriors in all of the Empire here, and all we can do is sit around waiting for that idiot to tell us what to do."

"I don't think he's an idiot," Bain allowed.

"Oh?" Qara shook her head. "You're not thinking then. If he wanted the throne, he could have had it. All he had to do was order the five of you to kill Daviland. Who would have been able to stop you?"

"Daviland defeated me," Clanless pointed out. "And he wouldn't have been alone. Others would have protected him."

"Even so, we could have done it," Sugh said, scratching his ear. "I think Qara's right."

"And then what would have happened?" Bain asked. "We kill Daviland. The city is full of his supporters. Would they all just give up and go home? Give everything to Ghouk? No. They would have risen up and killed him and us." He sat back. "And then chosen a new leader. No… Ghouk knew that. He's smart. He's aiming for greater power."

"How?" Qara's face wrinkled in confusion. "The mines? The crystal? How will that help him? Why isn't he trying to meet up with the rest of the army, the ones still loyal to his father?"

"I don't know yet," Bain admitted. "But it has something to do with the blood." He shot a glance at Clanless.

"Beyond me," Sugh said with a shrug. "I haven't known anything for years, besides how to kill. And that doesn't take much thinking."

The conversation meandered for a while, discussing the weather, the chaos moon, more speculation on Ghouk's plans, and how long their food would last. Clanless had enough and stood up. "Since it's not freezing, I'm going to walk outside."

"Good idea," Bain agreed. "We could use the exercise. I'll join you."

He'd wanted to be alone but didn't say so. The two fighters climbed out of the slow-moving carriage.

"What are you doing?" Ghouk demanded, eyes narrowed as he looked down at them.

"We've been three days without any exercise," Bain said. "While the weather's agreeable, we thought we'd walk instead of ride for a while."

"Follow the carriage then. But don't run off." Ghouk rolled his eyes and turned forward.

Bain and Clanless let the carriage pass them and followed in its tracks. The air was cold, but not frigid. After a few minutes of walking, Clanless no longer noticed the temperature. His wound complained, but he pushed through it. Bain was right: he did need the exercise. He swung his arms around every few steps.

"You know," he said after a few minutes, "Ghouk didn't order us not to damage the carriage. We could break one of those wheels. Give people time to catch up to us."

Bain shook his head. "You're still not thinking far enough ahead. No one knew we left, and even if they did, they wouldn't have followed in that weather. At earliest, someone might come out today. But even if they caught up to us, then what? Ghouk would only order us to fight. We'd have to kill whoever showed up."

Clanless kicked at a tuft of brown grass. He didn't want to admit it, but he was having trouble thinking straight. All of these new memories confused even his present thoughts. Maybe Sugh was right. Maybe he should only focus on the things he knew how to do without thinking.

"We have to let Ghouk play out his idea until we have a clearer understanding of what he's trying to do," Bain mused.

"And then what?"

Bain grinned. "Then I'll think of something."

After a couple of minutes, Bain chuckled. "The other day, when you told that story, it took me back to training days. I can't stop thinking about it now." He paused. "I hadn't thought about it in a long time," he added quietly.

Clanless grunted.

"Remember how crazy we thought Nerleson was? Always working so hard at everything?"

"Nerleson is dead," Clanless said. "They all are. We're the only ones left."

"We don't know that. Some of the others could still be around. Kan trained us well."

Clanless narrowed his eyes. "You told me Jik was dead."

Bain sighed. "We were in a duel, Clanless. I lied. I was trying to throw you off. It was the only way I thought I could win. Words are weapons just as much as your moonblade. You still haven't learned that."

Clanless didn't answer.

Bain rolled his eye. "You aren't still holding that fight against me, are you?"

"I don't know."

"I paid for it, remember." Bain gestured to his face.

"I never—" Clanless broke off. "You forced me into that," he whispered.

"People say that to me a lot." A moment later, he asked: "Does it matter that I saved your life the next time we met?"

"Did the Hawk King tell you to?"

Bain threw his head back and laughed. "Come on, Clanless. How could he possibly know you would be in that position and tell me to be waiting for it? The Hawk King was brilliant, but he couldn't see the future. I broke the arena rules to save you." He paused. "I'm lucky I didn't get executed for it."

Clanless didn't answer again. He didn't know what to think.

"We're friends, Aldan." Bain emphasized the name. "Or at least, I consider you a friend. We've been through a lot together. As you said, we might be the only ones left from our training class."

Clanless glanced at him. "Really? You keep telling me not to trust you, and yet we're supposed to be friends?"

Bain spread his arms and turned to walk backward. "You shouldn't trust me! I'm far too self-centered. Everything I do is for my own benefit. It's the only thing I truly learned from my parents." He paused. "By reverse example, I guess." He turned back around.

"That's not how friendship works," Clanless countered. He pointed at the carriage. "Hagh and Sugh? They're my friends. I can trust them. I know if I'm in trouble, they'll help me. And if they're in trouble, I'd do anything to help them. Not for my benefit, but for theirs."

"You mean like how I stole the healing blood for you?"

Clanless waited a few moments before saying, "Yes. Like that." He wanted to think of Bain as a friend, but when compared to Hagh and Sugh—or Zaluu—it wasn't the same. Friendship and trust went hand-in-hand. You couldn't have one without the other.

They trudged along in silence for half an hour or more. Clanless watched the snow melt, revealing more of the browns of the sand and dirt beneath. He wondered what it looked like during High Spring. Did the grass turn green? And what about animals? He asked the last question out loud.

"Some animals live up here," Bain said. "But most of them hide during High Winter, or so I've been told. The really huge animals are much further north, toward the Melkute Kingdom." He looked around. "We might have some difficulty at night if this weather holds."

"Wolves?" Clanless guessed.

"Possibly. But I was thinking of something else. Remember that creature you fought in the arena?"

He'd actually fought two different strange creatures during his time in the arena, but he knew which one Bain meant. His missing toe gave him a constant reminder of that particular fight. He shuddered at the thought of fighting one of those things again.

Then he shivered again for a different reason. The wind had picked up again. He looked up to see the sun surrendering to the goddess. Gathered clouds in the north looked to be heading their way. So much for the pleasant weather. Within a few minutes, all of them returned to the shelter of the carriage.

DAVIL'S DEDUCTIONS

Four days. It had been four days since Aldan and the other fighters had disappeared. Kekeen tried to keep busy, tried to accomplish… anything. But she was stonewalled at every turn. Borde continued to be "unavailable." The horrific weather kept everyone indoors most of the time. She couldn't follow up on any of the mysteries that bothered her. She braved the cold to travel between their inn and the palace over and over, without any success.

This morning, however, had brought an odd pause in the wind and snow, a welcome respite when venturing outside building walls.

Stymied once again in an attempt to see Borde, she crossed from the palace to the arena. She'd searched Aldan's room—and those of the others—twice, but each time, she'd felt guilty looking through someone else's possessions. Maybe one more time would reveal something.

Aldan's door stood open. Someone else moved around inside. Kekeen's heart quickened as she stepped into the doorway.

Daviland stood beside the wall. He ran his hand along the space where Aldan used to hang his famous moonblade. At her entry, he turned with a smile. "Kekeen. How pleasant to see you again. I needed some time to think, away from—" He waved in the direction of the palace. "I'm not sure how I ended up here."

"Maybe you're starting to be concerned about the missing arena fighters." Her voice sounded sharper than she'd intended.

"Maybe I am. None of them have turned up. It's… troubling."

Daviland moved across the room.

Kekeen frowned. Troubling? Two days ago, he'd behaved as if it didn't matter.

"I'm beginning to think someone took them somewhere," he went on. He paused and picked up a metal platter from Aldan's table.

Kekeen had wondered about that platter. She'd tried to clean it herself, but the bloodstains were deeply embedded, as if it had held blood many times. She couldn't help but wonder why Aldan would have such a thing.

Daviland traced the edges of the platter with a finger. He appeared completely lost in thought.

"But who would take them?" Kekeen asked. "No, who could take them? They're the mightiest warriors in the Empire!"

Daviland nodded. "Who indeed?" He set the platter down and looked at Aldan's bed.

"I've tried to figure this out for four days now," Kekeen said. "There aren't many people who could have forced them to go anywhere. One of the Lords, maybe? I don't think even they would have that kind of power. So maybe it was some kind of threat that coerced them. Or maybe an emergency that needed to be dealt with right away."

Daviland chuckled, an odd sound from one who'd looked so melancholy a moment before. He looked over his shoulder at Kekeen with almost a smirk. "Can't accept the idea that he might have left you of his own free will, can you?"

She stepped back. "No. No, I can't. He wouldn't do that. You, you don't know him like I do."

Daviland held up a hand. "I apologize. That was… not me. I shouldn't have said it."

Kekeen folded her arms across her chest. "Then what do you think happened?"

Daviland looked back at the table and platter. "You're right. There aren't many who could have forced them—all of them, that is. And threats wouldn't work." He picked up the platter again. "I suppose someone could have forced Aldan into doing something by threatening you. It's worked before, after all."

Kekeen took in a sharp breath through her nose, but didn't say anything.

"But," Daviland went on, "it wouldn't have worked on the others. Most of them don't have any loved ones, at least not in the city. Oh, I suppose they all had their favorites at Pasque House, like Aldan did, but they wouldn't take those kind of threats seriously."

"What do you mean by that? Aldan's… favorites?" Kekeen knew exactly what Pasque House was.

Daviland looked up with open mouth. "I'm sorry. I was sure you knew. All of the arena fighters were almost weekly visitors to Pasque House. The great Clanless was well known to have a special favorite among the girls there. Ask anyone."

Kekeen tapped her foot. Daviland gave an apologetic grin and returned the platter to the table.

"What is wrong with you?" Kekeen demanded.

"I don't—"

"You have been a completely different person since the Hawk King died! What happened to the man who talked for hours about changing the Empire, ending slavery, and, and elevating the poor?"

"All of that is still true!" Daviland broke in. "We will do it."

"When? You seem totally preoccupied with spending time with the same Lords who did all of it! And when a man who was instrumental in your victory disappears, you act like you don't even care! You—"

"It was Ghouk."

Kekeen stopped. "What?"

"Ghouk." Daviland slapped a hand on the table. "Why didn't I see it before? He's missing too, and he's the only one who might have the power to compel all of them!"

"How could he do that?"

"But where would he take them? And why?" Daviland muttered as he walked to the window and looked out at the swirling snow. "General Ghan. Would he go there? Would the general accept him?"

"How could Ghouk force them?" Kekeen demanded.

Daviland turned back. "I don't know. But as soon as the weather clears up, we'll find out."

"That could be weeks! Or months!"

"I know." Daviland nodded, his mouth set. "But we have little choice." He pointed at the snow. "We say we've overthrown the Hawk King and taken control of the Empire, but really all we've done is take control of this city… and that control is tenuous. Most of the rest of the Empire probably hasn't even heard about what happened here! I know I made this plan, but… maybe it wasn't the best."

"Then you still have a big job ahead of you, I guess."

"You're right." He strode toward the door. "I need to get back to it. Thank you, Kekeen, for this conversation. It's been enlightening."

"Wait, wait." She caught his arm. "I've been trying to visit Borde, but they keep telling me she's unavailable. Can you let me see her?"

"Ah." He hesitated. "She has not been feeling well the past few days. I am not certain, but…" He glanced out the door as if to make sure they were alone. "I think she may be with child."

((((●))))

Kekeen considered Daviland's words for the rest of the day. Borde with child? Here in the capital, such a thing wasn't quite the scandal it would be back in the clanholds or the smaller cities. But it would still be frowned upon in the upper class society… exactly the group Daviland was trying to win over right now. Not good.

The other claim made by Daviland—that Clanless had a "favorite" at Pasque House—troubled her even more, but she didn't know what to do about it. She considered going to Pasque House herself to ask questions, but both the impropriety of visiting such a place combined with worries about her own safety kept her from that course of action. She would have to wait to ask Aldan when he returned.

She continued to muse over both issues until her father arrived at her room that evening. Koland paced about grumbling, trying to get all of it out of his system before performing in the eating house. The crowd wouldn't be very large, but his performances paid for their room and board. Kekeen, on the other hand, hadn't sung since Aldan disappeared.

"What is going on with that man?" he griped. "I don't understand him any more."

"Daviland?"

"Of course, Daviland." Koland threw up his hands. "I've advised him for the past five years, but now he barely listens to a word I say."

"Who does he listen to?"

"The Lords think he's listening to them, but he's not. He doesn't seem overly interested in implementing anything they suggest… thankfully. And they're only stalling, anyway. They hope things will change when High Winter ends." Koland slumped into a chair and banged his fist on the table. "He holds meetings with them, meetings with the Ghamba Lam, meetings with merchants and military leaders, but I'm starting to think he only listens to himself."

"Does he?" Kekeen asked. "He doesn't seem much like himself any more."

Koland tapped his beard. "You're right, of course. Did you see him today?"

Kekeen related her encounter in Aldan's room, leaving out the reference to Pasque House. Koland shook his head at the final revelation. "That will not endear him to the populace at any level. What is he thinking?" He took a deep breath. "Maybe he's wrong about her. Maybe it's just a winter sickness."

"Maybe." Kekeen was not convinced. "But now what? I mean, what can we do?"

Koland put a hand to his face and leaned on his elbow. "I don't like the idea of using threats… but maybe I need to remind Davil whose stories built his legend." He sighed. "No… that's arrogant of me."

"But true!" Kekeen clasped his hand and pulled it from his face. "If not for you, Daviland's following would never have grown to the numbers it has now!"

He smiled at her. "While true, it's not something I should flaunt in front of him. But maybe I can slip it into a conversation somehow."

"You're the best storyteller in the Empire. You slip all kinds of things into conversations all the time. You can do this."

Koland nodded and got to his feet. "Speaking of stories, I need to go tell a few. Sure you won't join me?"

Kekeen lowered her head and shook it. "No… I can't. I just can't right now."

He sighed. "I understand. But I hope you'll try sometime soon." He headed for the door. "You can't mourn forever."

"He's not dead!" Kekeen's head snapped up, eyes wide.

"I'm not saying he is." Koland paused at the door. "But when you turn off the rest of your life, you behave as if he is."

Kekeen winced as he left. He had a point, of course. Her life wasn't all about Aldan, no matter how much she loved him. For the past few years, she'd been hard at work as part of the rebellion, traveling with her father and influencing people. Why? Because she'd believed in Daviland and what he would do.

And now he needed to be held accountable to do those things.

HERE WE SACRIFICE

Then

"It doesn't feel right without the cape," Zaluu grumbled.

Badaar rolled his eyes. "You've gone without it before when you needed to. Now you need to."

"But how will they know it's me?" Zaluu grinned as he fingered his throwing knives. "I want them to know."

"They'll know enough." Clanless tested the edge of his moonblade with his finger. "We'll make sure of it."

Badaar looked out from the alley where the three of them waited. "Not long now. If my sources are right, the cult should be gathering as the sun retreats." He pointed to a house down the street.

"I don't understand the cult thing," Clanless said. "They worship a different moon?"

"The chaos moon," Zaluu corrected. "Suirel."

"It only appears every thirty years," Badaar said, keeping his eyes on the street. "Messes with the weather. But sun take me if I know why they would worship it."

"Does Suirel ask for blood?" Clanless wondered.

"We'll have to ask one of them," Zaluu said, "if we keep one alive."

Badaar turned and lowered his eyebrows at him. "We're not here to slaughter them all."

"Are you sure? There goes one now." Zaluu pointed.

Badaar and Clanless looked back at the street to see a man walking at a normal pace. Clanless opened his mouth to ask Zaluu how he knew, but at that moment, the man turned to the cult house, opened the door and entered.

"That's one," Badaar whispered.

Over the next few minutes, sixteen more entered the house: thirteen men and three women. When no one else arrived after a space of ten minutes, Badaar decided they'd waited long enough. "Let's move in. Remember, we want to see what they're up to before we do anything else. After that…" He hesitated. "Well, we'll just see where this leads."

They hurried across the street to the house. Clanless lifted his moon-blade and glanced at Zaluu. His friend nodded, his face stone. Clanless fought against a rage rising up within. This cult, whoever they were, had kidnapped Koland and threatened Kekeen… all to get to him. The prisoner Zaluu captured claimed to have been hired by a Daghilch to kill the one they considered an abomination: Clanless himself. He strongly suspected he knew which Daghilch was in question.

Badaar held up a hand and eased the door open. When nothing happened, he motioned to them to follow and stepped inside. The front door opened into a dark hall which led straight ahead for longer than it should have. The house wasn't that deep. As they proceeded down the hall, Clanless realized it must continue into another building behind the original house. He hadn't paid attention to what might be behind it.

They passed only two doors along the way, one on either side. Badaar listened at each one and heard nothing. A dim light shone around the edges of the door at the end of the hall. The cult members must have gone through there.

The three warriors gathered outside the door and strained their hearing. Clanless thought he could hear a voice, but it sounded some distance away yet. He and Zaluu looked to Badaar. The trainer took a deep breath, grasped the door handle and eased it open.

Beyond the door lay a platform with stairs descending both left and right. A railing directly ahead overlooked a fire-lit area down below. A single man stood with his back to them.

With stealth beyond what Clanless would have expected, Badaar crept up behind the man. His powerful arm snaked out and around the man's throat, cutting off his air before he could cry out. Badaar pulled him back, squeezing until the cultist slumped insensate. Clanless glanced at Zaluu, and the two of them stepped up to look down over the railing. Badaar joined them a moment later.

Clanless didn't know what he had expected to see. Badaar called this a cult, which seemed to be some kind of religious group. The only religion Clanless knew, of course, was the worship of the goddess. Until now, he'd never even considered that people would worship anything else.

The remaining sixteen cultists gathered below in a surprisingly large space dug into the earth like an enormous basement. It could easily have held three times that number. The cultists stood together facing a platform on the far side. A large fire blazed against the dirt wall beyond it, adding to the flickering light provided by a scattering of torches around the rest of the room. Two men in dark red robes stood on the platform with a third man between them, arms outstretched toward the sky. Clanless couldn't tell if the robes matched those of the blood-priests. In this light, they looked darker. He looked up and saw a huge open space in the roof, revealing the moon. Such openings were common, but this one had an odd shape, as if a small circle had intersected with a larger one.

Voices drew his attention back to the cultists. He strained to hear their words.

"...wisdom of the ages?" one of the red robes asked.

"I do desire the wisdom of the ages!" the man in the middle proclaimed. "I seek truth, wisdom, and power from on high!"

"And you shall have it," the red robe answered. "Surrender yourself, and allow one of those beyond to enter you."

The other robed cultist turned to a table Clanless hadn't noticed before. He picked up a shallow bowl and held it up. Even in the flickering dimness, Clanless could see the blood filling it. Was this the answer to his question?

The cultist handed the bowl to the man in the center, who held it up toward the sky. "Suirel!" he cried. "Send one of your children, those who live within this blood, to me! Fill my veins with your power and wisdom!"

Clanless's mouth went dry. Those who live within the blood?

The man brought the bowl to his lips and drank. "Ewww," Zaluu whispered.

The empty bowl fell to the floor. The red robes backed away as the central cultist started to shake. His entire body convulsed in some sort of seizure, but he remained standing. The seizure continued for so long, Clanless wondered if the man would live through it. At last, the trembling stopped. The man swayed on his feet, but kept his balance somehow. He lifted his head and let out a shout.

"Brother?" One of the red robes stepped back. "Are you...?"

"At last!" the man shouted. "At last!" He looked about at the other cultists. "Ah, my friends. Loyal devotees of Suirel! Thank you. Thank you for your faithfulness. Suirel's time is at hand, and you will be rewarded. Less than six years remain until his coming. Be faithful to the end, and you will rule with him!"

The crowd cheered.

"Six years?" Clanless whispered to Badaar. "Is that right for the thirty-year gap?"

The trainer nodded. "But I've never seen anything like this. It's… insane. What has possessed that man?"

Clanless could put a name to it, but didn't. He might be wrong, after all. Zektel had never mentioned Suirel or a cult.

"Are we going to stop all this?" Zaluu asked.

"I don't know…" Badaar began.

"Who are you, great one?" one of the red robes asked.

"I am called Chinkis in your tongue. My true name cannot be uttered by you."

Clanless shifted. This was far too similar to Zektel for his comfort.

"This is bigger than I thought. We can't just slaughter them," Badaar whispered. "Perhaps we should tell someone else."

"Who would we tell?" Zaluu demanded. "The priests? Some of them might be down there right now!"

"The guard?" Clanless suggested.

"What would they do?" Zaluu scoffed. "We can't prove anything, and—"

"We have visitors, my friends!" The booming voice came from the newly-possessed cultist. The entire group turned to look up at the platform where the three warriors crouched.

"I think the decision's been made for us!" Badaar shoved Zaluu back. "Into the hall. Quick!"

Already, the cultists poured up the stairs toward them. Many pulled out weapons as they ran.

"Why are we running?" Zaluu demanded as they hurried down the hall. "We can take them!"

"I know!" Badaar answered. "But—"

His words were cut off as a stone slammed into his shoulder and spun him around. Slinger!

"That does it," Clanless growled. "Zaluu, your knives!"

"About time!" Zaluu whirled and threw one knife after the other down the hall at their pursuers. At least two struck home, including a hit on the slinger.

Clanless activated the Taint at once. The two cultists seized up, shaking in pain before they collapsed. The others kept coming, ignoring the bodies of their comrades. Clanless stood in the center of the hall, moonblade at ready. "Help Badaar!" he called over his shoulder.

"Help yourself!" Badaar grunted, getting to his feet.

"Make them bleed then," Clanless growled. "I'll do the rest."

In a moment, carnage filled the dark hallway. Clanless swung the moonblade up and back in the center. Badaar and Zaluu crouched to either side of him, lunging forward with their own weapons as the opportunity presented itself. Over and over, Clanless used the Taint. It took only a few short minutes before the attackers stopped coming. None were left standing... except one man who waited calmly beyond the fallen bodies. As Clanless caught his breath, the man slowly clapped three times.

"Impressive. Very impressive," he called. Clanless recognized the possessed voice from earlier but couldn't tell much of anything else about the man in the dark. "But especially you, clanless one. Your mastery of your talent is admirable."

"Then why are you trying to kill me?"

"A misguided effort from these." The man gestured at the bodies strewn along the hall. "It will not happen again while I am here."

"We need more of a guarantee than your word," Badaar said through clenched teeth.

"I have an idea," Zaluu said. A brush of air went by Clanless's ear. The cultist grunted as Zaluu's last knife hit him somewhere. "Burn him, Clanless."

"No. Wait—" the cultist began.

But Clanless activated it anyway. To his surprise, the cultist screamed far louder and shriller than anyone he'd ever burned before. He thrashed about, slamming into both walls of the corridor before collapsing backward over another body. Clanless thought he saw blood on his face.

"That... was strange," Zaluu said. "I think you hurt the thing inside him."

Badaar groaned and slumped against the wall.

"Let's get him to a healer." Clanless left the mystery of the cultist behind. But he knew he'd be asking Zektel some hard questions later.

Now

He never did talk with Zektel about the fight with the cultists. Or did he? Clanless lay still, staring up at the carriage ceiling. Zektel had repressed that memory as soon as possible, most likely. He'd learned too much. And if he did talk with her about it, she'd repressed that memory too. Maybe he'd remember it later.

Five whole days of travel had gone by. After the half a day of sunshine, High Winter returned with a vengeance. The cold grew so intense that the six travelers were forced to huddle closer together in the carriage to keep warm. All throughout the following night and day, they'd received no respite from plunging temperatures. At last, as the sun retreated on the fifth day, the winds died down a little and the temperature rose enough that they could bear it. They'd slept much better. Even now, Clanless thought he was the only one awake.

"We should get there today," Bain whispered beside him, proving him wrong.

Clanless rolled onto his side to face his fellow fighter. "What makes you say that?"

Bain gestured with his head toward the sleeping Ghouk. "He muttered it as he fell asleep last night. He didn't say how late in the day, though."

"Have you figured out what we should do?"

"We still don't know his plan." Bain stopped when Ghouk stirred. When the prince didn't get up, he continued: "We have to wait… and be ready to act."

Clanless didn't know how they could "act" when Ghouk controlled their bloodbonds, but he nodded.

A few minutes later, Ghouk woke up and ordered everyone to get things moving. Even without Bain's words, Clanless would have guessed something was up. Ghouk seemed more anxious and excited than he'd been since they left the city. While helping Sugh take care of the oxen, Clanless saw the nearest mountain looming close. They might not reach the mountain itself today, but some high hills in front of it might be their target.

Five or six days of travel in a slow-moving carriage. How many miles would that be? Clanless had no idea, but it seemed like quite a trip. Of course, he'd only traveled three other times in his entire life, so what did he know?

The hills and mountain grew ever closer each time they stopped or when he took a turn directing the oxen and looked through the front window. And as the hills grew, so did a strange feeling within Clanless. At first, he thought it was his gut wound, but the feeling extended to his nostrils and tongue, as if a familiar scent or taste were just beyond his perception. He opened his mouth to mention it, but stopped himself. Why reveal anything at all to Ghouk? He'd bring it up with one of the others if given the chance.

Late afternoon, they arrived at their destination. "We're approaching some gates," Qara reported from the driver's position.

Ghouk shot to his feet and bent over to look out through the front. "Pull right up there." He turned to the others. "Sugh. Clanless. When we stop, get out and open the gates."

"What if they're locked?" Clanless asked.

"There's no reason for them to be locked." Ghouk rolled his eyes. "Just shut. Open them and join us on the other side."

Sugh looked at Clanless and shrugged. They waited for the carriage to stop before jumping out into the cold air. At least the wind, though it cut right through their clothes, wasn't quite as bad as it had been earlier in the day.

Clanless stared up at a twenty-foot-high wall. It extended in a gentle curve in both directions, joining up with higher cliffs on either side. High hills leading into a mountain waited behind the gate, but he couldn't see much of it yet. The strange feeling grew a little stronger. He sniffed at the air several times but still couldn't figure it out.

Despite Ghouk's assurances, the gate could not be opened from the outside. They explored in either direction until Sugh found a rope ladder hanging from the top. He looked it over with suspicion before trusting his weight to it. Satisfied, he climbed quickly, reached the top, and disappeared onto the other side. After a moment, he called for Clanless to join him. "Can't do it on my own!"

Clanless climbed up the ladder much slower. His wounded gut didn't like this kind of motion. At the top, the wall was only about a foot wide. Down below, Sugh gestured for him to jump. Even though he knew it looked ridiculous, Clanless took the time to hang down over the edge before dropping down into a snowbank. He didn't want to risk ripping the wound open on impact.

Sugh hauled him out of the snow and helped him brush off. The walls muted the wind's power, much to their relief. "Over here," Sugh said, gesturing at the gate.

A heavy crossbar held it shut. Together, the two fighters strained to lift it and move it out of the way. One or two more men would have made a significant difference. It also took both of them working together to pull one side of the gate open and then the other. No sooner did they accomplish this than the carriage rolled right in. Clanless had to step out of the way in a hurry to keep from getting bumped by one of the oxen.

Only then did he turn and look at where they'd arrived.

The road—such as it was—entered a wide inner space within the walls. Here and there, empty carts bore testimony to the mining that had once taken place. A couple of ramshackle huts sat near the gate and the road, but they appeared empty as well.

"Is no one here?" Sugh wondered.

"Maybe up there." Clanless pointed up the road. From the inner yard, it turned left up an incline that worked its way up the hill until it reached a large cave opening. There, it switched back to the right, passing by more dark entrances before another switchback took it to the left. At the top of that one, the road divided. One final switchback led far to the right and to another hole in the rock. But to the left and higher, they could see some newer buildings set in against the rock. It was hard to see amidst a few snow flurries, but Clanless thought he discerned smoke drifting up from one of them.

The carriage rolled on to the base of the inclined road. Clanless and Sugh hurried to catch up. There, they discovered the road partially blocked by a rockslide.

Ghouk opened the carriage door and surveyed the problem. "Move those rocks!" he commanded.

Sugh started forward, but Clanless hesitated. "I don't think that will work. Look there." He pointed toward the top of the slide. "If we move the ones at the bottom, more will fall."

Bain climbed out behind Ghouk. "That's probably why it hasn't been repaired yet," he observed. "It'll take a lot of work to get this open again." He looked up at the zig-zag road. "I take it we're going up there?"

Ghouk looked over the rocks and the road with a scowl. "We'll walk then. Come on." He led the way around the rocks and started up the road.

Hagh brought Clanless and Bain their weapons. Qara exited the carriage last. Clanless glanced back at the open gates before following their master. He hadn't ordered them to close the gates. Or take care of the oxen. Qara patted one as they walked past. "We'll be back," she promised.

The six of them trudged up the rocky road. Ruts in the dirt made it clear heavy-laden carts had traveled this way on a regular basis. Clanless saw evidence of frequent repair jobs everywhere. Holes had been filled. Locations of other rock slides had been reinforced. The condition of the road seemed inconsistent with the abandoned materials below.

"It's like they're not doing much mining any more," Bain muttered, "but they're still using this road."

They hadn't ascended far before they left the protection of the walls, and the wind returned. They walked as far from the outer edge as possible. No one wanted to be blown over the side, a possibility that became more and more likely the higher they climbed.

They reached the first switchback and passed an enormous mine entrance. Clanless looked into the darkness but saw nothing but rock and snow. No one had used that one in a while. He looked up at the steep cliff leading to the next segment of the road. He supposed this back-and-forth made the most sense for ascending this height, but it certainly took a long time. Another mine entrance gaped empty and unused midway to the next switchback. They passed two more before finally reaching the division of the road.

Ghouk stopped and appeared to be thinking. Clanless shivered. At least while they'd been climbing, the movement and exercise provided some warmth. Standing here only made them colder than ever. At last, Ghouk seemed to make a decision.

"Hagh. Sugh." He pointed up the road to the left in the direction of the buildings. "Investigate those buildings. Kill anyone you find."

"Is that necessary?" Qara protested. "They're just mine workers, aren't they?"

"No. They're not." Ghouk's face was stone. "The mine workers left before High Winter began."

"Then who…?"

"I will brook no further delays in obedience!" Ghouk snapped. He reached into his coat and pulled out the bloodbonds. "Do you all need a reminder of who is in charge?"

Hagh patted Sugh on the shoulder and they started up the leftward trail.

"The rest of you, with me." Ghouk turned and continued up the road to the right. Clanless and Bain exchanged looks and followed. Qara hesitated a little longer before joining them.

This last stretch of the road was steeper by far. Clanless slipped multiple times, banging his knees against the rocky surface, but he wasn't the only one. Ghouk cursed every time it happened to him. Qara expressed dismay in her own way. Only Bain kept his footing.

Though the road ended at the cavern entrance ahead, Clanless noticed two more openings in the rock above them. About fifty feet above the road, the two holes gaped side-by-side in the cliff face. "Almost like eyes," Bain muttered beside him. Clanless agreed. Snow had begun to swirl down and around them again, making the two holes appear even more foreboding.

At last they reached the final entrance. Ghouk plunged right in, and the others followed. Once inside, they all stopped to catch their breath. The shelter from the wind and snow made an enormous difference. Clanless found himself sweating, even though the air had to be near freezing at best.

"You could drive wagons through here," Bain observed. The tunnel they'd entered made a slow curve up and toward the left, almost as if yet another switchback awaited them inside instead of out.

"They do," Ghouk said. He lifted his head, and Clanless almost shuddered. The look of predatory greed on Ghouk's face reminded him far too much of the Hawk King himself.

Qara took a few steps forward. "What are we doing here, Ghouk? This place is empty." She gestured at the walls. "I don't even see any crystal."

"We're not here for crystal." He pointed to a pile of discarded materials next to the wall. "Clanless. Bain. Make torches. It will be lighter further on, but we may need guidance on the way."

"Blood." The word escaped Clanless's lips before he realized what he'd been sensing for hours.

Ghouk's eyes shot to him. "What?"

Clanless didn't answer, overwhelmed by his senses. Now he understood. Somewhere nearby, there was blood. A lot of it. No. An enormous amount of it. Ever since the Taint became part of him, he'd been able to sense the presence of blood. Usually, it happened in the arena when his opponent bled. But this… the coppery taste filled his mouth. The smell of it flooded his nostrils. He hadn't felt like this since the raid in the temple where he'd Tainted huge quantities of blood at once. But if the sensation was so strong here, where he couldn't even see any blood yet, how much could it be?

Ghouk strode over and slapped him in the face. Clanless stepped back in surprise. "Snap out of it!" Ghouk ordered. "What is happening to you?"

Clanless looked around. Qara stared at him, mouth agape. Bain stared as well, but he appeared more curious than shocked. "What do you mean? What did I do?"

"You were mumbling to yourself," Bain said. "You dropped your blade and stared into the darkness."

Embarrassed, Clanless retrieved the moonblade. "It's… blood. A lot of it. I can… sense it."

Ghouk nodded and stepped back. "Because of your power, I suppose. Interesting."

"This is where they bring the excess blood!" Bain realized. "That's what you were hinting at."

"It's not far now," Ghouk said. "Torches, please?"

The smell and taste continued to permeate his senses, but Clanless obeyed. Together, he and Bain managed to create two rudimentary torches. "They won't last long," Bain reported.

"They won't need to." Ghouk took one and led the way into the darkness.

Clanless took the other torch and gestured for Bain and Qara to go ahead, while he brought up the rear. Trailing the others, he could try to keep the sensations under control. With every step they took up the path, it only grew stronger.

The tunnel continued its upward climb. If someone did bring wagons in here—wagons of blood, if Ghouk was right—the oxen would have to work very hard to get it up this incline. Unless… maybe some blood magic was involved as well. Clanless ground his teeth, both to distract himself from the taste of blood and out of frustration over his lack of knowledge. He hated not knowing so much about the blood-magic, this place, the world around him, everything. And yet, he'd be happy to stay ignorant if he could back to Kekeen and get away from all of it.

After another long ascent, the air grew cooler. A dim light shone ahead, almost right as the torches sputtered and died. A few moments later, they entered an enormous chamber, at least the size of the arena in Et-Baylak.

The two openings Bain had called "eyes" provided the light, though not as much as Clanless would have expected. Another look revealed why: the openings angled downward from the chamber. While it prevented direct sunlight, it also kept the snow and wind out.

But his attention immediately shifted from the light source to the dominant feature of this chamber. Clanless let the dying torch drop to the ground and gripped his moonblade with both hands. The smell and taste of blood so overwhelmed him that he swayed on his feet. He couldn't breathe. He reached for the Taint, desperate to do something, but it eluded him. For the first time in memory, he couldn't activate it.

A hand touched his shoulder. "Are you all right?"

He shifted his gaze to Qara; concern radiated from her face. For some reason, her presence calmed him. He took a deep breath. "I will be." Only after two more deep breaths did he manage to turn and face the chamber.

In simplest terms, it was a hole. But only if the hole had grown out of the floor, pulling rock with it like a liquid and then turned at an angle to face them. It almost looked like some sort of stone serpent without a head had erupted from the ground. Bloodstains coated the entirety of the opening and much of the rock around it. The opening descended into darkness, but not before crossing a ring of stone "teeth" that pointed back into the hole. It would be easy to get past them going down, but not so easy trying to get back out.

Ghouk walked to the very edge of the hole and put a hand on the rock. "We're here." His voice held… awe?

"It's a hole," Bain said. He looked around. "This is where they bring the excess blood?"

"Yes." Ghouk pointed into the depths. "They pour it here."

"That's it?" Qara asked. "All of that blood from sacrifices to the goddess… they load it up on carts, bring it all the way out here, drive up this ridiculous road into this cave… and pour it down a hole? Is this a joke?"

"I don't see the humor," Bain said, his brow wrinkled. "But I don't see the point either."

Ghouk pointed at him. "You're not as clever as you think, are you? This place is more than you know." He bent and stared down the hole. "This is the Throat of the Goddess, perhaps the most sacred spot in all the Empire."

"Why?" Qara wanted to know. "What makes it sacred? How is this possibly connected to the goddess?" She pointed up toward the moon, hidden by tons of rock above their heads.

Clanless glanced up. "Oh." Qara looked too, and her eyes widened. Etched into the ceiling was a huge rendition of the moon. Clanless stared; he'd never seen details on the moon like this. Mountains and valleys, canyons and hills: did the moon truly possess such things?

"Fascinating," Bain said, but his tone said the opposite. "This is all religious then?" He gestured at the hole. "The blood-priests come here, do some kind of ceremony and pour the blood down the goddess's blessed throat? This is the end result of our people's worship? That's it?"

"What a waste," Qara muttered.

"It's not wasted." Ghouk clenched his fists. "The Throat leads to a cavern lined entirely with almaz crystal. The blood is preserved." He paused. "*All* of it."

Bain's expression shifted from disdain to curiosity. "Blood from every clan, then."

Ghouk nodded. "This is the true source of my father's power. It all began here. It all began… down there." He pointed down the hole.

"You're saying he went down there?" Qara asked.

"I've heard the story since I was a child. The Hawk King descended the Throat of the Goddess and returned a new man. A powerful man. A man blessed by the goddess and empowered by her."

"Bathed in the blood," Bain whispered.

For a few moments, no one said anything.

Clanless shook his head. "No. No. It makes no sense."

"What do you mean?" Bain turned to look at him.

"Dunking yourself in blood doesn't give you any special power." Clanless struggled get his words out as the sensations of the blood continued to pressure him. "If it did, the priests would do it all the time. They have all they need back in the cities. Why come out here?"

"It's not just blood," Ghouk said. "It's all the blood. The blood of all the clans over hundreds of years. Some of my blood is there. Some of your blood, no doubt. Brought here from sacrifices we gave as we grew up. And before that, the blood of our parents, and their parents, and our ancestors so many generations back, we can't even grasp it."

"I still don't—"

"And the crystal," Bain interrupted. "It's not just the blood; it's the crystal. I always knew the crystal had strange properties; how else could it keep blood fresh?" He stepped closer to the Throat. "You're saying all that blood down there is still fresh?"

"And amplified." Ghouk smiled. "There's no place like this anywhere in the world. The crystal is only found here. And the Throat leads to the greatest amount of it. My father described it to me. There's so much power down there the crystals themselves provide constant light, reflecting on a veritable sea of blood."

Qara shuddered beside Clanless. "Sounds disgusting."

"Because you have no vision!" Ghouk snapped. "I will become as powerful as my father. And then you will escort me to the border encampment to the north where General Ghan waits with my army. I will return to Et-Baylak, and the Sar Empire will reach new heights under my leadership!" He looked around the room until he spotted what he wanted. "Over there, all of you."

Tearing his eyes from the Throat, Clanless looked to the side wall opposite the eyes and saw a pair of tables. A number of golden bowls rested on them, probably for use in sacrifice ceremonies. But beside the tables, anchored into the rock, stood an enormous winch with a thick rope wrapped around it.

"You will use that rope to lower me down," Ghouk commanded, "and bring me back up when I am ready."

Clanless and Qara started toward the winch, but Bain didn't move. "No," he said. "I don't think we will."

BLOOD AND PROMISES

Ghouk bristled. "What do you mean, 'no'? You do what I say!" He fumbled for the bloodbonds.

"In the end, you're just not as smart as you think you are," Bain said. Before Ghouk could do anything, he stepped forward and swung one of his spiked maces against the prince's knee. Ghouk screamed and collapsed. The bloodbonds clanged and scattered on the stone floor.

Clanless and Qara stared. How? How could Bain do that?

Ghouk lay on the ground, pathetically whimpering. He reached for the metal plates only to have Bain step on his fingers. "No need of that. Of course, it wouldn't do you any good."

Ghouk looked up at Bain, tears streaming down his face. "How?"

"You mocked me throughout the trip here." Bain did a rough imitation of Ghouk's voice, but with a whinier tone: "'You're the clever one.'" He bent down and picked up one of the bloodbonds. "Yet through this entire process, through everything that's happened… you never bothered to count these, did you?"

Qara sucked in a breath.

"There are only five here, you idiot." Bain tossed the bloodbond back with the others. It skipped across them and came to rest near Clanless's feet. "And no, you didn't throw Hawking's out after you got rid of him. It's here too." He chuckled. "But mine is not."

"Why?" Qara exclaimed.

Bain glanced back at her. "Because the Hawk King freed me the day before he died." He looked back at Ghouk. "I was never under your control. I played along to find out what you had planned." He seized the prince by the back of his clothing. "Do you know how annoying it was that you made me wait until we were all the way here?"

Bain dragged Ghouk across the room. The prince screamed as his shattered knee rubbed against the floor. "Clanless!" he managed. Bain smacked him across the mouth.

"Nope. Can't have you ordering him to fight me. We've done that too much already. Besides, you won't be his master much longer."

Clanless took a step forward. "Bain…"

With a heave, Bain launched Ghouk across the floor toward one of the "eyes." He teetered on the edge of the incline, scrambling desperately for some kind of handhold. But he found none. Ghouk plunged down the cliff with a wail.

Though Clanless couldn't hear the impact, he felt it. Or rather… he felt the end of the bloodbond. For a moment, a great weight pressed against every inch of his body. And then it vanished. He almost bounced upward at the relief.

"We're free!" Qara gasped.

Bain stood still, staring down through the eye.

Clanless shook himself, still fighting against the blood sensations. He wanted to celebrate, to cheer, to count this as day four of freedom. But one question dominated his thoughts: "Bain. Why did the Hawk King free you?"

"I didn't count on this," Bain murmured, still staring.

"What's going on?" Qara asked.

Bain looked back. All the mockery had vanished from his face. "The oxen are dead."

"What?"

Qara and Clanless moved to the edge of the incline and peered down. Snow swirled in front of the opening for a moment, obstructing their view. When it cleared, Clanless caught a glimpse of something he couldn't identify. Something moved near the carriage. With agility greater than any ox, it darted out of sight behind the carriage. The oxen lay on the ground in pools of blood and gore, still tied to their harnesses.

"We left the gate open." Bain slammed a fist against the rock wall. "We left the blood-damned gate open!"

"What is it?" Qara asked, still not comprehending.

More movement caught Clanless's eyes. Four—no, five—of the creatures galloped up the first incline toward the switchback. "The lizards." The same two-legged horror he'd faced in the arena. But an entire pack of them.

Bain waved his arms in the air as he stomped back toward the Throat. "All this time, all this waiting. Manipulating Ghouk. And everything falls apart because Sugh didn't close the gate!"

Clanless turned to him. "Why did the Hawk King free you?"

"We've got a more urgent issue on our hands right now, Clanless!" he snarled.

Clanless tightened his grip on the moonblade and took a step forward. "You... you could have saved Hawking!"

Bain pointed at the eye opening. "Creatures! Coming this way to eat us!"

"They're almost at the second turn!" Qara reported.

Clanless wanted to scream. So many sensations still tore at him, threatening to overwhelm him at any moment. And yet a dire thought kept coming to his mind.

"Bain. What. Did. You. Do?"

Bain grabbed the rope from the winch and yanked it toward the Throat. He kicked the scattered bloodbonds. "I freed you from slavery. You're welcome. Now help me with this!"

Clanless's jaw dropped. "You still want to go down there?"

"It may be our only way out of here! Do you want to stay and face those things?"

"They've paused at the third turn. They can't decide which way to go!" Qara kept them updated.

"We'll fight them," Clanless said. "Together, we can—"

"Be serious, Aldan! I had to save you from only one of them. We can't possibly fight them off... and protect Qara at the same time!"

Qara turned away from the eye. "They've split up. Three are heading toward the buildings. Two are coming this way."

Bain shook his head. "Not even two. Not in a wide space like this." He pointed at the Throat. "It's our only chance."

"I'm not going down there!" Qara exclaimed.

"You'd rather be eaten?" Bain continued to pull the rope from the winch.

"There's a smaller exit right over there!" Qara pointed beyond the Throat.

Clanless and Bain both whirled to look. The Throat had so dominated the chamber they'd never even looked to the back wall. Not much light made it that far from the eyes, but a dark opening not much larger than a doorway waited there.

"If you want to charge down a pitch-black hall with monsters chasing you, be my guest," Bain said. "I know where this one goes."

"Clanless?" Qara looked to him with a tremor in her voice.

"We'll take the passage," he said. "It's narrow enough to give me a chance against those creatures if I have to turn and fight."

"They can't even follow us here!" Bain protested. He pushed some of the rope down the Throat.

Clanless shook his head. "I'm not going near that hole." If the blood overwhelmed him up here, what would it do to him if he got closer?

A screech echoed through the chamber. Qara didn't wait any longer; she dashed for the passage. Clanless followed her, but paused at the entrance to look back. "Bain?"

"No turning back now." Bain's eye met his. "I'll be back, Aldan. Count on it." He yanked the rope further from the winch and launched himself into the Throat.

"Sands!" Clanless never quite understood the use of that word as an epithet, but it worked. He hurried down the tunnel after Qara. After a single turn, they lost almost all of the light.

"Bain was right about this," Clanless said. "We can't run through the darkness." He glanced back, wondering how well the creatures could see in the dark.

"I'll take care of it." Qara fumbled with something. In the darkness, it looked like a blood vial. "Give me a drop of your blood. Quick."

"What?"

"It'll be faster. Give me some blood!" When he didn't respond, Qara grabbed his coat and pulled him closer. "Trust me this once, Clanless. Please."

Clanless drew the heel of his left hand across the moonblade's edge, creating a shallow cut. He held the arm out to Qara. She ran a finger along the cut to gather blood, then applied it to the opening of the vial in her other hand. With a swift gesture, she slammed the vial against the wall of the tunnel. Light exploded from her hand, filling the tunnel in both directions. Clanless blinked, turning his eyes away.

"What was that?"

"Clan Dendsu blood. The light is a side-effect, and it might not last long enough, but it's what we need most right now." She trotted down the tunnel as fast as she could. The floor, fortunately, was smooth enough for them to walk at an accelerated pace.

"You know how to use the blood-magic?" Clanless demanded.

"My father was a Daghilch. I learned a lot before his… fall. Which led to my slavery."

The sound of claws scratching the floor at a fleet-footed rate grew loud behind them. Clanless turned and stationed himself, moonblade ready. "If it looks bad for me, turn and run as fast as you can," he said. "Maybe I can at least hold them off while you escape."

"You can do this," she said, her mouth almost directly behind his ear. "You're the greatest arena fighter in history."

As the light reflected off a pair of eyes approaching fast, Clanless took a deep breath. "We're not in the arena."

The monster slowed as it drew near, perhaps unsure about prey that didn't run. It appeared remarkably similar to the one he'd fought in the Hawk King's arena. As it advanced on two powerful legs, it bent forward, creating an almost horizontal line from the tip of its nose to the end of its whip-like tail. It hissed from between its massive jaws. Some of the feather-like scales at the back of its head and spine rose up like the fur on the back of an angry cat.

Clanless moved the moonblade back and forth. The creature's eyes followed it. Within the confines of the tunnel, the beast was limited. It couldn't leap at him, removing the danger of the huge claws on its feet. Even so, Clanless knew how deadly it could be. He'd buried the moonblade into the back of the last one, but it kept fighting. He couldn't afford that kind of mistake here. Bain would not be charging in for the rescue.

He stabbed forward, testing the creature's reactions. It hissed and backed up. Clanless took a step closer and stabbed again. It backed up again.

"Don't follow it!" Qara said.

He didn't intend to. If he followed long enough, it would lead him back into the larger chamber where it would have the advantage... and others might be waiting.

Instead, Clanless backed away, trusting Qara to do the same. The beast growled deep in its throat. It let him walk back five or six steps before it lunged forward, teeth bared.

Clanless swung the moonblade in an uppercut. He caught the edge of the creature's lower jaw. The moonblade almost stuck in it, but the force of his swing pulled it loose. The monster screeched and backed up, blood dripping from its mouth.

"Keep moving back," Clanless told Qara, following his own instructions. The tunnel angled upward from this point, which pleased him. Now the creature would have to come up to get to him, losing momentum.

Whether the creature understood this or not, it continued to follow them. Another screech resounded through the narrow space. It took Clanless a moment to realize it hadn't come from the monster in front of him.

"There's another one," Qara said.

The monster gave a screech of its own in answer. Asking for help from its fellow or warning it away? They'd arrived as a pack, but Clanless couldn't be sure they always worked together. There wasn't enough room for two of them to fight him here. Even so, he'd rather dispatch this one and try to outrun the second.

"Come on," he snarled at it. "Fight me!"

The creature understood a challenge, at least. It growl-hissed in response, gathered itself, and charged full-force. Qara shrieked. Clanless brought the moonblade down in a vicious strike directly into the beast's skull, but it kept coming. The sheer size and momentum of it threw Clanless to the ground and ripped the moonblade from his grasp. Claws and teeth cut at him in various places, tearing his clothes. For a few moments, confusion reigned in the tunnel. Qara had stumbled backward and fallen herself, and the light almost went out. Clanless experienced a view of ragged feather-scales, light, darkness, and light again. The creature's tail struck him in the face, but not as hard as he'd expected.

And then everything stopped. The beast lay still on top of him.

Qara scrambled to her feet and turned to run.

"Wait! I think it's dead."

She paused and stepped closer, holding the light up. Clanless pushed himself free and stood. The moonblade remained embedded in the creature's skull.

"You killed it with one blow," Qara whispered.

"One very lucky blow," Clanless said. He took hold of the moonblade's handle and pulled. He worked it back and forth several times to extract it. Before it came loose, another screech echoed from somewhere near.

"It's getting closer," Qara pointed out.

Clanless yanked the moonblade loose at last. "Then let's get further."

Holding her glowing vial aloft, Qara led the way as fast as they could move. The tunnel continued to ascend. It took a couple of turns, but Clanless had long since lost track of their direction.

"This has to come out somewhere," he muttered.

"It only makes sense," Qara said. "If the priests are the ones who used that… that Throat, then this tunnel was also for their use."

The passageway leveled out and continued in a straight line for a while. Then it grew narrow, and Clanless had to turn almost sideways to fit. He hoped their pursuer would have more trouble, but the tunnel soon widened again. The longer they walked, the more the blood sensations faded. They must have traveled far from the sea of blood at the bottom of the Throat… and far from Bain, if he'd made it there.

"I think I see something," Qara said. "We might be coming to an end."

Clanless didn't answer. He'd been straining his ears, trying to detect any sound of the beast following them, convinced he still heard claws scraping rock in the distance.

"Here." Qara came to a stop. "Look at this."

Clanless stepped up close behind her and stared at a dead end. This couldn't be possible. The tunnel couldn't have come this far only to just… stop. "There must be a door," he murmured. In Qara's light, he could make out the edges of something. The wall wasn't completely smooth. He moved past Qara and pushed against it, but nothing happened.

"Wait, I know." Qara dug through the pouch at her belt and drew out another blood vial. "Ha. Clan Shasin. Mostly priests. This one should work."

"Work how?" Clanless asked, looking back the way they had come again. He knew he'd heard claws this time. Closer.

"Quiet. Let me try to remember." Qara switched places with him again and explored the edges. She muttered to herself as she ran her fingers along a crack.

Clanless, though curious, turned back to face the tunnel. The creature was back there somewhere. Why hadn't it attacked like its companion? Could these things learn from each other?

"Got it!" Qara exclaimed. A moment later, a rumble filled their ears. Clanless turned and watched a rock door slide down, spilling light and frigid air into the tunnel. Qara hopped over it before it reached the bottom and hurried outside. Clanless followed, but stayed wary.

They came out onto a wide, flat area near the peak of the high hills. The mountains still loomed nearby, but Clanless couldn't see the mines at all. They must have come all the way through some of the hills to the other side. A light snow swept sideways through the air by the wind. Clanless became instantly conscious of the torn holes in his clothing. They couldn't stay out in this weather unprotected for long, but neither could they return to the tunnel.

"Look at this." Qara moved down a series of steps to a type of stone pagoda: a circular, wall-less structure with pillars supporting its roof. A pair of stone benches sat alone beneath it.

Clanless followed her. Qara brushed snow off one of the benches and frowned to discover it coated in ice. "What do you suppose they used this for?" She looked up and exclaimed, "Oh!" Clanless looked up and saw the answer to her question. The center of the circular roof was made of some kind of glass, not stone. Through it, partially obscured by snow, they could see the moon… but it was at least twice its normal size! Clanless stepped outside of the pagoda and looked at a normal moon, then returned to see the larger one. The glass magnified the moon's appearance.

"We can't wait here," he said, tearing his eyes away. "We don't know—"

He didn't finish the statement. One of the creatures burst out of the tunnel in a leap, bypassing the stairs and landing only a few feet from the pagoda. It raised itself to its full height and screamed in triumph.

"Run!" Clanless stepped toward the beast, raising his blade. It hissed and sidestepped, moving around the pagoda. Clanless stumbled around one of the benches, trying to keep the monster between him and Qara.

"This way!" Qara called. "There's a way down… I think."

The creature's head swung in the direction of her voice.

"No, you don't! Fight me, you monster!" Clanless banged the backside of the moonblade against one of the pillars. A clump of snow fell from the pagoda's roof at the impact. The creature turned back toward him and growled. Its head moved up and down, evaluating the structure.

Clanless shouted at it again, trying to goad the beast. It snapped its jaws in his direction before crouching down, preparing to jump. Clanless had a brief moment to brace himself before it happened. The creature leaped forward, almost hitting the edge of the pagoda roof. All four of its limbs stretched forward, claws hungering for its prey. Clanless sidestepped and swung the moonblade. He managed to cut a deep gash in the creature's left thigh. It roared as it tried to land on the benches. Its feet slipped on the ice, and it collapsed between the benches in a tangle of limbs.

Clanless bolted after Qara. He could stay and fight, but he'd rather be in a position to stop it from catching his companion. He knew how fast these things could be; it might choose to ignore him and chase Qara. No matter what, he had to cut off that possibility.

Qara had found somewhat of a path descending from the pagoda toward a wide, open plateau. Clanless didn't like the look of it: the wider the space, the more advantage the creature gained. The path itself was more of a series of ledges and rocks which the wind had kept mostly bare of ice and snow. But he could see it wouldn't stay that way much longer. Like the benches above, these rocks would soon be covered in ice as well. The path allowed for a slow, but relatively safe descent for around thirty or forty feet. Clanless hoped the beast would have more trouble with it.

Looking at the enormous plateau, Clanless would have thought they had reached ground level if he hadn't known better. On two sides, he couldn't see the edges. Only the rock wall behind him and a drop-off not far to the right defined the landscape. At first glance, he'd assumed the plateau to be completely flat. As he descended, he realized it was more varied than the desert they'd traveled through in the carriage. Rock outcroppings dotted the ground here and there, all of them coated with snow to some degree. Qara moved toward the nearest of them. Once he reached her level, Clanless followed.

He glanced back and saw, to his dismay, that the cliff descent was no detriment to his pursuer. The creature paused at the top for only a moment before jumping off the edge. It seemed to bounce from foothold to foothold, sideways to the cliff, tail extended for balance. Many of the ledges or footholds broke from its weight, and tumbled down the cliff. It would be difficult, if not impossible, to climb back up that way. The beast never stopped until it reached the bottom, a trip taking only a few seconds. Its final leap landed with an explosion of white in a snowbank.

Clanless caught up to Qara near the outcropping, an upthrust chunk of rock about eight feet high at its peak. He spun to face the monster. The wind picked up, swirling snow in heavier gusts, making vision difficult.

"Qara! Keep behind me! I can't protect you if you get too far to either side!"

The beast advanced in slow steps, keeping its eyes fixed on Clanless. If the snow and wind bothered it, it gave no sign. The head dropped lower and lower as it drew near. Clanless spared a quick glance for Qara, who appeared to be fumbling in her pouch again. He took one step back toward her.

The creature rushed the last few feet and leaped, high and fast. Its trajectory would take it over Clanless and right at Qara. It was also in range of the moonblade.

Clanless swung at the right moment. His blade sliced through the creature's stomach, leaving at least a seven-inch gash. But it did nothing to stop its momentum.

Qara screamed.

A dark blur slammed into the creature in mid-air. The two bodies landed at least ten feet away. Clanless spun, but the snow chose that moment to come down in a furious rush, blinding him. Sounds of jaws tearing, growls, and grunts were all the clues he had. He took a tentative step forward.

The snow lessened. A single dark shape stood over the fallen body of its foe. Whatever this new threat might be, it was larger than the lizard-creature, but appeared to be a quadruped. It moved away with sure steps, showing no signs of injury.

Clanless took several steps forward himself, his curiosity outweighing his caution. "Wait!" Qara cried.

The snow lessened further. The dark shape circled around another short outcropping and stood upon it, looking down toward them. Clanless took one more step, and the snow cleared.

An enormous wolf stood on the rock, gazing back at him with golden eyes. White streaks broke up its gray fur, but the closer he looked, the more Clanless noticed ragged scars on the beast's sides and back.

"It… it looks like the fur you wear." Until she spoke, Clanless hadn't realized Qara had come up beside him. He put a hand out to keep her from getting any closer.

"Don't. It's more dangerous than the beast it killed."

"You have nothing to fear from me, child of my fur."

Clanless took a step back and almost pushed Qara over. The voice resounded in his head, not through the air. The wolf's expression hadn't changed; its jaw hadn't moved.

"Did you hear that?" he whispered.

"It spoke in my head," Qara said.

"What do we do?"

"Answer it?"

Clanless swallowed. "Who are you?" he called out.

"You wear the skin I gave to another of your kind many years ago," the voice said in his head. "Did you take it from him, or did he give it to you?"

"He gave it to me," Clanless said.

The wolf's head inclined in a slight nod. "Then he knew you would need it. It is well. Keep it on you at all times."

"I usually do." Clanless wrinkled his brow, unsure of the point of this conversation.

"As long as you wear it, you cannot be controlled."

Clanless almost laughed. "I've been a slave most of my life. This fur hasn't stopped anyone from controlling me."

"You misunderstand. I do not speak of your own kind."

"Then…"

"I have bathed in the blood of your ancestors." The wolf's voice grew louder. "I bear the marks of my escape from that pit. You would do well to heed my words."

"Yes, of course," Clanless said. "I will. But—"

"The dark time is here. The winter of winters has begun. You will not survive long out here, neither can you return the way you came."

"Can you help us find shelter?" Qara asked.

The wolf did not answer for a moment. It turned to look to their right. The snowfall grew thicker.

"You will find assistance shortly," the voice in their head declared. "Do not fear. It will be well."

As the snow continued to increase, the wolf turned and vanished into the swirling white. For a few moments, neither of them said anything.

Qara moved closer to Clanless, trembling. "I hope he was right about the assistance."

Clanless shifted his moonblade and put an arm around her. "Let's try to get out of the wind at least." He considered heading back to the cliff, but couldn't imagine being successful. The beast had torn the descending path apart, and by now, more snow and ice would have formed. They couldn't get back that way.

Together, they pushed through the snow back to the larger outcropping. Only one side of it gave any sort of protection from the wind. They crouched down low against the rock. Clanless allowed Qara to hold him as tight as she wanted. They needed whatever warmth they could get. The temperature, already frigid, seemed to be sinking even faster. Only then did Clanless think about the time. The snow complicated his view, but the light was definitely fading. The sun must be finishing its daily retreat already. With this kind of weather, they could not survive the night. He thought his own situation might be worse than Qara's. The blood from his multiple wounds had already frozen on his skin and clothing. When he shifted his weight, more blasts of cold air pushed their way in through the tears.

However, a few minutes later, Qara whispered, "I don't think I'm going to make it." Her voice slowed as she went on: "At least no one will miss me…" Her eyes closed.

"Yes, we would!" he exclaimed, giving her a shake. "Stay with me, Qara! Don't give up now!" Clanless didn't know a lot about surviving in this kind of weather, but he'd remembered hearing sleep could be fatal.

"Too… cold."

Clanless dropped the moonblade and pulled her tight. He rubbed her arms and back. "No. You'll be all right." She had to be. While they'd never been very close, he'd known and worked with Qara for years now. He thought back to his words to Bain about friendship. "You're my friend, Qara. I won't let you die."

"'S sweet," she murmured. "Unless you have another way… to warm me…" Her head rested against his shoulder.

"Qara? Qara!" He shook her again, but she didn't respond this time. "No, no, no…"

"Use the Taint."

Clanless jerked his head around. Who said that? Was it even a voice, or his own thoughts? Had the wolf returned? The goddess? He couldn't think straight. Everything grew fuzzy. He shook his head.

The Taint. It burned. But what good would it do to burn Qara's blood? It might warm her up for a brief moment, but would only render her unconscious again. He needed her warm and awake!

He reached to his belt and drew Zaluu's throwing knife. Gently, he pulled Qara's arm from around his neck and pulled back her sleeves. He hesitated only a moment before drawing the knife across the back of her forearm. She muttered something without opening her eyes. The immediate smell and taste of her blood hit him, despite the cold.

Clanless put his hand over the cut and swallowed. "Goddess…" He didn't know what to say. He reached for the Taint.

Every time he'd used it in the past, it had been for violence, against an enemy. He'd burned their blood, hurting them as much as he could. Now… he didn't just trigger it, as he'd always done. He let it begin with a trickle, a touch, a gentle flowing. It worked its way through her veins like a gradual flow, rather than an instantaneous eruption. It required every bit of his concentration to control it, to keep it from ripping through her body like he'd always done.

She gave a soft moan, and her eyelids fluttered. "Oh… oh. That… feels good," she murmured. "Warm…"

If frost hadn't been caked around his eyes, Clanless would have cried. It worked. He could keep her alive. As long as he lived, she would live. He let the Taint finish its way through her body and then released it. He didn't know exactly how long it would take her body to repair her blood, or whatever it did, but after a rest, he should be able to use the Taint on her again.

If he could survive. He lifted his head and looked around. The sun, completing its retreat, took its light with it. The wind, thankfully, faded as well. The snow fell as heavily as ever, but it tumbled almost straight down instead of rushing at them from the side.

"What… did you do?" Qara asked.

"Shhh. I'll keep you warm. Just hold on."

The wolf had said not to fear. But what did a wolf know about humans and High Winter? They shouldn't be out here for any amount of time. Foolishness. They should have stayed in the tunnel. But more creatures might have found them there. Death awaited them at every turn, it seemed.

His thoughts drifted to the others. Bain and the Throat… he'd be safe from monsters and freezing, no doubt. But how would he get back out? Had the rope been long enough? Strong enough?

And Hagh. Sugh. They'd been sent on an execution mission. Had they completed it before Ghouk's death? And what of the creatures that had gone in their direction? All in all, they might have the best chance of survival.

He would never see Kekeen again. He was going to die here, on a desolate plateau in the desert, frozen with another woman in his arms. How pathetic was that? He almost wished Zektel were still with him. She'd be screaming at him not to give up, not to surrender, to use whatever it took to keep himself alive.

He heard and saw nothing but the snow… until a pair of heavy boots appeared only a few feet away. He lifted his head and saw a dark figure looming over them. Two more appeared to either side. Though man-shaped, something didn't seem right. The one in the middle stepped closer and crouched down where Clanless could see his face: orange-brown skin and long white hair.

Beastmen.

Part Two

BEASTMEN

# THE TAILOR

Kekeen left the throne room again, wearing a satisfied smile. Even if Koland didn't find time for it, she'd reminded Daviland of her father's importance herself. He'd even admitted she was right. Now maybe things would change.

The Hawk King's former aide stood in the hall, a now-freed slave who'd been in charge of scheduling meetings and such. He'd been happy to do the same for Daviland. The man smiled all the time now, a marked change from the fear he'd lived under with his former master. He nodded to her as she exited, then turned to the men who stood waiting.

"Daviland will see you now. I trust you've brought everything you need?"

The taller of the two men sniffed. "My good man, I've clothed half the Lords in this city. I always have everything I need."

Tailors? Really? Kekeen shook her head. She watched them enter and paused. Hadn't she seen the second man before? He wasn't easy to forget: short and extremely overweight, a balding head with a thin half-ring of stringy hair on the back, narrow eyes and a sharp nose. Ghoyor! He'd been at the arena in Ghoyor. She'd seen him there when she sought Aldan's help in rescuing her father.

When the aide returned to the hall, she pointed after them. "Do you know those men?"

"They're among the finest tailors in the city," he said. "I've worked with them before."

Kekeen obtained the name of the shorter man and waited. About half an hour later, the tailors emerged and started to leave. She waited until they passed before calling out: "Gogeku!"

The shorter man turned and wiped sweat from his wrinkled brow. "May I help you?" he asked in a nasally voice. His eyes looked her over—not in the way most men did, but still evaluating and not being impressed with what he saw. "If you're one of his"—he gestured to the throne room—"new elite, you'll have to make an appointment. We are so very busy, you know. High Spring fashions are only beginning to develop, and we have much to do for Clan Ghutalta, as well as many other new clients." He continued to eye her. "You have an excellent frame, but…"

"No, no. And, um, thank you. I just needed to ask you something. Didn't you used to work at the arena in Ghoyor?"

Gogeku glanced at his partner, who rolled his eyes and moved on down the hall. "Catch up to me when you can!" he called back.

The tailor frowned. "My cousin is not known for his patience." He turned back to Kekeen. "Yes, I did have the honor of working at the arena. The combatants wore the finest and most elaborate outfits of any in the Empire, if I do say so."

"I believe it." She smiled. "I remember seeing some of them. Zaluu's cape, for instance."

"Ah, yes, the capes. Poor Zaluu." He shook his head. "Memories are all that we have of that one, I'm afraid."

"So you knew Ald—Clanless, then?"

He brightened a bit. "I did work closely with Clanless. A real hero, that one. I knew from the start that he was different, you know." He pointed at her to emphasize his words. "From the day he arrived, I saw potential in him."

"Yes, I've… known him for many years myself." Kekeen clasped her hands in front of her. "Unfortunately, he's disappeared, along with the other Dohor. No one knows where they've gone or anything."

Gogeku fanned his face with his hand. "Disappeared? How troubling. And after that magnificent battle with Daviland to complete his career. His first real loss, you know, but I would think he wouldn't mind, what with the Hawk King's demise and all." His eyes widened as he realized what he'd said. "I mean, that is." He looked up and down the hall. "From his point of view, of course."

"There are no friends of the Hawk King here," she assured him. "I'm hoping you can help me, in fact."

He gave a short bow. "How may I be of assistance, my lady? As I said, we are very busy this time of year. The rebellion has thrown the fashion world into such consternation. We're hard-pressed to decide the proper colors without the Hawk King's predilections leading the way."

"It's about Clanless," she repeated. "I was hoping you might be able to share more about his time at Ghoyor… that maybe it would help shed some kind of light on his disappearance."

"Ah." He stood for a moment, tapping his foot and rubbing his chin. "I'm afraid I would be of little help. I… didn't know the man as well as you might think. I designed his clothes, and not much beyond." He eyed her again. "But this is personal, is it not?" He snapped his fingers. "You are the singer! The one he was obsessed with!"

Kekeen chuckled nervously. "Um, yeah. That's me."

Gogeku looked around her in the direction his cousin had gone. "I would be happy to assist you, if I were able to. I'm a firm believer in the cause of true love, after all. Even if Orgina almost banned him from seeing you. To her, his reputation—his personality—was more important. But I don't know that I could tell you anything you don't already know. He was a good man, I believe… but again, you already know this or you wouldn't care."

"Thank you. I'm not sure what I'm looking for," Kekeen admitted. "But I would love to hear any other little details you may remember."

"I think…" Gogeku's face suddenly lit up. "Oh, I know! If you really want to know everything, there is one other person you should talk to! And he's here, in the city, right now!"

"Who is that?"

The little man waved a finger. "I will take you to him! I know exactly where he is staying." He took two steps down the hall, then stopped. "Oh, but he doesn't want people to know he's here. That is a problem."

Kekeen's shoulders slumped.

"Never you fear." Gogeku took her hand and patted it. "I'll speak to him and persuade him to see you. I promise. Now. You come to our shop at closing time tomorrow—no, make it the day after, and I'll take you to him. He knows everything. He'll tell you all your precious little heart desires."

"A-all right." Kekeen shook her head. This was happening a bit fast. "Where is your shop?"

"Oh yes, you wouldn't know that, would you? After all, my name is not on the sign." Gogeku gave out a sigh far larger than Kekeen would have expected from his size. "My cousin has promised, of course, but after over two years, he has yet to fulfill that promise. Now he says he'll deal with it once the current 'crisis' has passed." He made a vague gesture toward the sky and the moons. "Anyway, my name will be on the sign, sooner or later, and I won't have to have these kind of troublesome conversations."

"But where is it?" Kekeen persisted.

After babbling on a bit about the condition of the road and the snow, Gogeku finally gave her an address and an approximate time for the closing of the shop. She thanked him and let him hurry on down the hall.

"Two days," he called back at her. "Day after tomorrow. He'll tell you everything. I promise!"

SWIFT CLAW

Then

Aldan burst into his home, eyes wide. "Father? Mother?"

"Here, here, don't worry." Uncle Sejikdi came in behind him. "Everything's all right."

Aldan spun around. "Why? Where are they?"

"Your mother has gone to the temple to deliver the baby," his uncle explained. "Your father and Borde are with her. It will probably take many hours."

"Should we go too?" Aldan moved toward the door. "I've never seen a baby come out of a mother!"

"No, no." Sejikdi waved a hand. "Men are not allowed."

Aldan wrinkled his brow. "But Father is there."

Sejikdi chuckled. "Yes, he's the exception. But he'll be in the way until they tell him to stand over to the side and wait." He nodded. "Believe me. I remember Borde's birth very well."

"Then… what shall we do?"

"Worry not." Sejikdi patted him on the shoulder. "You and I can wait together. We'll have some fun." He bent down to look Aldan in the face. "Let's play a game. Show me where you sleep."

Now

Clanless sucked in a breath through his nose and forced his eyes open. He would not relive that memory. Not now, and not ever, if he had any choice.

A fire blazed in front of him. He blinked and shook his head, trying to erase the dream memory and remember where he'd been. Snow. He and Qara had been freezing to death in the snow. And then...

He sat up and looked around. Qara lay beside him, sound asleep. Both of them lay atop a wide cushion of some kind, in front of the huge fire providing welcome heat. It wasn't a fireplace, exactly, but the flames roared within a niche in the rock wall. The smoke rose up into a shaft.

As Clanless turned his head, he saw rock in every direction, including the floor and roof. They were back in a cave! But if so, it was a more sophisticated cave, considering the fire and the smooth surfaces. An opening across from the fire appeared to lead into another passage.

He flexed his fingers and hands and examined his injuries. He saw no lasting damage from the cold, thankfully. Now if Qara were all right...

She stirred at that moment. With a grunt and a yawn, she pushed up from the cushion and opened her eyes. "Clanless! Oh, thank the goddess!" She threw her arms around his neck and hugged him, much to his surprise. He took her hands to pull her back.

"Are you all right?" His eyes immediately looked to the place he'd cut her arm.

She glanced down at it. "I'm fine." She pulled a hand free and touched the cut. "I don't remember that."

"I did it. I'm sorry, but I—"

"You did something! To keep me warm!" She looked up at him, her face bright. "You saved my life!"

"I tried, but we wouldn't have made it if not—" He broke off, his eyes darting to the doorway.

A beastman stood there, watching them.

"Oh." Qara gasped as she also turned, pulling her other hand from Clanless.

The beastman turned and shouted something that sounded like "hrout!" to his right. A moment later, two other beastmen joined him. All three entered and stood a few feet away, blocking the exit. They were similar in appearance, in that they all possessed the orange-brown skin, white hair, powerful muscles, long arms, and animalistic claws on their hands and feet. Beyond that, they were as different as any three human men might be. The central figure stood several inches taller and broader than the other two, wearing what looked like an armored vest above a black skirt. He also possessed the shortest beard of the three. A scimitar hung from his belt. The one on his right gave an appearance of greater age with wrinkled skin and a narrow beard that reached almost to the ground. He wore trousers and a tan-colored open-chested shirt. The one on the left wore only a black skirt, but also had more hair than the other two. Long sideburns connected with his beard, which had a black ribbon wrapped around it. Behind those three, Clanless saw others gathering in the passageway.

The one on the left stepped closer and pointed at Clanless's chest. Qara seized his right arm and held it tight.

Only then did Clanless realize his necklace had been pulled out from beneath his clothes and hung free on the outside. He lifted it up, remembering its origin. The disc-shaped ornament on the chain had come from the beastman he'd killed in the arena.

The beastman in front of him nodded. "Saved your life, it did," he said in a guttural voice. The central beastman grunted. "For now," the speaker amended. "How did it come to you?"

"I fought him," Clanless said. He saw no reason to lie, at least not yet.

All three beastmen nodded. "Did you kill him?" the speaker asked.

"I did. He gave this to me." Clanless hesitated. "He said… to tell his wife that honor was served."

The speaker said something to the others in their language, apparently translating his words. A murmur ran through the crowd of beastmen. The ones in the passage spoke to each other in rapid conversation, as the words passed throughout the crowd, followed by intense discussion.

The central beastman raised a clawed fist, and the conversation faded. The speaker glanced at him before turning back to Clanless: "How long? This was?"

Clanless had to think about it. "Two years and… three or four months, I think."

The speaker pressed him for more details about the fight. Clanless answered to the best of his ability, his eyes darting from one beastman to the other, trying to judge their reactions. The central figure appeared to be a warrior and leader of some kind. From the way the translator kept deferring to him, Clanless suspected the leader would be deciding their fate. When the story had been fully told and translated, the leader barked out something else.

The translator pointed to Clanless's shoulder. "Now this."

Clanless put a hand to his shoulder before he realized what they meant.

"The fur? It was given to me."

"But we met the wolf!" Qara put in.

This created a stir when the translator reported it. On a word from the leader, the translator looked at Clanless with his teeth showing. "Is this true?"

He nodded. "The wolf saved us from a… uh… lizard-beast. It told us you were coming."

The teeth vanished. At the translation, even the leader appeared impressed, assuming Clanless was interpreting their facial expressions correctly.

The leader turned to the older beastman and whispered a question. The old one studied Clanless and Qara for a few moments before answering. He gave a long speech while continuing to watch them. The leader grunted in return. He and the old one turned together and left the room. The beastmen outside parted to make way for them. Most of them also moved away, although a handful remained outside the door, watching. Qara finally loosened her hold on Clanless's arm.

The translator sat, crossing his legs in a manner Clanless was sure would be extremely painful if he tried it. "You are Wolf Chosen. You will be agreed to stay until the Wind is gone," the translator said.

"Thank you," Clanless answered. "But we don't have to stay long. If you can get us near one of our cities, we—"

"Are you a fool?" The translator pulled his head back in alarm. "Shall I call back the lead one? I tell you the Wind has come. You must stay here."

"Yes, we know it's very windy." Clanless glanced at Qara.

"No. No." The translator shook his head. "The Wind of the Dead Lord. It has come. Long time before it come again."

"Long time… maybe he means the chaos moon," Qara whispered.

"Yes. We understand," Clanless said to the translator. "But we don't want to wait until the end of High Winter before we leave. If we can find a city not far, and wait for the right weather, we should be able to make it."

"This is not correct." The translator continued to be agitated. He glanced toward the other beastmen in the entrance. "You will stay here. You will not test the Lord of the Dead. His wind will take your wind."

His wind will take your wind? Maybe he meant "breath?"

"We can't stay here for all of High Winter!" Qara exclaimed. "It's barely begun! Why do they fear the wind? They came out in it to find us!"

"We were sent by the True Wind." The translator nodded rapidly as if that explained everything. He glanced at Qara and back to Clanless. "This woman? She is yours?"

"What? No. She isn't mine."

The beastman's eyes grew larger and his mouth wider. "Ah. Good." He called to the ones at the door. Two of them came forward. They conversed with the translator for a few moments before he turned back. "We will find a good match for her. These two will fight to see."

Qara screamed as the beastmen came forward, reaching for her. "Clanless! Don't let them take me!"

Clanless leaped to his feet. "No, no. I… didn't understand." He stood over Qara and looked about. He had no weapons. Could he possibly fight even one of these clawed creatures without one?

The translator held up a hand and cocked his head. "What do you mean?"

"I mean… uh… she is mine. My woman." He reached down, and Qara seized his hand.

The translator considered for a moment. He held out both hands, palms up, then returned them to his sides. Was that an agreement? Or a shrug? He barked an order to the other beastmen. They returned to the doorway, grumbling to each other, with many backwards looks at Qara. Clanless could feel her shudders through her grip on his hand.

"We find a space for both of you," the translator declared. "You will rest. Be warm together."

"Thank you." Clanless hesitated. "I… did you find my weapons when you brought us here?"

"This I will see. You are a warrior, Wolf Chosen?"

"I am."

"He's the greatest warrior in the Empire!" Qara inserted.

The beastman nodded. "This is good. Much honor for warriors. I will see for weapons." He lifted himself with his palms and unfolded his legs. He stood to face Clanless. "Take you to space now."

The translator motioned for them to follow. Clanless helped Qara to her feet and obeyed, noticing that two other beastmen fell in behind them. Perhaps they were guests, perhaps prisoners, or perhaps somewhere in between.

Clanless tried to watch everything as they walked. The passageways through which they traveled were clean and smooth, though at times they grew extremely narrow. The humans had to duck from time to time when the ceiling grew too low. The beastmen, who walked hunched over, had no great difficulty. Clanless ran a hand along the stone wall, amazed at the even surfaces. "Did your people, ah, dig all these tunnels?" he asked.

"Dig?" The translator lowered his enormous eyebrows.

Clanless gestured at the wall. "Dig. Um, carve out? Create?"

"Mmh." The sound came out like a grunt combined with a growl in the throat. The beastman nodded. "You speak of the Formation. The ancestors formed it. We continue. We are safe here from the Dead Wind."

"I would think so," Qara murmured.

The passageway branched off in many directions as they walked, but their guide never hesitated at the intersections. They passed through several larger caverns as well, where Clanless saw buildings, made from stone and wood. They weren't crude by any means, but they lacked any kind of decorative touches. Their path led between some of the buildings and back into another passage.

Everywhere they went, oil lanterns lit their way, mounted periodically along the walls. Clanless wondered how many beastmen—perhaps the young?—were assigned to keep the lanterns burning. Almost as often as the lanterns, he spotted small, round openings in the ceiling. The light didn't reach far into them, so he couldn't discern their purpose.

Occasionally, a brief gust of air indicated some movement somewhere. Perhaps from the small openings? Away from the fireplace, the temperature dropped, but did not become uncomfortable. It wasn't much different from the inside of a well-built home during winter.

The smell was another matter. The beastmen themselves radiated a musky smell, not unlike large animals, and the odor permeated the caverns. Clanless hoped his nostrils would adapt to it soon enough.

At last, the guide stopped beside another opening. He gestured inside. Clanless and Qara walked past him, turned a sharp corner, and entered a space about the same size as the one they'd left. A large bed took about a third of the room, and a heavy cloth lay on the floor like a rug.

"This will be for you," the beastman announced.

"No door?" Qara asked.

He cocked his head as if the question were odd. "No one will enter unless you say."

"They can't see around the corner," Clanless pointed out. Not that the lack of a door concerned him. He was thinking more about other bodily requirements.

Anticipating his thoughts, the beastman pointed to a smaller opening across from the bed. "You will find a place for cleanliness in there."

"Thank the goddess," Qara said.

"Let your winds be at peace," the beastman said with a bow. He departed, leaving them alone for the first time.

Qara sat on the bed and bounced. "This is much nicer than I expected.

These beastmen, they're… far more civilized than any of us knew."

"No doubt." Clanless fingered the necklace. He suspected it might be the only reason they were alive now.

"But I haven't seen any… beastwomen yet," she went on. "Do they keep them hidden, do you think?"

"I don't know." He looked around their room aimlessly. Bad enough Ghouk had taken him away from Kekeen. Now he was separated from the other fighters and even his moonblade.

Clanless took a deep breath. Did this count as freedom? Three days for sure, back at the arena, and maybe a half a day after Ghouk died, but now? He might not have a bloodbond any more, or a master, but…

They might have to spend three months here? No matter how civilized it might be, how would he cope with that? He'd somewhat enjoyed High Winters in the past, taking a break from the grueling arena schedule… but he'd never been able to take the inaction for very long. He often trained himself, even in the snow and wind, just to get out of his room. Here, he would be indoors the entire time. A strange sense of pressure erupted all over his body.

"Hey!" Qara crossed the room and grabbed his arm. "It's going to be all right. We're alive, thanks to you." She pulled herself closer. "And I'm safe, thanks to you." She reached for his face. "How can I repay you?"

He pulled away. "Qara…"

"What? We're alone, Clanless. We're the only people—humans, I guess—here. And we're going to be stuck together for a long time." She gestured to the bed. "They think we're a couple. We have a bed. We might as well enjoy each other's company, you know."

"I'll sleep on the floor."

She rolled her eyes. "What is wrong with you?"

Clanless thought for a moment. "There are many ways I could answer that."

"Then maybe you should choose one." She put her hands on her hips. "We may be together for months. We have plenty of time to talk, at the very least."

"You're right, and…" He hesitated. "I will tell you more. But not right this minute, please. Just… give me time. It's not easy."

Qara sighed. "I suppose you're right. We've been through chaos the last week or more." She snorted and stepped back. "Chaos, like the extra moon up there. Maybe there is something to that."

Clanless pulled his outer coat off, wincing as some of his scabs tore loose from the movement. "Why? What have you heard about the chaos moon?"

"Really?" Qara sat on the bed again. "You won't talk personal feelings, but you want to talk about that?"

"Sorry. Forget I said anything."

"No, no. I mean, Suirel is an interesting topic, I guess. I know the priests talk about him endlessly."

Clanless looked at her. "You said 'him'? You think of the chaos moon as a person."

"I didn't say I did. I was talking about the priests and their talking." She shrugged. "Some of them think he's a god, like an enemy to the goddess of the regular moon."

"And some of them worship him," Clanless said. "That explains some things."

"There you go being cryptic again." She leaned forward. "There is so much more to Clanless the arena fighter than what you show the rest of the world. I just want to understand you better. For starters, why don't you have a real name? Clanless isn't a name. And neither is 'Wolf Chosen.' Why can't you have a normal name?"

He headed toward the side room the beastman called a "place for cleanliness." Pausing at the entrance, he looked back at Qara. "I had a name. Once. I… don't use it much any more."

"Don't take too long in there!" she called after him. "Or I'm coming in too."

He stopped, staring at the interior. "Actually… you should come in here and see this."

Qara jumped off the bed and joined him. "Oh. Oh my."

The lavatory—as Clanless called it in his head—contained two different spaces. One curved around to the side, away from everything else, and included a deep, narrow hole presumably for human—beastman—waste. The other contained a bath: a small pool deep enough to sit in without difficulty. Bubbles and movement continuously erupted from one end. A faint odor similar to boiled eggs filled the air, overriding any smell that might come from the waste hole. Qara put her hand in the water and gasped.

"It's so warm!" She looked at Clanless. "Are you going to use it? If you don't, I'm getting in right now. Even if you do, I might get in with you."

"I would love to get in," he admitted. "But if you can't wait, you go first."

Qara rolled her eyes. "You go ahead. I'm not the one with dried blood all over my body." She turned back to the room. "I'll take a nap. Wake me when you're out."

Clanless waited until she left. He carefully removed the rest of his clothing, tearing open more wounds as the material pulled away. For the first time, he paused before removing the wolf pelt, thinking about what the great wolf said about control. He would be all right in the bath, wouldn't he? He'd taken hundreds of baths after all. He couldn't be expected to wear it everywhere. Stripped at last, he lowered himself into the delightful water. He gasped and tensed when water reached each open wound.

"I wasn't thinking," Qara called from the other room. "I'm sorry. Would you like me to heal your wounds? I can, you know."

Clanless considered it. "How much of the healing blood do you have?"

"Two vials."

"Then save it. We may have more need of it later. None of these wounds are bad." He gritted his teeth after saying it. The water sloshed against a gash under his left armpit. That one would leave a scar. But still nothing he couldn't deal with. The wound in his gut had not completely healed either, but it was too late to waste magic on that one. Better to save the healing in case of something major. Who knew what might happen between now and… whenever they reached somewhere with healers?

Finally settled into the water, Clanless relaxed with only his head and arms dry. After days of sleeping in the cold carriage, followed by their harrowing time in the snow, he'd begun to wonder if he'd ever be warm again. Even sleeping in front of the fire earlier had not brought warmth like this water. He sighed and closed his eyes. The gentle pulsing of the water lapped against his shoulders and neck. His arms grew cold by comparison, so he let them slip in as well, leaving only his head above water. It would be almost too easy to fall asleep here.

He opened his eyes and glanced toward the entrance, suddenly paranoid. Qara might come in anyway. He wouldn't put it past her. But no… she wasn't a liar. She said she'd take a nap.

What to do about that situation? The longer they stayed together, sleeping in the same room, the more she would pressure him to sleep together. Would she be satisfied with his insistence of remaining true to Kekeen? Or would he have to tell her more?

He'd worked with Qara for over two years. In that time, he supposed they'd become friends, of a sort. She'd made romantic insinuations toward him on any number of times, which he'd ignored or turned down, but she'd never shown any anger about it. Aside from that, he knew almost nothing else about her. The revelation about her use of magic yesterday: that had come out of nowhere.

What kind of friend did it make him? Not knowing anything about someone after over two years of living in the same building? Clanless sighed. As if he didn't have enough guilt in his life.

He let the back of his neck sink down into the water. So good. All these other issues could wait until tomorrow. And hopefully, this bath would make up for sleeping on the floor. He could have easily stayed in the water for hours, but after thirty minutes, he got out and let Qara have her turn. Wrapping himself in his clothes, he stretched out on the floor and fell asleep.

❨ ❨ ❨ ❨ ● ❩ ❩ ❩ ❩

Clanless didn't dream of memories this time. Instead, he saw someone walking through darkness, leaving bloody footprints wherever he went. The vision forced him awake. He'd never experienced anything like it before. Not a memory, and not a particularly horrific nightmare either. His confusion lasted only a few minutes before he fell asleep again.

He dreamed no more. The rest of the night, Clanless experienced his best sleep since leaving Et-Baylak. Despite his injuries and the flat stone floor, he awoke rested and relaxed. He patted the thick rug-cloth gratefully.

"Mmmm. Have you arranged for breakfast? I'm starving." Qara, wearing only a thin shift, sat on the edge of the bed and stretched.

Clanless looked away. "I wonder. Are we free to go looking for food?" He got up and went around the corner to the exit. Two beastmen stood in the hall watching. He smiled, but couldn't tell if they smiled back. Learning facial expressions on a different-shaped face would be another challenge. He returned to the room. "Looks like we're prisoners, despite the nice quarters."

A discrete cough came from the exit. "May I enter?" a voice called.

Clanless glanced at Qara, who grabbed up her clothes and headed for the lavatory. "Come in," he answered.

A beastman entered the room, bowing his head as he did. Clanless thought he was the translator from the day before. At least he spoke their language.

"I have come to help you," the beastman announced. "Have you questions?"

"We were wondering about food." Clanless paused. "And about the guards at the door."

"Food will be arriving soon. The men at the door are for protection." The beastman sat on the floor in that odd cross-legged manner again.

"For our protection or yours?" Clanless sat down as well.

"Both. The… Formation is vast and…" He squinted with the effort of finding the right word. "Long? There are many turns. We do not wish you to become lost. And many do not know you yet."

"So if we went wandering, someone might attack us."

"It is possible. Also, most do not know how to speak."

Clanless assumed he meant their language, not the capability of speech. But then again…

Qara entered, pulling on her outer vest. "Did I hear something about food?"

"They'll be bringing some soon," Clanless reported.

"What about a drink?"

The beastman cocked his head. "You have much water."

Qara glanced around before her eyes widened. "The bathing water? We can't drink that!"

"We are… not accustomed to drinking warm water," Clanless added.

The beastman straightened his head. "Ah. You wish colder drink. I understand and will arrange."

"What is our status here?" Qara settled on the edge of the bed again. "Are we guests or prisoners?"

"You are visitors," he answered. "Once you learn things, you can see our places. Let your winds be at peace."

"That right there." Qara pointed at him. "You keep using the word 'wind' for all kinds of things. Why is that?"

He cocked his head again. "I do not understand."

"Why do you talk about our winds? What do you mean by that?"

"Do you mean our breath?" Clanless asked, blowing air out with a hand gesture to demonstrate.

The beastman tapped claws against the stone floor. "I must think of this. I do not wish to give you a false answer." He ducked his head. "My understanding of your words is better than many, but I do not know all."

"We are very thankful for how much you do know!" Clanless hastened to say. Though the beastman's voice sounded far more guttural than a human's, they had little trouble understanding his actual words.

The beastman lifted his head. "I am thankful for your words."

Clanless laughed. The whole thing was just crazy.

"We must understand each other better," the beastman said. "That is why I am here. The elders have sent me."

"What's your name, then?" Qara asked.

"Mmh. My people call me…" He enunciated a series of syllables Clanless knew he couldn't repeat. Most of them involved some kind of "hn" sound which resonated in the beastman's snout. "In your words, it would be… Swift Claw." He looked at Clanless. "You are Wolf Chosen, and…" He looked back at Qara. "You are Wolf Chosen's woman."

"I'm Qara."

"Kharha," Swift Claw repeated.

"We're very glad to meet you, Swift Claw." Clanless got to his feet and gave a bow. Qara repeated the gesture.

The beastman's eyes and mouth grew larger, without showing a lot of teeth. "You show me much honor. I will do my best for you."

"Then… how about that water?" Qara grinned.

Swift Claw unfolded his legs and got to his feet. "I will see to it at once."

He left, but returned only moments later, carrying a large metal bowl. He set it on the floor, his head down as he explained, "I apologize that you must wait a few minutes more."

Clanless laughed. Fresh snow filled the bowl. He scooped up a handful and nibbled at it. "This will be wonderful," he assured Swift Claw. Qara agreed, though she shook her head in amusement.

Two more beastmen entered, carrying a large platter. They set it on the floor beside the bowl and left the humans with their translator. Clanless examined the food on the platter with curiosity. He hadn't even thought about what to expect. To his pleasant surprise, he didn't see anything too unusual. Meat dominated the platter, as he would have expected, but he also saw a number of root vegetables and what he assumed to be some kind of large seeds. He and Qara both set to with delight.

Swift Claw appeared anxious about their reactions to the food. They both assured him of their delight.

"I am sure our cooks will be pleased. Shall I leave you while you eat?"

"No, please stay," Clanless said. "We have so much to learn." He picked up one of the seeds and found it warm. Roasted? He took a tentative bite. It was crunchy and a bit bland.

Swift Claw nodded and re-settled himself. "I am here to instruct. What else would you know?"

"You said you would see about my weapons," Clanless said with trepidation. "Have you located them?"

The beastman lowered his head again. "I am sorry. The elders do not wish you to have weapons. Until…"

"Until they know they can trust us," Clanless finished.

"You understand."

He understood, but he didn't like it. He hadn't been separated from the moonblade this long since… since he'd owned it. It felt wrong.

"Why can't they trust us?" Qara asked. "Didn't you say some great wind sent you out to find us? And there was that wolf too."

"These are strong portents." Swift Claw nodded. "But it is… hard for us. We have little dealings with your people. Too often they hunt us, or capture us and take us away."

"Did that happen to you?" Clanless wondered. "Is that how you learned our language?"

"Mmh. No. I have traveled far in search. I spent much time with people far from here. Very different from you." His eyes narrowed. "But we trust them less. They promise good while doing bad. Much lying. We lost entire tribe to them."

Clanless tried to think of who he might be referencing. Qara figured it out first: "The Melkute Kingdom!"

"They're worse than our people?" Clanless took another handful of the seeds. Their flavor improved the more he ate. Before the Hawk King's death, he'd wondered if the northern kingdom might be a safer place for he and Kekeen to live. It didn't sound very promising now.

"Have you more questions?" Swift Claw asked without answering the last one.

Clanless shrugged. "We could probably ask you questions all day. Would you like to ask us any questions?" It seemed the polite thing to do.

Swift Claw hesitated. Then he pointed at Qara. "The woman carries blood. We would like to know why this is."

Qara's hand went to the pouch at her belt. "It's not much. Just a few vials."

"We use blood for, uh, trade within our people," Clanless explained.

Swift Claw shook his head. "We know of this. The blood she carries is different."

Clanless hesitated. He didn't want to get into a discussion of blood magic right now. "It is for ritual," he said at last. "For religious purposes."

The beastman cocked his head. "You worship with it?"

"Yes," Qara said. "Worship."

Swift Claw couldn't exactly frown, but the way he showed his teeth and squinted his eyes appeared to be some kind of equivalent, unless it meant something stronger, perhaps anger. "There is much we do not understand about your people. But some we know to be wrong."

"Wrong in what way?"

"Wrong," Swift Claw repeated. "Not right. Bad instead of good. It is what you do with the blood."

"We do… many things with blood."

"You seek power with it. Some of you do. And this brings the dark winds."

Wind again. But… "Do you mean the magic?"

"When we use the blood to heal and other things?" Qara added.

"Yes." Swift Claw nodded. "Mmh. This is what I mean. It is not good."

"Only the priests know this magic," Clanless said, glancing at Qara. "We are not priests."

"It is good. You will do no… magic while you are here. We do not wish the dark winds in this place."

"Of course." Clanless opened his mouth to ask about the dark winds, but Swift Claw got to his feet.

"I am sorry. I must report to the elders." He gestured at the food. "Continue. We will question more when I return."

"This is wonderful," Qara said. "But if I eat much more, I won't have room for lunch!"

Swift Claw cocked his head. "What is this lunch?"

"The meal in the middle of the day?"

"Mmh. We have two meals in one day, one when we awake, and one before we sleep." The beastman paused. "And some say it is twice as much as we need."

No lunch. All right. Clanless wondered how many other ways their cultures differed. Living here might be a continual adjustment.

"Eat." Swift Claw gestured again. "I will return soon."

FREEDOM OR SLAVERY

After they'd eaten and cleaned up, Swift Claw returned. "Come! I will show you things." Clanless and Qara followed without hesitation. At least they'd get to leave their room. The guards at the door fell in behind them a few paces back.

As they passed by other tunnel entrances, Clanless asked, "How many of your people live like this?" He gestured at one of the side passages. "I'm guessing there are dozens of rooms like ours?"

Swift Claw cocked his head. "Dozens? No, hundreds. Yes. Maybe more. We form new ones every year."

"Hundreds?"

"You make them?" Qara asked. "You mean you dig these out of the rock? How?"

Swift Claw stopped and pointed at the wall. "The ancestors formed first. We continue. The rock is hard above, but soft beneath."

Clanless wrinkled his brow. "You mean on the surface and down here?"

"Yes." Swift Claw reached out and ran his claws down the side of the wall, leaving furrows. "See? We can form."

Qara fingered the furrows. "Maybe you can. Goddess."

"I saw buildings earlier," Clanless said. "This is like an underground city, isn't it?"

"Mmh. That is correct."

"Amazing. How far does it stretch?" He waved his arm. "Are we still near the mines where you found us? Or are we closer to any other human settlements? A city or a clanhold?"

Swift Claw shook his head. "You are trying to find us. I will not tell you." He paused and faced them. "Please. Forsake this idea of leaving. The Lord of the Dead's Wind has come. I have told you this. You cannot go out."

"We traveled for many miles in the wind for the past week," Qara said. "We're not afraid of it."

Swift Claw regarded them without expression, or at least without one Clanless could identify. "Then you are very fortunate to still possess your own wind." Before they could ask any more, he gestured them on. "Come. I will still show you things."

Over the next couple of hours, Clanless and Qara saw an underground civilization beyond what either could have imagined. Swift Claw's estimate of hundreds of rooms had not been an exaggeration. In some of the larger caverns, he pointed at walls where they could see lanterns alongside a multitude of doors to living quarters lining passages built into the side of enormous cliffs.

Within those larger caverns, they also got a closer look at some of the buildings they'd spotted earlier. They included places for communal gatherings, places to eat, and even some marketplaces. Qara expressed interest in the latter, but decided against it after a few moments inside one. The cacophony and physical interactions were much more frenzied and aggressive than a human marketplace.

After more exploring, they entered another large cavern. Their path wound its way around the outer edge of the chamber, elevated above a large flat surface where a couple dozen beastmen were gathered. Clanless paused, watching. "Is this what I think it is?"

"This is a training area," Swift Claw confirmed. "They learn to fight."

The beastmen appeared to be engaged in mock combat. Two of them would rush each other and grapple until one succeeded in throwing the other to the ground. Somehow, despite the claws and teeth, the bouts appeared almost bloodless. The goal was to succeed with strength alone.

"Do we need to watch this?" Qara asked.

"For a few minutes," Clanless said. "I want to see it."

One beastman with multiple scars across his chest appeared to be the champion. Multiple challengers came forward, but he bested them all. After slamming another opponent into the ground, he turned and caught sight of the humans.

"You!" He pointed at Clanless and yelled something in his own language.

"Wolf Chosen, he says he heard you are the mightiest human warrior," Swift Claw translated. "He asks if this is true."

"I don't—" Clanless began.

"He is," Qara interrupted. "He definitely is."

Swift Claw called something to the warrior, who responded by pounding his chest with a fist. He yelled even louder than before.

"He challenges you," Swift Claw said.

"I got the message." Clanless frowned. "I can't possibly beat him in a strength competition. He knows that, of course. Will he accept an alternate form of challenge?"

"Using weapons to kill in the Formation is forbidden," Swift Claw said. "A weapon challenge cannot be controlled."

The champion paced back and forth, growling. He smacked his chest with a fist again.

Clanless pointed to what appeared to be a bundle of wooden staves leaning against the far wall. "What about those?"

Swift Claw nodded. "It is permitted."

The champion saw where Clanless pointed and showed his teeth. He said something, obviously protesting. Swift Claw argued with him for a few moments. The other combatants and spectators watched with great interest. At last, Swift Claw turned back to Clanless. "He is willing, but he questions your… valor. He says the sticks are for cubs."

"We'll see about that." Clanless strode across the open area and examined the staves. He selected two and tossed one to the champion. The beastman caught it and laughed derisively. He pointed at the staff in Clanless's hands and roared.

"He says you have chosen the…" Swift Claw hesitated. "The most cub stick."

Clanless smiled, then took a defensive stance. The champion was probably right. The staff he'd chosen was shorter than all the others. But he held it near one end and extended it forward… exactly like his moonblade.

The champion held his staff and took a casual stance. He growled something and Swift Claw started to translate, "You are not—"

"I get it," Clanless said. "Let's begin."

The beastman surged forward, swinging the staff with expert speed and deliberation. Clanless sidestepped at the last moment and tapped his opponent's left bicep with his stick. "You lose that arm."

With a roar, the beastman swung a backhanded fist at him. Clanless ducked and raked his stick across the beastman's ribs. Swift Claw yelled something, but Clanless couldn't make it out. He rolled to his right to dodge his opponent's staff again.

The beastman went berserk, leaping and swinging the staff with wild abandon. Clanless ducked, parried, and dodged, but the rapid pace strained his existing wounds. "All right, all right!" he called. "I concede. Can we end this?" His opponent didn't answer, but Swift Claw yelled repeatedly. Clanless thought he heard Qara yelling too.

When an opening came, Clanless dodged away, rolled several feet, and leaped up. He tossed his stick away and held up his hands. "The fight is over! I won't do any more!"

The beastman, eyes wide, charged him, lifting his staff for an overhand blow. Clanless dropped to his knees and threw both arms over his head to protect it. The blow that would have shattered at least one of his forearms never came. He looked up. Swift Claw and another beastman had jumped in front of him and seized his attacker by both arms. Swift Claw spoke rapidly in their language for what seemed an entire minute.

At last, the warrior tore free of the other two, glaring at Clanless. He snapped the staff over his knee and stormed out of the cave.

Qara hurried to Clanless's side. "Are you all right?" She put a hand on his shoulder. To his own surprise, he didn't flinch away.

Swift Claw also turned to him. "I apologize. He became... not himself."

"Yeah, I understand. The bloodrush." Clanless got to his feet. "I'll be fine." He winced and put a hand to his side. "I'll be hurting for a while, but fine."

The second beastman who had interceded for him said something to Swift Claw. "Ah. This is Wind Tooth," the translator explained. "He leads some of our warriors."

Clanless gave him a respectful nod before wiping sweat from his own brow.

"Wind Tooth wishes to know if you would consent to teaching us some of your fighting. After you are fully healed, of course."

"He wants me to help train his fighters?"

Swift Claw nodded. "He saw you do things he does not know. He wishes you to teach. This is a good thing, I believe. You will need a place to work until the Wind is gone. It would not be good for you to do nothing."

"You mean sit around the cave all day?" Clanless chuckled. "All right. I agree, as long as you can help me communicate with them."

"That is my task." Swift Claw turned to Wind Tooth and spoke for a while.

"I've seen you fight in the arena," Qara said, "but never this close.

Or…" She glanced around and shuddered. "Or with this kind of audience."

"It was a new experience for me too." He watched the two beastmen talk, then lowered his head to speak to her in a quiet voice: "I'm only agreeing to this idea for the moment. I still want to get us out of here. I don't plan to stay here through all of High Winter."

She nodded, but didn't answer. Swift Claw had finished his conversation and moved closer. "I have made the arrangements," he said. "When you are ready, as I said." He looked at Qara. "Now we must find a place for you to help."

"Do we need to do that right away?" Qara glanced at Clanless. "I'm… still not comfortable here. Maybe I should just help Clanless until he recovers."

"This is acceptable." Swift Claw gestured. "Do you wish to continue seeing our place?"

"I think we've seen enough for now," Clanless said. "I could use some rest."

☾☾☾☾●☽☽☽☽

Swift Claw took them back to their own cave and left them alone for the afternoon. At least, Clanless assumed it was the afternoon. Keeping track of the time of day wasn't easy inside a cave.

"I'm terrified of what they might ask me to do," Qara told him, pacing their small living space. "What do their women do? Cook the food? Make clothes?"

"Maybe they're warriors too," Clanless said. "I wouldn't be surprised."

Qara stopped pacing. "I didn't think of that. Goddess." She waved an arm. "I don't know how to do any of those things. I managed arena fighters. I told other slaves what to do. I didn't do any of it myself."

Clanless relaxed on the bed. At her insistence, he'd agreed to use it for resting, alone. "I think you're more capable than you give yourself credit for."

"It's not just that." She moved beside the bed. "They frighten me, Clanless. Walking around with them today was, was horrible. Their claws and teeth… even that smell! We're guests now, but I don't think they all like it. Like the one who fought you. I think some of them would be very happy to tear us apart and eat us."

"They don't eat people."

"Are you sure?"

He didn't answer. He couldn't.

"And there are two of them outside the door," she went on. "All the time! The only reason I slept at all last night was because I knew you were lying there." She put a hand on his forearm. "You made me feel safe, at least for a while."

Clanless pulled his arm free and sat up. "I will do everything in my power to keep you safe," he promised. "But I don't think we need to fear that much." He sighed. "It doesn't mean I want to stay, of course."

"How can we escape? We don't even know our way around." Qara gestured widely. "These caves go for miles, it seems. And even if we got out, how would we know where to go?"

"We'll have to convince Swift Claw to take us."

She shook her head. "He's too scared of some dead lord's wind or whatever it was."

"We'll have to convince him," he repeated. "Show him how important it is to us."

"Good luck." She glanced at the door. "Just don't, uh, mention your girlfriend. I'm your woman here, remember? I'm even more terrified of what would happen if they suspected that wasn't true."

"We'll keep up the act."

"It would help if you slept in the bed," she pointed out. "If they discover you're sleeping on the floor…"

Clanless closed his eyes. "Qara… please. I love Kekeen. I won't betray her."

"And if they take me away to be part of some beast king's harem, how will your conscience feel about that?"

"I won't let that happen to you. I promise."

She folded her arms. "You make a lot of promises."

"None that I don't intend to keep."

Qara put her hands on her hips. "When did this girlfriend thing begin, anyway? You spent plenty of time at Pasque House with the other fighters." She paused. "Right up until the end, in fact. Unless you met this girl right before the Hawk King's death… you weren't being very faithful to her back then."

Clanless sighed. "I… had an arrangement with one of the girls at Pasque House."

"I'll bet you did."

He turned to look at her. "I never did anything with her. I mean, we never slept together. Ever."

"You…" Qara lowered her arms. "You visited this girl almost every week for over two years… and never bedded her?"

"Yes. She's a good friend." He looked back toward the ceiling, wondering where Salkhi was now. He'd bought her freedom, but the onset of High Winter would have kept her in the city, most likely.

"I'm not sure I believe that." Qara shook her head. "But I guess it sort of makes sense. I did hear things, you know."

"Like what?"

She put her hands on the edge of the bed and leaned over. She drew her words out: "All kinds of things…"

Clanless rolled his eyes.

"It was no secret you had a favorite at Pasque." She chuckled. "But someone—probably Sugh—let it slip that she wasn't your favorite; she was your 'only.' And that's where the rumors began."

"What rumors?"

Qara spun and took several steps across the room. "Oh, you know how people talk. They said Clanless is in love with this girl. That he's going to steal her away someday. Or that the Hawk King likes the same girl, and they're destined to fight over her. Or that you'd arranged the death of another fighter—Silence, I'm assuming—because he slept with your girl. Or—"

"None of those things are true!"

She laughed again. "Of course they're not. But people love their stories. It gives them something to talk about." She paused. "Besides their own pathetic lives."

Distracted, Clanless didn't hear her last line. Of course, he'd known people made up stories about him. They always had. His earlier master, Orgina, spread them deliberately. It was all part of the system, part of being famous in one way or another. People wanted more. What was it Kan, his first trainer, had said?

"They come to watch… because they wish they could do it."

"Are you talking about the arena or Pasque House?"

"The arena. Famous people, I guess." He shifted to look at her again. "The crowds want more than just a short fight in the arena. They want to know the story behind it, the story of the people involved. They wish they could do what I can do, so they make up more about me, to satisfy their curiosity, their desires. Kan said it was about wanting to be the villain, but I think it's more than that."

"Who's Kan?"

"My first trainer." Clanless lay back, his mind racing. He felt like he was on the verge of understanding something important. Koland, of course, talked a lot about the power of stories. Maybe he was right.

"Of course, those rumors came mostly from the men. Should I tell you what the women came up with?"

"Uh, not now, thank you. I… need to rest."

◖ ◖ ◖ ◖ ● ◗ ◗ ◗ ◗

Swift Claw returned with the evening meal. Clanless was pleased to see this meal included bread—not quite the flat bread he'd prefer, but thin and soft nonetheless.

"We've been giving more thought to your proposals for our time here," Clanless said after taking a few bites.

Swift Claw sat cross-legged across from him. "Have you suggestions?"

"Not… specifically. But I wanted to talk about how long we'll be here."

"Until the Dark Wind is gone," the beastman answered without pause.

Clanless gave a short nod. "Yes, so you've said. But I want you to understand how important it is to us to get back to our people, to those we love."

Qara shot him a look.

Swift Claw's expression didn't change. "I do understand. But matters not. You cannot leave."

"Listen to me, please." Clanless tried to look the beastman in the eyes. "I want you to hear me." He'd thought a lot about how to communicate his desires, and trying to keep it in terms the beastman would understand.

Swift Claw nodded.

"I've been a slave since I was a boy. Do you know what that means?"

"We understand slaves, yes." He cocked his head. "You were a warrior and a slave?"

"I was a slave. I got my freedom only a couple of weeks ago." He paused. Had it been weeks or just days? He couldn't remember. "And then another man made me a slave again. He died only a few days ago, and now I'm free again. Or I thought I was."

"You are not sure?"

Clanless shook his head. "No, I'm not. Because this"—he gestured at their surroundings—"feels like slavery again."

"You are not our slave!" Swift Claw leaned back, almost falling over.

"I cannot leave. I cannot be with the people I want to be with. I'm being asked to work in the same kind of forced work I had before."

"But you agreed to do the warrior training. Were you untrue?"

Clanless stopped himself in the act of rolling his eyes. "That is not what I'm saying. I was a slave forced to be an arena fighter for years. I am tired of fighting, but it is all I know. You tell me I need to train your warriors too, to pay for our food, I guess. I accept that. But it's the same thing again. And I'm not really free to make my own choices."

"You are Wolf Chosen. You are not our slave!" Swift Claw appeared genuinely offended at the concept. "We do not do this. We do not keep slaves. Our ancestors may have done so, but the True Wind says no. We do not." He jumped to his feet, shaking his head. "We ask for you to work, to be a part of us. Not a slave."

Clanless held out both his palms. "Do you see how I would feel different? Do you understand my feelings?"

"How am I to tell you? Not a slave. Not."

"Am I free to leave? To make my own choices?"

Swift Claw did not answer.

Clanless stood and pointed at the doorway. "Can I even leave this room?"

"It is for your safety."

"You won't even give me back my own property, my weapons. How am I not a prisoner? Or a slave?"

Swift Claw shook his head again and again, but he also lowered it in the method Clanless thought meant shame. "You are not slave." He took a step back. "I must talk with the elders. I will be back." He left the room before Clanless could say anything else.

"So…" Qara slid off her seat on the bed. "You really confused him. If he was left alone, he might come around. But not if he's going to talk to his leaders. They won't be on our side."

"I had to try." Clanless sat back down and reached for his food.

"Do you really feel that way, though?" Qara sat down beside him. "That you're a slave again?"

Clanless thought for a moment while he chewed and swallowed.

"Yes."

THE WEAPONS MASTER

Two interminable days passed in agony for Kekeen. She showed up at Gogeku's workplace almost a full hour before the designated time. While she waited for the partners to close down the shop, she walked around and admired—and in some cases, tried not to laugh at—the rich fashions. How could these tailors possibly be this busy when most of the city's residents were holed up in their homes? Why would people be concerned about fashion in the midst of High Winter? She would never understand the upper class. Her impatience escalated until at last Gogeku joined her and headed for the door.

"Well? Are we going to see this friend of yours?"

"Yes, certainly. He is quite willing to meet with you," the short man said as he pulled open the door. A blast of wind threw snow in their faces. "In fact, let us go as swiftly as we may!"

Kekeen agreed. The tailor had a small carriage waiting, a luxury Kekeen rarely experienced. While its interior could never be warm, at least they could escape the wind and snow. "How far is it?" she asked once they were settled inside and the carriage set off.

"Not far. Not far at all." Gogeku appeared nervous, arousing her suspicions. He'd worked with Aldan and seemed nice enough. What more did she need to know? But her father's warnings about men filled her head.

"Is there really another person?" she demanded, sitting up straight. "Where are you taking me?"

Gogeku's eyes widened. "What? Why would I lie to you? Of course he exists. Whatever do you take me for?"

"I don't know. I don't know you."

Gogeku wiped his forehead and raised his hand. "May I never sew another thread if I intend any harm to you whatsoever."

Kekeen settled back. He sounded sincere, at least. But even if he were telling the truth, what about this other person? She took a calming breath. She hadn't told her father or anyone else where she was going. Stupid.

In fact, she hadn't seen much of Koland the past two days. Daviland had summoned him and kept him at the palace for hours and hours. Apparently, Kekeen's words had made a difference. She smiled at the thought. She'd done something right, at least.

The carriage came to a stop. "We're here," Gogeku announced. He pushed open the door and hopped out.

For a moment, Kekeen considered running. This little man would certainly not try to pursue her. But where would she go? Bang on a random door somewhere? No. If this mysterious person might help her find Aldan, she had to take the risk. She pulled her scarf over her face to shield from the cold and followed Gogeku.

A quick glance confirmed they were in the middle range of Et-Baylak: not the central region filled only with the richest elites, nor the outer circle of those who were always on the verge of financial disaster. These were people who lived comfortably, for the most part, but would never know the excesses of the true elite. Gogeku knocked three times on the door, grasped the handle, and pushed it open. He gestured for Kekeen to go in. She hesitated for a few seconds before ducking her head to step into the house.

The entry hall was dark and still, lit only by a flickering, almost-dead candle. "We're here!" Gogeku called. He rubbed his hands together and stomped his feet to shake off the snow. "Confound the man," he grumbled in a lower tone. "Why does he sit in the dark so much? There's no telling how long ago the fire went out." He shivered. "Quite some time, I would think."

"Geku?" The voice came from a darker room beyond the entry. "Who is with you?"

"I told you I was bringing the girl today, you idiot. The least you could have done is have the lights on for us and a fire stoked! Two-time Hero of the Empire, and you waste away in the darkness. How the mighty have fallen!" Gogeku looked up at Kekeen. "He wasn't always like this, you know. Time was, he was—"

"Stop your babbling, tailor. I can speak for myself." Someone struck a flame and lit an oil lantern. The warm glow spread throughout the room, illuminating its sole occupant. A short man—though nowhere near as short as Gogeku—bulging with muscles. His gray hair, though short, lay flat on his scalp. Stubble decorated his face in patches. He held up the lantern with his left hand. Kekeen held back a gasp when she noticed his right arm ended in a stump.

"So you're Clanless's girl, are you?" The man stood up and stepped closer. "I don't think we ever met directly, though I heard plenty about you. All that trouble with the cult of Suirel." He nodded. "I'm Badaar. I trained Clanless in the arena."

"Of course," Kekeen murmured, her anxiety fading. "Aldan told me about you." She wrinkled her brow. "But why are you here? Living like this?" She glanced around the room, now visible in the flickering lantern light. Badaar set the lantern on a rough-hewn side table, the only other piece of furniture in the room besides the cushioned chair in which he'd been sitting. A fireplace dominated one wall, but nothing burned within. The floor had not been cleaned any time in recent memory. A few pieces of clothing and even some remnants of former meals lay scattered about. Something might have moved in the corner. Kekeen shuddered.

Badaar snorted and waved his stump at her. "Not much use for a weapons master with only one hand."

"That wasn't it, and you know it," Gogeku said.

Badaar slumped back into the chair, his shirt hanging open. "Enlighten us then, tailor. What happened? Why am I here?"

"It was the barbarian attack." The short man looked up at Kekeen. "All of our fighters died, except for Clanless. I couldn't stay after that. We lived with death hanging over those young men every day, but to lose them all at once…" He shook his head. "I couldn't stay. I left Orgina and came here to work with my cousin." He looked back at the trainer. "I thought Badaar was all right. He put on a brave show when the Hawk King came, turning down a job offer, even. We all believed he was fine, even after losing the hand. We were wrong. It broke him."

"Are you done?" Badaar grumbled. "Then leave me. I shouldn't have let you back in here, Geku."

"But… I came for information about Aldan!" Kekeen exclaimed. "He's missing!"

Badaar's head shot up, the fastest movement he'd made since they arrived. "Missing? What do you mean?"

"All of the fighters, the Dohor, disappeared over a week ago. No one knows where they went or, or anything." The words spilled out. "Daviland thinks Ghouk, the Hawk King's son, is involved. But we've seen and heard nothing!"

"Geku, why haven't you told me anything about this?" Badaar demanded.

The tailor sputtered. "Y-you yell at me every time I come here! Why would I tell you anything about anything? Until just now, I didn't think you would have listened to me!"

Badaar pushed himself back up. "The only one of my fighters still alive, and you didn't think I would listen?" His voice shook. "Tell me everything, everything you know. Please."

"There's not a lot to tell," Kekeen said. "After the fight with Daviland, Aldan was badly hurt, and we didn't have enough healing blood—"

"I heard about that fight. Almost went to see it." Badaar shook his head again. "But I couldn't... couldn't go near an arena again. Geku told me all about it." He sighed. "The only real loss for the mighty Clanless. It had to come someday."

"He didn't lose! He let Davil win!" Kekeen wrung her hands together. "It's mostly my fault, I think."

"Your fault? How... Never mind. Go back to the rest. What happened after the fight?"

"Daviland killed the Hawk King, and the fighters were free! I tended Aldan for three days. He... he struggled with nightmares, I think." She looked down. "He always woke up suddenly, sometimes yelling. I pretended not to notice."

"Ghosts," Badaar murmured.

Kekeen looked up. "Then when I went to his room on the fourth day, he wasn't there! I searched the whole arena. All five of the Dohor were gone, and the girl, Qara, who managed them. They'd disappeared."

"Search the city! Go through every house!" Badaar's intensity surprised her.

"Our people have searched as much as they can. We think they may have left the city. A royal carriage went out that morning, but we don't know who was in it."

Badaar held up his left hand, fingers clenched like claws... an effect magnified by fingernails that hadn't been trimmed in far too long. He let out a sigh and dropped his hand. "Then... Clanless is gone too." He almost fell back into the chair. "It was only a matter of time."

"He's not dead!" Kekeen snapped. "We just have to find out where he's gone. I thought that by talking with you and, and Gogeku here, I might learn more about him. Something that might provide a clue or..."

Badaar shook his head, but looked up at her. "Nothing back then would explain why he's gone now. I'm sorry, child. You've wasted your time."

"That much is obvious!" She spun around and moved toward the door. She stopped at Badaar's voice again, but he wasn't talking to her.

"Durken? No, don't be ridiculous. Use the mace, like you've always done."

Kekeen looked back. Badaar stared off into a darkened corner of the room. Was someone else there?

"Keep going," Gogeku whispered. "I'll explain in the carriage."

Both of them stopped out into the snow. Kekeen took one more look inside before the tailor shut the door. Badaar leaned over and blew out the lantern, returning to the darkness.

☾☾☾●☽☽☽

In the carriage, Kekeen wanted answers. "What is wrong with that man?"

Gogeku sighed. "As I said, he's broken. I think he came here to the city to be near Clanless, but he never went to speak with him or even watched any of his fights."

"But…"

"Clanless is the only survivor, remember? He's special. Badaar wants… well, I don't know what he wants, exactly. But that's why he's here. I had hoped that your story would yank him out of this." Gogeku looked through the carriage window back at the house. "And for a brief moment, it did. He almost sounded like himself. But it didn't last."

"I still don't understand…"

Gogeku motioned for the driver to start. The carriage jerked and moved down the street, its single ox plodding through the snow. "How can I explain this to someone like you? When you work in the arena, no matter your job, death is a constant. You live with that possibility. For those of us who didn't work closely with the fighters every day, it wasn't as… as profound. As serious." He looked down. "Most of the time. That cape…"

"But Badaar… he was their trainer, right?" Kekeen prompted.

"Yes." Gogeku straightened. "And so he worked with them every day. His entire job was to teach them how to stay alive. Every single day, he would teach them, prepare them, train them. How to stay alive. And yet they died."

Kekeen hugged herself, feeling a chill beyond the ever-present cold.

"One by one, over the years, everyone died. It had to take its toll on him, if he had any kind of heart at all." Gogeku sniffed. "And Badaar has a bigger heart than most know. The first time he was proclaimed Hero of the Empire proved that, at least. Not many people know the full story, you know. And then, after all those years of watching these young men die, he lost all of them—except Clanless—in one horrible, horrible day." He sighed. "The fact that he lost his good right hand as well only reinforced his belief in his own failure, his own uselessness."

"Who was he talking to in there?"

"He said Durken, didn't he?" Gogeku nodded. "That was one of the youngest of the fighters who died that day. He talks to him a lot. And others. Allaka. Darghan. Patch. Zaluu."

"Are... are they real? They're spirits, I mean. Do they actually speak with him?"

Gogeku scoffed. "Don't be ridiculous. The dead don't speak with the living." He paused. "But the living may speak with the dead. Or believe they do..."

Kekeen put her hands in her lap and sat quiet as the carriage rolled on. "How incredibly sad," she said after a few minutes.

Gogeku stirred out of his own thoughts. "Sad? Yes. Yes, it is sad. It's why I keep coming back to see him ever since I discovered him here over a year ago. I keep hoping he'll return to some semblance of the man he was." He shook his head. "A fool's hope, I suppose. And I should admit it and move on."

"No! I think it's very compassionate of you to keep visiting your friend," Kekeen protested.

The tailor gave her a sad smile. "Is it? We weren't really friends, you know. We almost never interacted back in Ghoyor, unless Orgina called a meeting of all the staff."

She wrinkled her brow. "Then why do you do it?"

He didn't answer for a moment. "When I came here..." He broke off, then started again: "When I came here, I was broken too, or almost broken, at the least. I didn't do well at first. My cousin almost dismissed me. But I sought comfort and encouragement where I could find it. At the temple, and... other places." He shot a glance at her. "And I came through. I recovered. Or so I tell myself. So when I discovered Badaar was here, I didn't want to see him at first. I didn't want a reminder of that time. It's why I never went to the arena, either. But then I found out his condition, and... I couldn't leave him there like that." He shrugged. "I wanted him to recover, to be all right. Because then I, I could accept that I was all right. Truly all right, and not just pretending." He looked down.

"It's still a kind thing to do," Kekeen said.

"Maybe it is. I don't know. All I know for certain is clothing." He adjusted his vest and looked back at her. "Since you appear to be in the good graces of our new leader, perhaps you might be wanting a new wardrobe? I know I said we were extremely busy, but I might be able to squeeze you in. You could come by the store tomorrow for measurements, and—"

Kekeen laughed. "I'm not suddenly rich. My father tells stories for our bread and butter. I sing. We don't have the blood for your kind of business, I'm afraid."

Gogeku shrugged. "As you say. But don't be surprised if your leader suddenly decides that everyone around him should look the part. If so, you know where to find me."

"Thank you."

The tailor fell silent for most of the remaining trip. Kekeen replayed the evening's events and conversations in her head, looking for anything worthwhile. "He... Badaar said something about Suirel, didn't he? What was that?"

"Hm? Oh." Gogeku took a deep breath. "That business. I didn't have anything to do with it, but I know Clanless and Badaar—and Zaluu, I believe—had some kind of trouble with the cult of Suirel. Actually fought outside the arena, if I remember right." He swiveled to look at her. "In fact... wasn't it all about you? Some business where Clanless had to save you or something?"

"He, he and Zaluu rescued my father once. But I don't know anything about a cult."

"How curious."

When Kekeen exited the carriage at their inn some time later, she tried not to be too disappointed. She'd gained almost nothing from her conversations with Gogeku and Badaar. If anything, she'd found more people in need. But none of it was getting her anywhere closer to Aldan. The only new thing she had to contemplate was this bit about the cult of Suirel, and that seemed linked to her father more than Aldan. She hurried to her rooms to ask him about it.

Koland did not return to the inn that night.

MEMORIES

Kekeen didn't sleep well, wondering about her father. The innkeeper didn't know anything and grumbled about Koland's absence on the stage. Throughout the night, she imagined all sorts of problems that could have kept him away. The most recurring thought pictured him lying dead in the snow.

So when he breezed into their room just after dawn, she leaped out of bed and rushed into his arms. "Where have you been?" she demanded when she could breathe.

He smiled, though his eyes drooped with fatigue. "With Daviland." He yawned and gently pushed free of her embrace. "We were up all night debating how to spread the word of our revolution to the other cities."

"It's our revolution again, then?"

"Yes, yes, it is." Koland rubbed his face and yawned again. "Davil is… he's much more like he was before the Hawk King's death."

"That's wonderful. Did you hear anything else about Borde?"

Koland blinked a few times. "Oh, uh… I don't think so. I don't remember talking about her."

"You were with Davil for a day and a night and she never came up?" Kekeen put her hands on her hips. "I know men can be ignorant sometimes, but that's beyond belief!"

"Maybe we did." Koland shook his head. "I'm sorry, dear. My head is swimming. I need sleep."

"Of course." She stood aside and let him head for his bed, torn between conflicting emotions. On the one hand, Koland spending this much time with their leader harkened back to the earlier days of the revolution. An all-night conversation was not unheard-of back then. But considering everything that had been happening in the last week or more, could anything be considered normal?

Koland paused after pulling off his boots. "Oh… didn't you have a meeting with someone? How did that go?"

"I'll tell you when you're awake."

Koland nodded slowly. He twisted and fell across his bed, asleep in almost an instant.

Kekeen envied him in that moment.

(((●))))

When Koland roused himself in the early afternoon, he seemed a different man entirely. After cleaning himself up, he asked Kekeen to sit with him at their table.

"Something is not right," he announced. He held up his hands. "I know, I know. A lot of things have not been right the last few days. But I mean specifically the past two."

Kekeen frowned. "What do you mean? I thought the past two days were the best since… since the revolution."

"Yes and no." Koland tapped his beard. "I don't know quite how to say this."

Kekeen opened her hands. "I'm right here, Father."

"I'm missing some time."

She waited for him to explain.

Koland blew out through his teeth. "I said I didn't know how to say it. Um… you know I've been at the palace with Daviland a lot the past two days."

"Yes?"

"I can't remember all that time."

Kekeen lowered her eyebrows. "Isn't that kind of normal? I know when I've been talking with someone for a long time, I don't always remember all of it."

"No, not like that." He shook his head. "I remember my conversations, dear. All of them. I remember each story I tell, every bit of advice I give. And every story and bit of advice I hear. It's part of what makes me so good at what I do."

"All right." She had heard him say things like this before, though she'd never quite grasped what it meant.

"For the past two days… I don't remember large parts of it. I can remember conversations we had, but they weren't enough to take up that much time. Somehow, I've forgotten things. And I don't know how!"

Kekeen started to smile and open her mouth to make a joke about her father getting old. But she stopped at the look on his face. "This is serious?"

"Yes." Despite his request that they sit together, Koland got up and paced around the room. "It's not natural. I'm losing time from each day, and I don't know how or why."

"Then I'll stay with you from here on," Kekeen suggested. "And maybe I'll see something. Or maybe it will stop happening."

He nodded. "I was hoping you'd say that. I know you've been trying to find clues to Aldan's disappearance…"

She looked at the table's surface. "I'm getting nowhere. No one knows anything."

"Today, I'm staying here." Koland sat back down. "I need more rest, anyway. And I need to perform this evening and make up my absence to the innkeeper. But tomorrow… I want you with me when I go back to the palace."

"Is something happening tomorrow?"

He nodded. "Daviland is assembling a full advisory council tomorrow morning. I do remember discussing that. It will include myself and at least one other member of the revolution, along with some of the existing city leaders."

"Like those three Lords?"

"And the Ghamba Lam."

Kekeen pulled back. "Really? I thought… well, I thought Davil would be decreasing the power of the priests."

"I argued against it, but it was a concession to the Lords, I think. He also promised to bring someone in to counterbalance the Ghamba Lam."

"What does that mean?"

Koland shrugged. "I guess we'll find out tomorrow."

Then

Clanless relaxed and let the warmth of the water penetrate into his muscles. Three warriors, all of them using Clan Dalbai blood-magic, had fallen to the moonblade this evening. The Hawk King was pushing him harder and harder. But he could handle it.

A large splash shook the water. Clanless opened his eyes to see Sugh sinking down only a few feet away. "Ahhh. The water is good today," he announced.

"You had a good fight," Clanless said.

"So did you! Well done. You are surpassing all of us. And at such a young age." Sugh closed his eyes and shook his head. "Soon the crowds will not want to see the mighty Sugh and his axe. Only Clanless."

"I can't do every fight." Clanless chuckled.

"No, I suppose not. There will be room for me still."

Clanless closed his eyes again, listening for the distant sound of the crowd. Hagh and Silence were fighting together for the final bout. It would be a good one too. They were all good fights. Badzorik knew how to run a schedule.

Sugh muttered something he could barely hear. It sounded like "You were right."

"What did you say?"

"Oh. Sorry. I was not speaking to you."

Clanless opened his eyes and glanced around. "I'm the only one here."

"That you can see."

"What does that mean?"

"I like to talk sometimes. That is all."

Clanless didn't respond, thinking about what Hagh had told him about Sugh when he first arrived. Since then, he'd heard for himself a few times. Maybe now was the time to find out the truth.

"Sugh, can I ask you something?"

"Always. I am right here."

"Who… who do you talk to in your room?"

"Who do you talk to in your room?" Sugh countered.

"Uh, myself." Clanless swallowed. He always tried to keep his conversations with Zektel quiet, but he supposed someone might have heard him. Did Sugh have something similar going on?

"I am joking. I have never heard you in your room." Sugh stretched and lowered his shoulders into the water. "But I know people hear me. It is all right."

Clanless waited.

"I speak to the goddess."

"Oh." Praying. He hadn't even thought of that.

"It is not what you think. I am not a religious man. I do not go to the temples."

"Then…"

"She has spoken to me a few times," Sugh explained. "So I speak to her. She does not usually answer me, but I talk anyway. Just in case, you know."

"I don't understand." At least, he hoped he didn't understand. When Zektel had first spoken to him, he thought she was the goddess. Maybe another wraith was deceiving Sugh. Or maybe it was all his imagination. Or… maybe he told the truth. That seemed the least likely.

"It is all right." Sugh sank down until only his face protruded from the water. "She said you were coming, and you would be good for us."

"Really?"

"It is so."

"Huh."

Now

Swift Claw did not return the next day. Clanless worried that he'd pressed the translator too hard. Maybe he should have waited to be so adamant about leaving. The new memory baffled him. Why would Zektel suppress that? She didn't want him to know Sugh thought he talked with the goddess?

Qara, on the other hand, busied herself with another worry. "We've been wearing these same clothes for over a week. It's disgusting!"

Clanless wrapped himself in the bedclothes and waited while she worked to resolve the problem. Using the soap they had for themselves, she washed all of their clothes in the bath. Drying would probably take hours, though.

"If only there were a way to get some more clothes," she grumbled behind him. Clanless sat facing the wall, unsure whether Qara wore anything at all.

"I don't think we'll find much here," he said.

"The beastmen don't wear very much," she agreed. "Most seem to wear a skirt and nothing more. I still haven't seen the women or what they wear."

"They have so much hair. Maybe they don't see the need for clothes as much as we do."

"Clothes aren't just for warmth, you know."

Clanless didn't answer her. Maybe the beastmen had different thoughts than human men or women. Who could say? It wasn't on his mental list of questions for Swift Claw. He was far more curious about a great many other aspects of beastman culture. But would he even get to ask the questions? Aside from those who brought the morning meal, no one had entered their room.

"What about your fur?" Qara asked. "Do you want me to clean it?"

Clanless picked up the wolf pelt and ran his hand over it. "No… it's old. I wouldn't want to risk damaging it."

Qara moved closer behind him. "All right, 'Wolf Chosen'. What do you think the wolf meant about it protecting you?"

"I'm not sure." But he had an idea. During all the years with Zektel, she had hidden his memories and messed with his thoughts. But only once had she seized control of him. He couldn't remember whether he'd been wearing the fur then or not. Is that what the wolf meant? Could blood-wraiths take complete control of a person? In Bain's stories, they did it all the time. If so, someone like Daviland would be in great danger.

When had he encountered others with a blood-wraith? There was the barbarian leader, though he only knew that from Zektel. And the cultist he'd just remembered, which did seem like full control. And the Hawk King… or so Zektel claimed; he'd never seen any evidence of it. Maybe she'd lied. If so, she might have lied about the Daghilch not being possessed.

He shook his head. Too many lies made everything unsure. How could he know?

Thinking of the Daghilch reminded him of something else. "Qara… you said your father was a Daghilch?"

"He was. Why?"

"Just curious." He turned his head to the side, but couldn't see her. "As you said, we're stuck together. I think you've heard a lot of my story. I was wondering about yours."

Qara snorted. After a pause, she said, "No one's ever asked about my story before."

"Then tell me. We appear to have time."

"All right. The clothes are all spread out to dry." She climbed onto the bed. "I grew up in Conchaga. It's not a big city, not like the capital. It didn't even have an arena. My father was the Daghilch for the whole region. I suppose he was a good one. I don't really know.

"When I was fourteen, he started making mistakes. He… drank too much and put what was left of his blood into bad ideas."

"Bad ideas?"

"He was trying to become rich, because he felt like he didn't get enough blood for the Daghilch job." She paused. "We didn't care. We liked our life until he ruined it."

"Did you have a large family?"

"Two younger brothers. Much younger. So when my father's problems became our problems… I was the logical choice to solve them. My own mother sold me. I didn't… I haven't spoken to any of them since."

"Couldn't you have been married by then? Escaped before all of it?"

"Look, clanhold boy. They may get married at twelve where you grew up, but in the cities, it's not so early."

"Thirteen," he mumbled.

"Thirteen. That's crazy."

"Wouldn't it have been better than becoming a slave?"

"Maybe. I don't know. Depends on the man, I suppose. Anyway, it wasn't an option for me. I didn't get any choice in the matter."

"I'm so sorry."

He could almost hear her shrug. "Happens every day in this Empire. Maybe Daviland will change all that… or maybe he won't."

"How did you end up at the arena?"

"It wasn't easy. Young slave girls are usually considered worthwhile for only one job."

Clanless winced.

"I started that way, but got out of it after a couple of years. I made myself essential to the master who ran the house. I took care of all the other girls, organized things, made sure everything ran smoothly… I did so well at those other tasks that I didn't get called on much for the clients." She paused again. "Though I wasn't bad at the original job, in case you ever change your mind."

"Qara…"

"We're still stuck here. Just keeping the invitation open. Anyway, my master sold me to a businessman in Et-Baylak, where I did well enough to eventually be noticed by some of the Hawk King's servants. One thing led to another, and I ended up as the manager for the Hawk King's very own arena fighters."

"You did well for yourself."

"Maybe. Still a slave. And… not all that different from my very first job, when it came down to it. I had to keep the fighters happy, you know."

"Oh." Clanless didn't want to think about that. His fellow Dohor had frequented Pasque House, of course. But Qara was… She was a friend. And you didn't treat friends like that.

"You're so naive, Clanless."

"Maybe. What will you do when we get back? Now that you're free, I mean?"

"I don't know. It's been so long since… since I could make my own choices, like you told the beastman. I guess I'll look for a real job. Organizing things. It's what I'm good at."

"I think you'll be great, no matter what you choose." He meant it.

"Thank you. I'm going to take a nap now," she announced. "I didn't sleep well last night, and these clothes are going to take a long time to dry."

"Go ahead."

He heard her shifting around on the bed for a moment or two. It would be so easy to climb up there with her. She wanted it. He… wanted it too, if he could admit it. She was lying there naked right now: that simple reality tempted him more than he would tell her. He closed his eyes and tried to think of something else.

For the next hour, while she slept, he diverted his thoughts by considering all the information they'd learned about the beastmen so far. Nothing jumped out as anything they could use to either escape or persuade Swift Claw—or anyone else—to help them leave.

When the clothes finally dried, he pulled his on as soon as he could. They were stiff and uncomfortable, but clean. Qara grumbled about the feel of the stiff cloth, but appeared pleased overall.

The beastmen who brought the evening meal remained as silent as the morning team. If either of them understood human speech, they did not respond in kind. Clanless and Qara ate alone again. The day ended as it had begun.

（（（●））） ）

The next morning, Swift Claw arrived with the early meal. He appeared pleased, but Clanless still had trouble identifying that emotion in a beastman's face.

"I apologize for the delay." Swift Claw lowered his head briefly. "It took longer than I had hoped. But I have something for you." He gestured to another beastman who entered behind him. This one carried something wrapped in a blanket. He placed it on the floor beside the food, lowered his head, and left them.

Clanless knew before he unwrapped it. He could almost feel the cold metal within the blanket calling to him. He flipped the last bit of the cloth away and drank it in. The moonblade.

"It is… a most unique weapon," Swift Claw said.

"You don't know the half of it," Qara said, moving around Clanless to see for herself.

Clanless said nothing. He picked up the moonblade and let his eyes roam its familiar surfaces, from the terebinth handle to the engraved craters to the single chip in the blade from the beastman's sword—a reminder to explore their forging processes when possible.

"You have this weapon a long time?" Swift Claw asked.

"Long enough," Clanless answered. "Years."

The beastman nodded. "A bond must exist then. I understand. And these others?"

Clanless took up the throwing knife, smiled at it, and tucked it into his belt. "A reminder of a lost friend."

"And this one's mine." Qara bent down and grabbed the thin dagger that remained.

"I didn't even know you had that!"

"It's a last resort," she said, concealing the dagger within her skirt.

"Our women carry weapons as well," Swift Claw said. "Some are fierce fighters also."

"We haven't seen any of your women." Qara glanced toward the door. "Have we?"

"Not as yet. It was agreed to keep them from your eyes at first. That will change soon. I hope."

"You've kept a lot of things from us at first," Clanless said.

Swift Claw lowered his head. "I apologize. You are not trusted."

Clanless spread his arms. "What are we going to do? Fight our way through hundreds of your warriors?" He displayed the moonblade. "Even with this, I wouldn't get very far."

"When the winds have passed, you will be leaving us," Swift Claw pointed out. "The elders are concerned about what you will tell your people about us." He crossed his legs as he settled on the floor. "Now, we are not known much by your people."

"Some don't even believe you exist."

"Yes. It is good. Those who do believe stay away. Most of them. But if you tell all you know, then it may change. Already they hunt us. If they knew more, it might be worse."

"I understand. We will tell nothing about you, if you ask." Clanless glanced to Qara. "We have no reason to."

"Except to explain how we survived the winter," she said.

"We stayed in a cave. Simple and true, right?"

Qara laughed. "True enough, I guess."

"You will not speak of us at all?" Swift Claw seemed amazed.

"If you don't want us to, we won't. We would rather be your friends," Clanless said.

"Mmh. We have no friends among your people."

"Then that needs to change."

Swift Claw leaned back. "It would be… good to have friends."

"It is good," Clanless agreed. "I hope my, uh, pressuring you the other day didn't hurt our chances."

Swift Claw tilted his head. "I do not understand."

"I was forceful in my speech about wanting to leave. That doesn't mean we can't be friends."

"Mmh. I see. You separate this"—he gestured at the cave around them—"from us." He pointed at himself.

"Yes. Exactly."

"It is good." Swift Claw's eyes and mouth grew larger. "And how do you heal?"

"I'm sorry?"

Swift Claw pointed at him. "Your injuries. Do you recover?"

"Oh. Yes. I'm getting better."

"When do you wish to help with the training? Is it good tomorrow?"

Clanless stretched. "I think so. I don't want to spend too many days in this room. I need… movement."

Swift Claw nodded. "It is good." He turned to look at Qara. "And the woman, Kharha? We could—"

"I want her with me," Clanless cut him off. "I've been thinking about it, and it would be best if she were with us at the training."

"I do not understand." Swift Claw cocked his head.

"If I were to be injured, I would need her," Clanless explained. "Your people do not know how to treat humans. Am I right?"

Swift Claw considered. "There may be wisdom in this. I do not know. But we can allow it."

Qara reached out and squeezed Clanless's hand. He resisted the urge to yank it away.

Swift Claw unfolded himself and stood. "Rest this day then. I will see you with the next meal. Tomorrow, we will do more."

Clanless also stood. "Thank you, Swift Claw. For all of this."

The beastman nodded and left them alone.

Qara let out a long sigh. "I will sleep better tonight with this dagger handy."

Clanless fingered the moonblade. "Me too. Did he seem different to you, somehow?"

"What do you mean?"

"I don't know." He shrugged. "Maybe I'm imagining it. But he seemed nervous. I think he wasn't sure what would happen when he gave us the weapons. I hope we reassured him."

"With all that talk about friendship, I would think so. Did you mean all of that?"

"Of course. Why wouldn't we want to be friends?"

Qara sat down and reached for the food. "I don't know. Maybe because we want to get out of here as soon as possible."

"We can still be friends." He picked up a piece of the bread. "I don't know about you, but I haven't had a lot of friends in my life."

"I thought all of you Dohor were the best of friends."

"Hagh and Sugh, sure. And Bain... sort of. But I never really got to know Hawking. Or Silence. And at the city before, I only had one real friend." Thinking about Zaluu stirred up thoughts of his recently restored memories. Maybe two friends. He'd apparently spent more time with Badaar than he used to think. The suppressed and returned memories complicated so much of his past life.

"Thank you, by the way," Qara said after a moment, "for including me in your training plans."

He nodded. "You said you were scared of what they might ask you to do, and I know you don't want to sit around in here all the time. It just seemed like the best idea."

"It was. You've saved me again." She looked around their room. "And now we have one more day in here while you rest and heal. Good thing we have these meals or we'd never be able to keep track of the time. Assuming they're telling us the truth about it, I guess. For all we know, it could be late evening when they're telling us it's time for breakfast."

"I don't see why they would do that."

Qara made a disgusted noise in her throat. "It's a joke, Clanless. Humor. Remember how that works?"

"Sometimes. I've never been very good at it."

"I'll add that to the list of things I should teach you."

"You have a list?"

"It's been growing since we left Et-Baylak." She took a drink and eyed him over the cup. "Should we begin today?"

Several responses ran through Clanless's head, a couple of which he considered to be quite funny. But rather than risk the attempt, all he said was: "I'm supposed to rest today, remember?"

COUNCIL MEMBERS

The next day, Koland and Kekeen bundled up and made their way to the palace. The High Winter of the chaos moon showed no signs of diminishing. If anything, the temperature had dropped further and the wind grown stronger. Kekeen was thoroughly miserable by the time they reached the warmth of the Hawk King's former abode.

She wanted to swing by Borde's room, but Koland was summoned directly to the former throne room. "Just wait inside near the door," he whispered to her as they hurried down the hall. "The others might not even notice your presence. If they do, I'll explain that I need you there for medical reasons."

"Medical?"

He handed her a small vial and winked. "Of course. You have the medicine I might need."

Kekeen raised the vial and peered at it. "Isn't this—?"

"It's medicine," Koland repeated. "Just hang on to it. Here we are."

Once past the huge double doors, Kekeen slipped off to the side to wait and watch. A large table, moved from somewhere else in the palace, sat at the base of the Hawk King's throne. Daviland welcomed Koland, who pointed toward Kekeen and spoke with animation. Davil smiled and waved toward her. Lord Ezen already waited at the table. A moment later, the other two Lords entered and joined them around the table.

"What is this?" Lord Ulakan asked. "The palace has three or four meeting rooms. Why move a table in here?"

Daviland gestured at the surroundings. "I thought it fitting, gathering in the shadow of this symbol of the Hawk King's rule. Just a constant reminder of how things have changed."

A servant brought Kekeen a chair, which she accepted gratefully. Who knew how long this meeting might last? She wondered if anyone had suggested the chair, or if the servant had taken his own initiative. The smile he gave her hinted at the latter.

A heavy-set man beginning to lose his hair entered next. Kekeen recognized him: Sonkogh, a man who'd been by Daviland's side almost as long as Koland. His presence made her feel a little more confident.

And then the Ghamba Lam swooped in, red robe billowing. Kekeen rolled her eyes. Without waiting for instruction, the priest took a seat at one end of the table and stared imperiously at Daviland, as if daring him to challenge his seating choice.

"This is a good start!" Daviland proclaimed, clapping his hands. "Almost everyone is here. Good, good."

"Almost?" Lord Ulakan asked. "Who—?"

"Please have a seat, gentlemen. Thank you. I'm so glad you could all make it." As the men sat, eyeing each other across the table, Daviland moved to the opposite end. "As you know, I have come here to change the Empire, to remake it in… in a way that spreads its riches and security to all its people."

While Daviland talked, Kekeen tried to watch each of the men around the table. Koland and Sonkogh sat with their backs to her, so she couldn't see their faces, but she knew them the best. The three Lords appeared sullen and uneasy… except for Lord Ulakan. A smile never left his face. Kekeen wondered again about his meeting with the priests. She watched for any connection between Ulakan and the Ghamba Lam, but the two never seemed to look at one another.

As for the religious leader, he fidgeted. Something bothered him, clearly. But he'd met with Daviland before, and his inclusion here was an acknowledgment of his importance. What could have disturbed him so?

"I led the rebellion that overthrew the Hawk King," Davil went on. "You all know this, of course. I bring it up only to point out that it would be easy—expected, even—for me to sweep in here with only those who came with me." He gestured toward Koland and Sonkogh. "We want to remake the Empire, after all. Many of my followers would doubtlessly expect us to cast out everyone else and confide only in ourselves."

Kekeen had expected something like that. She still didn't fully understand why he needed these others.

"Et-Baylak remains on edge, buried beneath the snow as it is. Open fighting between my followers and those still loyal to the Hawk King could break out again once the weather is more reasonable. And that's here, in this city. What of our other cities? What of the clanholds? News of our rebellion has not reached all of them yet, a topic that we should discuss later today.

"I want a balance in our leadership. An equal representation for every group or faction. In time, we will develop this into a more organized assembly, but for now, this advisory council will suffice. Koland and Sonkogh here have been with me for a long time. The three of us will be balanced by the three Lords present, those who helped the Hawk King in running this great city for so many years."

Kekeen could see some wisdom in that, but hoped Daviland would not take every man's word equally. The rebellion had to count for something other than just a seat at the table. They'd won.

"The Ghamba Lam is here, of course, to represent the religious beliefs of our people." Daviland gave a half-bow toward the priest.

"I cannot help but notice an empty chair," the Ghamba Lam inserted, gesturing to the offending piece of furniture. "Who else will be joining us?"

Daviland's smile never moved. "I'm rather surprised that our final member has not arrived yet. I'm sure he'll be along at any moment. For you see, Ghamba Lam, we must have someone to balance you as well."

"Preposterous. I am the embodiment of our people's beliefs, the emissary of the goddess herself. What balance do I need?"

"Not everyone shares your beliefs," Daviland said. "There are growing numbers who have rejected them entirely. Or those like myself who still believe in the goddess, but reject your methods. Or those who believe in… something else."

The doors opened. Kekeen jerked her head to see who the final advisor might be. She wrinkled her brow. She'd never seen this man before. Like everyone before him, he removed his heavy coat and handed it to a servant before turning toward the table. He looked affable enough, dressed in clothing nicer than the rebels but not on the same level as the Lords. Average height, black hair and beard… Aside from a tiny scar that split his right eyebrow, there was nothing to distinguish him from most of the city's general population.

"Ah, here he is," Daviland announced. "Gentlemen, may I present the final member of this advisory council, Demujin."

The Ghamba Lam leaped to his feet. He pointed at the newcomer, his hand trembling with rage. "You cannot possibly be serious!"

Demujin only smiled and walked toward the table.

The Ghamba Lam looked at the other men. "Do you not know who this man is? What he represents?" With a thunderous voice and a slap on the table, the priest shouted, "He is a leader in the cult of Suirel!"

The cult of Suirel. Badaar said they'd been involved in Koland's kidnapping, in trying to kill Aldan! With a gasp, Kekeen remembered the last time she'd overheard Suirel mentioned. Her eyes shot to Lord Ulakan. His smile grew as he watched Demujin join them at the table. That was the connection. Those priests he'd met with must be part of the cult as well.

Daviland spread his hands while he attempted to calm the furious Ghamba Lam. "You admit he has a different set of beliefs, then? Isn't that what we need here?"

"It is preposterous!" The Ghamba Lam looked ready to storm out of the room. "You cannot give any credibility to this... this fringe group!"

"Two weeks ago, I was considered the leader of a fringe group," Daviland responded.

"You have thousands of followers. This group, this cult—"

"Has more followers than you're willing to admit," Demujin interrupted. "Have you surveyed your own priests lately?"

While Kekeen enjoyed seeing the Ghamba Lam in such a predicament, she couldn't help but think he might be right this time. From what little she'd heard of the cult, they didn't sound like a group that should be given any power. They worshipped a moon known for creating chaos, for the goddess's sake!

Her father appeared to agree with her. "Davil, this is... highly unusual. I wish you'd sought our advice on this."

"We needed another voice on this council," Daviland said. "I considered my choices thoroughly. Demujin is the man we need. A leader of a different faction within our population. A voice of—shall we say—disruption."

"You mean chaos!" Lord Ghayaktal exclaimed. "Anarchy! Disorder! Confusion!"

Demujin took his seat. "I'm afraid, Lord Ghayaktal, that you've been listening to idle gossip. That's hardly a fair assessment of our beliefs."

"How would you describe them then?" Sonkogh asked.

"We celebrate the return of our Lord Suirel to the skies above, it is true. But referring to him as a force for 'chaos' is... not accurate."

"Have you stepped outside lately?" Lord Ezen asked drily.

Demujin laughed. "High Winter? It happens every year around this time. Some years are more severe than others. Yet our elders always have stories of the worst winter of all time when they were children."

"Yes," Koland agreed with a chuckle. "Thirty years ago."

"Let us be clear," Daviland said, putting both hands on the table. "This is not a topic of debate for this council. I have chosen the seven of you to advise me. I made that choice. If you do not want to be here, the doors are easy to find." He took his own seat at the head of the table.

The Ghamba Lam still stood at the other end. Even from her vantage point, Kekeen could see the man trembling. He would leave, wouldn't he? How could he stay…?

The Ghamba Lam sat down.

Kekeen blinked. She hadn't expected that, and from the look on Davil's face, neither had he. But he recovered quickly. "Excellent. Let us begin."

The first few topics of discussion were boring, from Kekeen's point of view. Discussions of things like water storage and street repair weren't enough to arouse any strong emotions from anyone at the table. Occasionally, someone would throw a snide remark or jab in someone else's direction. But tempers stayed under control throughout these discussions.

Kekeen perked up when Daviland introduced a new topic she hadn't heard about: "I have been thinking about visiting the almaz mines."

"Why would you do that?" Sonkogh asked. He appeared to be speaking for the entire table, all of whom looked at their leader with curiosity.

"I've always wanted to see them." Davil shrugged. "And they are a… significant historical and religious site to our people. Isn't that correct, Ghamba Lam?"

"It is," the priest answered slowly. "But I fail to see what a visit there would accomplish for you."

Davil sat back. "First you object to the presence of an unbeliever"—he waved at Demujin—"and now you object to my learning more about our faith?"

"That is not what I meant." The Ghamba Lam sighed. "You know very well the significance of the mines, as we had this discussion a week ago."

"I don't," Lord Ezen piped up.

"Going there will not affect anything one way or another," the priest went on, ignoring him. "But once this chaotic winter has passed, and you have consolidated your rule, perhaps we can arrange something."

"I was thinking much sooner than that," Davil said.

"You would take a trip in the middle of High Winter?" Koland asked. "When we haven't even solidified things here?"

"It does not seem… prudent," Lord Ghayaktal said.

"Didn't the Hawk King possess special carriages for traveling in High

Winter?" Davil asked.

"Yes, but…" Koland spread his hands. "I'm sorry, Davil. I fail to see why such a trip will do any good at all, not when there is so much else to be done."

"There's another reason not to travel in that direction," Sonkogh said. "A topic we seem to have avoided so far. What about General Ghan and the army?"

"What about them?" Daviland asked.

"Tell us, Lord Ezen, where is the bulk of the Empire's military might right now?" Sonkogh asked across the table.

"The Hawk King sent General Ghan and the majority of our army to the fortress of Tzhambul, near the border with the Melkute Kingdom. It was seen as a deterrent against invasion." The Lord recited the facts in a monotone, as if it meant nothing to him.

"And that very move is why we were able to achieve our victory," Daviland said quickly.

"Traveling to the mines would take you much closer to the General," Sonkogh persisted. "He was known for his fierce loyalty to the Hawk King."

"Let's be really honest about it," Koland said. He gestured to the three Lords. "You three are hoping the General returns in High Spring and kicks us out of here."

The Lords didn't answer.

"We have time to prepare," Koland went on. "But it is the most serious issue facing this new government. What are we to do about General Ghan?"

"I have met the General," the Ghamba Lam offered. "I believe he can be reasoned with."

"And what if Ghouk, the Hawk King's son, has fled to him?"

The rest of the table reacted with surprise. "Is that a possibility?" "I thought Ghouk was dead!"

"Ghouk is probably behind the disappearance of the Dohor warriors," Daviland explained. "But we do not know where he has gone."

"It sounds as if we should prepare the city for a siege come winter's end," Demujin said.

"Perhaps. Or perhaps we can negotiate with the General, and come to an agreement that satisfies both parties. At any rate, it is not a decision we need to make at this time." Davil looked around the table. "Well. I suppose we've done enough for this morning. I should allow you gentlemen to eat lunch with your families. Thank you all for coming." He stood up.

The others followed suit, though Kekeen could tell the abrupt end to the meeting had caught them off guard. One by one, they left, most grumbling.

Kekeen met her father halfway. He shook his head, brow wrinkled. "Confusing," he muttered.

"Storyteller!" They both turned to see Demujin approaching with a wide smile.

"Demujin." Koland stiffened ever so slightly.

"You were the most logical, clear-headed voice of reason at that entire table," the cult leader declared. "I'm including myself in that number, as I'm afraid I contributed little of substance."

"Why are you here, Demujin?" Koland asked. "Aside from being an irritant to the Ghamba Lam." He glanced at the priest as the red robes swept through the doors. "Daviland has never mentioned you in all the time I've known him."

"You've known him far longer than I," Demujin said. "I only met him a few days ago when he sought me out."

"That couldn't have been easy," Kekeen put in. "If I were to walk around asking people where to find the leader of the cult of Suirel, I doubt I'd get many good answers."

Demujin chuckled. "No, I imagine not. But please: I am a leader, not the leader. And we do not like the term 'cult.'"

"Fair enough," Koland said. "But you haven't answered my question."

"I am here because our leader sought me out and asked me to come. It's no more complicated than that." Demujin lifted a hand. "But! I am more interested in your story. The storyteller who lifted a rebel leader from obscurity to emperor!"

"He's not an emperor," Koland protested, glancing toward Daviland. "He would greatly object to that title."

Demujin shrugged. "Perhaps not in name, I suppose. But effectively, that's what he's becoming. Regardless, I would love to hear more about it. And maybe I can offer you some stories in return, meager though they may be."

"I am interested in learning more about your beliefs." Koland tapped his beard. He gave Demujin the name of their inn and suggested he come that evening. "When I take a break between stories, we can talk together. You can learn a lot about a man over a few drinks."

"True that!" Demujin clenched a fist in the air. "I will be there!" He nodded to Kekeen and left the room.

"What is going on?" Kekeen wondered, stepping closer to her father.

"I don't know. But the more I can learn about that man and his cult, the closer we may come to some answers."

Kekeen hesitated. "Speaking of the cult, there's something else I need to tell you…"

Demujin did come to the inn that evening. After Koland's nightly performance, the two sat and talked for a long time. Kekeen joined them at first, but soon grew uncomfortable. The cult leader didn't ogle her in front of her father, but any time Koland's back was turned, Kekeen felt Demujin's eyes on her. She excused herself and returned to her room.

When Koland joined her hours later, he expressed his frustration: "Demujin is a man full of contradictions representing a belief system full of contradictions."

"How so?" Kekeen set aside the book she'd been reading.

"He's very knowledgeable about the inner workings of the Empire, so far as it applies to religious things." Koland collapsed into his chair. "But he knows next to nothing about the political realm. He hardly seems like the kind of man to advise the leader of the Empire.

"And his beliefs!" Koland threw up his hands. "He freely acknowledges that everyone has always considered Suirel to be the chaos moon, a bad omen. But he claims everyone's wrong. That Suirel doesn't represent chaos, but freedom." He paused. "When you press him on the meaning of freedom, he starts ranting against the blood-priests and their version of morality. I believe his idea of freedom is the ability to do whatever you want whenever you want."

"Is that such a bad thing?"

"If everyone believed they were free to do whatever they wanted whenever they wanted…" Koland shook his head. "It would be a horrible world. What happens when someone's wants conflict with someone else's wants?" He tapped his beard. "Let me give a simple illustration. Let's say I wanted to take all of Demujin's property? But he wanted to keep all of his property. We both have wants. Who decides?"

"Did you ask him that?"

"He pontificated some nonsense about how true desires don't conflict, so I suppose taking someone's property would be evidence that my desires weren't true or something. Then he went on about how we all had a responsibility to seek out the true desires within us, and so on."

Kekeen wrinkled her brow. "So they reject any standards, and base everything on… individual desires?"

"Exactly. It's totally self-centered." Koland sighed. "That's only the beginning of it, of course. We know they engage in various rituals and treat Suirel like some kind of god, but he wasn't very forthcoming in discussing all that." He paused. "He did invite me to join them some time, though."

"You aren't going to, are you?" Kekeen sat up straight in alarm.

"Probably not." Her father got up and removed his jacket. "Still… it might help with a story or two…"

（（（（●））））

High Winter grew so fearsome over the next few days that no one wanted to step outside. Even a short trip around the corner could be an enormous risk. Snow piled up in the streets, swept along by the strongest winds anyone could remember. The eating house had no customers three nights in a row.

When the winds finally let up enough for people to escape their homes, Daviland summoned another meeting of the advisory council. Kekeen sat in again, listening intently. Despite Daviland's attempts to change the subject, the council focused almost exclusively on the problem of General Ghan and the army. The Lords of Et-Baylak offered no suggestions other than waiting until the General arrived to negotiate with him. Kekeen could easily see their desire to stall until High Spring, although they did grow uncomfortable when Ghouk's name was brought into the mix. The Hawk King's son had not earned many loyal fans, it seemed.

The rest of the council floated various ideas, from preparing the city for a possible siege to sending a messenger of peace to the General, offering him a place in the new government. Nothing was resolved.

Demujin embraced his role as counter to the Ghamba Lam, provoking the high priest at every opportunity. Despite her dislike of the man, Kekeen had to cover her mouth more than once to keep from laughing at some of Demujin's barbs.

Following the meeting, Kekeen made another attempt to visit Borde. And yet again, she was prevented from seeing Aldan's cousin for "health reasons."

Stymied in every direction, Kekeen sought out Gogeku. "I need information on the Suirel cult," she explained. "Your friend Badaar is the only person I know who's had experience."

The short man sighed. "I'll speak to him, but I don't think he'll want visitors again."

"Would he like to hear a storyteller?" Kekeen asked with sudden inspiration. "Do you think you could persuade him to come to our inn? We would provide food and drink and entertainment."

Gogeku considered the proposal. "I will attempt it. I can make no promises, though."

Kekeen patted him on the shoulder. "I have faith in you."

BECOMING A TEACHER

The training sessions changed everything.

After breakfast, Swift Claw brought them to the large open space used for warrior training. Clanless deferred at first, wanting to watch the beastmen, to compare their training with his own. He would be no good as an instructor if all he did was tell them things they already knew. The three of them watched from the higher level as Wind Tooth began training a couple dozen younger beastmen.

At first, the training looked similar to what Clanless endured as a boy: a lot of running and practicing stances. They also spent a good deal of time practicing various moves with wooden practice weapons. But there were significant differences, as well. The beastmen spent as much time leaping as they did running. They practicing jumping over things and jumping for distance. Some of those leaps involved attacking with claws upon landing. In fact, the use of claws appeared to be as much of an emphasis as any other part of the training. It made sense. The beastmen possessed fearsome weapons as part of their own bodies. Developing their use made even more sense than the use of handheld weapons.

Those weapons fascinated Clanless. In his arena duel with the beastman, he'd been impressed with the quality and craftsmanship of his opponent's sword. The beastmen swords were curved like scimitars, but none of them were identical. Serrations ran down the back edge, but always in different patterns, sizes, and shapes. Clanless fingered the small chip in his moonblade. He had to get a closer look at those weapons and their forge, if possible.

After observing for an hour, Wind Tooth approached them and spoke with Swift Claw. The translator turned to Clanless. "He has told his students that you fought in the humans' arena for many years. He would like you to tell them how you survived for so long."

"How I survived?" Clanless almost laughed. What could he say to that? He didn't want to tell them about the Taint, especially since it hadn't worked the one time he'd tried to use it on a beastman. He also couldn't tell them anything about Zektel. He had a feeling they would be repulsed by that part of the story. But he wasn't completely unique in his survival. Bain had survived as long as he, as had Hagh and others he'd known.

The younger beastmen gathered, looking up at him expectantly. He took a step forward and glanced at Swift Claw. "Do I talk to you or...?"

"Just speak to them as you would your own people," Swift Claw said. "I will speak your words after you. But do not speak fast, please."

Clanless smiled. "Right." He looked out at the group and tried to ignore the... inhumanity of the scene: the teeth, the claws, the hair. He took a deep breath and began. As he finished each sentence, Swift Claw spoke rapidly in their own language beside him. It was distracting, but he pushed on.

"I was taken from my family as a boy and trained to kill," he said. "As a slave, I was forced to fight for my life in the arena. I fought almost every week for eight years. I only lost once, against one of the lizard creatures outside. If another fighter hadn't intervened, I would have died that time." Technically, he'd lost his final fight against Daviland, but they didn't need to know about that one. It had been his choice, after all, making it a different kind of victory.

"I don't know how many I killed, but I did it for one reason: to survive." He paused a moment longer. Swift Claw finished translating and waited for him.

"I was taught not only how to fight to win, but how to fight for entertainment, so the watchers would enjoy the fights." A confused murmur went through the crowd at that. They didn't quite understand, and he didn't blame them. "But all of that would go away if the fight were dangerous. If I thought I might lose. When that happened, only one type of training saved me: the training to be brutal.

"In the arena, I couldn't think of my opponents as real people. I had to fight to kill, and sometimes that meant killing as hard and as fast as I could. Because that's what the other man would be trying to do to me. In the arena, brutality wins. Every time."

When he stepped back and said no more, Wind Tooth spoke quickly to Swift Claw. "This is a harsh lesson, but no less true," the translator said. "Wind Tooth thanks you. He asks if you could demonstrate some of your techniques."

Clanless nodded. "It will feel good to do some practicing again. Clear out some space and I'll do some showing off."

"Showing off?" Swift Claw didn't understand that one.

"I'll… demonstrate my techniques."

Wind Tooth babbled some instructions and the students stepped back. They opened up a large space and gathered around it, watching as the human warrior strode in between them.

The light from the walls barely reached this part of the room, putting it all into somewhat of a dark twilight. Clanless wondered if the beastmen could see better in lower light. It would explain a few things. He took a stance in the center and adjusted his grip on the moonblade.

If Qara's calculations were right yesterday, it had been two weeks since the fall of the Hawk King. Two weeks since Clanless had any kind of physical workout. He needed this. He took a practice swing with the moonblade, enjoying the feel and balance he knew so well. He took a step back and began.

The movements came with ease and a smoothness he'd been worried might not be there. With all the confusion in his head from Zektel, he'd wondered whether he would forget how to fight, or get things mixed up. But his body knew what to do, even if his mind sometimes drifted. He executed stroke after stroke and movement after movement without difficulty. The gut wound gave him some twinges of pain, as did a few of his other recent injuries, but none of them prevented him from doing what he wanted.

In a few moments, sweat drenched his body, despite the coolness of the cavern air. He finished his series of exercises with a leap of his own ending in a low kneel as he swept the moonblade out with only one hand. He paused at the end of the stroke and held it for a few moments. Then he stood and brought the blade back to its resting place on his shoulder.

The beastmen reacted in a surprising fashion. As a group, most of them pointed their noses skyward, howled, and beat their chests. A few did not participate, instead glaring at the human warrior. Clanless wiped the moisture from his face and looked to Swift Claw.

"I'm guessing that's how they applaud," Qara said.

"They give their praise," Swift Claw said. He listened to Wind Tooth for a moment, then turned to Clanless. "Will you answer questions?"

"From them?" Clanless gestured at the trainees. "I guess so."

Swift Claw listened to the other beastmen and relayed their questions to him.

"How do you carry that large weapon?"

Clanless wrinkled his brow. "Um, like this?" He paused. "Oh, does he mean when I'm traveling?"

"I believe so."

"Heh. I don't know. This is the first time I've been anywhere outside the arena for very long." He hefted the moonblade. "It was made for arena fighting, and not intended for just warrior stuff, I guess." He looked down at it. "I've never even thought of that."

One of the beastmen shoved his way forward, pointed at Clanless, and almost shouted his question. Swift Claw responded to him, but the young beastman insisted. Swift Claw turned back to Clanless. "This one wants to know why you kill beastmen."

"What? I don't."

Swift Claw lowered his head. "I apologize. He sees the... necklace you wear and assumes you took it from one of our people."

"I've answered that already. You know this."

"Yes. But they must see me speak with you before I answer." Swift Claw turned back to the questioner and gave a lengthy response.

The young beastman snarled an answer, pointing at Clanless again.

"What did he say?"

"It does not matter." Swift Claw said something to Wind Tooth, who gave the young beastman an order. The warrior snarled again, but retreated back with his comrades.

"Swift Claw." Clanless stepped closer. "What did he say?"

"He says you speak falsehoods. That you killed a noble warrior by treachery and took the necklace." Swift Claw looked at him. "He says all humans are liars."

"Pleasant attitude," Qara murmured.

More questions followed, easier to answer. Most of them wanted to know about his fights, how many opponents he'd fought at one time, and so on. After more questions than he'd anticipated, Clanless stepped back while Wind Tooth addressed his students.

"He is telling them that you will be part of his training staff during the winter," Swift Claw said. "He says they should respect you like they respect him."

The concept unsettled Clanless. In the past, he'd always been the student, learning from others. The idea of being a teacher himself felt... unusual, to say the least. He was too young to be a teacher. He wondered if the beastmen understood that… then realized he didn't understand beast-men aging. How old were these students? Did their age mean the same as it did to humans? Maybe twenty-one years was an elder among these people.

His eyes strayed toward the angry one who'd asked the question about the necklace. When Wind Tooth dismissed the trainees, a group gathered around the dissenter. They shot angry glares at Clanless, while they talked amongst themselves. They were obviously not pleased about a human giving them instruction.

"Maybe it won't lead to trouble," he said to himself.

"And maybe High Winter ends tomorrow," Qara said, stepping up beside him, "but I wouldn't count on it."

((((●))))

Clanless and Qara soon appreciated the change in their routine. Spending part of the day outside of the single room helped the time pass. They ate breakfast each morning, after which Swift Claw would escort them to the training center. Once there, they would observe the earliest parts of the training before Clanless joined the process. He helped run the young warriors through various drills and supervised some of their sparring, giving pointers through Swift Claw.

Clanless learned from the beastmen, as well. Their emphasis on weaponless fighting enabled him to learn more about grappling and throwing. He couldn't match their use of claws and teeth, of course, but he enjoyed learning about new ways to fight. The scratches he accumulated were a small price to pay for the experience.

A small group remained adamantly opposed to Clanless's presence. Some of them left the training altogether, but most stayed, content to express their displeasure through glares, snarls, and muttered grumblings. Clanless couldn't understand them, of course, but he got the meaning.

Other beastmen appeared at the training sessions every day to watch, fascinated or offended by the humans. On the first two days, Clanless noticed the leader they'd met on the first day, the one with the armored vest, standing in the crowd, arms folded.

Qara watched the proceedings, but had almost nothing to do herself. She chatted with Swift Claw whenever he wasn't needed to translate for Clanless. Through him, she learned more about the beastmen culture and society.

Both of them tried to learn a few words and phrases of the beastmen language, but the sounds would not come out right. Swift Claw tried and failed to hide his amusement.

"It's the shape of their snouts," Qara complained. "Our mouths can't do the same things. We can't howl like wolves either."

"Then why can Swift Claw speak our language?" Clanless wondered.

"Maybe ours is easier? I don't know."

The beastmen provided them with extra clothes, much to Qara's relief. Though simple in design, they were surprisingly well made. Clanless, however, struggled with the problem of his right shoulder. The new clothing didn't leave it open to the air. He'd grown so used to that since his branding so many years ago, covering it created discomfort. He kept rolling his shoulder, convinced the new clothes were restricting it. Over time, he grew used to it, but he still flinched every so often when the cloth brushed against his brand.

After training and cleaning up, they alternated afternoons between days of rest and times of further exploration with Swift Claw as their guide (and the ever-present guards). Through him, they learned more about life within the Formation.

Clanless found himself fascinated by the beastmen's religion. They worshipped the True Wind, Swift Claw explained, who ruled above all other powers in the universe. Swift Claw kept translating this word as "wind," but it showed up in so many ways. In this case, Clanless was pretty sure it meant something like "soul" or "spirit," and not an actual movement of air.

The True Wind appeared to have no connection to the moon or any other visible phenomena, although the great wolf was considered to be one of its agents. The beastmen attributed kindness and wisdom to the True Wind, among other positive aspects. It wasn't a great divergence from the Empire's worship of the moon goddess... but without the blood requirements. As far as Clanless could tell, the True Wind did not require any specific kind of sacrifices, though the beastmen did gather once a week for a solemn assembly of worship. Clanless and Qara attended one out of courtesy and curiosity. They found it quaint and a little bit humbling. Their own remembrances of temple worship back home, with all of the blood, appeared almost barbaric in comparison.

Beastmen seemed to have little regard for blood at all. They used bladed weapons in combat, which the Empire would regard as "dishonorable." Blood spilled regularly in training—more from teeth and claws than swords—and no one paid any attention to it.

The experience left him wondering about greater powers. He'd met the moon goddess, assuming it hadn't been some kind of personal insanity. She'd mentioned Suirel, who appeared to be some sort of god himself, and "war in the heavens." She'd also said she'd been "assigned" to his people. Assigned by who? Did the beastmen beliefs fit into this concept? He tried asking Swift Claw, but the translator laughed at the very concept of a moon goddess. Clanless didn't ask again.

He did try asking about the name they'd given him: Wolf Chosen. Swift Claw would only point at his fur, as if that explained everything. He couldn't tell if being chosen by the wolf meant he was also some kind of divine agent, or if he'd merely been blessed by one, or something else altogether.

Everywhere Swift Claw took them, Clanless and Qara noticed a division among the beastmen. Most watched them with curiosity, welcome, or indifference. But a minority always displayed visible anger at their presence, much like the group within the trainees. Clanless observed how their guards took notice of these instances as well.

High Winter's hold outside grew stronger. Though it didn't become too unpleasant, the temperature within their room slowly decreased. Clanless experienced it most at night as he slept on the floor. It grew more and more difficult to resist the warmth of the nearby bed and its occupant. Every night, he asked himself why he resisted. The covering grew less effective as the chill increased. Qara noticed his discomfort and requested an additional blanket. Swift Claw at first expressed surprise, but then noted the humans' paltry hair coverings.

As the days progressed, something else nagged at Clanless. It took him some time to identify the discomfort. "It's the moon," he told Qara.

"What about it?"

"I've never gone this long in my life without seeing it." He paused, considering how to articulate his issue. "Even when I lived beneath arenas, I spent a great deal of time outside, beneath the moon's gaze."

"Even during High Winter?"

He nodded. "Even then. I needed to train, to practice. And I needed to do that outside. I endured the cold, but I had to be out under the moon." He gestured at their ceiling. "Here, we sleep under rock. We eat under rock. We walk around under rock. I train under rock. It's..." He sighed. "I'm not religious, Qara. You know that. The priests despise me. But the moon... it's part of my life. And I can't see it."

Qara stared up at the ceiling. "I hadn't thought about it like that, but you're right. It's like a part of me is missing." She paused. "A small part, mind you, but I can feel it."

Clanless stretched out on the floor, looking up. "Do you think there's more to it than belief? That maybe we are connected to the moon, somehow? Our people, I mean."

Qara regarded him. "I don't know. And I have to say: it was simpler to answer the questions of arena fighters than philosophers."

"What's a philosopher?"

She laughed. "Now we're back to normal."

FEW THINGS ARE SO BROKEN

Gogeku proved to be more persuasive than he gave himself credit for. Two nights later, he and Badaar (cleaned up and well dressed) showed up at the eating house. Koland played his dovshuur and told a pair of stories, while Kekeen assisted in serving the two men. Badaar listened intently to the storyteller, but Geku could barely contain his annoyance with the lower class nature of his surroundings.

Koland plucked his dovshuur before launching into a third story: "In ages past, a king died, leaving the kingdom to his only son. Now this king had been powerful and prosperous… but not especially loved by his people. In order to gain his power and wealth, he had been somewhat fierce. He never approached the level of a tyrant, I should say, but his taxes and labor were excessive.

"Upon assuming the throne, the new king, being quite young, sought advice. First he went to the elders of the kingdom, those who had served and advised his father. 'Your father became great,' they told him, 'but you can be greater. The people have sacrificed enough. Decrease their burden, and they will love you. With them behind you, you will become the greatest king we have ever known.'

"The new king then turned to his friends, those his own age who had grown up observing the kingdom under his father. 'What do you think?' he asked them. 'How did your father become so great and powerful?' they answered. 'Would you now turn from what he did? If you want to be greater than him, then be greater! He showed you the way. Do what he did, only stronger! Then your power and prosperity will rival the rest of the world!'"

Koland plucked a discordant note.

"The young king chose to listen to his friends instead of the elders. He announced new initiatives, bold plans, all designed to increase his own wealth and power, at the expense of his own people. It should not have come as a shock, then, when the people rose up against him.

"The kingdom split, with half of the people remaining loyal to the king—mostly out of respect for his father, and half of them choosing their own king to follow. In a very short time, armies were assembled. War was inevitable... until a prophetess appeared.

"She stood alone in the road, directly in front of the king and his army who were marching from the capital to meet the rebels. Seeing her, the king called for a halt. He'd seen her before, bringing word to his father from time to time. Everyone knew that she spoke for the goddess.

"'Hear me, oh king,' she proclaimed in the hearing of all his leaders. 'The goddess is not with you in this. Do not seek war against your own people.'

"'Seek it?' the king exclaimed. 'They have rebelled against me! They brought this upon themselves!'

"'Nevertheless, the goddess says you should let them go. She is not with those who fight against their own.'

"The young king fumed, and his pride boiled over. How could he accept this? Split the kingdom? Lose half of it to these rebels? How could he be greater and more powerful than his father with only half the kingdom? 'Move out of the way,' he told the prophetess. 'We have places to be.'

"She shook her head in regret. 'Your dynasty could have been so much more,' she said before leaving the road.

"The king turned to his lead general and ordered the continuation of the march. But the general had heard all that the prophetess had said. He was an older man, a hero who had served the previous king for many years. He hesitated, considering the cost of fighting against his own people and against the will of the goddess.

"'What are you waiting for?' the king demanded. 'Let us be on our way!'

"With deep anguish in his soul, the general drew his weapon. To the shock of all around, he struck quickly and killed the young king. Some of the other leaders demanded his death in return. But because the general was well loved by his men, the entire army rallied to his side. They returned to the capital where he was crowned the new king.

"So began a dynasty blessed by the goddess herself, for the new king wisely made peace with the rebels. Two new kingdoms grew out of the old, and both became prosperous and powerful… but not for the kings only."

Koland plucked another note and stopped speaking.

"Is that story true?" Gogeku asked.

"All stories are true," he answered, "in the sense that all stories communicate truth."

Gogeku growled. "You know what I mean, fabler. Did it actually happen?"

"This story has been passed down over many generations of storytellers." Koland paused and looked pensive for a moment. "Some say it tells the origin of the Sar Empire and the Melkute Kingdom, that they were once united in a far greater kingdom. Some even say the general in the story became the Hawk King."

"That doesn't sound like him," Badaar observed.

"Perhaps not." Koland got to his feet. "But… that is the story I have to tell tonight." He sat down across from Badaar. "I understand we have a Hero of the Empire with us."

"Twice," Gogeku sniffed before turning to Kekeen. "Are you sure these utensils were thoroughly cleaned?"

"Thoroughly," she promised. "Father, Badaar was also one of Aldan's trainers back in Ghoyor."

"Oh, really? You're the man behind the success of the mighty Clanless, are you?"

"I wouldn't say that," Badaar mumbled, looking down at his plate.

Gogeku rolled his eyes. "The boy would never have survived a month without you guiding him, and you know it."

"I'd love to hear more," Koland said, accepting a drink from Kekeen. "We storytellers always have a need to hear more true stories, you know. Helps us work on the other kind."

"There's not much to tell." Badaar shrugged. "I trained a lot of arena fighters over the years." He jerked and looked off to his right, as if he'd seen someone else walk by.

"Aldan told me once that you fought some cult members together," Kekeen prompted.

"Oh. Yes." Badaar turned back. "It was because of you two."

Koland's eyebrows went up. "Now you must tell me!"

"Clanless and Zaluu…" Badaar glanced off to the right again. "Um, they rescued you from some bandits. Zaluu brought one of them back to the arena. When we questioned him, we discovered he was part of this cult."

"I had no idea." Koland tapped his fingers on his mug. "I thought they were just after Clanless."

"It was the cult," Badaar repeated. "I tracked them down. Took a while. And then we saw…" He shook his head. "Sun take me, but they did some strange things. We saw a man get possessed by something." He reached across and massaged his right shoulder. "We had to fight our way out. Slinger got me right here. Still acts up in High Winter."

"Possessed by something? What do you mean?"

"Some guy asked for it, did something with the blood, and everything about him changed." Badaar broke off and glared off to the right. "I'm telling them what I remember, Zaluu. If you think you can do better, feel free to step in."

No one said anything. Gogeku caught Kekeen's eyes and gave a knowing nod.

"That's what I thought." Badaar grumbled a little bit to himself, then looked back at Koland. "He said something about the children of Suirel that live in the blood. Or some such nonsense."

Koland put his hands together and rested his chin on them. "Fascinating. There are multiple connections to legends about the creatures known as blood-wraiths. Do you think that's what they meant?"

Badaar shrugged. "Beyond what I know."

Silence again. The only sound came from the innkeeper cleaning up the kitchen.

Gogeku piped up: "Any news on Clanless?"

"We think he was taken north," Koland said. "Perhaps by Ghouk, the son of the Hawk King. They may be connecting with the rest of the army, under General Ghan."

"Hmm. There's a name I haven't heard in a while." Badaar shook his head. "He's a mean one. I fought with him against the barbarians years ago."

"Really?" Koland perked up. "Tell me about him."

"What's fiercer than a hawk?"

Koland traded looks with his daughter. "I'm not sure."

"The Hawk King got his name from the ferocity of his battle tactics." Badaar made a swooping motion with his stump. "Ghan, though… he was tougher. Fiercer. So we asked ourselves: 'what's fiercer than a hawk?'"

"Did you find an answer?" Gogeku asked.

"A leopard." Badaar nodded solemnly. "Not just any leopard. The big ones that live in the mountains, with the huge teeth. They hunt even during High Winter. A little cold doesn't stop them. You never see them coming." He looked down at his plate again. "That's what we took to calling the General behind his back: the Leopard Warrior." He looked back up. "His most loyal soldiers—and there's a lot of 'em—even called him the Leopard King."

"Do you think he had aspirations toward the throne?" Koland asked. "That he wanted to be king himself?"

Badaar shrugged. "He knew what the men called him. He never said anything about it. But he did everything the Hawk King ever asked him, without complaint. Seemed loyal, at least from the outside. I can't say as to anything else."

"Well." Koland sat back, tapping his beard. "Very interesting. You've given me some things to think about, Badaar. I'm glad we met."

Badaar scratched his head. "Not sure how I helped any. I usually don't."

"Nonsense." Kekeen leaned across the table and grasped hold of his hand. "You've been a big help to us. And I know you were a huge help to Aldan. Clanless."

Badaar almost smiled. "I wish I could see him again," he whispered.

"You will," Kekeen promised. "As soon as we have any information, you'll be the first person I tell. We might need your help again!"

"If you say so." His eyes wandered around until he fixed on Gogeku. "Geku? There you are. Allaka says he needs some new shirts."

"I'll be sure to get on that." Gogeku looked at the others. "I think I should get him back home now."

Koland stood. "You do that. Be safe out in the cold. And thank you both."

As Gogeku led Badaar out to his carriage, Kekeen leaned against her father. "He looked better than when I first met him," she said. "But still..."

"He's a broken man." Koland sighed and put his arm around her. "But give him time. Few things are so broken they cannot be repaired."

ᗈᗈᗈᗈ●ᗕᗕᗕᗕ

Kekeen resolved she would do whatever it took to see Borde. A few days later, when Daviland's advisory council met again, she accompanied her father as usual. But once the council began its discussions, she slipped out of the door. Nothing had happened at these meetings to give any clues to Koland's earlier claims of losing time, so she doubted anything would happen at this one. And she needed the distraction.

The hardest part had been finding Borde's location. The Hawk King's enormous palace possessed dozens, perhaps even hundreds of rooms.

Kekeen had no idea why he'd needed so many. Most of them appeared empty now. But by observing the servants still at work, she deduced the hallway and narrowed her choices down to two doors.

Kekeen made her way to the hall and hid around a corner. A steward stood near the two doors that interested her. He dressed like the other servants, but his bulk implied a soldier or fighter of some kind. He shifted his weight, scratching at the fingernails on one hand with the other. After a minute or two, he glanced around and then wandered down the hall in the other direction.

As soon as he turned the corner, Kekeen slipped out and rushed to the first door. The handle wouldn't turn. The second door, however, opened. Kekeen hurried inside and shut it behind her. She leaned against the door and stared at the room before her.

An enormous canopied bed dominated the room, leaving little room for any other furniture. A small desk with a mirror and chair barely fit in a narrow space against the far left wall. Next to it, an open door led to the room whose door she'd found locked. Borde lay on the bed, leaning on one elbow while she read a book.

"They already took the breakfast tray," she said before looking up. Upon seeing Kekeen, she gasped. She let go of the book and slid off the bed. The two girls rushed to each other and embraced.

"How did you find me?" Borde cried.

"It wasn't easy." Kekeen separated and looked her over. Aldan's dark-haired cousin looked much the same as she had the last time they'd seen each other. Had it been two weeks? "Are you all right? Are you healthy?"

"Yes, yes. I'm fine. What about you? And everyone else? What's happening out there?"

"Davil doesn't tell you? He told me you were ill, that you might be with child." Kekeen couldn't help looking down at Borde's stomach. It didn't appear any larger.

Borde gasped and clasped a hand to her mouth. "That man! I don't know what's happened to him!"

"So… you're not…?"

Borde stamped her bare foot. "I am most assuredly not with child! Neither am I sick. He's kept me in here for days. I haven't seen anyone other than servants until you came through the door."

Kekeen glanced back. "I saw a very large man out there. Is he your guard?"

Borde nodded. "One of them. You're lucky you got past him. Oh, Kekeen. Tell me everything. What's been going on?"

"First tell me about Daviland. Why is he doing this to you?"

Borde bit her lip. She glanced around and then pulled herself back onto the bed. She patted it. "Come. Sit. There's obviously plenty of room."

Kekeen climbed up beside her. "I believe six people could sleep in this bed."

"Seven, I think. And it's only one of the Hawk King's personal bedrooms. He had five, scattered around the palace. He slept wherever he wanted, on a whim. The servants had to keep all of them in perfect condition, since they never knew which one would be in use." Borde put her hands in her lap. "I've heard a lot of stories from the servants since I've been here."

"And Davil?"

"He's changed." Borde shook her head. "After he killed the Hawk King, it's like he became a completely different person! I don't know him any more. Sometimes…" She looked toward the door. "Sometimes, I think I see my Davil peering out at me through his eyes, but then another voice speaks through his mouth. He's become cruel, Kekeen. So cruel. He doesn't care about me, or anyone else now."

"We've been wondering. He's been acting very strange." Kekeen hurried through a recital of everything that had taken place since the Hawk King's fall. "And there's another council meeting happening right now," she concluded. "That's why I'm here."

Borde picked up one of the many pillows from the bed and hugged it. "I don't know how else to say this… but I think Davil is the Hawk King now."

"What do you mean?"

Borde looked at her with wide and trembling eyes. "I think when he killed the Hawk King, the Hawk King's spirit possessed him. Or something like that. I can't think of any other explanation."

"The spirit of the Hawk King," Kekeen murmured, thinking of Badaar's story of possession. "Maybe. Or some other spirit."

"I'd already heard a little bit of what you just told me," Borde admitted. "I beg the servants to tell me things. And Daviland visits me from time to time. I think he likes gloating." She frowned. "You know, he mentions Aldan an awful lot. Sometimes, it feels like he's baiting me somehow. I really don't understand it."

"Does he ever mention… Suirel?"

Borde looked down at the pillow. "That… that's the most disturbing part. He's even brought that man, Demujin, in there"—she gestured toward the adjoining room—"for supposedly private conversations, even though he knows I'm right here and can listen in."

"What do they talk about?" Kekeen swallowed. This was worse than she'd thought.

"I can't hear everything," Borde clarified. "But what I do here is troubling. There's a lot of talk about Suirel and blood and ceremonies."

"Is there anything more specific?" Kekeen glanced at the door. "If he's keeping you in here and isn't afraid of what you'll hear, maybe it's really important."

Borde bit her lip again. "They want Suirel to come here."

Kekeen leaned back and caught herself before she lost her balance on the bed. "To come here? What does that even mean?"

"I don't know! I thought Suirel was just a moon." Borde threw a hand upward. "But they talk about him like he's a god."

"If the goddess lives in our moon, then I guess it makes sense that another moon would have another, um, such being," Kekeen mused. "So for him to come here, does that mean they want to convince everyone to worship Suirel instead of the goddess?"

"I think it's more than that. They talk about it like he's actually coming here. As if he were a person taking a trip, I guess. Do gods take trips?"

Kekeen suppressed a giggle. "I've never heard anything like that. But I don't understand the appeal." She leaned back on her hands and looked up at the bed canopy. "The goddess is right there in the sky above us all day and night, all the time. Why would they want to worship a god who only shows up once every thirty years?"

Borde shook her head so rapidly her hair swung into her face. "That's part of the point. They don't want him to show up every thirty years. They want him here, with us, all the time. Like we could see him and talk with him."

Kekeen shivered and straightened up. "All right. This is all crazy. Let's see if we can get you out of here."

"No. Please."

"What?" Kekeen paused in the middle of getting off the bed.

Borde licked her lips, nervously watching the door. "He's... Davil's still in there. I know it. The man I love is still there. I just need to find a way to get him back out."

"Borde. If he's really possessed by the Hawk King or something, then you could be in great danger!"

"I know, I know." She pushed the pillow aside and got off the bed herself. "But isn't that the true measure of love? Risking yourself for someone else?"

Kekeen slid off the bed and embraced her friend. "You're absolutely right. But that doesn't mean I won't worry about you."

"You need to go. The longer you're here, the more danger you're in too."

Kekeen smiled. "I know you're right. I just hate to leave you here."

Borde hesitated. "They… they talk a lot about someone else, Kekeen. It's your father."

"What about him?"

"They're planning something. Davil wants him on their side, and he thinks Demujin can do it." Borde's eyes bored into hers. "Don't let them be alone together."

Kekeen gave her another quick hug and hurried to the door. She listened for a moment before easing it open to check the hall. Seeing no one, she smiled back at Borde and raced away.

She found the throne room empty. Kekeen grabbed the servant who had given her a chair the first time. "Where is everyone?"

"The council ended, my lady. They've all gone."

"My father. Did you see him leave?"

"They all left," he repeated. "He left with, uh, someone else."

Kekeen grabbed his other arm. "Think carefully. Please. Was that someone else Demujin? The cult leader?"

His eyes widened. "Oh. Yes. I believe it was."

Kekeen released the servant and spun around in place. What could she do? If her father had gone with Demujin, he was in grave danger. But where would they have gone? How could she find them?

"The cult. The cult. Where do they meet?" she murmured to herself.

Demujin was a leader of the cult. Aside from him, who else did she know that was part of it? Some priests, and… Lord Ulakan. She turned back to the servant.

"Tell me everything you know about Lord Ulakan."

"Ah, I don't know much, my lady. He's of clan Ghutalta. He and the other two Lords basically ran the city under the Hawk King's supervision."

"Ghultalta, Ghutalta. That means banking, mainly. Very rich." Kekeen paced toward the door of the throne room and back. "Do you know where he lives?"

"That's not a secret." The servant pointed off to his right. "Two houses that way. It's the largest mansion up here, outside of the palace, of course."

Kekeen gave him her best smile and put a hand on his shoulder. "You've been so helpful. What was your name again?"

His whole face lit up. "Badu, my lady."

"Badu, I will thank the goddess for you by name. And maybe you could come hear me sing sometime. Would you like that?"

He swallowed. "Of-of course I would."

"Wonderful. There's just one more thing. Can you send a message for me?"

His smile faltered. "Ah, messengers who will go out in this weather are hard to come by…"

She stepped a little closer. "I would appreciate it so much, though."

"I'll do it. I'll take it."

"Good. It's not a big message. It's just to a tailor…"

☾ ☾ ☾ ☾ ● ☽ ☽ ☽ ☽

Twenty minutes later, Kekeen banged on the door to Lord Ulakan's mansion. Drenched by the snow, the wind tearing at her clothes, she knew she had to look utterly pitiful. She hoped that worked to her advantage.

It worked enough to get her through the door, at least. Lord Ulakan's steward took pity on her and let her in to escape the weather. But that was as far as his mercy extended.

"You will have to leave as soon as you've warmed up," he insisted.

Kekeen shook snow from her coat and stepped closer to the roaring fireplace. This was only the entrance room to this mansion, and it was as big as the eating house! One enormous window faced the street. Kekeen was amazed it could withstand the winds of High Winter. It seemed the truly rich could accomplish almost anything.

"I need to speak to your master, Lord Ulakan," she repeated.

"He is not going to see a lower class girl from the streets," the steward answered, rolling his eyes. "And should Lady Ulakan finds you here, it will be even worse."

Kekeen's mouth fell open. "What do you think I am?"

"I think I just made that clear. You need to leave."

"No." Kekeen shook her head. "You will tell your master that the daughter of Koland, of Daviland's advisory council, is here and needs to speak to him. Urgently."

The steward blinked and stepped back. "The advisory council? But he's just come from there."

"Precisely. Tell him it's urgent."

The steward regarded her for a few moments longer, as if trying to ascertain the truthfulness of her claims. She straightened up and looked him in the eye, pushing confidence with her posture. At last he nodded. "Stay here." He left the room.

Kekeen relaxed with a huge exhale. She'd passed the first test. The next one would be much harder.

She didn't have long to wait. Lord Ulakan had only returned a few minutes ago, so he hadn't had time to change or get started on anything else important. He pulled his gloves off as he entered the welcoming room.

"Koland's daughter? Yes. I've seen you at the palace." His eyes wandered over her body in that manner she'd long since grown used to but could never respect. "Just because your father somehow has the ear of our new ruler doesn't give you the right to barge into my house. What do you want?"

"I need to know where the cult of Suirel meets for their ceremonies."

Lord Ulakan recoiled, shocked but trying to appear confused. "What a bizarre request. I certainly can't help you with that."

"Yes, you can." She took a step toward him. "I have seen you meeting with the rogue blood-priests who are part of the cult. I saw your delight when Demujin joined the council. Others inside the palace have confirmed that you're a part of this group. Right now, it's not public knowledge, of course." She paused. "But it could be."

"Are you threatening me?" He chuckled.

"I am. My father is in danger, and I will do whatever it takes to save him."

He laughed a little harder. "You have no concept of true power, little girl. You think you can walk in here and threaten me, a Lord of Et-Baylak! And with what? A rumor about an obscure religious group?" He walked forward, and Kekeen stepped out of his way. Still chuckling, he leaned on the mantle, watching the fire.

"I need to know," Kekeen said. "I'm only asking for a location." She tried to look more impressive. "You may think my word won't mean anything, but I've been a part of Daviland's rebellion for years. I know everyone. When I tell them you're a part of the cult—"

"But you won't," he cut her off. He looked up, the fire creating red shadows across his face. "You won't be leaving this house. You've come alone into my home. That was the most foolish thing you could possibly do." He straightened up, and now held a poker from the fireplace. "I could snap my fingers and let the servants get rid of you, but I think I'll do it myself."

Kekeen backed away. "It's not that simple," she said.

"Oh, no? It seems so to me." He advanced toward her. "You see, I'm not at all pleased with your whole rebellion, the one you've been a part of for years, you say. Since I can't deal with Daviland until General Ghan returns, I'll have to take out my frustrations on you."

"I told someone to meet me here," Kekeen blurted, dodging around a large padded chair.

"Another low-class friend of yours? I'll inform Dok not to let them in."

"A Hero of the Empire, actually. Twice."

Lord Ulakan paused. "I admire creative lying. But it's not enough."

"I'm not lying. Before coming here, I asked Badaar, Hero of the Empire, to meet me outside this house in half an hour. If I don't come out, he'll break down your door to find me." The last part was made up, but she could hope.

Lord Ulakan lowered his weapon. "Hm. Either you're more creative than I thought, or…"

"Badaar trained Clanless the arena fighter," she persisted. "That's how I know him. Surely you know that I'm… I'm the beloved of Clanless." Somehow, saying it out loud hurt more than thinking about where he might be.

"I know nothing of that." He paused. "But I do remember you singing at that arena fight. Regardless, Clanless is missing along with the rest of the Dohor. He's not coming to save you."

"No. Badaar is."

Lord Ulakan didn't move.

"Hero of the Empire," Kekeen repeated. "Twice."

"I'm aware of Badaar's history," he growled. "Fine. I don't know if you're telling the truth, but it's not something I can risk at the moment." He tossed the poker next to the fireplace. "I warn you, though: if I find out you are lying, I will have you and your father arrested."

"For what?"

He shrugged. "It doesn't matter. I'll make something up and find someone to testify to it. Easy enough. Now, what was it you wanted today?"

She licked her lips. "Where does the cult of Suirel meet for their ceremonies?"

"You've just come from there. In the palace."

The palace? If true, it meant she had even less time to find Koland. She'd been counting on them traveling somewhere. "Where in the palace?"

"You know… I haven't met a Hero of the Empire in years. Let's wait for him together, shall we?" Lord Ulakan gestured toward the front window. "We have only to watch here."

Kekeen looked out the window. From here, despite the snow, they would be able to see when or if a carriage pulled up in front of the mansion.

She hoped she'd allowed enough time for the message to reach Gogeku and then Badaar. If not, she didn't know how to get out of this one.

Lord Ulakan stepped closer. Kekeen could feel his eyes on her. "You know," he said a few moments later, "your hair color is… unusually pale. Quite rare. You must attract a lot of attention from the younger men."

"I, I told you my beloved is Clanless."

He chuckled. "I'm not interested myself, dear. I'm just calculating how much blood I could make were I to sell you to one of the high-end brothels, such as Pasque House."

Kekeen somehow felt colder than she'd been outside. She whispered a prayer to the goddess.

"I'm beginning to think you may not have told the truth," Lord Ulakan said after another minute or two passed. "Perhaps…"

At that moment, a heavy carriage pulled up in front of the mansion. Even through the snow, Kekeen could recognize it as the one used by Gogeku. She spun around to face the Lord. "I've told you the truth. Where in the palace will I find the cultists?"

"The lower levels somewhere." He shrugged. "I've never been myself, but I've heard stories."

Kekeen hurried to the door. "Thank you for your assistance today, Lord Ulakan."

"I'm sure we'll speak again soon," he answered with a smile that haunted her all the way out to the carriage.

Badaar and Gogeku both waited inside. They demanded to know what was going on the instant she shut the door behind her.

"Back to the palace," she said. "We have to rescue my father from the cult."

On the way, which took longer than expected since the carriage had to turn around in the street, Kekeen explained all that she'd learned from Borde and Lord Ulakan. Gogeku listened with wide eyes the entire time, while Badaar's intensity forced her to include every detail.

"So, to sum up," the warrior said, "we're charging to the rescue without knowing the exact layout or even the exact location, and we have no idea how many enemies we'll be confronting."

"You'll be confronting," Gogeku said. "I want no part of this!"

Badaar didn't even spare him a glance. "I believe I have an idea that will help us." He picked up a small wooden box from the seat beside him. He opened it and withdrew two purple ribbons with a hawk-shaped medal hanging from each.

"You utter clod," Geku said. "You never let me see those before, and now you're going to wear them?"

Badaar hung both ribbons around his neck. "There was never any reason before."

Gogeku shook his head. "You could at least have let me help you coordinate your outfit to match them." His hands gestured futilely. "They don't stand out. There's no, no synergism here at all!"

"I think they'll be fine," Kekeen said, trying not to smile too much.

At the palace, she and Badaar hurried inside where a pair of guards met them. In the past two weeks, Kekeen had become known by them and allowed inside. But before she could speak, Badaar stalked up to both of them. He held out the medals. "Do you know what these are?" he demanded.

One of the guards, a good bit older than his companion, gasped. "Hero of the Empire!" he exclaimed.

"You are correct." Badaar let the medals fall to his chest. "I am Badaar, weapons master, trainer, and two-time Hero of the Empire. I need you to give me a mace, and for the two of you to come with me at once. Something dire is happening inside this palace."

The guards hesitated. "We serve Daviland now," the younger said. "You aren't going to cause trouble for him, are you?"

Kekeen stepped up. "You know me. My father is on Daviland's advisory council. Believe me when I say, this is of vital importance to all of them. We need your help."

The older guard unhooked his mace from his belt and handed it to Badaar. "Where are we going, sir?"

"The cult of Suirel is doing something in a lower level of this building," he answered. "Show us the way down."

Without another word, the guard led the way into the palace. Kekeen, Badaar, and the other guard followed as he took several turns into an unfamiliar area. He took one last corner and started down a wide staircase. "There is a lot of space down here," he explained. "Storage, mainly. Keeping everyone in this palace warm and fed throughout High Winter takes a lot."

"So it's all one huge basement?" Kekeen asked.

"Oh, no. There are more rooms down here. Some servants' quarters. Another kitchen. A barracks for when there are soldiers staying here."

"That sounds like a large space," Badaar said. "Let's try that one. And pick up the pace."

With every stair, every hallway, Kekeen's anxiety grew. In her head, she kept imagining Badaar's story of possession with her father in the victim role. What if they were too late? Was there any way to free someone already possessed?

"There's nothing here, sir," the guard reported on their arrival at the barracks.

Badaar looked up and down the way they had come. "Is this it? Is there anything else down here?"

"The prisons," the younger guard spoke up.

The older guard frowned. "We sealed those up after Daviland took over," he said. "No one goes down there."

"We do," Badaar said. "Take us now."

The guards led the way to a set of double doors. The younger guard pointed to a loose chain on the floor. "Not sealed any more."

Badaar lifted the mace to a ready position. "Then we're in the right place. Let's go."

The guards pulled the doors open to reveal another staircase descending into darkness. The older guard took an old torch from the wall and lit it with an oil lantern nearby. Holding it up, he and Badaar strode side-by-side down the stairs. After ten steps, the stairs smoothed out and became a simple ramp instead. They were entering the base bedrock of the city. Kekeen wondered how long ago this had been dug out and how long such a project would have taken. And all to house prisoners of the Hawk King. So much effort for such an evil purpose.

When they reached the bottom of the ramp, they found the prison: tiny, dark cells, their doors all hanging open. Without this torch, the darkness down here would have been horrid. Kekeen shuddered just thinking about it.

"Hold the torch back," Badaar ordered. He took several steps forward. "Yes, there's more light ahead. I think we've found our prey."

Kekeen started to rush forward, but Badaar held out his stump. "Wait there, girl. Let me take the lead on this. If all goes well, we may be able to avoid any kind of fight." He looked to the guards. "But you two be ready, just in case."

With that, the Hero of the Empire strode forward into the depths. The other three hurried to keep up with him. The light in the distance grew even as the passage curved to the right and then back to the left. Kekeen lost count of the number of cells along the way, certainly a few dozen at least.

They emerged into a much larger space, an empty, undeveloped cavern. Some of this space appeared natural, not carved by human tools. Perhaps those who'd dug out the rest of the prison had stumbled into this cave by accident. But the cultists had taken it for their own usage. At least a dozen men stood together, facing a small platform on the far side of the cavern. Half of them held torches, providing a flickering, inconsistent light to the scene. Three men in dark red robes stood on the platform. Two of them held another man by the arms. He appeared barely conscious; his head made a slow roll to one side and the light illuminated his face. Koland! Kekeen wanted to rush forward, but a strange trance seemed to have fallen over her. Her legs didn't seem to want to obey her mind.

The third man held up his arms toward the ceiling. "We seek the wisdom of the ages," he cried. "Bring truth to this poor soul. Truth, wisdom, and power from on high!"

"Demujin!" Kekeen hissed. She shook her head, trying to shake off the strange ennui that held her back.

The cult leader bent and retrieved a shallow bowl from the floor. He held it up in front of everyone. "Suirel! Send one of your children—"

"That's enough!" Badaar bellowed, breaking the trance. Every face in the room turned to look at him.

Demujin pulled back his hood and looked across his cultists. "Who dares interrupt our sacred ceremony?"

"I, Badaar, Hero of the Empire." He pointed at all of them with his mace. "You are gathered here in a place which does not belong to you, holding captive a friend who does not want to be here. I order you all to disperse at once!"

The two guards stepped up to either side of him, holding their torch and mace at ready.

"You have no authority here," Demujin answered. "We are gathered here with the full knowledge of Daviland, ruler of this Empire now. And two of us are part of his advisory council."

"Release my father at once!" Kekeen finally stepped forward. "He is not a part of your pagan nonsense!" With the grumbles that followed, Kekeen realized she might have chosen her words a little more carefully.

Demujin smiled at her. "Ah, Kekeen. Your father was looking for you after our meeting earlier. He wanted you to join us. I'm glad you found your way on your own."

Koland mumbled something.

Badaar leveled his mace to point straight at Demujin. "I am Badaar, weapons-master and Hero of the Empire. I have faced down barbarian hordes, Melkute marauders, and the great armored beasts of the north. If you do not fear me, then you are welcome to step forward and discover how I earned these medals. You will surrender our comrade and disperse, or I swear by the goddess that you will suffer the same fate as all those who have opposed me in the past."

Kekeen caught her breath. Was this the same man who mumbled to imaginary ghosts in a cold, dark room? He seemed completely transformed, a man of power and authority. She almost wanted to kneel and surrender to him herself.

Apparently, she wasn't the only one feeling the impulse. The cultists murmured and backed away.

Demujin hesitated, but his smile never left his face. He looked down at the bowl in his hands. Closing his eyes, he took a deep breath, as if inhaling something from the bowl. He knelt and placed it on the floor again.

"Very well." He stood and gestured to the two holding Koland. "You may take him and go. Koland came here of his own free will, but if you insist on disrupting our worship together, we will allow it. We only want peace and harmony for all of the Sar Empire's subjects, after all."

Kekeen pushed forward toward the platform. Badaar motioned to the younger guard who put his mace away and joined her. Together, they took Koland's arms from the other robed cultists and helped him back toward the exit. Demujin and the others remained where they stood.

Once they passed Badaar, he addressed the crowd again. "I have also ordered you to disperse. I grant you five minutes to wrap up your business while we leave. Once back in the palace, I will send a full squadron of guards. If you have not dispersed by the time they arrive…" He paused. "Well, then. These cells behind me may have new occupants."

The Hero of the Empire nodded to the older guard, turned on his heel, and left the scene of his latest victory.

THE ATTACK

"No, no, no. It's my turn!" Shool Baina insisted.

Yeltek threw up his hands. "Fine! Anything's got to be better than another Oteral story from Clanless!"

Clanless scowled. "It's Okteral," he muttered.

Bain spread out his hand in dramatic fashion as he began his story. The other boys leaned in closer, straining to hear over the sound of food preparation in the adjacent kitchen.

"In times past, legends grew around a great warrior of the Empire. Second only to the great Hawk King in his power, this warrior grew bored during a time of peace. No barbarians, no wars. He had nothing to do! So he set off on long journeys to find new challenges."

"He could have just gone to the arena," Jik said.

"He did fight in the arena!" Bain said. "But it was boring. So he got on a ship and sailed to a distant island."

"It's always an island," Yeltek grumbled.

"On this island, he sought out their greatest warrior and challenged him to a fight. This warrior was a magician who used magic no one in the Sar Empire has ever seen."

Tunt leaned over to Clanless. "You gotta admit Shool Baina's good at this. Kind of like the storyteller we heard in town."

"He's not that good." But mentioning the storyteller made him think about the storyteller's daughter, Kekeen. She'd accepted his scarf. What if someday…?

A moment later, he realized he'd missed part of the story. Bain's legendary warrior had defeated the island foe, apparently.

"But as the enemy lay wounded, something happened. Something rushed into the warrior's body, chilling his blood." Bain paused for effect. "Because, the secret of the island magician's power was… a blood-wraith."

"It's always a blood-wraith!" Yeltek exclaimed. "You don't know any other stories!"

"Let him finish," Duurald snapped. Yeltek's eyes widened, no doubt shocked that his minion would talk back to him.

"The blood-wraith took complete control over the warrior," Bain went on. "Though he'd been honorable and upright before, the blood-wraith used him for dishonorable and evil means. The first thing he did was to kill the wounded magician so he could not tell anyone the truth.

"When he returned home, his own family didn't know him. Because of course, it wasn't him. It was the blood-wraith controlling his body. He exiled his own son." Bain's voice lowered to almost a whisper. "And you wouldn't believe me if I told you what he did to his daughter."

"Ewww." Jik turned away.

"When his wife was found murdered, all the evidence pointed to him," Bain continued. "And so, he was taken before the Hawk King for sentencing. He showed no remorse, sneering—"

Duurald jumped to his feet, shoving the bench he'd been seated on backward. Uyan lost his balance and flailed wildly before grabbing the table to stop his fall. "Hey!" Duurald stomped out of the room, leaving all the other boys staring after him.

"What's his problem?" Tunt wondered.

"I don't blame him," Yeltek said. "Bain's stories are stupid."

"They're not stupid; they're true," Bain countered.

"Then why are they all about the same thing?"

"Maybe someone needs to hear it."

"Maybe you need to make up a story with a different monster." Yeltek snapped his fingers. "What was that one we were talking about the other day? A death worm? Or was it a blood worm?"

Bain shook his head. "Yeltek, sometimes you make the barbarians look civilized."

"What's that supposed to mean?"

((((●))))

Now

Clanless jerked awake and water sloshed. Had he fallen asleep in the bath? He must have been working hard with those young beastmen. Either that, or he hadn't been getting good sleep on the floor. Probably a combination of both.

Curious memory that time. Why repress another story time with the trainees? Maybe Zektel had been offended by Bain's portrayal of blood-wraiths. Or maybe...

Qara screamed.

In an instant, Clanless lunged out of the water. He heard pure terror in that scream. He grabbed the throwing knife where he'd left it with his clothes. Slipping once on the wet floor, he rushed around the corner.

Qara crouched on the bed, pushed up against the wall. Two beastmen advanced across the small room. Clanless didn't recognize them, but knew at once these weren't their daily guards.

The moonblade! He'd left it leaning against the bed. Before he could even think of rushing for it, one of the beastmen charged him, claws outstretched. Clanless ducked and sidestepped, using the beastman's momentum and trusting the slickness of his wet body to help. Hair brushed against him, but the claws missed.

He swept a backhanded slash at the beastman as he passed, unconcerned whether it actually hit. His eyes focused on the second beastman, one of the largest ones he'd seen, ripping the bedclothes away to get at Qara. The moonblade tumbled to the floor, tangled within the sheets. With hardly a thought, Clanless threw the knife. It slammed into flesh right beneath the beastman's arm as he lifted it. He shrieked and staggered back.

Maybe the shriek would bring help. But if Qara's scream hadn't been enough, he doubted it. Something had happened to their guards, and no one was coming to save the humans now.

Training with the beastmen had given him a healthy respect for their speed and agility. Even so, the first beastman caught him by surprise. As Clanless lunged toward the entangled moonblade, a powerful hand seized his ankle. His chin slammed down on the floor. Stars spun around his vision. The beastman yanked him back.

Clanless grabbed the floor covering and took it with him. He flipped over and tossed the cloth into the attacker's face. With a snarl, the beastman tore it away, distracting him for only a moment.

Clanless activated the Taint. He hadn't used it since they'd arrived in this cavern, the last beastman he'd tried it on had been unaffected, and he didn't even know if this one was bleeding. But he tried anyway. To his shock, the beastman in front of him released his ankle and fell to his knees. He howled at the ceiling as his face blurred with red. The redness, like a thin mist of blood, tore from the beastman and faded into the air. He wavered and fell forward. Clanless barely managed to get out of the way. Had that been a blood-wraith?

"His wind was not his own. I wondered sometimes." The voice of the second beastman growled behind him. Before Clanless could turn, claws wrapped around his neck. He struggled as the beastman dragged him back into the lavatory. He tore his fingernails against the hard flesh of the beastman's fingers. The skin of his knees and toes scraped against the rock.

"I could gut you now, eat your entrails." Despite his situation, part of Clanless's mind couldn't help wondering why this one could speak the language so well. "But the others want a way to deny it." He shoved Clanless's face down into the water of the bath, then yanked him back up. "This is a more deserving death for you anyway." He shoved him back down under the surface and held him.

Clanless fought with every bit of strength he could muster. It was no use against the much larger beastman. He managed to activate the Taint again, but detected no change in his assailant. The warm water pushed its way into his nostrils and tried to get past his clenched lips. At the same time, what little air remained to him sought exit, ascending from his face in a surge of bubbles that merged with the eddies and bubbling already present. Darkness gathered on the edges of his vision. He tried to brace both hands below him and shove upward, but the sloped surface made it impossible to gain the correct leverage.

Against his own thoughts, his body inhaled, seeking desperately for the air it needed. Instead, water flooded down his throat. A burning sensation filled his chest as his eyes grew ever darker. His strength fled.

The pressure holding him down vanished. His head bobbed to the surface, and he rolled, spewing water and gasping at the precious air. More than just water erupted from his mouth, adding a horrid taste to the burning sensation throughout his throat, lungs, and stomach. He thrashed in the water, trying to regain any kind of balance.

Another hand grabbed his. He almost yanked it down before his brain told him it was a human hand. His eyes cleared enough to see Qara trying to pull him up. With her help, he pulled his head and chest out onto the rock. He vomited again. Air flowed into his lungs, providing some relief, but the burning remained.

The beastman lay beside him, barely moving. Clanless at last managed to push himself up on his hands and knees enough to see Qara's dagger embedded in the attacker's neck. After one last, feeble attempt to grasp the small blade, the beastman fell still. His arm splashed down into the water.

Clanless closed his eyes, breathing hard. The burning sensation diminished, but didn't go away. As he regained more control over his consciousness, he became aware of other pains: his throat might be bruised, and his ankle throbbed.

"So…" Qara said, sliding down against the opposite wall, "You might want to put some clothes on."

Clanless snorted and opened his mouth to respond. Another beastman voice cried out in their room: "hrout!" It wasn't over.

Ignoring his pains, Clanless scrambled over the dead beastman and around the corner. The first beastman still lay next to the wall, the floor covering bunched up next to him. Two more beastmen had entered the room and struggled against each other. His vision still blurring, it took Clanless a moment to realize one of them was Swift Claw. His eyes searched the room until he spotted the moonblade still tangled in the bed sheets.

Swift Claw's opponent spun him around and slammed him to the ground. The attacker clawed at him, blood spraying.

Clanless dove, his wet body sliding easily across the floor. He crashed into the bed and yanked the sheets out of the way. His hand found the moonblade.

Swift Claw howled in pain and fury.

Clanless pulled himself up onto his knees and spun around. The moonblade slammed into the enemy beastman's chest. He stared at it for a moment, then started to fall back. Swift Claw shoved him the rest of the way and scrambled to his own feet. He turned toward Clanless, eyes wide. Long gashes covered his chest and part of his face. Blood ran down his skirt and legs.

"Are you…?" Clanless tried to ask, but his throat burned too much. He collapsed back against the bed.

"You have saved me," Swift Claw said. He dropped to his knees. "You hold my life and my honor, Wolf Chosen."

Qara peeked out. "Is it safe?"

Clanless nodded, unable to muster the strength for anything else.

Koland took two days to recover from whatever the cultists had done to him. Throughout it all, Kekeen kept an anxious eye on him, wary for anything out of character, anything that might indicate a willpower at work other than his own. But as he improved, he behaved and sounded exactly like the father she knew and loved.

He remembered very little of what had happened. "It appears either Daviland or Demujin or both have a power over memories," he mused. "It would explain a lot." After the advisory council adjourned for the day, Demujin had again approached him, suggesting a visit to their service. Koland declined, saying he needed to find his daughter. "After that, I'm not sure what happened," he admitted. "I have vague memories of walking through dark passages, but nothing specific."

Kekeen told him how they had found him and what happened. After seeing them safely into Gogeku's carriage, Badaar returned to the prison with a full complement of guards. The cultists were gone by then. Kekeen thanked the weapons master with profuse words, but he shook his head. "It's the least I can do for Clanless and Zaluu," he said, before asking Gogeku to return him to his home.

"I don't know what to think of that man," Kekeen told her father. "You should have seen him in there. I think the Hawk King himself would have submitted to his demands. And yet, the further we traveled from that moment, the less like that person he became. He seemed to… I don't know. It was as if once the need for him passed, he shrank up inside himself."

Koland nodded. "He's a man who lost his purpose and needs to find another," he said weakly. "You gave him one, but it didn't last long."

Of course Koland was interested in the sequence of events that led Kekeen to his rescue. He wasn't pleased about the dangers, and ranted about Lord Ulakan, but in the end, he praised her courage and resourcefulness. "I wouldn't be here now, if not for you."

Kekeen sat down across from him at their room's small table. She took a breath and changed the subject: "Borde thinks Davil is possessed by the spirit of the Hawk King or something." She elaborated a bit more on their conversation.

"I've never heard of someone's spirit possessing anyone else, at least outside one of my stories. But the Hawk King was a unique person. We have no idea what he was capable of. Or if he's capable of anything after his death." Koland frowned. "But we know there are other kinds of possession."

"You think it's a blood-wraith?"

"Maybe." Her father sighed and sat back. "I feel like something unusual is going on, and not just our rebellion and the fall of the Hawk King. I've heard more talk of blood-wraiths this year than… any time I can remember."

"And it's more than just talk, if Badaar's story is true," Kekeen pointed out.

"Yes. I can't help but wonder…" Koland's eyes flickered toward the ceiling.

"Suirel? You think there's something real there?"

Koland stood up and walked toward the room's door. "I don't know. You weren't alive the last time the chaos moon appeared, and I was only a child myself. I remember a bad winter and lots of doom and gloom from the adults, but nothing like this. It's hard to give it any credence."

"You, of all people, know there's bound to be some truth behind the old stories," she said. "You always taught me that."

"You're right. But strange as it is for a storyteller to say, I need more facts." He chuckled.

"So now what do we do?"

"We're not going back to the palace until Davil calls another council meeting. And then… well, we'll see what happens."

（（（●）））

"This is a horror and an outrage." Swift Claw's head hung lower than Clanless had ever seen it. "I am shamed. We are all shamed."

Clanless massaged his own neck and didn't answer. An intense ache filled his throat, inside and out. It had been at least two hours since the attack, but he didn't feel much better than Swift Claw looked. Their translator had cleaned his wounds, but the gashes would almost certainly become scars. Here and there, blood still oozed in small droplets.

"What happened to our guards?" Qara asked.

"We are trying to find them now," Swift Claw answered. "We do not know. When I arrived, I did not find them." He peered earnestly at Clanless and shook his head. "And the water. Such horror."

"He said it was the death I deserved," Clanless croaked. "What does that mean?"

"To lose one's wind to the water is the most terrible death one can have." Swift Claw almost hit his snout against the floor in lowering it further. "A shame to us."

"And no one heard us," Qara said. "No one came… except you. Not until the fight was over."

"It is a shame to us," the translator repeated. "We will find out. We do not know how or why this happened."

"What about the one who survived? Did you learn anything from him?"

"The last thing he remembers is from many days ago." Swift Claw waved a hand absently. "It is not understood."

"His wind was not his own," Clanless said.

"What?"

Clanless pointed toward the lavatory. "The dead one. That's what he said." The words were hard to get out through his burning throat.

"What does that mean?" Qara asked. "His wind? His spirit? Like he had a different spirit in him?"

Swift Claw did not say anything.

"A blood-wraith," Clanless said. It had to be what he'd seen. And for some reason, the Taint made a difference there. Had it always? When had he ever fought someone else possessed like that? Maybe it only happened because the blood-wraith was inside a beastman. And what happened to it? His eyes shot to Qara. It hadn't gone into her, had it?

"I do not know how such a thing could happen," Swift Claw said at last, without raising his head. "We... we work to prevent it."

"You take precautions against blood-wraiths?" Qara asked.

"We work."

Qara threw up her hands. "Why is it half of our questions never get answered?" She stood up and pointed at the translator. "There's always been a group that wants us gone. And now we know it goes beyond just snarling at us. They planned this. They knew our routine. They knew Clanless likes to get clean after the training time. They chose this specific time and got rid of the guards while they were at it. How do we know the guards weren't in on it? How do we know you weren't? Your arrival time is suspicious."

Swift Claw almost fell over backward. "I am your friend! I brought your weapons! I fought with you!"

"We thank you," Clanless intervened. "We are alive because of you. Qara is... upset."

"It's about trust!" Qara did not back off. "Who can we trust here, Swift Claw? Besides you? Your elders? New guards? Who?"

Clanless cocked his head and waited for Swift Claw's response. He had the same questions.

The beastman ran both hands through the hair on the sides and back of his head. Clanless didn't remember seeing any of them do that before. Frustration? Anxiety?

"We knew of those who oppose you," Swift Claw said. "But they are few. We did not believe they would do something like this. Perhaps the false wind did this. And now they will stop."

"They failed to kill us once, so they give up?" Qara snorted. "That's not how hate works. They'll try again."

"But the false wind—"

"Even if that's the problem," she cut him off, "can you guarantee no more of your people are, are possessed?"

He shook his head. "No more than you can."

Qara's eyebrows went up. "We're not carrying blood-wraiths around."

Clanless wondered how she would react to knowing about the one he carried for so long.

"We will place new guards that I will select myself," Swift Claw said. "Four of them, guarding both directions from your space. And I will speak more with the elders."

"Thank you," Clanless said.

"You hold my life and honor. I will do all I can for you."

"Your life is your own," Clanless said. "I am not your master."

Swift Claw considered for a moment and nodded. "My honor then. It is enough. I will go now."

Clanless nodded back. Qara grunted, but said nothing else until Swift Claw left. "What do you think?" she asked. "Are we safe here?"

"I think," Clanless said slowly through his aching throat, "we might have a way out of here now."

GIVING UP

The next morning, a summons to another council meeting came to the inn, requesting Koland's presence as the sun began its retreat. Kekeen and her father arrived at the palace early, but Koland hung back and waited until all the other members were present. Only then did he make his entrance.

"Ah, here he is," Daviland said as Koland strode to the table. "Now we can begin."

Kekeen's eyes darted around the table. Demujin's smile looked no different than always. Lord Ulakan leered at her, the scum.

"Before we start, I need to make an announcement," Koland declared, standing behind his chair.

"We need to talk about General Ghan right away," Lord Ghayktal said. "Unless this is urgent, can it wait?"

"It cannot." Koland looked to Daviland first. "Davil… I have been by your side for over three years now. It was an honor and a privilege to work with you throughout it all, to spread your message, to find new recruits for you, and everything else we did together."

Daviland acknowledged him with a nod.

"I am sorry that has to come to an end today."

"What?"

"The events of the past few days have led me to this decision," Koland went on. "It is hard… no, it is impossible for me to—" He broke off and shook his head. "Look at me. The storyteller struggling for the right words."

"What is wrong, my friend?" Daviland asked.

Koland looked at him and shook his head sadly. "The fact that you could sit there and ask that question, pretending you know nothing, seals my decision more than anything else could have. You are not the man I fought with. I don't know what has happened to you, but I can no longer stand by your side."

"Koland!" Sonkogh exclaimed. "Are you certain of this?"

"I apologize for not speaking with you ahead of time," Koland said to him. "You deserve a longer answer, and I will be happy to share it with you later." He turned back to the rest of the table. "Three days ago, I was abducted by Demujin and his cultists. Had it not been for my daughter and a most heroic friend, I would not have escaped."

"Outrageous!" The Ghamba Lam leaped to his feet. "This is precisely the kind of behavior I would have expected from him! Good storyteller, you are not the one who needs to leave. This criminal should be ejected from our presence immediately!"

"There are two sides to every story," Daviland said. "Let us hear what Demujin has to say for himself."

"To be utterly honest, I do not care," Koland countered. "Let him say what he wants. His behavior is only the second reason I am leaving you, and the third is the most serious."

"What else?" Sonkogh muttered, putting his face in his hands.

"In the course of trying to rescue me, my daughter faced deadly danger from someone here." Koland gripped the back of the chair and glared across the table. "Lord Ulakan, were this a… less civilized time, I would be coming after you with murderous intent. As it is, I cannot stomach the presence of a man like yourself who would so threaten my daughter."

"I'm sure I have no idea what you're talking about," Lord Ulakan said placidly.

"To repeat: Demujin abducted me, Ulakan almost assaulted my daughter, and we have spent the past two days recovering." Koland released the chair and stepped back. "Between these attacks and the fact that I can no longer believe or trust our leader, I am leaving this advisory council. I will no longer be a part of whatever you plan. Ghouk or Ghan or the barbarians can take all of you. I no longer care."

Koland turned and strode from the room. Kekeen joined him, with a quick glance over her shoulder as the council erupted in accusations and chaos. The Ghamba Lam and Sonkogh demanded answers, the Lords countered, and Daviland tried to regain control.

"You've thrown off the balance," Kekeen said as they left. "The other

Lords will back Ulakan and Demujin."

"There never was a balance," her father replied. "Not with Daviland compromised." He took one last look at the council table as the doors closed. "My every waking moment for the past few years has been wasted."

((((●))))

Though he wouldn't admit it to Qara, Clanless had experienced more fear in the short fight with the beastmen than any other he could recall. Over the next few nights, only one memory resurfaced over and over again: his head being held under the water, his air disappearing, and the burning water in his lungs.

From that moment, the moonblade never left his side again. While bathing, it sat in easy reach. He fell asleep each night with it by his hand. Every time he awakened, whether from dreams or morning, he instinctively seized it.

He'd faced death in the arena hundreds of times. But never like this. Never helpless, unable to fight. And never... without blood. So strange.

Zektel had taken some of his fear away during training. In spite of everything yet again, he wished she were still with him. And then he chastised himself for even thinking such a thing. But at least he could talk with her. She knew everything about him; he could be honest. He'd never had to worry what she might think or who she might tell. As close as he and Qara might be right now, he could never think of her the same way. Not like Zektel... or Kekeen.

He truly missed Kekeen. Weeks had passed now since Ghouk tore them apart. They'd had such a short time together after the fall of the Hawk King, and he'd been recovering from his injuries. How he longed to just sit with her. To hold her. To listen to her sing. To fully experience the true companionship of lovers.

Would he ever see her again? So many powers and forces seemed to be conspiring to keep them apart. If his vision of the goddess had been real, even spiritual forces were warring over him somehow. And the ones against him appeared to be winning.

With these dark thoughts, Clanless sank deep into gloom. He refused to go to the training for several days. Qara tried her best to pull him out of it, but her efforts only pushed him deeper or made him angry. The last time he'd gotten this depressed, he'd only come out of it after a talk with Orgina in which she promised him new books. Nothing like that would happen this time.

After several days of this, Qara changed tactics. She emerged from the bath to find him sitting against the wall, staring at the front entrance and fingering the moonblade. "All right, I've had enough." From her meager pile of belongings, she took out her dagger and a vial of blood. She crouched down in front of him.

"Clan Zavi blood," she explained. "They use it to create bursts of speed; you've fought people like that. But with the right amount, it can just accelerate your heart. Maybe that'll wake you up and get you out of... whatever this is." She held up the dagger. "I just need a drop of your blood for catalyst. I could do it on my own, but it's such a process, and it's so much easier with the clanless one's blood."

He stared at her, so close and so... here. She wore only a simple robe provided by the beastmen. Far too large for her, it hung open in the front. It would be so easy to reach forward... and she wouldn't object. So easy. It would be a way to escape the dark thoughts, a way to enjoy himself, to lose himself in her... He lifted his left arm, reaching forward. And an image of his uncle reaching toward him filled his head.

Instead of reaching further, he turned his arm, exposing the underside. Qara took it with her left hand and brought the dagger in close. "Wait." She set the dagger down and twisted his arm toward the light. She ran a finger along the underside of his forearm and gasped.

"What is this?" Qara let go of his arm and stared at him. "You have dozens of tiny scars here. How often have you... No." She shook her head. "This isn't from the arena. These are deliberate, like what I was about to do. Why?"

Clanless didn't answer.

Qara grabbed a handful of his hair and pulled his head away from the wall. "Why, Clanless?"

He met her eyes. "It's none of your business."

"Wrong." She let go of his hair. His head fell back and smacked the rock wall a little too hard. "We are the only two humans trapped among hundreds of beastmen, half of which want to kill us! Everything about you is my business." She paused before adding, "And everything about me is your business."

When he didn't say anything else, she sat back and sighed. "Clanless. Please. I want to help." She watched for a moment. "Fine. If you won't tell me, I'll figure it out on my own." She thought for a moment, watching his face. "The first and most obvious answer is the same thing I was about to do: you've been using your own blood to help with blood-magic. But I don't think that's it." She frowned. "I've never seen any evidence that you're using magic. I'm good at spotting that. And it wouldn't make much sense for you, anyway. But maybe someone else is doing it for you… or using you. That's a definite possibility."

"Let it go," Clanless mumbled.

Qara tapped her chin. "What other reason could there be? You like cutting yourself? I've heard about that kind of thing. But it doesn't seem like you. And I haven't seen you do it since we've been here… or evidence of it." Her eyes widened. "It has to do with your power, doesn't it? You shed your own blood because… no, that doesn't make any sense. Do you test it on yourself?"

Her guesses were getting too close to the truth. Clanless set the moon-blade down. "If I tell you, will you let me alone?"

"No. I need you back." Her facade cracked just enough for him to see real fear in her eyes. "I don't know what's going to happen here. I need you." She reached out and took hold of one of his hands. He flinched a little, but didn't pull away.

Clanless closed his eyes and took a deep breath. "You're right. I'm… I'll be all right." He opened his eyes and tried to smile.

Qara lowered her eyebrows. "And the scars?"

"You're… not far wrong. In, in the past, I needed to test my power. I would spill some blood in a bowl or something and practice. It's how I became so good at it." A lie, but mixed with a good bit of truth.

"Hmp." Qara watched him, as if evaluating his truthfulness. "All right. Let's get things back to normal. Or as normal as it can be in here."

Clanless nodded. "I'll do my best."

She released his hand and got back to her feet. "And start by taking a bath. You stink."

☾☾☾☾●☽☽☽☽

Sonkogh came to the eating house that evening, hoping to convince Koland to change his mind. They talked far into the night. Koland shared everything he now knew with his friend.

"I understand your anger, but…" Sonkogh shook his head. "This is not like you, my friend. You're the weaver of stories. You are particular and careful, planning everything. That's why you were so invaluable to Daviland in the first place. This… this is not careful."

Koland grimaced. "You're right, of course." He glanced toward Kekeen, who hovered nearby to listen. "It was rash of me. It might have been better if I'd stuck it out, endured the hostility and overlooked the attempts against my daughter and myself. But…"

"I know." Sonkogh nodded. "Part of me wants to quit as well."

"Oh no." Koland pointed at him. "You have to stay, if only to keep an eye on what is happening. We will all depend on you. True, you probably won't be able to sway this council in any major way, but you can keep us advised of what they're doing."

"My thoughts exactly. Who could have foreseen this?" He laughed. "That I would sit on Daviland's council, only to be most closely aligned with the Ghamba Lam, of all people!"

"We live in unusual times." Koland toyed with an empty mug. "I am… disappointed—but only a little—in myself for making such an emotional decision. But even when I think it through, I am not sure I would have done anything differently."

Kekeen moved away from the table. She had mixed emotions about the whole thing. On the one hand, she applauded her father for standing up to the council and especially Demujin and Ulakan. On the other hand, he'd quit because of her. Was that a good thing or bad? Koland had become completely invested in Daviland's cause over the past few years. Could he really be all right with leaving it so abruptly?Koland threw himself back into storytelling and playing his dovshuur. He spent hours each day writing down new story ideas and composing new melodies. He also took to pouring over maps of the Sar Empire, muttering about the different cities and the people in each one.

Kekeen had never cared much about maps before, but now she took an interest. She studied the regions north of Et-Baylak, wondering where Aldan might be now. She traced the roads that led to the northern military base where General Ghan waited for High Winter to end. Answers to most of her questions came much sooner than she expected but brought with them a host of new questions.

Around a week after Koland's resignation from the council, two bedraggled travelers wearing heavy clothes entered the eating house in the early evening. Koland continued his story for the five other guests, barely glancing at the newcomers. Kekeen watched them, feeling like she should know these two. Both were very large men, though one towered over the other. Only when the shorter one removed the cloths wrapped around his face did Kekeen squeal and rush toward them.

"Hagh!" She threw her arms around the arena fighter. "And Sugh!" She embraced the larger man as well, before he could even uncover his face.

"Careful now!" Sugh said, returning her hug. "We don't want to make Clanless too jealous!"

"Then he's alive! Where is he?"

"Ah." Hagh glanced from her to Koland, who'd paused his story to watch them, along with his audience. "Truth is, we were hoping to find him here with you."

Kekeen's shoulders fell, but she recovered quick enough. "Have a seat, both of you. Let me fetch you something warm to eat, and you can tell us everything."

"Is it safe here?" Hagh asked with a short cough. "We only just entered the city. We haven't been to the arena or anythin'."

"You are very welcome and safe here," Koland said from the stage. "We are glad to see you. Allow me to finish regaling these others, and I will join you."

In a few minutes, Kekeen had enlisted the help of the staff in bringing food and drink to the two arena fighters, who set to with gusto. Koland sat down with the three of them, a bemused smile on his face. "You act as though you haven't eaten in days."

"Nothing this good," Sugh confirmed. "We've had little enough for weeks."

"Eat as much as you like," Koland said. "But between bites, please satisfy my daughter's curiosity before she bursts."

"I wish we had better news for you," Hagh said. "We haven't seen Clanless in…" He looked to Sugh. "Two weeks? No, more'n that."

"A good story starts at the beginning," Koland suggested. "Tell us how you all left the city. That was certainly three weeks ago."

"Twenty-three days," Kekeen said.

"It was Ghouk," Sugh said. "He had our bloodbonds. He forced us to go with him."

"All of you, then?"

"Aye. All five Dohor," Hagh said. "And Qara too. Uh… speaking of which, since Clanless hasn't returned, have any of the others? Hawking? Bain?"

"No. You're the first." Koland accepted a drink of his own from the innkeeper. "We'd guessed you'd gone north, possibly with Ghouk, but we had no other information."

"North it was." Hagh sighed and took a quick bite of bread before continuing. "Ghouk took us to the mines. He kicked Hawking out of the carriage halfway there. I suppose that's the last we've seen of him."

"Either of them," Sugh said around a mouthful.

"Ghouk is dead?" Kekeen asked.

"I'm getting to that." Hagh gave Sugh an annoyed look. "Ghouk had some crazy idea of gainin' his father's powers at the crystal mines. After that, I think he was going to find the rest of the army."

"We anticipated that much," Koland said, "but not the mines. That's unexpected."

"When we got there, he sent the two of us to kill the priests, while he went into the mines with Clanless, Bain, and Qara."

"But we didn't kill any," Sugh said with a chuckle.

"It was Bain who worked it out," Hagh said. "Gave me the idea, anyway. Clever, that one. He said in the carriage that just because Ghouk could order us to do stuff, we could find ways to interpret his orders differently if we didn't want to do them."

"He told us to kill anyone we found," Sugh cut in. "So we—"

"I'm tellin' it!" Hagh snapped. "It was my idea. As we walked up to the buildings, you see, we started shouting: 'We are two slaves who have been ordered to kill everyone we find!'"

Sugh threw his arms out. "I hope we don't find anyone!" he bellowed. "That's what I shouted," he added a little quieter.

"So they shut themselves in and didn't let us see them." Hagh laughed. "It felt good to twist that bastard's orders. Ah, sorry for my language, my lady."

"Just go on," Kekeen said impatiently. "What happened to Aldan?"

"Oh, of course." Hagh shook his head. "We didn't see him again after that. We were still shouting our intentions when we felt it."

"Ghouk was dead," Sugh said.

"The compulsion to obey his order disappeared. We let the priests know we didn't need to kill them any more, and then we tried to find the others."

"First we had to fight the lizards," Sugh put in.

"I doubt she cares about that part, lad." Hagh glared at him. "Yes, we fought some of those big lizard things. Then we went into the mines. We found Ghouk's body. Looked like he fell off a cliff somehow. But the others had disappeared."

Koland leaned forward. "They disappeared in the crystal mines?"

"Up near the top," Hagh explained. "In a place the priests called the Throat of the Goddess."

"Lots of tunnels," Sugh added.

"Yah. We searched them as much as we could over the next week, when the winter let us. We found a dead lizard beast that someone killed, but nothing else." Hagh shook his head. "No sign of Clanless, Bain, or Qara. We hoped they found a way out and came back here."

"If they got out, they froze to death," Sugh argued. "Just like Hawking."

"They're too smart to try walking," Hagh said. "Way too smart."

Kekeen clenched her hands together. It wasn't much; it wasn't the news she'd wanted. But it was better than nothing. Now she knew Aldan's movements for the first week after his disappearance, at least. After that... well, at least he'd been free and with friends.

"They're most likely holed up somewhere, waiting for High Winter to end," Koland said, watching her.

"I'm sure of it," she answered. She looked back at the two fighters. "Do you think they might still be in those tunnels somewhere?"

Hagh and Sugh exchanged looks. "We couldn't explore all of them, so it's possible," Hagh admitted. "But why wouldn't they come out after Ghouk died?"

"The caves would be safer than the outside," Koland mused. "But what about food and water?"

"That would be a problem."

"I'm sure they're all right," Kekeen repeated. "How did you two get back here?"

"We couldn't just hop back in the carriage," Hagh explained. "The lizards killed our oxen. So we had to stay with the priests up there for a while."

"They were very friendly, once we stopped trying to kill them," Sugh said.

"It took a while, and some solemn promises, but we managed to convince them to loan us another pair of oxen," Hagh said. "And so we came here as fast as we could."

"Thank you," Kekeen said. "Thank you for coming here."

"And for all you've told us," Koland added. "It explains a few things, but still..." He shook his head. "I don't understand why he went to the mines."

"We didn't understand it either. Bain kept trying to get him to tell his plans, but..." Hagh shrugged. "Even when he told some of it, I didn't get it. Made no sense. He wanted his daddy's power, and he thought he could get it there. Something about the blood too."

"How far is it to these mines?" Kekeen asked.

Hagh coughed. "It's a week's travel, at least. Took us longer coming back. Suirel's Winter is getting worse out there. I wouldn't want to go back in it. Better to wait until it clears."

Kekeen sat back, thinking. She would need to check Koland's maps again. Hagh and Sugh must have missed something. If Aldan had gone into the mines, he must still be there.

"Should we report this to Daviland?" Sugh asked. "I was thinking I would like my own bed tonight."

"That might not be the best idea," Koland said slowly. "Some things have happened since you've been gone."

"Can't be any crazier than our story," Hagh said. "Tell us."

Koland gave a brief outline of occurrences in the capital. Both Hagh and Sugh immediately offered to kill Lord Ulakan, but Kekeen assured them she didn't want that.

"I think you'd better stay here," Koland suggested. "There are plenty of available beds in the inn." He frowned. "But word of your return will get out, no matter what we do."

"If they summon us, we'll say no," Sugh declared. His face split open in an enormous grin. "We are free men now, you know!"

☾ ☾ ☽ ☾ ● ☽ ☽ ☽ ☾

Clanless threw himself back into the training exercises. As he did, he found he actually enjoyed teaching, to his own surprise. He tried to incorporate the best of what he'd learned from Kan and Badaar. He also found that some of things he'd hated most while under their training turned out to be the most essential parts of teaching younger warriors (even when they weren't human).

He and Qara also started more serious discussions of escape routes. By paying attention to the temperature within tunnels, he began to get an idea of which ways led toward the surface.

"But all of those exits are sure to be guarded," he told Qara as he sat against the cavern wall one evening. "We would have to fight our way through. And without knowing how many guards, or how many might be nearby, we can't make a plan."

"Maybe there are ways out that aren't guarded."

"What do you mean?"

Qara slid off the bed where she'd been sitting and walked to the lamp on the wall. She pointed at the ceiling. "See the hole? That's where the smoke goes. These are all over the place. Otherwise, we'd be sitting in smoke all the time."

Clanless nodded. "I noticed them early on, but hadn't thought through their purpose. But what good does that do us?"

"Remember when we first woke up here?" Qara folded her arms. "The big fireplace? That had to have a much larger exit for the smoke. If we can find something like that not in use, maybe we could climb out."

"Large fires…"

"Like the kitchens!" Qara paced their small room. "And they would have to be closer to the surface, probably. They wouldn't want the air holes to be too long, I'd guess."

"The forge," Clanless said. "That would have large fires also. I've asked to see it, but Swift Claw hasn't been forthcoming on that request."

"Let's assume we found one of these smoke tunnels, and that we could get to it without being caught." Qara stopped and looked at him. "Do you think we could climb? Have you ever climbed anything like that?"

Clanless chuckled. "Did you ever see any mountains in the arena? My life has been sand."

"I've never done it either. I just didn't know if the Wolf Chosen had more special abilities I didn't know about."

"What does the wolf have to do with this?"

"I don't know! We don't even know why they call you that!" Qara threw up her hands. "And I don't even know your real name!"

Clanless hesitated for a moment. "It's Aldan."

Qara lowered her hands and stared. "Are you being serious?"

He nodded. "It's the name my parents gave me. The priests said they took it from me when they sold me as a slave. From then on, I was Clanless." He shrugged. "It's hard for me to think of myself any other way now."

"Aldan," she repeated. She sat on the bed again. "I… thank you. I'm guessing not many people know that any more."

"Kekeen does. And her father. And Bain." He scratched the back of his head. "Daviland too, I guess, since they told him. Oh, and my cousin Borde."

"Your cousin? Do you have any other family left from… from before?"

"I don't know." He shrugged. "Borde said they're all right, but I haven't seen them in eight years… maybe nine now. They've forgotten me by now."

"You can't believe that."

"They let the priests take me. They did nothing to stop it. And they had another son afterwards. They didn't need me any more."

Qara slid off the bed onto the floor. "You have a brother you've never met?"

"I guess." He hadn't thought about that in so long. His little brother would be eight or nine years old now, old enough to help Father in the fields, old enough to carry rocks for the back wall, old enough… His blood ran cold. Uncle Sejikdi. Would he treat this new nephew the same way he'd treated little Aldan?

"What is it?" Qara asked, sliding a little closer. "What's wrong?"

"I don't… I don't want to think about this now."

"We all have families left behind somewhere, Aldan. That's part of the tragedy of being a slave." Qara reached out toward him.

Clanless jumped to his feet and stalked away, pushing past her outstretched hand. "Escape. That's what we need to talk about. What else have we not considered?"

Qara sat back on her heels. "I don't know, Clanless. Maybe using your sword to dig a tunnel?"

"The rock's not soft enough for that."

She let out an exasperated sigh. "That was sarcasm, you dolt." She got up, shaking her head. "If you don't want to talk, we won't." She climbed into the bed, grumbling. "Arena fighters. Idiots. All idiots."

ALDAN WAS NEVER ALONE

At a late breakfast, Kekeen questioned Hagh about a return trip to the mines. "Can we use the carriage you came back in?"

"Afraid not." Hagh shook his head while spreading butter on his pastry. "On the trip with Ghouk, we had six oxen. For the return trip, the priests were only able to loan us two. Sugh and I stripped the carriage down to make it easier for them to pull. What's left of it barely made it here intact."

Kekeen frowned, both at his words and his culinary choices. "Are you certain? Couldn't we repair it a bit?"

"I don't think so." Hagh took a huge bite. After swallowing, he added: "I don't think it would make it more than a couple miles outside the city by now. You're welcome to look at it, of course. Maybe if you got a master carpenter to work on it. But I still doubt it."

"So we need a new carriage and oxen to pull it," Kekeen concluded.

"The only place you'll find that is the Hawk King's stables," Hagh said. "Or maybe the Ghamba Lam's."

"Maybe we should take what we need!" Sugh said. "It is for a good cause."

"I don't think that would work out, lad." Hagh eyed Sugh over the top of his pastry. "Both of them have guards. And the penalty for that kind of theft is either death or slavery."

"We are free men now!"

"Yes, and I'd like to stay that way." He coughed and looked back to

Kekeen. "As free men, we need to think about our future. It's not much, but I do have some blood stored away at the arena. I'd like to pick it up."

"Ah, so do I," Sugh said. "And some more clothes."

"You should certainly take what is yours," Kekeen said. "I don't see how anyone would question that."

"Will you go with us?" Hagh asked. "I don't know any of this Daviland's people, and if we get confronted, it would be good to have someone who knows people." He glanced toward the door. "I'd ask your father, but I've yet to see him this morning."

"He sleeps in a lot when he entertains late." Kekeen thought about it. She had no desire to get anywhere near Daviland again, but it made sense to help the two fighters. Besides, how much safer could she be than with two of the most celebrated warriors in the Empire?

The three of them bundled up and found their way to the arena. No guards confronted them when they entered. Hagh and Sugh hurried to their own rooms to gather their things.

While she waited, Kekeen made her way into Aldan's room. She knew exactly what she'd find, but maybe it was time to take Aldan's personal items out, like the other two were doing. She knelt beside his chest and opened it, bracing herself for the emotions she knew she'd experience. She'd searched it before, but only while looking for clues to his location.

Clothes made up the bulk of the chest's contents. She packed them all into a large bag. Gogeku must have made some of these. She'd seen Aldan wear some of them, but others were brand-new to her.

She also collected all of his blood vials, far less than she'd expected. She wondered if he'd taken some with him, or if thieves had helped themselves to his stock. But if so, wouldn't they have taken all of it? Two of the vials caught her attention. One had to be the oldest vial in the collection; its crystal edges were worn smooth all around. Though larger than most, it only held half as much blood as it could. She wondered at its significance, as she did at the second one. While at first glance, it looked like any other average crystal vial of blood, something felt wrong. The blood appeared darker, maybe. A different consistency? She held it up to the light and turned it back and forth. So strange.

Kekeen almost missed the last item in the chest. As she tightened the cinch on the bag, her eye caught something off-color on the chest's floor. She bent down and picked up a weathered and folded piece of paper. She opened it and read:

My dear Aldan,

Father woke me early this morn...

It was her letter! The one she'd sent him after Koland rushed them out of Ghoyor that one time. Her eyes welled up. He'd kept it all this time.

Sugh stuck his head in through the door. "We've got trouble!"

Kekeen took the note and the bag of Aldan's things and hurried into the hall. Hagh stood further down, near some other rooms. He motioned for them to join him. Kekeen recognized the arena's dining hall as they approached. She stiffened, seeing what awaited them.

Daviland sat in one of the dining hall's chairs, his feet resting on a table. Six guards stood at attention behind him. "Did you all find what you were looking for?" he asked with a smile. "Because I certainly have."

He gestured, and the guards spread out around the room. "I must say, I'm disappointed." He continued smiling. "The Dohor return. The answer to our biggest mystery of the winter. And no one comes to tell me?"

"We don't answer to you," Kekeen said. "And we're not really on speaking terms any more."

"Word is you're not yerself," Hagh added.

"Who else would I be?" Daviland took his feet from the table and stood up. "I'm afraid you've been listening to wild rumors, Hagh."

"You know our names?" Sugh asked.

"My dear Sugh, I know all about you. Every detail."

Hagh scowled. He'd dropped his own bag of belongings and held his twin maces in a tight grip. "We've never even met you."

"And yet I know you. For example, I know you're about to cough. Violently, I might add."

The two men stared at one another. Hagh turned his head and coughed five or six times, his whole body shaking.

"I know that Sugh talks alone in his room a lot, and has delusions about who he's talking to. And that his favorite scar is high on his left hip," Daviland went on.

Kekeen glanced at the big man. His face confirmed it.

"I've watched you both for so long, I've come to think of you as my friends too. It's so disheartening when the feeling is not returned."

"But we don't know you," Sugh said, his brow wrinkled.

Daviland waved at the leader of the guards. "Would you men mind waiting just outside? I'll call you if I need you."

The guards, clearly confused, obeyed him nonetheless.

"You sure you don't need them?" Hagh asked.

"Maybe you should be afraid of being alone with me," Daviland said.

"I did defeat Clanless and the Hawk King, after all."

"Aldan let you win!" Kekeen couldn't help herself.

"I know what happened better than anyone, Kekeen."

She took a step toward him. "Who are you?"

"I would think you would know me by now."

"You're not Daviland. You don't act or sound like him at all."

"Should I tell you how much I know about you, then? Do you still have the scarf?"

Kekeen's eyes widened.

"Who was the boy who claimed your first kiss? You know, the one you said didn't count before the real kiss on the stage in Ghoyor?"

Kekeen gasped. Her voice trembled. "How could you know that?"

Daviland shrugged. "You told me."

"No, I didn't. I told Aldan. And we were alone!"

Daviland leaned forward. For a brief moment, his eyes turned almost red. "Aldan was never alone."

Sugh grabbed Kekeen's shoulder and yanked her back. Hagh stepped closer to Daviland, holding his maces at ready. "What are you, then? Blood-wraith?"

Daviland shook his head. "You would think slaves would show more respect for the man who set them free."

"You didn't free us, whoever you are!" Sugh cried. "We weren't free until Ghouk died."

"Ah, so the Hawk King's son is dead. Good news for me. But where is Aldan in all of this?" Daviland put a hand over his heart. "Don't tell me he's dead!" Before they could answer, he went on: "But no. Kekeen wouldn't be here if that were true. She'd be mourning. No…" He studied the three of them. "Aldan is somewhere else, but in trouble. You want to help him. Maybe you even need my help."

"We don't trust you," Hagh said with a short cough.

Kekeen couldn't resist. "We need one of the Hawk King's winter carriage. And oxen to pull it."

Hagh shot her a look. "Don't listen to him! He's not even human any more!"

"What do you know of being human, Hagh?" Daviland took a step closer. "You lived your life in blood and sex. When you weren't killing, you were working your way through every woman at Pasque House and beyond." He cocked his head with a condescending smile. "But then you'd go to the temple and cry about it to the priests and give them your own blood, so it's all good with your goddess, isn't it?"

Hagh lowered his maces, staring.

"Aldan thought of you as his friend, maybe one of the best," Daviland went on, stepping right in front of Hagh. "But out of all the arena fighters he met over all those years…" He shook his head, leaning even closer. "You disgusted me most of all with your attempts at piety. Do you think your goddess really forgave you?"

"I don't… what are you?" Hagh whispered.

Before Kekeen or Sugh could react, Daviland whipped a dagger from inside his cloak and thrust it up into Hagh's chest.

"My name is Zektel. And I rule the Sar Empire."

Time froze. No one moved. It… it couldn't be real. Not Hagh.

Sugh's bellow of rage split Kekeen's eardrums. The giant warrior shoved her aside, lifting his axe as he charged Daviland.

The wraith-possessed man yanked the dagger from Hagh's chest, seized one of the fighter's maces, and swung it with both hands to block Sugh's attack.

Kekeen regained her balance. "Hagh!" she finally screamed.

Sugh swung again and again, his massive axe slamming down at Daviland, driving him across the dining hall. Kekeen rushed to Hagh's side as he slumped to the floor. Blood poured from his chest. She held both hands over the wound, trying to staunch the flow.

"I'll find a healer," she found herself saying. "You'll be all right. Just hold on."

He coughed, and blood appeared on the corners of his mouth. "Too late for me. Save that big—cough—lunk, will ya?"

"No, no, no." She kept trying to hold back the blood. "I need your help. I need you."

Hagh gave one last cough and stopped moving. Kekeen stared at him. The sound of weapons clashing faded in her ears. Was… was he dead? The rush of blood around her hands subsided. "Hagh?" His eyes didn't move. He… he…

Kekeen had not seen a dead body since… since her mother died. She'd only been seven years old at the time. Aldan talked about all the deaths he'd been a part of, but she'd never… She lifted a hand to cover her mouth, only to freeze at the sight of it coated in blood.

Daviland's guards charged back into the room, screaming for Sugh to stop his attack. Kekeen whimpered and wiped her hands on her skirt, already spattered with Hagh's blood. She stared about in shock and fear. Sugh shouted, swinging his axe in a wide circle to keep the guards back. They would kill him. He couldn't fight all of them. Not all at once. He—

Kekeen jumped to her feet, Hagh's last words in her head. "Everyone stop!" she screamed.

The guards paused. Sugh's head jerked back and forth watching them and Daviland, but he stopped attacking.

"Daviland. Let us go."

The rebel leader wiped sweat from his brow and lowered Hagh's mace. "Ah, I suppose I should let you leave, or your father might go beyond simply yelling at my council." He stepped around the guards encircling Sugh. "But it's a shame. You look good in red."

Kekeen's breath came hard and fast. "Sugh also. We'll take Hagh's body with us."

Daviland cocked his head. "I don't think so. This one attacked me. All of these guards witnessed it."

"You killed Hagh!" Sugh shouted, lifting his axe over his head again.

"Wait, wait!" Kekeen cried, holding out a hand to him.

"I have this great big prison that's totally empty right now," Daviland said. "I think it's time to move in at least one new occupant."

"You can't. I know the truth. And, and I'll tell everyone." Kekeen's eyes darted from Sugh to the guards to Daviland. "Sugh is one of the Dohor. He's popular with the people. They won't like this."

Daviland looked up at the ceiling. "I could argue that I'm more popular now. But then you'd probably show up at my door with that one-handed antique again. It's just too much trouble, I suppose." He shrugged. "Let them go."

The guards backed away from Sugh, keeping their weapons up and staying between him and Daviland.

Before leaving, Davil paused in front of Kekeen again. He handed her Hagh's mace, then touched her hair. "You really do look good in red. I'll have the tailors send you a dress. And an invitation to sing at the palace. Everyone should have a chance to hear your voice."

Kekeen shivered under his gaze. When she didn't answer, he smiled again and left. The guards followed, leaving them alone with Hagh's body.

Sugh dropped his axe and fell to his knees beside the body of his friend. Kekeen stood awkwardly holding the mace while the largest man she'd ever seen sobbed like a baby.

RESOLUTIONS

One morning, after four weeks among the beastmen, Swift Claw entered their room as usual, but he did not come alone. An older beastman accompanied him. Clanless couldn't be sure, but he looked like the elder who had been present at their first arrival in the caves. His narrow beard, paler than most, hung almost to the floor.

Swift Claw confirmed it: "This is White Horn, one of our elders. You have met before."

Clanless and Qara both rose and gave a short bow to the elder. He gave a nod of acknowledgement before launching into a lengthy speech. The humans stood waiting until he finished, then both looked to Swift Claw.

The translator appeared unsure of himself. "I… that… the elder here is…"

The elder barked something harsh. Swift Claw straightened and looked at the wall beyond Clanless while he spoke: "The elder wanted to come and inform you himself about a decision that has been made regarding your status here."

"We appreciate the elder's personal attention," Qara said.

Swift Claw did not translate her words, but continued: "The elders have held many discussions. They spoke many words over many days. It was not easy. They have decided… you are to stay with us."

"Until High Winter ends," Clanless said. "So you have told us."

Swift Claw glanced at the elder. "You do not understand. You are to stay with us. For… all times."

"You can't be serious!" Qara exclaimed.

"I… don't understand," Clanless said. "What do you mean by all times?"

Swift Claw looked down at the floor. "You will not be allowed to leave."

"They want us to stay here forever!" Qara's face turned red.

Clanless looked at the elder. "This can't be right. Why would you do this?"

"They fear you will tell others," Swift Claw said without looking up.

"We've been over that." Clanless continued to focus on the elder. "We promise not to tell anyone about you or this place."

"They do not accept your word," Swift Claw said.

"Why?" Qara demanded. "Why won't you trust us?"

Swift Claw glanced at the elder before answering: "Humans lie. This is what they believe." The elder gave a little growl. "This is what they have experienced," Swift Claw corrected.

"How can we convince you?" Clanless asked. "What guarantees will satisfy you? There must be something."

"We can't stay here," Qara added.

White Horn replied and Swift Claw translated: "There will be no more talks. The decision is complete. You will stay until your winds depart."

Qara made a disgusted noise.

"What are you afraid of?" Clanless demanded. He pointed toward the door. "Don't think I haven't noticed what's happening in the training sessions. You keep the class size small, but the students keep changing. You have many, many young warriors. Enough for a small army. And that's not including your older warriors. You have more than enough to defend yourselves. Even if we told our people everything we know, even if the Sar Empire gathered their own army and marched here… you'd still probably win!" He waved his arm. "You have soldiers. You have weapons. You have incredible hiding places with amazing defenses. Why are you so afraid?"

Swift Claw translated the speech for the elder, but before he got halfway through, White Horn interrupted with a firm rebuke. He looked at Clanless. "You have blood," he answered in a much thicker accent than the translator.

Clanless took a step backward. "The blood? Blood-magic? Really? That's what you're afraid of?"

The beastmen didn't answer.

"Blood-magic is powerful, yes." Clanless looked from Qara to the beastmen. "But not that powerful. I've fought against men using blood-magic, and I've won every time."

"Army," Swift Claw said in a low voice. "Not one only."

"I'm sure the Empire's army uses blood-magic," Clanless conceded. "But to empower an entire army with multiple blood-powers… it would… that would take…"

"It would take sacrifices," Qara said softly. "It would take people in every city and clanhold giving up blood on a regular basis. It would take a massive organization to gather that blood and stockpile it for the military's use."

Clanless froze. Was it true? They'd seen where the priests took the excess blood, according to Ghouk. He'd seen storage of blood in the city. Yet, even all that couldn't account for the quantity of blood being sacrificed on a weekly basis throughout the Empire. He'd always been told the priests used it for magic, and that the military was the primary recipient of that magic. But an entire army with the ability to use blood-magic? Even if it were only the strength and speed magic, they would be devastatingly powerful.

Daviland was doomed. His only protection was High Winter. Once it ended, the army would return. Nothing could stop them. The Hawk King might be dead, but the nobles and priests would choose a new leader, and everything would return to the way it had always been. The entire revolution was a fraud. Killing the Hawk King had been pointless.

None of which mattered now. He had to get out of here. "We will not stay," he said aloud.

White Horn's eyes shrunk. He showed his teeth.

"You must not disagree," Swift Claw said. "He is not pleased."

"I'm not pleased," Clanless shot back. "And we're not living the rest of our lives here, no matter what he says."

White Horn barked something. "The choice is not yours," Swift Claw translated.

"I will not be a slave!" Clanless snarled. "I will fight. You'll have to—"

"Stop." Qara stood in front of him and put a hand on his chest. "Don't say anything else."

He stared. "What are you doing?"

She leaned in close, and he tensed up. "Trust me," she whispered. "Don't say any more."

He took a deep breath in through his nose and let it out. He didn't say anything but glared over Qara's head at the beastman elder.

White Horn grunted. He said a few words to Swift Claw and turned for the door.

"I will return soon," Swift Claw said before following the elder out.

As soon as they'd left, Clanless pushed Qara away. "What was that?" "You were going to get us killed!"

"Better that than living here forever!"

"We can't escape if we're already dead!" she snapped. "Think, Clanless!"

He didn't answer.

"Yes, I would rather die than stay here," she said. "But if we have to die, let's do it trying to escape, instead of just telling them to kill us and get it over with!"

"You're right," he grunted.

"Besides." She glanced at the door. "You've been trying to convert Swift Claw to our cause all along. And he didn't look very pleased by what the elder had to say either."

The wait for Swift Claw's return might have been only twenty or thirty minutes, but to Clanless, it felt like hours. He paced about their small room holding the moonblade at ready. How many times had he paced like this, waiting for the arena door to open to reveal his latest opponent?

Life had been simple in the arena. He trained. He fought. He lived. He hated it, but it was simple. Since Ghouk dragged him away, everything had been so confusing. Everyone still wanted to control him, but they no longer fell into simple categories like master, fellow slave, or opponent. Or maybe they did. Which one would Swift Claw be, then? Fellow slave or opponent?

When the translator did return, he entered with head down. "My friends," he began, "I am sorry. They do not know you."

"But you do," Qara said. "What can we do, Swift Claw? Can you help us?"

"I have spoken to them three times. They do not honor me."

"Then we will not honor them," Clanless said. "We will leave on our own terms."

Swift Claw looked at the door. "You must not say this."

"I will say it. And you will help us."

Swift Claw took a step backward. "I cannot! If I act against the elders, I will lose my honor."

"And if we stay here, we will lose our lives," Qara said.

"I thought I held your honor," Clanless pointed out.

The translator hesitated. "It is so."

"What does that mean, exactly? If I hold your honor, and you refuse to help me when I ask, what does it mean?"

Swift Claw's head drooped. "I cannot deny you. My honor would be gone forever."

Clanless stepped closer to Swift Claw. "We cannot stay. I will not be a slave again. You know this. Please. Help us."

Swift Claw covered his face with his hands. "It is not possible. The Lord of the Dead's wind will take your winds. And you know not where to go."

"I've been thinking about that," Clanless said. "This is the chaotic High Winter, caused by Suirel. It's not consistent. There are days where the sun shines and the wind isn't bad. We had one of those days on the way here."

"Yes!" Qara almost jumped up and down. "We could leave on one of those days!"

"But only if we're near a human shelter: a clanhold or city," Clanless added. "It would need to be a short trip." He looked at Swift Claw. "Is there an exit from the caverns near such a place?"

Swift Claw removed one hand from his face but kept the other in place. "I know exit closest to a city, yes. But that would be secret elders most want you not to know."

Clanless closed his eyes with bowed head for a moment. "Let me walk through this for you, as a suggestion." He opened his eyes and pointed up. "You can monitor the weather. I don't care how; someone reports to you or you stick your head out yourself or whatever. You wait until we have one of those clear days. In the meantime, we'll keep going as if we've given in."

"We can play our parts," Qara put in.

"When the weather is right, you can lead us to this exit and point us in the direction of the city. We give you our word we will never try to lead anyone else here. We won't try to find this exit from the outside."

"Besides, we probably can't," Qara added again. "Clear day or not, it's still High Winter out there. Snow and everything."

"Not good, not good enough." Swift Claw shook his head. "The way to city is confusing. Without guide, you would be soon lost. And the Dark Wind would come for you."

Clanless clenched his fist. "Goddess! There's got to be a way to make this work!"

Swift Claw took the other hand from his face. "Maybe. Maybe. I will think. I will speak to a friend. We will see."

"Careful who you talk with!" Qara cautioned. "You don't want the elders suspecting you."

"You are friends." Swift Claw gave a short bow. "I do not believe the elders have done right. I do not know what I can do, but you hold my honor. I will think."

"Don't think too long," Clanless said. "If you keep me here long enough, I might start thinking of fighting my way out."

Swift Claw's eyes widened. "You would do this?"

Clanless picked up the moonblade. "I will not be a slave. Not again."

"Aldan was never alone."

Kekeen held her pillow against her chest, trying to prevent a new bout of trembling. That line kept reverberating through her head, shaking her up more than Hagh's death.

Sugh had carried Hagh's body through the wind and snow back to the inn. After hearing the whole story, Koland arranged to store the body in a shed near the city wall until High Winter ended. Sugh wanted a true burial, but the frozen ground was too hard right now.

"Aldan was never alone."

Kekeen looked at her hands. No matter how much she'd scrubbed and scrubbed them to remove the blood, she still saw red. Her fingers shook, and she clasped them together. She wanted to go find Sugh and comfort him. Wouldn't that be the right thing to do? Yet how could she encourage someone when she felt horrible and horrified herself? Her father had held her and comforted her far into the night, but he thought she was just upset about Hagh's death. She hadn't told him the full truth about Zektel.

Zektel. The blood-wraith. With four words, Kekeen's whole world had been destroyed.

"Aldan was never alone."

She shivered all over again. She didn't want to, but she had to think this through. All the way through, no matter where it led.

Borde believed Daviland had been taken over, possibly by the spirit of the Hawk King. But that wasn't it. He was possessed by a blood-wraith who claimed to have been in Aldan for years. Was that really what had happened in their arena fight? The wraith left Aldan and entered Daviland? It would explain why he'd been behaving different since then.

What did the blood-wraith want? If it ruled the Empire through Daviland, what would that mean? Davil had sounded cruel, at the least. Kekeen couldn't see how this would be an improvement over the Hawk King.

She hugged the pillow again. Contemplating Daviland was a distraction, something to keep her from thinking about the real issue.

Aldan had been possessed by a blood-wraith ever since she'd met him.

Did that mean she'd… fallen in love with a wraith? Had anything he'd ever said to her been his own words, or those of Zektel? Who had said, "I love you, Kekeen"? Was it Aldan, the slave boy grown into the greatest arena fighter of the Empire? Or was it Zektel, the blood-wraith, laughing inside Aldan's body at the naïveté of this motherless girl?

"He never loved me," she whispered. "Not really." How could he? Men only liked her for her voice and her looks. She thought Aldan was different, that he saw beyond those things to her true self. That he loved her for who she was. But it was all a lie. Everything was a lie. She buried her face in the pillow, letting the tears flow again.

Aldan's mastery of the arena. His power over blood itself. It was all because of the blood-wraith, wasn't it? He'd only lost a fight when the wraith left him, not because he cared about the person singing over the battle. Everything. All of it. All lies. All fake. All deception by an evil creature.

And yet…

She lifted her face as a new thought struck her. Aldan hadn't changed after the fight. In the days she'd tended him, he'd been… Aldan. Nothing more or less than the one she'd known and loved all along.

How could that be? Kekeen rubbed her eyes. The wraith had said things, known things, that she had shared only with Aldan. So it had to have been there, possessing Aldan. But the wraith now possessed Daviland, and he'd completely changed. She'd seen the wraith's personality take over him, control him. But Aldan never behaved that way. He'd never shown this kind of attitude, let alone murderous intent.

She pounded the pillow with her fists. Everything contradicted everything else! How could she know what was true, what was real?

It was a choice. Her choice. She could choose to believe the words of a creature for whom lying seemed to be part of its nature. Or she could choose to believe her own heart—no, more than that: her own experiences, the facts of her relationship with Aldan. She knew beyond any doubt which choice she wanted to believe. But faced with Zektel's words, it was still hard.

Hagh had been one of Aldan's friends. If Zektel had controlled him all these years, why kill that friend now? Another inconsistency.

Enough. She would make her choice. She would believe what she wanted to believe until she could speak to Aldan himself. Only then could she know the full truth.

Kekeen wiped her eyes and got to her feet. She needed to go to Sugh.

She found him alone in the eating house, sitting cross-legged on the floor, far too close to the fireplace. The big man stared into the flames, but his eyes didn't seem to be seeing anything at all. His mouth moved as though talking. Kekeen couldn't make out any of the words. She came up behind him and put her arms around his neck. She almost didn't need to bend over. Sugh fell silent and didn't react for a few moments. Then he reached up one hand and patted hers.

"I am sorry you had to see that," he said. "Such things should not be done in front of women."

Kekeen almost laughed. Hadn't Sugh's entire career consisted of doing such things in front of audiences that included hundreds of women? But she thought she understood his intent.

"I didn't know him very well, but Hagh seemed like a good man," she said.

"He was the best, no matter what that filthy bas—forgive me." Sugh shook his head. Kekeen had to loosen her embrace to keep from being jostled side to side. "Hagh was the best friend a man could ask for."

"Can you… tell me about him?"

"I will." Sugh got to his feet. Together, they sat at a table further from the fire.

"I came to the Dohor perhaps a year before Clanless." He thought about it for a moment. "Maybe less. Hagh was there, and some others. But they died. So he became my friend."

"Oh." Kekeen wasn't sure how to react.

"The others were not worthy," Sugh explained. "Except Silence. I forget him sometimes. It was not easy to be friends with one who cannot talk."

"What made Hagh worthy?"

Sugh grinned. "He said what he wanted to say and did not care what I thought." He gave a short laugh. "You may think that is strange, but before I came to this city, everyone feared me. I was the biggest and strongest. Even my former master feared me. I think he was happy when the Hawk King bought my bloodbond.

"Hagh… Hagh did not fear me. I liked this. We talked a lot. We fought together. We ate together. We—uh"—he glanced at Kekeen—"went other places together. We were friends."

"True friends are a gift from the goddess," Kekeen whispered, quoting something she'd heard from her father.

Sugh smacked the table with his fist. "Just so. I am not a religious man, like Hagh. But I can believe that." He looked away and ran his fingers over his bald head. "But I do not know what to believe now."

"You get to choose what you believe," Kekeen said. "We all do. I choose to believe that… that thing inside Daviland was lying to us yesterday, about a lot of things."

"I do not know that." Sugh looked at the table's surface. "He knew my favorite scar. Only the other Dohor know that." He paused. "And a few girls. Maybe more than a few."

"It doesn't matter," Kekeen insisted. "He's evil, and we'll resist him, just like we resisted the Hawk King."

Sugh looked up. "Do you think we will fight him then?"

"I don't know. I have to find Aldan—Clanless—most of all."

He nodded. "Then I will help you."

To Kekeen's surprise, Sugh slid off his chair and knelt on the floor. "Noble lady of song," he declared, "I will serve you until we find Clanless, or you have no need of me."

Her mouth fell open. "You're not a slave any more! I'm not your master!"

His eyes twinkled. "I am not asking to be a slave. I am a free man. And I can choose my path. I choose this."

Kekeen looked around to make sure no one else was seeing this.

"Clanless is my friend," Sugh said, "perhaps the only one I have left. Since we cannot go find him now, I can help him by serving you." He shrugged. "Besides, she said it would be a good idea."

"Thank you, I guess?" Kekeen blinked. "Who is 'she'?"

"The goddess." Sugh grinned and got to his feet. Before Kekeen could ask anything else, he picked up his axe and left the room.

21

ESCAPE

Clanless couldn't be sure what Swift Claw meant about holding his honor. It might be a kind of blood-debt since he'd saved the beastman's life. Swift Claw didn't offer any further details. Could he regain his honor? Pay back the debt? Clanless didn't want to be a slave master. But he also needed to escape the caverns, and persuading Swift Claw was the only way.

Two days later, over their evening meal, Swift Claw told them: "Someone watches the weather for me."

Qara almost dropped her food. "You're going to help us?"

Swift Claw nodded with a quick glance toward the door. "When the time comes, I will come for you. Be ready always."

"We will be," Clanless promised.

No more was said until the meal ended and Swift Claw left.

"We're getting out!" Qara exclaimed.

"Assuming everything falls into place," Clanless cautioned. "We don't know when another one of those clear days will come, and if everything will be all right in here that day."

Qara leaped forward and threw her arms around him. He stiffened at first, but then relaxed. "Stop being so negative," she whispered into his ear. "It could happen tomorrow! This is the best news we've had in weeks. Just think: soon we'll be back in regular beds somewhere. And when High Spring rolls around, we can go home!"

Clanless didn't answer. When High Spring came, the Empire's military would return as well, putting an end to Daviland's rebellion. What would that mean for him? For those he cared about? His mind couldn't think of any positive outcomes.

Qara relaxed further against him. "You haven't let me hug you like this before. It's nice."

He tried to smile. "I'm trying."

She shifted, brushing a little harder against his body. "Since this might be our last night here—it's possible; don't argue!—maybe you should try sleeping in the actual bed tonight."

"Qara, I—"

"One night with me, Clanless. Aldan. Is that such a horrible thing?"

No. It wouldn't be. And he'd never been more tempted, not even with Salkhi. He'd spent every day with Qara for weeks. He enjoyed her presence, her personality, her body pressed against his right this moment. He wanted it. But… "I have hope of getting back to Kekeen now," he whispered. "I… can't."

She pushed away. "You wouldn't do it when you had no hope, either. You were always going to have an excuse, weren't you?" She stormed off into the lavatory.

Clanless sighed. He couldn't tell her how close he'd come to saying yes. So very close. He'd thought about climbing into that bed almost every night. But something always stopped him. On good days, it was thoughts of Kekeen. On bad days, it was thoughts of Uncle Sejikdi. Physical contact with anyone still bothered him, awakening irrational fears. But Qara's touch, especially just now… that was different. Only Kekeen had been able to touch him like that before.

His hand rested on the bed. It would be so easy. And no one else would ever know. Maybe.

Qara reemerged from the lavatory. She didn't look up. "Aldan… I'm sorry. I shouldn't have done that. You're a good man." She finally looked up with a sad smile. "Kekeen is lucky, very lucky, to have someone like you."

He swallowed. "Thank you," he whispered. The temptation and the opportunity faded. He couldn't very well change his mind now. With a nod, he prepared his usual spot on the floor.

Then

"Long ago, so long ago… before your ancestors' ancestors… I had a body. We all did." Zektel's voice tinkled more than usual as she spoke.

Clanless thought that sound meant she was laughing, but this didn't sound funny.

He wrinkled his brow. "But you're made of blood. Literally. How did you have a body?"

"I'm trying to tell you. This was another place. Another world."

Clanless pointed to the moon shining down on the arena. "Like that one?"

"Something like that." She sounded exasperated. "Just let me talk. Save the questions."

"All right." He glanced around. He didn't think any of the other boys would come out here, but it wouldn't hurt to be cautious. Tunt and Bain knew, of course, but he definitely didn't want Yeltek or Duurald discovering Zektel. Or any of the others, to be honest. They wouldn't understand.

"We were the children of the gods, the gods who came down to the world and found mates for themselves. We were born, like anyone, but we grew more powerful than even the gods expected. For a time, we ruled our world. No one could stand against us."

She stopped talking. Clanless waited a full minute before prompting her: "And then?"

"Then we were cast down. Destroyed. Disembodied. All our work undone. Everything we had, taken away. All because we would not bow the knee to a tyrant."

"Like the Hawk King."

"Your petty squabbles cannot possibly match the celestial conflict I am describing to you."

He flinched a little at her tone. "All right."

She waited a while before speaking again. Clanless wasn't sure whether she was doing so to punish him or because she didn't like this part of the story.

"We wandered. We had become spirits, shades, wraiths. Mere remnants of our former glory. With no bodies, we had no hunger, no thirst, no lust. But we had desire. We longed for what we had lost. We desired to rule again, to exalt ourselves to the place where we belonged, to revenge ourselves against the one who deceived us and brought us down."

Clanless wanted to ask who had done all this, but he focused on keeping his questions to himself. He wanted to hear the end of the story.

"But most of all, we longed for bodies again." She shook her head. "You have no idea what it is like to wander the plains ethereal. I said we did not hunger, thirst, or lust. But we wished that we could do those things. We hungered for hunger itself. We thirsted for thirst itself. We lusted for lust itself."

Clanless shifted uncomfortably. He didn't like the discussion of lust.

"We despaired of ever feeling again, of tasting, seeing, smelling, touching… with a physical body. Until…"

"Until what?"

"Our prison, the world on which we existed… it broke free and sailed across the universe."

"Worlds can move?"

"Your world is always moving, dearest."

"It doesn't feel like it." He pointed at the moon again. "The moon never moves."

"It's not allowed to. Your moon is a slave to your world, much like you are a slave to Kan."

"How? The goddess lives there!" He slumped. "But she's probably not real, is she?"

"Don't worry about her. She doesn't matter."

"I don't… this is all confusing."

"I'm almost done," Zektel promised. "Our world spent ages crossing the darkness between the stars. And then one day, everything changed. Your world captured ours as well." This time, she pointed at the moon. "Like the moon you know, but not always there."

"Another moon?" He rolled over on the sand until his face was only a few inches away from her form.

"Sort of. Even so, we were trapped there. We couldn't escape. Until…" She trailed off again.

"I think you like doing that," Clanless complained.

Zektel smiled. "Until your priests weakened the barrier."

"What does that mean?"

"I think I've told you enough for now. You should get some sleep."

"But I want to hear the end of the story."

Her face leaned toward him. "The story hasn't ended yet, love. You're a part of it now."

Now

Clanless woke up but didn't move. He hadn't experienced a "lost" memory for weeks now. He didn't know what had prompted the emergence of another one, but he could see why Zektel had repressed this one.

She'd been far too honest about the blood-wraiths and been forced to make him forget. The world she spoke of had to be Suirel, of course.

But she'd told him other stories about where she'd come from. At first, she'd claimed to be a part of him. She'd told so many lies. How much of this story was true? He couldn't possibly be sure.

He looked up at the bed, hearing Qara stir. It must be almost time to wake up for the day. A new day, with hope of escape. And an end to this living arrangement. In some ways, he would miss it, he supposed. He shook his head at himself. What was he thinking?

They did not leave that day, as Qara hoped. Or the next. In fact, nothing changed for over a week. They continued helping with the warrior training and pretended to be resigned to their fate.

Clanless thought long and hard about the situation with Daviland and the army. He could think of nothing good coming of their meeting. Ghouk mentioned a general, whom he believed would be loyal to the Hawk King's son. Clanless couldn't remember the name. Ghouk would have made things worse, but his death ultimately didn't make much of a difference. Once the chaos winter cleared up, the general would lead his blood-magic-enhanced army home. The army would want to keep things the way they'd always been, because of the power it gave them. The priesthood would want the same. Between those two forces, what hope did Daviland have? He possessed the city of Et-Baylak, but it wouldn't last. It couldn't last.

Looming over those problems was the mystery of Zektel and the blood-wraiths. The memory he'd just dreamed provided one motivation for them: they wanted bodies. But more than that; she'd talked about ruling a world. Did they want the same thing here? With Zektel possessing Daviland, how would it change his plans, his possibilities? What seemed hopeless might not be… but it might lead to an even darker place.

Either outcome led to more slavery. Clanless resolved to find Kekeen and escape. He didn't care where they went. Maybe back to the clanhold where he grew up, though that posed a different set of problems. Maybe the Melkute Kingdom, even though Swift Claw made it sound worse. He couldn't stay; that's all he knew.

Kekeen would still be in the city. Ever since Ghouk dragged him out, he'd wondered what she would be doing. How far would she have gone looking for him? Koland, of course, would be involved in Daviland's plans, whatever they were. If only Clanless had told them about Zektel. They would have no way of knowing about her influence or control over the rebel leader. Yet another reason to get out as soon as possible.

Clanless fretted over all these issues for hours, often descending into his own thoughts and ignoring Qara's attempts to pull him out. He wasn't depressed as he'd been earlier. Instead, he made plans, rejected them, made new ones, and generally tried to imagine every possibility.

Having outwardly accepted his fate with the beastmen, Clanless resumed his push to visit the forge. After all, if he would be spending the rest of his life here, why hide things any more? Swift Claw relayed his request to the elders multiple times. Five days after the ruling, the elders at last relented.

They stipulated, however, that Swift Claw could take Clanless—and only Clanless—to visit the forge for one brief visit. Qara was not allowed to go, as no women were allowed in the forge area. She grumbled, but accepted it only after Swift Claw promised to keep the trip short and double the guards at her door.

Swift Claw led Clanless through passages he hadn't seen before. As anticipated, the path sloped up toward the surface. Clanless's pulse quickened the closer they came.

At last, they turned a corner and arrived at the forge. Clanless stopped and stared. He'd expected a number of different things, and while many of his expectations were accurate, others weren't.

The forge cavern spread out over a wide space, but surprisingly did not have a high ceiling. This created a dark haze across the room. As he'd hoped, Clanless saw an opening in the ceiling above the primary forge fire pit. But he soon realized that climbing into it would be nearly impossible. Even if the fire were out, the sides of the chimney were coated in black ash, which would probably be slippery. As they drew closer to the fire, Clanless couldn't see the sky up the chimney; it must twist and turn. It made sense, now that he thought about it. A straight up shaft would allow snow and other debris to fall down. The beastmen also would have thought about where the smoke would be exiting, making sure it wasn't somewhere that would arouse curiosity from passers-by. Escaping up the chimney would not be an option.

With that thought thrown out, Clanless took time to satisfy his curiosity about the actual forge. Three or four beastmen moved through the haze, hard at work on various tasks. The largest of the group hammered red-hot metal on a stand vaguely resembling an anvil. As Clanless watched, the beastman dropped his hammer, picked up the metal with a pair of tongs, and thrust it back into the nearby fire.

"They will do this many, many times," Swift Claw said. "Look here." He pointed to a table by the wall. Clanless stepped near and looked down at six new scimitar blades, all without handles. As he'd noticed with other scimitars he'd seen here, every one of them was unique in shape, size, and serrations.

One of the beastmen smiths approached and said something while looking expectantly at Clanless. "He wishes to know if you would like your weapon sharpened and polished," Swift Claw translated.

"Oh. Sure." Clanless glanced around to make sure their guards were still present before he handed the moonblade to the smith. The beastman said something to Swift Claw, then hurried off to another workstation. Clanless watched him through the haze, amused to see the smith start by carefully measuring every part of the moonblade. Were they hoping to duplicate its design? He imagined a dozen beastmen armed with moonblades, charging into battle. That would be a sight to see.

"Have you questions?" Swift Claw broke into his thoughts.

"Yes. Why are the weapons all different?" Clanless pointed to the scimitars. "We make special weapons like mine for arena fighters, but the rest all look mostly identical." He thought of the maces carried by guards and soldiers he'd seen.

"Each weapon is a… Mmh. I am not sure how to say it. An art?"

"A work of art?"

"Yes. Work of art. Something special. Since a weapon may decide your life or death, it must be a part of you. So each may choose his own from those available." Swift Claw drew his own scimitar and displayed it. "Each choice is for life."

"You never trade it in for a different weapon?"

Swift Claw cocked his head. "Why would we do that? The weapon is for life."

Clanless watched his moonblade being sharpened. He'd never thought about it in that way, but he never felt right when the moonblade was apart from him. "Life or death," he repeated.

Swift Claw picked up a piece of unused metal from near the forge. "This will be a weapon someday."

"Where does the ore come from?" Clanless gestured at the walls. "From here?"

"No, no. The ore comes from deep, deep in the Formation. It is not easy to find. Then combined with other things to make stronger."

"Our smiths do something similar." Clanless watched the various processes for a while longer. Yes, human smiths worked metal in a similar way, but the first beastman scimitar he'd encountered had put a chip in his moonblade. They were obviously stronger somehow. He wished he knew more about these processes, about what made the difference.

After the smith returned his polished and sharpened moonblade to him, Clanless thanked them all and let Swift Claw escort him away. He hadn't discovered all that he'd wanted at the forge, but it had been a learning experience all the same. He hated going back to the waiting.

And then the day came.

☽☽☾☾●☾☾☾☾

"The wind blows not," Swift Claw announced.

Qara slid off the bed. "Does that mean what I think it means?"

Swift Claw nodded and glanced toward the door.

Clanless picked up the moonblade. "What about the guards?"

"Two will stay here, to protect your space," Swift Claw said. "The other two will come with us until I tell them."

"They'll abandon their job?" Qara pulled on her coat.

"When I tell them," Swift Claw repeated.

Clanless didn't quite understand what the translator meant, but as long as it worked, he didn't care. He had no desire to fight any of the beastmen unless it became absolutely necessary.

"Follow." Swift Claw beckoned.

Clanless look one last look around the room they'd spent weeks in. Perhaps months now. He'd lost track. As his eyes wandered over the bed, Qara nudged him. "Missed your chance," she whispered. He smiled and followed Swift Claw.

At first, they traveled through familiar passageways. After all this time, Clanless knew much of the way around the caverns, or at least the parts they'd visited on a regular basis. He'd paid attention, considering his own plans for escape. But having a guide made things much simpler, especially when Swift Claw turned an unfamiliar corner and the tunnel began to ascend. The gaps between lanterns became further, creating larger regions of darkness.

Swift Claw stopped and spoke with the guards. They nodded and stationed themselves where they stood. Clanless wondered what Swift Claw had told them. He hoped they wouldn't get into too much trouble over losing their assignments.

The further they traveled, the more the temperature dropped. Their own room had grown cold enough. If the surface were even colder than this, they would have to travel fast. Even without wind, the cold would make survival difficult enough.

"We are here," Swift Claw said after two more turns. He pointed to a solid wall. "Door is there. Are you certain?"

"We're not turning back now," Qara answered.

Swift Claw glanced at Clanless, who nodded. The beastman went up to the wall. He concealed his movements with his own body. Whatever he did, the cavern rumbled. The stone wall rotated to the right. A rush of even colder air blasted into the cavern. But with it came sunlight. Clanless caught his breath. The surface. They'd made it.

A shout came from behind. Clanless spun and saw four beastmen approaching from below. Wind Tooth, the warrior trainer, led them. Clanless braced himself and readied the moonblade.

Swift Claw stepped in front of him and put a hand to his chest. He turned to Wind Tooth and spoke rapidly. The other beastman answered in kind. Swift Claw punched both of his fists to his chest and pointed at Clanless while he answered. White Horn shook his head and put a hand on his sword hilt.

"What's happening?" Qara asked.

Swift Claw exchanged a few more words with Wind Tooth before turning back to them. "Wind Tooth knows of the elders' decision. He has come to stop us."

"We gathered that much." Clanless kept his eyes on Wind Tooth.

"I have explained that you hold my honor," Swift Claw hastened to add. "He understands this and will not try to stop me. But he will stop you."

"How does that make any sense?" Qara shook her head. "Men."

"It is honor." Swift Claw put both fists to his own chest again. "Wind Tooth would lose his honor if he allowed you to violate the elders' decision."

"So we have to fight."

"Yes." Swift Claw pointed at Wind Tooth. "He will fight you. If you win, we may leave. If he wins, we return. And all retain honor."

"What about the others?"

"They are young. They have no voice. Wind Tooth's word is all that matters."

Clanless took a step forward. "Take Qara out of the way."

Swift Claw again put a hand to Clanless's chest. "Not here. Wind Tooth understands. A tunnel fight is not good." He pointed to the door. "You will fight out there."

Clanless stepped past the door into the open air for the first time in weeks. He took a deep breath and savored it, though the frigid air chilled his throat. His eyes darted at once to the heavens. The moon held its usual position, dominating the center of the sky. But Suirel, the chaos moon, remained visible as well. The sun hung low in the east, beginning its pursuit. A breeze carried the chill of High Winter, but only a few small clouds drifted across the pale blue sky.

Snow dominated the ground-level view everywhere he turned. The landscape looked much as it had during their carriage trip with Ghouk. Here and there, a tuft of brown grass managed to extend its reach above the ever-present whiteness. A haze hung over the horizon, obscuring the view of a mountain range in the far distance.

Clanless kicked the snow aside. He bent and touched the ground with one hand. He dug his fingers into the cold earth, relieved to feel something other than solid rock.

"Are you prepared?" Swift Claw asked.

Clanless straightened and looked to the others. Swift Claw and Qara stood with the three young beastmen. Wind Tooth walked a dozen yards away and turned back. He drew his sword and called out.

"Wind Tooth is prepared," Swift Claw translated.

"I will not return to the caves," Clanless said. "If I lose, I die. Please take special care of Qara for me. Do not… don't let anything happen to her that she does not approve."

"It is a charge of honor," Swift Claw said. "I will do it."

"Aldan…" Qara stepped forward.

He waved her back. "Don't say anything else. I'm pretty sure I'll win here, but you have to be ready if I don't."

"No. I can't. Don't you dare lose a fight on me now."

He smiled. "When have I done that?" He turned away before she could bring up the fight with Daviland. He lifted the moonblade into the air. "Let's go!"

He jogged forward. Wind Tooth lifted his own sword high and charged, shouting a war cry. Clanless recognized the charge; the first beastman he'd fought in the arena had done the same. If Wind Tooth used the same strategy… Sure enough, Wind Tooth dropped both hands down into the snow. He flipped into the air, his clawed feet outstretched toward Clanless.

But this time, Clanless knew what to expect. He sidestepped at the right time and swung the moonblade at the leaping beastman. Somehow, Wind Tooth twisted in mid-air to avoid the full slash. But the tip of the moonblade scoured across his right side. Qara cheered from her vantage point.

Clanless pivoted and slipped a few inches in the snow. He had little experience with this type of surface. A couple of times, Orgina had staged a special winter battle in the snow-filled arena in Ghoyor. He'd fought well enough then, but low audience turnout kept those events from becoming a regular thing.

Wind Tooth advanced with more caution. Clanless reminded himself this was no ordinary warrior. Wind Tooth taught the younger fighters. This was like fighting Kan or Badaar, neither of which he ever wanted to face. The beastman would not go down easy.

Clanless feinted to the left as his opponent drew close. Wind Tooth didn't take the bait, keeping his eyes fixed on Clanless. The beastman slashed low. Clanless stepped back to protect his legs and countered with his own slash at mid-body. For a few moments, the combatants repeated this process in a series of attempted attacks, neither connecting.

Clanless activated the Taint out of habit, but Wind Tooth barely flinched. Except for the one possessed by a blood-wraith, none of the beastmen had been strongly affected by the Taint. He still couldn't figure out why.

When their fight slowed enough for the fighters to split apart and circle one another, Clanless felt the cold again. His lungs burned for some reason. He'd expected them to be cold instead. He took deep breaths, trying to calm his body.

Wind Tooth scooped up a huge ball of snow in his left hand and threw it at Clanless. Despite knowing it was only snow, he couldn't help blinking and jerking his head aside. In that moment, Wind Tooth lunged forward. Clanless twisted to his right, dodging the outstretched sword. But Wind Tooth's left hand also came forward and scratched at his stomach. Clanless grunted at the pain. He'd had worse, but four deep cuts across his stomach would slow him, especially if the fight lasted long enough for him to bleed too much. It wouldn't make travel easy if he won, either.

He put a hand to his stomach and staggered back, exaggerating the seriousness of the wounds. Wind Tooth took the bait, rushing to take advantage of his weakened opponent. At the last moment, Clanless seized the moonblade with both hands and slashed it upward in a ferocious strike just as Wind Tooth's attack arrived. The moonblade's edge cut into the beastman's right forearm, almost splitting it in half.

Wind Tooth howled and stepped back. His sword fell into the snow. Blood poured from the useless arm.

Clanless adjusted his grip and took a step. But Wind Tooth held up his left hand and barked something.

"Honor is served!" Swift Claw shouted, running to join them.

The younger beastmen hurried to Wind Tooth's side and encouraged him toward the tunnel. Swift Claw traded some more words with all of them as Qara arrived and examined Clanless. "That's bad," she whispered. "I'll try to heal it for you later, when they're not watching."

He nodded. Now that he wasn't moving, the cold air cutting through his torn clothes bothered him more than the actual wounds. "Are we free?" he called to Swift Claw.

The translator turned back to them as the other beastmen disappeared into the ground. "We must go."

Clanless took a deep breath. Would this be the fourth day of freedom? "Lead the way."

Part Three
SUIREL

COVENANT AS ONE

From that day on, Sugh stayed near Kekeen wherever she went. For most of the time, she rarely left the inn and eating house. High Winter kept them inside most of the time. On the days where it let up, Kekeen didn't find many reasons to leave. She considered trying to visit Borde, but sneaking in to the palace would probably be much more difficult now. She didn't want to risk getting anywhere near Daviland, especially with Sugh following her. One of them would end up dead.

Sonkogh kept them updated on the council doings. Not much seemed to be happening there, either. High Winter kept Daviland from executing any of his plans.

And then the red dress arrived. Gogeku entered the eating house one afternoon, followed by his assistant, a stone-faced young woman. She carried something wrapped in leather. Once inside, she set it on the nearest table and dusted the snow from its surface.

"Kekeen, my dear, I have the loveliest news for you," Gogeku called.

"What is it?" She approached the tailor with curiosity.

"Despite my many, many other pending jobs, I have managed to complete… this!" He gestured with a dramatic flourish, which ended up being wasted since the assistant hadn't finished unwrapping the item. Once she finished, the girl swept out a gorgeous red dress and held it up for Kekeen's perusal.

Kekeen's heart skipped a beat, and she put a hand over her mouth. Even though she knew who had sent it, she couldn't help it. The dress was so much finer and more beautiful than anything she'd ever owned. A base layer of almost pure red fell to ankle-height, covered by a second layer of darker, embroidered red with gold and blue highlights. The neckline was a little more daring than she'd normally prefer, but she could wear a scarf or heavier coat over it… and maybe Aldan would like that.

She closed her eyes and shook her head. "No," she said with effort. "I can't accept it."

"W-what?" Gogeku stammered. "But it's yours! Commissioned by Daviland. He provided me with a complete set of your measurements and everything!"

Kekeen winced. The blood-wraith knew her measurements. The creepiness of the idea made it easier to reject. "No, take it away."

"What's this?" Sugh appeared and took the dress from the passive assistant. He held it up much higher and shook it a little. Gogeku whimpered and lifted a finger, but didn't say anything.

"It's from Daviland," Kekeen said. "Well, from the one who looks like Daviland, anyway."

"What?" Gogeku bit his finger.

"It's very nice," Sugh said. He brought it down and tossed it to Kekeen, much to Gogeku's wide-eyed disbelief. "You will make it nicer."

"I can't keep it. It's from the wraith."

Sugh shrugged. "It's a nice gift. You might use it sometime to get into somewhere they wear nice clothes."

Kekeen started to answer but stopped herself. Sugh made a good point. How many times would it have been helpful to look more like a member of the upper class? She didn't have to wear the dress for Daviland, after all.

Gogeku looked back and forth between them. "Ah, so does this mean you will be keeping it?" he asked in a hopeful tone. "My cousin would be displeased if I returned with it, you know."

Kekeen draped the dress over her arm and smoothed it out. "Thank you, tailor. I know you did amazing work, regardless of where it came from."

Gogeku brightened, made quick farewells, and hurried out before she could change her mind again.

Sugh wandered back toward the fire, muttering something to himself or the goddess.

Kekeen spread the dress out over the table again. It really was quite lovely. Wearing it, she would look like a member of the upper class. Or at least the women that hung around the upper class, like… the girls of Pasque House.

Despite her resolution to believe in Aldan, that part of Zektel's accusations still hurt. It had troubled her for weeks, since Daviland first mentioned it in Aldan's room. Even that early, Zektel had been trying to hurt her. She would have dismissed the whole thing as a lie, except... She'd confronted Sugh about it, and he'd reluctantly admitted the Dohor's regular visits to that place.

Kekeen traced the dress's neckline with her finger. Aldan had always been so cautious with her, physically. It didn't make sense. How could he be... like that... with another woman? Maybe those were the times when the blood-wraith did take control of him! Maybe Zektel had the favorite, not Aldan. Not really.

She sighed. She could make up as many theories as she wanted, but... "I made my choice," she told herself. She would believe until Aldan gave her reason not to.

She swept up the dress and took it back to her room. She had work to do.

Weeks passed with little to mark them. When the weather did let up, people crowded into the eating house, giving them all plenty to do. On those nights, Koland earned their keep and then some.

Kekeen started to sing again. She joined her father at least every other night on the stage. She could only bring herself to perform songs with a sad theme, especially ones about lost love. To her surprise, these turned out to be insanely popular with the locals. More and more of them braved High Winter's cold to visit the eating house. Somehow, word got out that she had sung at the arena when the Hawk King fell, and many came just to see her and ask about that day. She deferred to Koland to tell the story, which he handled with pleasure.

And then Sonkogh informed Koland that he would be receiving a special guest the next day...

)(((●)))

Swift Claw knew exactly which way he wanted to go and started at once, setting a rapid pace. Qara and Clanless struggled to keep up. They pushed their way through far too much snow. Though the wind remained nothing more than a breeze, the deep cold cut through their clothing.

"How far is this city?" Qara asked after about half an hour of this.

Swift Claw glanced toward the sun. "Not too far. Some hours perhaps."

"Hours!" Qara looked back at Clanless. "I'm sorry. We need to stop and let me treat Aldan's wounds. Maybe you could scout ahead, check out the best path?"

Swift Claw paused. "Yes. Good. I will look ahead." He hurried away.

Clanless pushed snow from a large rock and leaned against it. Qara hurried back to him, pulling a vial of blood from one of her pouches. "There's more than enough of your blood here to be a catalyst," she murmured. "It should work right away." Clanless leaned back and let her pour the Clan Kurav blood on his wounds. He clenched his teeth against the immediate pain, worse than the actual injury.

Qara cut off part of his hanging coat and wrapped his stomach. "They didn't close all the way. I don't understand."

"Maybe the blood lost some of its potency," Clanless suggested.

"That doesn't happen," she argued, "not if it's sealed in crystal. Maybe I did something wrong."

Clanless pulled himself upright. "Or maybe it's me. Maybe it just doesn't work as well on me as it used to."

Qara's eyes widened. "That's terrible! You wouldn't be able to fight any more without risking serious injury!"

He chuckled as he adjusted her bandaging. "I'm hoping to avoid any more fighting, you know."

They started following Swift Claw's steps. "Would you ever go back?" Qara asked a few moments later. "To the arena, I mean. If it was as a free man. You know, to earn your own blood. For yourself."

"No." He shook his head. "I have no desire to see the inside of an arena ever again."

"It was your whole life for so long," she pressed. "That doesn't pull at you, even a little bit?"

He hesitated. Qara couldn't know about the bloodrush, of course, and how much he enjoyed it. "Just because I'm good at something and… well, just because I'm good at it doesn't mean I want to do it. I suppose I do want it, somewhat, but only because it's what I've always known." He looked up. "Kind of how I missed the moon while we were underground."

Swift Claw bounded across the open land in front of them, scattering snow in all directions. "Moving again? Good. We must hurry. The Dead Lord's Wind could return at any time."

Clanless and Qara did their best to accelerate their pace. "What will you do, Swift Claw?" Qara asked. "Once we reach the city. Will you go back to the formation?"

The beastman did not answer for a few moments. "Mmh. I can return. Wind Tooth knows my honor. But others would not believe. I will not be welcome with some."

"You are welcome with me always," Clanless said.

"I would not be welcome with your people. Less welcome."

Clanless stopped walking. Swift Claw turned to him with a cocked head. "Hear me," Clanless said. "I will not forget what you have done for us. If not for you, Qara and I would be dead long ago. We owe you everything."

"I hold your honor?" The concept seemed to catch Swift Claw by surprise.

"If that is how you see it, then yes."

Swift Claw cocked his head one way and then the other. "We must cut," he said at last.

Clanless wiped frost from his face with his glove. "What does that mean?"

Swift Claw nodded rapidly. "When we stop again, we will cut. You will see." He hurried on, not waiting for them to keep up with him.

At one point, the beastman left them to struggle on together while he raced away into a large area of the protruding brown grass. When he returned much later, a small, dead animal hung from his belt. It looked like a rabbit. He said nothing about it, but kept moving, guiding them on through the desolate land.

The steady pace helped with the cold, but not nearly enough. More than once, Clanless experienced the temptation to stop and rest, maybe even sleep. And if he felt it, Qara must be feeling it much more. As the sun began its surrender after midday, he called out to Swift Claw: "I don't think we can keep this up for much longer."

The beastman paused. He pointed ahead. "We stop soon. Rest. Make the cut."

A few minutes later, he led them onto the surface of an enormous flat rock. Exposed to the sun and wind, very little snow clung to it. Clanless and Qara gratefully sat down, relieved to be off their feet. The cold seeped into their bones. Clanless glared at the sun, shining as bright as ever. Why didn't it provide heat? Yet another reason why no one talked about the sun's stability.

Swift Claw busied himself a few feet away. He cleared any last vestiges of snow, then set the dead rabbit on the rock. He drew his sword, positioned the rabbit at a certain angle, and cut it in half lengthwise, nose to tail.

"He isn't going to ask us to eat that, is he?" Qara whispered.

"You know as much as I do," Clanless answered.

Swift Claw pulled the two halves of the dead animal apart, leaving a gory mess of blood between them. He stood and looked down at it, shaking his head. "Not much. Should have three. But one will do for now." He turned around and extended a hand toward Clanless. "Now?"

Clanless set the moonblade aside and got to his feet. "What are we doing?"

"We cut." Swift Claw lowered his head and turned it from side to side as if searching for something. "Covenant!" he burst out. "It is covenant."

Clanless had a vague idea of what he meant. "We're making a covenant? An agreement with each other?"

"Yes. Agreement. But more." He pointed at the dead animal. "Blood seals."

"How so?"

Swift Claw gestured. "Walk through. Better if more, but this is all we have for now. I go first." He walked between the two halves of the animal, making sure that both his feet contacted the blood on the rock. As he did, he held out his hands toward the halves. Once through, he turned and came back the same way. "Now you."

"What am I agreeing to?" Clanless asked. "I don't fully understand what we're doing."

Swift Claw pointed down again. "Blood seals." He pointed to Clanless and to himself. "We make covenant. Hold each other's honor for all time."

The seriousness of the ceremony struck Clanless. Swift Claw wasn't doing this lightly. This was a pledge, one man to another, a blood pledge. For all time? His chest grew tight, and he swallowed. No one had ever offered him something so significant. He imitated Swift Claw in walking through the blood. As he did, his eyes focused on the dead animal's unseeing eye. Maybe the walking symbolized more? A way of saying only death could break this bond? Or should break it. There didn't seem to be any magic involved, like a bloodbond.

He returned through the blood and stopped. "What now?"

"It is done. We are as one."

Qara snickered. "You're married?"

Swift Claw recoiled. "No. No. You do not understand. We are as, as brothers."

"Works for me," Clanless said. "Blood brothers, I suppose."

"Yes." Swift Claw nodded. "Blood brothers. We hold each other's honor. Cannot be broken." He looked toward the sun. "We must keep moving now."

"Sure." Clanless turned and bent to pick up the moonblade.

"You have no idea what you've just done, do you?"

Confused, Clanless turned back, but Swift Claw was already moving away. Had he imagined that final question?

"I was getting too cold sitting still, anyway," Qara said, following after the beastman.

Clanless joined her, and they continued walking through the frozen wasteland.

((((●))))

"There it is." Swift Claw stopped and pointed.

Clanless bent over to catch his breath first. Then he joined Qara in peering ahead. Just ahead, the ground dipped, leading into some lowlands. Here at last, they saw more plant life. The slope and the lowlands were dotted with scrubby trees, most no taller than Clanless himself, all of them bare and seemingly lifeless. But far in the distance, a frozen river wove its way through the scrub. And straddling it stood a walled city. From this distance, Clanless couldn't tell its size, but it had to be a major city to be seen from this distance.

"Do you know it?" he asked Qara.

"I'm pretty sure it's Ulken," she answered. "It's the only one that I remember to the north and sitting on a river."

"Ulken." Clanless didn't remember much about that particular piece of the Sar Empire. It had an arena, one of the top eight outside of the capital. Beyond that, he couldn't think of anything else.

"It will be night before we get there," Swift Claw said. "Not good."

Qara hugged herself. "The temperature is already dropping."

"The sun has almost finished its retreat," Clanless noted. "We need to hurry."

"I don't think we're going to make it," Qara murmured as they started down the slope.

Indeed, as the shadows deepened, the air grew more and more frigid. Before long, Clanless knew it had to be at least as cold as the evening when the beastmen found them. He and Qara could not make it all the way to the city in this.

"Swift Claw! We need heat or we'll die!"

The beastman paused and turned, frost cracking from his fur. He hesitated before answering: "You are right. We must make a fire."

At least they had fuel available. All three of them worked to gather branches from the ground and snapping them off the barren trees. Swift

Claw led the way to a sheltered place where the rock formed a low semi-circle. The beastman produced flint and soon made sparks fly. It took far longer than the humans wanted, but in a few minutes, the fire blazed up. They crowded in as close as they dared, letting it warm their extremities.

"We must stay all night," Swift Claw said after a few more minutes.

Clanless considered their options. They could attempt to make it the rest of the way to the city after warming here. But the warmth would fade in minutes, if not seconds.

"The city gates are probably closed," Qara said. "We might not be able to get in at night."

On the other hand, if they stayed here, they would have to keep this fire going all through the night. And they had no guarantee the wind and snow would not suddenly return, dousing the flames and their hopes. Neither option offered more chance of success than the other.

"We stay," Swift Claw repeated, making the decision. "The fire will burn all night."

Qara settled herself down. "I've never slept on the dirt before. But after this day, I'm more than ready to try it."

"Go ahead," Clanless said. "Swift Claw and I will keep the fire going."

"We will take turns," the beastman said.

Clanless could not remember a longer night in his life. He and Swift Claw sat beside the fire, taking turns tending it and dozing. Every so often, one of them would have to gather more fuel. Each time he stepped away from the flames, Clanless thought he would freeze in moments. He worked as fast as he could and rushed back to the warmth. The longer the night progressed, the colder it became. Even the warmth of the fire diminished. How cold could it get? In his sleep-deprived mind, Clanless imagined the fire itself freezing into tongues of red and orange ice.

Shaking his head and blinking, he checked on Qara. She slept fitfully at first, but toward the middle of the night, she settled into a deeper slumber. Clanless worried she might fall into one of those sleeps from which she wouldn't awake. He touched the skin on her face from time to time, making sure it stayed warm. If her condition changed, he would consider using the Taint on her again.

And so the night passed, hour by hour. Neither he nor Swift Claw felt inclined to speak. Between thoughts of cold and heat, Clanless considered what might happen the next day, his fifth day of freedom. Despite his assurances earlier, he knew it would not be easy to convince people to accept Swift Claw. They would have to make some kind of arrangements to keep him hidden most of the time. And then he could come along when

Clanless took Kekeen away from everything.

He looked across the fire at the beastman, who stared into the flames without expression. He still didn't fully understand the meaning behind the strange ceremony earlier, but brothers… that he could understand. It would be nice to have a brother. But of course, he did have a brother, far away in a clanhold with his parents and sister Ot. And his uncle. He closed his eyes. No. It wasn't his responsibility. He couldn't think about that now.

He looked up toward the moon. The sight of her, long denied, comforted him. He always preferred her steady glow at night, when she needed no shield against the sun. But the presence of Suirel, dimmer than before but still visible, added an uneasy element. He didn't like to think too hard about the cosmic forces in play either. He had enough troubles down here.

Dawn, the beginning of the sun's pursuit, arrived far later than Clanless ever would have expected. He and Swift Claw stoked up the fire one last time, then woke Qara. "You'll have to watch for a little while," he told her. "We need some rest before the final hike."

She nodded, blinking slowly. "Of course," she murmured. "We made it this far."

Clanless pushed some rocks and sticks out of the way to stretch out on the ground, facing the fire. His last thoughts, before losing consciousness, were of the city in the distance. He felt he should know something more about it, something he'd forgotten long ago…

☾ ☽ ☾ ☽ ● ☾ ☽ ☾ ☽

"Clanless! Aldan! Wake up!" Qara's voice penetrated the haze within his mind. His eyelids, like frozen weights, struggled to open. "Hurry," she hissed. "I think someone's here!"

Clanless inhaled the chill air and jerked himself up. His hand grasped the moonblade. He pulled himself up to his knees and reached out to shake Swift Claw. The beastman murmured and lifted his head.

"That's far enough!" a voice called out. "You won't be needing that fancy sword!"

Clanless jerked his head around, searching for the source of the voice. Swift Claw jumped to his feet, claws at the ready.

"Whoa, whoa, whoa," the voice exclaimed. "That's a beastman there!"

Another voice, this time from above their sheltering rock, called back, "Do you know how much Chuluun will pay us for that one?"

"Who are you?" Clanless demanded. "Show yourselves!"

A figure stepped out from hiding among the small trees, not far away.

With the bulky clothing, Clanless couldn't tell what kind of man he might be, but the leather sling dangling from his hand commanded attention. A good slinger could take a warrior down before he could take three steps.

"There are five of us here, friend," the man said. "Don't try anything."

"Oh, thank the goddess!" Qara exploded. She stumbled toward him. "You're here to rescue me! Thank you, thank you!"

The man took a step back. "Wait right there, lady. What are you talking about?" He moved the sling out of her reach, but held it ready to go.

"This man, and his, his pet," she babbled, waving at them, "they've kept me here. You can't imagine. Please, take me back to the city!"

Swift Claw growled at the betrayal. Clanless leaned toward him. "It's all right," he whispered. "She's trying to deceive them."

A second man stepped into view not far from the first, also with a sling poised to launch. "I think we might get a good bounty for the man too," he said. "Or at least his sword. That's fancy."

The first man took a step closer, peering toward Clanless. His eyes widened. "I know that sword! Only one man in the Empire has a sword like that!"

"Sands!" came the voice from above again. "He's got the wolf thing too. You don't think it's him, do you?" Clanless glanced up to see the speaker looking down at them, another sling at ready.

"Only one way to find out." The first man pointed at Clanless. "Show me your right shoulder, stranger."

"I don't think I should."

"We've got five good slings aimed at you two. I'd rather bring you in alive, but there's blood to be made from your dead bodies too."

Clanless considered the odds. He and Swift Claw might be able to charge the two in front, especially if Qara distracted them. Five stones would fly. While they wouldn't all hit, depending on the skill of the slingers, two or more probably would. And those kind of wounds could be enough to stop them, or even kill. Even if they survived the first round and took down the two visible hunters, the other three would have time to attack again. It wasn't worth it. He lowered the moonblade to the ground. With both hands, he pulled his clothing apart to reveal the brand on his right shoulder.

The hunters erupted. "It's him!" "Clanless!" "What is he doing here?" "I saw him fight once."

The lead man raised one hand to silence the others. "We'll take them both in. Keep your eyes on them all the way back. They're dangerous."

"Thank you," Qara exclaimed. "Thank you so much." She paused. "I can come with you, can't I?"

He barely spared her a glance. "Sure, lady. Whatever you need."

Swift Claw looked at Clanless. "What are we to do?"

"We don't have much choice. We'll go with them." He covered his shoulder again. "I'm sorry. This is not going to be pleasant. I should not have got you into this."

Swift Claw put a hand on his shoulder. Clanless didn't flinch. "We are as one. Whatever happens, we face it together."

So much for day five.

FAMILIARPLACES AND FACES

Kekeen held the door as their guest swept into the eating house, his blood-red robes in stark contrast to the snow billowing in around him. The Ghamba Lam stopped and sniffed, removing his gloves as he looked around.

"It's not what you're used to, I'm sure," Koland said, approaching. "But we welcome you, nonetheless."

"Not at all." The Ghamba Lam wiped frost from his face. "I grew up in a much smaller city far from here. I've been in much more disreputable locations."

"Then please… have a seat."

Once the Ghamba Lam had seated, Koland sat across from him. Kekeen offered to bring them something to drink, but the priest turned her down. She sat at the end of the table, in hearing range, but not close enough to claim a place in this meeting. Sugh stood behind her, arms folded across his chest.

The Ghamba Lam brushed more snow from his robes and took a deep breath. "Thank you for agreeing to meet with me."

"It's not a problem at all," Koland said. "I am very curious to hear the reason for this. I've never had much of a relationship with the priesthood."

"You were part of Daviland's rebellion and the subsequent advisory council. You also led a raid on some of my blood stores the night before the Hawk King's fall."

Koland's eyebrows went up. "I suppose there's no use denying that last part."

"I knew all about it. I wanted it to happen. The Hawk King had grown dangerous and was toying with some dangerous ideas."

Kekeen kept herself from exclaiming aloud. The Ghamba Lam had wanted the Hawk King removed?

"Unfortunately," the priest went on, "Daviland has proven no better. He is considering some of the very same ideas. And the consequences could be devastating for the entire Empire."

"You'll have to be much more specific," Koland said.

"High Winter draws near to a close." The Ghamba Lam held up a hand. "I know. Perhaps you would not call it 'near.' But we are over halfway through. It is at this time every year that I must make a trip."

Kekeen's ear perked up.

"I am already overdue, thanks to the… severity of this winter. But this trip is absolutely necessary. I must make a delivery to the almaz mines to the north."

"When are you going?" Kekeen burst out.

The Ghamba Lam started. "Soon," he said, with a glance at her. "It is a trip we make four times every year, without fail."

"Can we go with you?" Kekeen clenched her fists. Could such an opportunity just drop into their laps like this?

"Kekeen, let's hear the rest of his concerns," Koland said.

The Ghamba Lam seemed perplexed at the request. "I… yes. At any rate, the problem is Daviland. He is suggesting on a near-daily basis that he will go with us."

Koland frowned. "That seems reckless. Didn't we have a discussion about this in one of the earliest council meetings?"

"Exactly! Not only does it serve no good purpose for him, it takes him dangerously close to General Ghan, the one man who can put an end to his reign." Before Koland could respond, the priest kept going: "More than that, he's dropped hints that his very purpose might be to disrupt our work there!"

Koland tapped his beard. "And what might that be?"

The Ghamba Lam hesitated.

"It is where they take the blood," Sugh broke in.

The priest's head jerked to look at him. The moon emblem on his necklace clattered against the table. "What?"

"Your priests explained it all to us. They were very friendly once we stopped trying to kill them."

The Ghamba Lam stared. "When did this happen?"

"It seems we are in possession of information you did not know," Koland said. "Ghouk took the Dohor to the almaz mines. Fortunately for all of us, he died there."

"Tell me more." The Ghamba Lam leaned forward.

"First, you tell us more. Why is this so important to you that you would take a trip during High Winter? Why not schedule it at a less difficult time?"

"It is vital to our world. We must replenish the blood store there." He glanced at Sugh.

"You pour it down the Throat of the Goddess," the big man said.

"But why right now?" Koland repeated.

"It would be better at a different time, of course," the Ghamba Lam admitted. "In fact, the schedule used to allow for that. But the disruptions caused by your rebellion and the threat of the Melkute Kingdom required changes in the schedule over the past year. And now it is absolutely necessary."

"But why?" Kekeen burst out. "Why is it necessary to take the blood there?"

The Ghamba Lam looked down.

"It is a valid question," Koland said. "If it is this important, we should know why."

The Ghamba Lam put his palms together and touched them to his face. "The blood protects us. I have tried to explain this to Daviland. Without the blood..." He hesitated before continuing: "Without the blood, evil would be unleashed on our land such as no one alive has ever seen. The blood makes certain this does not happen. So it has been for centuries."

Kekeen traded looks with her father. He had to be thinking the same thing she was: Suirel? The blood-wraiths?

"That is all I will say on that matter," he went on. "I have told you more than anyone outside the priesthood knows. Please do not spread this. There is no need to cause a panic among the lower classes."

"Of course," Koland said. "There are already a thousand theories about what happens to the blood you collect from sacrifices and the arenas as it is. Even if I were to speak of this, it would be but one more."

"Now. Tell me more of Ghouk," the Ghamba Lam insisted.

Sugh told what he knew, taking obvious delight in delaying his words to frustrate the Ghamba Lam. When he concluded, the priest drummed his fingers against the table. "So you say two of the Dohor—Clanless and Bain—remain unaccounted for?"

"We could not find them."

The Ghamba Lam leaned forward, staring intently at Sugh. "Could they have gone down the Throat?"

Sugh scratched his head. "I couldn't say. We didn't go down it." He looked at Kekeen. "It was not a pleasant looking place."

"Think carefully," the Ghamba Lam said. "Was there any evidence they went that way?"

"I don't know. It's possible." He frowned. "No, maybe not. We did find a dead beast in one of the tunnels that they killed. Probably Clanless, Hagh said. It bled a lot."

The Ghamba Lam relaxed. "I am relieved to hear that. There is no more dangerous place on this world for Clanless to be."

"Why is that?" Kekeen demanded. "Why do you say that?"

"If Clanless were to use the Taint—his power—down there..." He shook his head with a shudder. "All the blood we could bring would matter not. He would destroy the very thing protecting us all."

"Then all the more reason we need to find him! Please, your grace, can we travel with you to these mines?"

He stared at her. "Have you not been listening? The very reason I'm here now is because Daviland wants to travel with me! He is not pleased with any of you. There is no way to conceal you from him on such a journey."

"Let's get back to that," Koland said. "I'm still not clear on why you came to me about this. What do you suppose I can do? As you said, Daviland is not pleased with me. I can't convince him not to go."

"Maybe not with your words." The Ghamba Lam rubbed his hands together. "Is it always this cold in here?"

"The inn must conserve its firewood stores, like most of the city at this point," Koland explained. "Since you come from a 'smaller city,' I would think you would remember that."

"Of course, of course." The priest glanced around the room. "As I said, I don't expect you to talk with him. But throughout the rebellion, you all showed a predilection and impressive ability to, ah, take matters into your own hands to prevent certain outcomes."

Koland closed his eyes for a moment. He took a deep breath. "People have called me a master of words at time. But I don't think I could have ever come up with the words you just used to describe what I think you're saying." He chuckled. "Are you suggesting some form of sabotage?"

"Whatever is necessary."

"I'm afraid I fail to see a way that could succeed just now."

"Your blood is worth more. You people were quite creative during the rebellion."

"Yes, but…" Koland glanced at Kekeen and Sugh. "The most obvious form of sabotage would be to damage or destroy the carriages or wagons for the trip, but you need those. How could we stop him without stopping you?"

The Ghamba Lam threw up his hands. "How should I know? Treat him as you treated the Hawk King!"

Silence fell. Koland sat back and tapped his beard. "Are you saying what I think you're saying?"

The priest looked at Sugh and made a point of lifting his eyes upward to see all of the fighter. "It seems you have one of the mightiest warriors in the Empire right here. One with very special talents, I might add."

"That's enough." Koland put his hand flat on the table. "Despite what Daviland has done lately, I spent more than two years at his side. I have to believe the man I knew can come back. I will not be involved in any assassination plot."

The Ghamba Lam folded his arms across his chest. "I am afraid you have misunderstood me. I would never suggest such a thing."

"Of course you wouldn't."

The priest got to his feet. "It appears I have taken too much of your time. At the very least, we exchanged information that may be of use to the other."

"Indeed." Koland also stood.

"If you do… think of anything that may help with this situation, do be sure to take action on it."

"I will think long and hard about your words," Koland promised.

"That is all I can ask." As he pulled on his gloves, the Ghamba Lam looked again at Sugh. "Such a shame," he murmured almost too quietly to be heard.

Kekeen narrowed her eyes. He meant something more by that, more than just his failed assassination idea. But before she could ponder it further, the Ghamba Lam pulled the door open, unleashing a fury of wind-driven snow. Once he exited, they worked together to clean up the mess.

"We have to find a way to get there," she told her father as they finished.

"I'm not arguing with you. I saw something in the Ghamba Lam I've never seen before."

"What was that?"

"Fear. Whatever he thinks could happen at the mines, it goes far beyond whoever rules the Sar Empire."

The last stage of the journey was the most miserable. The hunters took the moonblade and Swift Claw's sword and marched the two prisoners ahead of them. Five slings remained ready to launch at their backs the entire time. Qara trailed along behind. The hunters were so excited about their prospective payment, they didn't much care about the woman.

The walk from their shelter to the city itself took close to two hours. Midway there, the wind started to pick up. Clouds gathered overhead. By the time they reached the city gates, the glacial wind was unbearable, sweeping a few snowflakes along before it. High Winter wanted them inside.

Clanless gathered as much information as he could from observations. The city of Ulken appeared larger than Ghoyor, but nowhere close to the enormity of Et-Baylak. Its walls were at least as thick as either of them and might be taller. The open gates seemed smaller in proportion to the walls itself, but a second set of closed gates to the right drew Clanless's attention. The city had been built atop a river flowing down from the mountains and southeast toward the sea. He'd noticed that much from a distance. Now he observed gates across the frozen river, at least twice the size of the ground-based gates. Metal spikes descended from the lowest part of the gate into the ice. Clanless guessed the spikes were meant to prevent enemies from swimming under the gates when the river wasn't frozen, but he had no more time to examine it.

Once inside, they gained shelter from the wind, but the temperature continued to drop. Instructed by their captors, Clanless and Swift Claw followed the empty streets to a huge arena. Somewhere along the way, Qara slipped away. Clanless breathed a sigh of relief when he noticed her absence. Qara was smart. She'd find a way to survive in this city, and possibly even a way to get back home.

To Clanless's experienced eyes, the Ulken arena had seen better days. In size, it didn't quite rival Et-Baylak, but came closer than any other he'd seen. Yet everywhere he looked, he saw patchwork repair jobs on the walls, the stands, and even some of the doors. Some of the work looked ready to fall apart. Either this arena wasn't earning its blood, or the owner didn't feel it necessary to spend on upkeep.

The hunters escorted their prisoners through one-such battered entry and down a disheveled and dark hall. The lead hunter met a young man, spoke briefly, and sent him running away. "We can wait here," the hunter announced. The others spread out, but kept their slings at ready and their eyes on Clanless and Swift Claw.

The young messenger returned, followed by a tall, severe man who leaned on a cane. He stopped and stared at the captives. "What have you brought me, Gucukur?" His voice matched his looks: firm and sharp.

The lead hunter displayed the moonblade. "It's Clanless, Chuluun. We found him and this beastman outside the city."

The arena owner pointed at Clanless. "The shoulder. Let's see it."

Clanless didn't move. One of the other hunters stepped forward and yanked his clothing to the side, revealing the brand.

"Clanless." Chuluun shook his head. "The most famous arena fighter in the Empire. What are you doing out here?" His eyes wandered to Swift Claw. "And in such interesting company."

"I am a free man," Clanless said. "As such, I can travel wherever I want, with whoever I want."

"Is that so?" Chuluun's expression didn't change. "When did this supposed freedom occur? You were still in the Hawk King's arena before High Winter began."

"I fought my last fight on the day the sun surrendered. I've been a free man ever since." He glared at the hunters. "Your men here had no right to take us prisoner."

"No? Whether you gained your freedom or not, you are clearly in violation of the law." Chuluun leaned on his cane as if he couldn't survive without it. "Your branding is a lifelong requirement, and as such, must always be exposed. You were brought here with it covered, disguising yourself. The priests will demand a punishment for this violation."

Clanless didn't answer.

"Yes." Chuluun nodded. "I think you will make me a good deal of blood. What better way to celebrate the end of High Winter than arena fights featuring the mighty Clanless." He paused. "And a beastman too. Very well done, Gucukur. You know who to see for your reward." Throughout the conversation, Chuluun's voice never altered its tone or volume.

The hunter bowed and backed away. A group of soldiers carrying maces, presumably the arena's own guards, surrounded the prisoners.

"I will not fight for you," Clanless declared. "I am a free man. You don't have my bloodbond."

"There are other ways to compel a man. You will fight when I tell you to fight." Chuluun shook his head slowly. "I made a mistake in not buying you when you graduated from Kan's training. I thought I needed someone larger then." He stretched out his cane and tapped Clanless in the chest. "But I see your muscles have grown along with your reputation. Ah well. I expect you'll make up for my mistake in time."

"I am not a slave." Clanless clenched his fists.

Chuluun gave a short wave. "We'll see. Och! Take the beastman to the lower pits. Put this one… in the chains."

"Stay strong!" Swift Claw shouted before the guards crowded around him to take him away.

Clanless struggled against the guards who seized his arms. He knew it was pointless, but he couldn't help it. They dragged him through halls and down two flights of stairs before throwing him into a dark cell. He scrambled back to his feet. A fist slammed into his face, and his vision blurred. Before he could react, a second guard punched him. He flailed back at them, without success. In the darkness, he couldn't tell how many guards crowded into the cell, but every one of them seemed intent on leaving him a reminder of their presence.

Once they'd beaten him enough for their desires, they pulled him up. Two guards held his right arm up in the air while a third locked a manacle around his wrist. They did the same with his other arm and attached his legs to something. He blinked, trying to clear his vision while he worked his bruised jaw. He couldn't see much through the swelling around his left eye. Blood leaked from multiple injuries. The chains held him high enough that he could choose to put his weight on the balls of his feet, which barely touched the floor at an awkward angle, or let it hang from his wrists. Either way was unpleasant, to say the least.

Chuluun appeared at the cell door, accompanied by a pair of larger figures Clanless couldn't make out. Arena fighters?

"We'll leave you here until you've lost some of this unnecessary resistance," the arena owner said. "I hope you'll give in before the chains do too much damage."

Clanless pulled at the chains with all his available strength. Nothing happened, of course.

"It really is him," said one of the fighters. "I never thought I'd see it."

"Yes." Chuluun turned to go. "I thought you would be interested, seeing as how you're old classmates, after all."

Classmates? Clanless squinted with his good eye. He couldn't make out much about the fighter. He looked very large, maybe Sugh's size.

"Ha! You thought you were something, didn't you, taichin? Not so tough now, are you?"

Yeltek? No. Yeltek wouldn't be that big, and his voice wasn't that deep. "Duurald," he realized.

"Yeah, it's me. Had to think about it, didn't you? You never were the brightest."

"Compared to you, I was the pursuing sun." Clanless didn't know what made him taunt the other man, but Duurald hadn't ever brought out the best in him years ago.

"Shut up!" Duurald punched him. Clanless's head snapped back. More blood oozed from his battered face. Something bled inside his mouth too. He spat some out.

"You're good… at beating a defenseless man. Surprised you've survived this… long."

"I hope they let me fight you in the arena!" Duurald snarled. "I've come a long way since training!"

Clanless lifted his face and gave Duurald a bloody grin. "You might remember… I had a trick or two back then. And I've had eight years to get better at it."

"You're nothing!" Duurald shouted. "I don't need taichin tricks!"

"Duurald," his companion finally spoke. "Leave him. It's not worth it."

"Eh, you're right." Duurald jerked his shoulders in an odd manner before turning to disappear into the darkness. "We'll have a reckoning, Clanless!" he called back.

Clanless let his weight sag against the chains for a few minutes. The pain in his arms was worth the relief to his legs, at least for a little bit. Blood dripped from his face to the floor, pooling on the stone. What a disaster this had turned into. At least Qara was free. More blood gathered in his mouth. He spat it onto the growing puddle.

"Use the Taint." The thought came to him like an audible voice. He blinked and glanced around. None of his tormentors had returned… and none of them knew his power by that name, as far as he knew. Where had the voice come from?

He looked down at the puddle of blood and snorted. Why not? With a thought, he activated the Taint. A spark flew from the pool, fading as quickly as it appeared. And then a face formed in the dark red liquid.

Clanless jerked hard, yanking the chains fiercer than when he'd first tested their strength. Panic surged through him.

"Relax," said the face in the blood with a distinctly deep male tone. "I'm not Zektel."

"Who are you? Where did you come from?" Clanless spat the words out, spraying more blood from his mouth.

"I said relax. I've been here a while, but now it seems like we really need to talk."

Clanless didn't answer, glaring at the face as best as he could with one eye.

The blood-wraith sighed. "Listen, Aldan. Things aren't looking good here. I thought you could use some help."

"I don't need help from a wraith."

"Of course you don't. And you absolutely haven't been wishing you could talk with Zektel for the past few weeks."

Clanless didn't want to answer, but he coughed. More blood pooled beneath his tongue.

"See that? You're bleeding inside somewhere. The beating probably brought back your old wound from the Daviland fight. That's not going to help you in whatever fight they force you into here. Especially if you spend too much time strung up like this."

"Who are you?"

"You can call me Yul. It's close enough. I've been with you for... oh, two and a half years, I think. Remember the barbarians?"

Clanless closed his eyes. "Zektel... said there was another wraith there. You were in the barbarian leader."

"And when you killed him, I decided to join you. I'd been controlling him for four years. I needed a break."

Clanless struggled to understand. He'd had two blood-wraiths inside him all that time? A horrible thought struck him. How could he trust any of those new memories now? If Zektel had been hiding them, maybe this wraith had done even more...

"I've only spoken to you a couple of times," Yul said. "I haven't done anything else. I've never tried to control you... can't, anyway, with that wolf pelt. And I've never messed with your head. That was all Zektel. And you, of course."

In the distance, Clanless heard a groan. Someone else lived down here. Maybe they'd brought Swift Claw. He considered yelling, but decided to save his strength—what little remained.

The wraith's words made a kind of twisted sense. He did remember moments where he'd heard a voice, or thought he had. And then there was the odd memory of the two words: "I'm staying."

"You stayed when Zektel left."

"Yes. I told you I needed a break. You remember how Zektel told you we crave bodies?"

"Because you lost yours."

"Something like that. I felt that way for… oh, for generations." Yul's face rolled side to side. "But I grew tired. It's a lot of effort to control someone against their will. I'm not ready to try that again."

Clanless snorted.

"I'm not!" Yul insisted. "I've been content just to ride along, to observe the strangeness of your mortal life. And the violence that comes with it. I do enjoy that part. But I've left you alone."

"Not any more?"

"Well, you're all alone. I thought you might want someone to talk to."

"I'm not interested… in the words of a blood-wraith." He knew enough about them now.

"Yes, you are. You've lost everyone else. And you hate being alone."

Clanless kept his mouth shut.

"Unfortunately, I have more bad news for you. You think things are bad now? They're going to get a lot worse if Suirel gets his way."

"I don't care."

"You should. I know there are still people you care about. Kekeen, of course."

"Don't talk about her."

"Pick any of your other friends then. Hagh. Bain. They're all going to die, if they aren't dead already."

Clanless coughed again. "So glad you're here to cheer me up."

"Did I say I was here to cheer you up?" The face shifted rapidly. "No, I'm here to motivate you. Whatever this place has planned for you, you need to deal with it and get back to the mines."

"The mines? Why?"

Yul's face faded. "Your friend Bain. You shouldn't have let him do that."

Clanless shifted to put weight back on his feet. "This is pointless."

"No, it's not. I've introduced myself at least. You know I'm here now."

"I don't… want you here."

"I still don't believe that." The face faded a bit more.

"How do I get rid of you?"

"You can't get rid of one of us unless we want to go."

"What about the beastman?" Clanless coughed again. "I drove a wraith out of him."

"Yes," Yul acknowledged. "And yet Zektel and I stayed when Daviland did the same to you, didn't we?"

Clanless didn't answer. He struggled to think clearly through the pain from his face and chest. There would be no healing for him down here.

"I may be able to help you out here," Yul said after a minute had passed. "I think I've already figured out a few things about this Chuluun and the way he handles things. Unless you think you can do everything without me."

Clanless's good eye sagged closed. "I don't know," he admitted. "There's a lot I don't know now."

"Good. If you can say that, then we can work together. I'm not as devious as Zektel, but I do believe I can contribute." He paused. "Oh. You're not going to be conscious long enough to continue this conversation. That's all right. We'll talk more later. I'm looking forward to it. It's… good to finally speak with someone again. I rather like it."

RETURN TO THE ARENA

Then

"Zektel… I'm scared."

The face in the blood bubbled as it shifted. "Now why is that, dearest?"

Aldan shifted, trying to ignore the horrid smells in this room. "I don't want to die. But this graduation thing they're talking about… a lot of us might die. Except Nerleson, of course. He's crazy."

"We've talked about this, remember? You're going to be the best. You don't have to worry about it."

"Yeah… I'm still scared."

"Do you trust me, Aldan?" Zektel's face faded.

"I… think so. I haven't known you that long."

"Trust me in this. Your fear will go away. I'll help with that."

Aldan wrinkled his brow. "How?"

"Don't worry about it. You should get back to your bed before the other boys notice you're gone."

Aldan pulled himself up to his hands and knees. "But—"

"I told you not to worry. Go to sleep. When you wake up in the morning, you won't even remember being afraid. I promise."

Now

The chains rattled as Clanless shook awake. He'd only dozed off for a few minutes, but another memory returned. Huh. Zektel had hidden his memories of being afraid? Not all of them, of course. He could remember being afraid many times. But his earlier fears during training… Maybe that explained how he'd advanced so well facing boys like Nerleson and Yeltek. And Duurald. Maybe his presence is what triggered the memory.

After a few hours, the guards let him down from the arm manacles, but left his feet chained to the floor. Grateful, he curled up on the filthy ground to get some more sleep. After weeks of sleeping on the floor in the beastmen caverns, he didn't care about the comfort level. His injuries, however, kept his sleep from being truly relaxing. He woke often and suddenly when a burst of pain shocked his system. In those moments, he thought he saw the blood-soaked figure in darkness again. Maybe he saw himself, considering how he felt.

No sunlight trickled down to his cell, which he assumed to be somewhere below the arena. When he did wake up for good, he had no idea of the time. By the light of a distant lantern, he noticed a metal plate with some bread and a cup of water on the floor. A guard must have brought it while he slept.

He had just finished the bread when a door opened down the hall. Several figures entered and approached his cell. He blinked against the brighter lights. His left eye remained swollen, but a trickle of light came through it. He recognized the slender figure of Chuluun and his cane. Duurald towered behind him.

"I assume you've had time to think over my offer?" the arena owner asked.

"Which offer was that?" Clanless asked.

"You will fight for me."

"And in return?"

"I won't turn you in for hiding your brand." After a pause, he added: "And I won't have you outright killed."

"What about Swift Claw?"

Chuluun showed no visible reaction. "I'm afraid I don't know that reference."

"The beastman who came with me. What about him?"

"Ah. What is your concern with that creature? He will fight as well."

"Let us fight together," Clanless suggested. "The two of us against all challengers."

Chuluun tapped his cane on the stone floor. "You are hardly in a position to negotiate."

Clanless pushed himself up and stood. "You want me to fight for you, so you can attract a big crowd."

"An enormous crowd, I rather think."

"Of course. But think about the draw. The mighty Clanless and his beastman companion: the undefeatable combination!"

"Is it your pet?" snorted Duurald.

"No. He's my friend, a concept you've never understood, Duurald." Clanless shifted his gaze to Chuluun. "Keep us together, and I'll fight for you without complaint."

Chuluun studied him. "And how long do you anticipate this arrangement lasting?"

"You tell me. You're the one with the power here."

"Hm. You're trying to appeal to my ego. It might be an effective strategy if I cared about things like that." He tapped his cane on the floor again. "Even so, you're not inaccurate. Very well. You and the beastman will fight together."

"I want him brought to me."

"No. He is restrained elsewhere. I cannot risk moving him about this place. You will see him when it is time." He snorted. "And now you have influenced my language in referencing the creature like a person. Well done." He turned to go.

"We won't be at our best if you keep us locked up like this until fight time," Clanless called after him.

"We'll discuss that another time." Chuluun left the way he had come, followed by Duurald and the others.

Clanless slid down the wall and sat on the floor again. That had gone better than he expected. At least he would get the chance to fight with Swift Claw. He'd been worried the beastman would get the same treatment as wild animals in the arena: a show for the masses only until death, which would be certain.

Unfortunately, Chuluun had given no indication of how long he expected them to fight. If the arena owner had his way, Clanless would never leave. Even if he died here, Chuluun would come out ahead. He'd paid a ransom to some hunters and gained arguably the greatest attraction his arena would ever see. The hunters' reward could be nowhere near the price of a slave, let alone what it would normally cost to capture and restrain a beastman.

There had to be a way out of this. Clanless would have to disguise his intentions, work to gain trust, and then make his escape. But doing so with Swift Claw would be much harder. Chuluun would never relax security on a beastman. Clanless gritted his teeth. He needed another option.

He glanced at the metal plate. It reminded him of the many times he'd spilled blood in just such a plate for summoning Zektel. Maybe Yul could help him think… No! He didn't need a blood-wraith. In fact, he needed a way to get rid of a blood-wraith. Yet another problem.

The door opened again, spilling light back into the hall. Clanless looked up. A meal already, perhaps?

A single guard entered, holding a lantern. He peered into the cell. "Better make yourself presentable again," he said. "You've got another curious visitor."

Clanless tried to roll his eyes, but his left one hurt too much. "What now?"

"It's the personal assistant to Lady Chinua. She's one of the big patrons of the arena, so be on your best behavior."

Clanless snorted. "Could you set out the zokin and flatbread? I haven't had the time."

The guard cocked his head. "Flatbread? You're a strange one."

"Show her in. I know how the game is played."

The guard retreated through the door. Clanless watched the open doorway with some curiosity. It wasn't the rich lady herself, but an assistant. Maybe she wanted an eyewitness to confirm his presence before she came herself to see the curiosity. He wondered if she helped run this city the way the three Lords of Et-Baylak ran theirs. In any case, she had become another factor to be considered in this game, as he'd just called it. A sympathetic rich woman could be a powerful ally.

The guard returned, leading a woman in a sparkling blue dress covered with a thick fur pelt around her shoulders. She shook snow from it as she approached, keeping Clanless from seeing her face.

"Here he is, my lady," the guard said, holding the lantern high and stepping to the side.

"Oh, good. I was hoping we wouldn't have to go much deeper into this rank place. Really. I doubt my mistress knows about the inhumane conditions down here. I will be sure to bring them up."

Clanless got to his feet and tried not to show his surprise. The woman lowered the pelt so he could see the face he already expected from the voice: it was Qara.

"Hmmm. How do I know this is really Clanless the arena fighter?" she asked the guard.

"There's his brand. Hey you! Show the lady your brand!"

Clanless somehow kept from smiling as he pulled his clothing aside to reveal the mark on his shoulder.

"Yes, well. That does seem definitive." Qara fanned her face. "This smell is quite overwhelming. It's even in my mouth. Be a good man and fetch me some wine, would you? I need something to wash it out."

"I can't leave you alone with him!"

Qara fanned herself more, making an irritated sound in her throat. "What do you think I'm going to do? Break open his cell door, snap his chains, and run away with him into High Winter?"

The guard looked confused. "No, my lady. But he—"

"I will be fine," she cut him off. "He's not going to ravish me from behind the bars. Please. My tongue cannot handle this much longer."

He nodded and hurried back to the door. "I'll be right back." He stopped and looked down at the lantern in his hand. "Um."

"Leave the light," Qara ordered.

The guard set the lantern on the floor and stumbled through the doorway.

Qara turned swiftly back to Clanless. "I don't know how far he has to go to find wine, so we'll need to talk fast."

"I don't suppose you are going to break open the cell and snap the chains?"

"No more than you're going to ravish me. You had plenty of chances for that already. The best I can do is give you some hope. At least for now."

He shook his head. "I want to ask how you did this, but I shouldn't be surprised. You've always been resourceful."

"I'm glad you recognize that at last. I would love to brag about how I got in here, but that would probably use all our time."

"Chuluun is going to make Swift Claw and me fight in his arena," Clanless said in a hurry. "I don't see any way out of it just yet."

"I know. Word is already spreading through the city. He'll probably stage your first appearance soon. He might not even wait for High Winter to end." She glanced toward the door. "That's why I need to hurry. I'm going to Et-Baylak."

"How?"

"Have you forgotten how Ghouk took us north already? There are ways to travel, even in High Winter." She stepped close to the cell door. "I'll be back with help as soon as I can, Aldan. I won't leave you here."

"Find Kekeen and Koland. They have Daviland's ear and—"

"I know what I'm doing, Clanless." She reached through the bars. He took hold of her hand. "You kept me safe from Ghouk, from the monsters, and the beastmen. I'm not leaving you here to die."

"Thank you, Qara." He swallowed. "I, I don't know what to say."

"Tell me you'll stay alive until I get back, you big idiot."

"I'll do my best."

She looked at him, staring into his eyes with an expression… an expression he didn't want to acknowledge. He knew what it meant. He released her hand.

"I…" She swallowed. "I'll be back."

The guard appeared at the door with the wine. Qara turned and swept past him.

The cell felt much colder once she left.

((((●))))

For the next several days, Clanless did what he could to exercise within his cell. His injuries didn't make it easy. If he were going to fight, he needed to stay as ready as he could. The guards brought better meals as he showed no signs of causing trouble. The food was simple and bland, but substantive. After two days, they even removed the chain from his feet. After three days, a blood-priest entered and threw some healing blood on him. It made a difference, but some aches, especially in his gut, remained.

After spending only one day outside, Clanless hated being shut off from the moon and sun even more. He kept track of the passage of time by the regularity of his meals. He hoped the guards were maintaining a schedule and not randomly delivering meals when they felt like it.

One day, after at least a week had gone by, five guards entered his prison at once. "You're to be taken topside for exercise," one of them informed him. "The weather is clear enough and Chuluun wants you to get some practice."

"How considerate of him." Clanless waited while they opened the door. For a brief moment, he considered whether he could seize one of their weapons and fight his way through. Conceivable, but… he would be abandoning Swift Claw.

The guards escorted him up the two flights of stairs and through halls until they exited a large opening into the arena itself. "You have two hours," the lead guard said, "or until the snow returns." He and the others backed away.

Clanless looked to the sky and sighed. The clouds hid the moon, but he could tell the sun's pursuit was well on its way. Mid-morning. His meal schedule was accurate. Little wind reached down this far right now, thankfully. A few flakes of snow drifted until caught by short gusts that sent them spinning across the arena.

Relieved, he took some time to stretch and examine his surroundings. This was the actual arena, not a training ground like in Et-Baylak. The floor looked to be about the same size as the arena in Ghoyor. He shivered from the cold, but as he exercised, that wouldn't be a problem. Someone—slaves, presumably—had pushed all of the snow to the sides, leaving huge piles all around.

A weapon rack stood nearby. Clanless checked it and found a collection of maces and swords of varying sizes, none of which were high quality.

"Hey, what about my moonblade?" he called to the guards. "The crowds will expect me to use it."

"Chuluun says you'll have it when the time comes," the guard answered. "Until then, you are instructed to use these."

He'd assumed as much, but it didn't hurt to ask. Clanless selected a two-handed sword, roughly the size of his moonblade, from the rack and took a few practice swings.

At that moment, shouts came from the guards. A few moments later, they shoved Swift Claw out into the arena. The beastman snarled at them, but then noticed Clanless. "Wolf Chosen!" He bounded across the sand and greeted Clanless with a bowed head that almost smacked him in the chest. Clanless took a step back. He considered embracing Swift Claw, but he'd never seen the beastmen hug one another. It might not mean the same thing in their culture. Instead, he lowered his head in the same way.

"Are you all right?" Clanless asked. "Have they mistreated you?" He looked over his friend and didn't see any obvious injuries until he reached his legs. Both of Swift Claw's ankles showed signs of tight shackles. Clanless frowned.

"They have. But it is well. I am well. I am pleased to see you."

"I'm pleased too." He glanced toward the crowd of guards inside the opening. "They let us out here to exercise. I suggest we do, but we can talk at the same time."

Swift Claw nodded. "They intend for us to fight then?"

"Yes." Clanless positioned himself to start a practice session with the sword. "But I've convinced them to let us fight together."

"Mmh. That is good. We are covenanted. We will fight well." Swift Claw looked through the weapons and selected a short sword. "But should we not try to escape?" He waved toward the door. "They could not stop Wolf Chosen and Swift Claw."

"Maybe not." Clanless started his progression. "But they would not be the only ones. We would have to fight many more. And if we did get out, what then? We couldn't hide in this city anywhere. We don't know anyone here. We can't go back out in the wilderness. And we can't go back to your people."

Swift Claw swung the sword a few times. "Then we will die well."

Clanless stopped. "I'm sorry, Swift Claw. This is all my fault."

"Your fault?" Swift Claw cocked his head. "You command these men?"

"No, no. That's not what I mean."

"Then it is not your fault."

"If you hadn't been with us, you wouldn't have been captured. I got you into this."

"It matters not. I chose to help you. I chose to covenant. They chose to, ah, catch us. And now we all choose to fight."

Clanless stepped close to him and lowered his voice. "Listen, Qara got away. I spoke with her, and she's on her way back to my home to get help."

Swift Claw's mouth and eyes grew wide. "Your woman will fetch your tribe?"

"Uh, something like that. I don't know how long it will take. If we can survive until then, we can escape all of this."

"Then we will live, not die." Swift Claw ran a few feet and leaped into the air, swinging his sword in a wide arc as he did.

Clapping came from the door. Clanless turned and saw Duurald approaching, gloved hands smacking together. "I'm shocked the thing knows what a sword is!" he declared. "Watching you two fight is going to be more interesting than I thought."

Clanless swung the sword onto his shoulder. "Care to start early?"

Duurald scowled. "The master won't let me fight you yet."

"Oh? Does he think you're not good enough? Do you need a bunch of other people to fight me first, wear me down?"

"You—!" Duurald waved a finger at him but cut himself off. "You are trying to goad me into attacking you," he said more calmly.

"Maybe." Clanless resumed his exercise. "Is it working?"

Duurald watched Swift Claw, who continued to run and leap about. "Until now, I didn't know taichin had powers over the beastmen too. How do you do it? What magic do you use?"

Clanless sighed and lowered the sword. "Duurald, can I be honest with you?"

The other fighter looked at him with suspicion. "What do you mean?"

"I'm not a taichin, or whatever fairy tale word you want to use. I have the one trick I can do with blood, and that's it. The priests didn't like it, and that's why I ended up in the arena."

Duurald played with a lock of his own hair. "Why are you telling me this?"

"Because you and I? We survived, Duurald. We survived Kan's training, his graduation, and eight years in the arenas. Not many people can do that." Clanless pointed at him. "The fact that you're standing here today, alive, proves how incredible you are."

Duurald grunted, but Clanless could see the praise had an impact. Maybe only a small one, but he could try. He'd persuaded Swift Claw with words; maybe he could do the same here.

"Listen to me. Daviland killed the Hawk King right before High Winter began. I don't know if that news has made it here yet. But it means all the slaves are being freed." He pointed to himself. "I'm a free man, Duurald. You can be free. Free of all of this." He waved at the arena.

"Ha." Duurald snorted a laugh. "Chuluun has never freed a slave in his life. He won't release our bloodbonds on the word of some upstart."

"That upstart rules the Sar Empire now."

Duurald's whole face wrinkled up. "I don't… Ugh. What difference does it make?" He pointed toward the luxury box. "Chuluun has my bloodbond here and now. He's the master. I do what he says or pay the consequences."

Clanless glanced up at the box. He thought he could make out a shadowed figure standing there. Between Bain's stories and these past few days, he was starting to understand how incredibly fortunate he'd been the day that Orgina bought him from Kan.

Swift Claw came to a stop next to him, panting. "Wolf Chosen. Is this one to practice with us?"

"No, I think Duurald was just leaving."

Duurald looked at both of them, snorted again, and walked away.

"He is a warrior, yes?" Swift Claw asked.

"Yes. Someone I knew long ago." Clanless shook his head. "Come on, let's work up a sweat. It's too cold out here."

❨❨❨●❩❩❩

The guards allowed Clanless and Swift Claw to exercise for two more days after the first. On the third day, Duurald approached them again after their workout.

"Chuluun is pleased with your work and obedience," he reported, almost mechanically. "You'll be fighting in three days."

Clanless looked around at the softly-falling snow. "It's still High Winter!"

Duurald shrugged. "He's not willing to wait for good weather. He's done this before. We'll have one or two special Arena Nights." He paused. "Which aren't really nights, I guess. We fight when the sun's pursuit is ending."

"Midday," Clanless clarified for Swift Claw. He looked up at the stands. "There will be crowds here in the cold?"

"To see the mighty Clanless and his beastman pet?" Duurald snorted. "Chuluun is convinced they'll come."

Clanless didn't feel convinced himself, but three days later, he had to admit he'd been wrong. As he and Swift Claw stood just inside the arena entrance, he could hear the size of the crowd. He looked back at the group of heavily armed guards behind them. "What about our weapons?"

"They are there." Swift Claw pointed out into the arena. The moonblade and the beastman scimitar stood protruding from the sand about a dozen feet out.

Only a few snowflakes drifted down from the overcast sky. Every so often, a sudden gust of wind would send them swirling horizontally instead. Cold as he was right now, Clanless knew the battle would soon warm him up. It would be nice if Chuluun would let them use the baths afterward, but he doubted that kind of privilege would be forthcoming.

"And now the fight you've been waiting for!" The presenter's blood-magic enhanced voice echoed across the arena. "From Et-Baylak comes the arena fighter of this age, the wielder of the massive moonblade, tamer of beastmen, and hero to the common man… Clanless!"

The crowd roared. Clanless gestured to Swift Claw to follow and jogged out to get the moonblade. "Remember what I told you," he said as they retrieved their weapons. "Ignore the noise, the presenter and the crowd. Focus only on the opponents. We're here to survive, not give them a show." He was telling himself as much as Swift Claw. Despite everything, he felt the thrill of the upcoming fight. The crowd chanted his name as he'd heard so many times. Almost against his own will, he lifted the moonblade into the air for them to cheer even louder.

"It will be well," Swift Claw said, raising his voice to be heard. "We will fight as one."

"Let's see what they have for us."

Clanless separated from Swift Claw, standing a good ten yards apart as they watched the opposite entrance. Clanless didn't expect anything serious this time. Chuluun wanted to bring in a lot of blood from them. He wouldn't make it deadly from the start.

Six armed men emerged from the other side, advancing with care. Three carried maces and shields, two carried two-handed mauls, and the last wielded a long spear. Clanless watched their movements as they approached. These were not trained soldiers or arena fighters. Most likely, they were prisoners or even volunteers desperate for a chance to earn some blood. He had no way of knowing exactly. Either way, he couldn't afford to show mercy if it endangered him or Swift Claw.

"Which one?" Swift Claw asked.

"Plan two." In their handful of exercise days, Clanless had established six plans of attack for them to use. He started to circle toward the right while Swift Claw bounded away to the left.

As anticipated, the attackers weren't sure which opponent to move against. Clanless didn't blame them. Should they try to attack the acknowledged greatest arena fighter in the Empire or the mysterious and frightening beastman? The spearman shouted to his fellows and apparently convinced them the beastman would make the easier target. He and three of the others moved toward Swift Claw. Two of the shield-carriers kept facing Clanless but moved backward after their comrades.

Swift Claw raced toward them and leaped from a full dozen yards away. He spun in the air, sword and claws outstretched. He arced over the spear and crashed into two of the others. With a roll across the sand, he leaped back to his feet and raced away, having accomplished nothing more than shallow cuts on the two he'd hit.

But shallow cuts were all Clanless needed. He lifted a hand and dramatically brought his fingers together in a fist as he activated the Taint. The two enemies collapsed, screaming, much to the delight of the crowd. Four more to go.

It felt good to unleash the Taint, but Clanless cursed himself for the extra dramatics. Why entertain the crowd? He'd gain nothing from it. Chuluun hadn't even given him a Siphon to gain his own blood portion after the fight.

Swift Claw circled back to his left, and Clanless continued to advance toward the two shield-carriers. The spearman was shouting something again.

Heart pounding, Clanless breathed faster and faster. The bloodrush was already taking over, and he hadn't even engaged anyone yet. Did he truly miss this life that much?

In that same moment, Clanless felt something else awaken. Even though Swift Claw had moved out of his sight, he had sudden and exact knowledge of the beastman's location. The pounding of his own heart was matched by an almost simultaneous pounding of another. As Swift Claw moved faster, so did he. What was this?

Clanless shouted as he closed the distance to the two opponents in front of him. Swift Claw bellowed as well, charging straight at the spearman.

Clanless swung a two-handed blow that knocked one of his opponent's shields aside. At the exact same moment, Swift Claw swung a one-handed uppercut that sliced the point from the spear. They fought in sync, almost mirroring each other's moves. The crowd erupted as they realized what was happening.

"That's a beautiful thing," a deep voice said within him. Yul. Clanless had tried to forget about him.

"Is this your doing?" Clanless asked before dodging a mace at the same time Swift Claw dodged a thrust from the broken spear.

"Not at all. I wish it were," Yul answered. "What a delightful potential for destruction the two of you have together."

Clanless wanted to ask more, but he had no time for talking. A slash of the moonblade took down one of his immediate opponents. He rolled to the right to avoid a counterattack from the second. Swift Claw also rolled, though only to gain distance on his opponent.

The beastman regained his feet, ran a couple of steps, and leaped at the spearman. Clanless also leaped, a strategy he would ordinary never have tried, and brought the moonblade down with a powerful overhand strike. Even with his shield, the fighter couldn't withstand it. He collapsed beneath the blow even as the spearman collapsed beneath the shredding claws of the beastman.

"What… is… happening?" Clanless gasped, standing over his foe.

"I think this is that covenant thing your friend talked about," Yul said within him. "You'll 'fight as one,' remember?"

Only one opponent remained, standing between Clanless and Swift Claw. Seeing the fall of his comrades, he took a few steps backward. He dropped his maul and fell to his knees, pleading for mercy.

Swift Claw started to advance on him. Clanless felt pulled in the same direction, but he resisted. "No!"

The beastman paused and looked toward him. "Do we not finish the fight?"

"He's beaten. We won."

Swift Claw pointed a bloody finger. "He still lives."

"We don't have to kill them." Clanless experienced a sensation of pulling someone back while standing in the same place. "Come here."

"A living foe is a future threat," Swift Claw grumbled but turned and joined Clanless in the center.

"Lift your sword," Clanless said, doing the same himself. From the corner of his eye, he saw blood-priests and attendants hurrying out to deal with the wounded and dead.

"I thought we ignore them." Swift Claw lifted his bloody scimitar.

"We do. We're showing off for Chuluun. We keep things valuable for him so we can survive long enough for Qara to get back."

Yul's voice resonated within his head: "But he has to know this won't last much beyond the onset of High Spring. He's surely heard some of what's happened in the capital by now."

The blood-wraith wasn't wrong. Clanless knew the fights would only escalate from here. Chuluun would do his best to get a performance out of them, which meant bigger threats. The next one would not be so easy.

WHAT IS TO COME

Chuluun came to visit Clanless that evening. He and Swift Claw had been allowed to clean up after the fight, but not in the baths. Afterwards, they were separated again and taken to their respective cells. All of it left Clanless in a poor mood.

"That was well done," the arena owner observed. He leaned on his cane outside the cell. "Quite a trick you performed with the beastman. How on earth did you train it to do that?"

"I didn't train him to do anything."

"Hmm. I find that hard to believe. The synchronization was far too perfect to be accidental. If you did not train it, that implies the use of magic somehow." He tapped the cane on the floor. "I am not aware of any magic that provides such a link, nor has anyone observed you using blood at all. That returns us to the training theory."

"Believe whatever you want." Clanless didn't feel like defending or explaining himself. "If you won't even treat us right, why should I tell you anything?"

"Very well. What is your request?"

Clanless finally looked up at him. "What do you mean?"

"What do you want? What should I give you in order for you to share this secret with me?"

"Set us free."

"Obviously, that is not happening. Come, let us compromise."

"All right." Clanless got to his feet and approached the bars. "Stop treating Swift Claw like an animal. Bring him in here with me, or a better location. Allow us access to the baths after we exercise or fight." He paused. "And add some flatbread to the meals."

Chuluun regarded him without immediate reaction. "That's a bit much for one piece of information. I will arrange to have the beastman moved to the cell beside you. That is my only offer." He paused. "But I'll check on the bread."

"All right." Clanless took hold of the bars with both hands. "It's beastman magic. They have their own, you know."

"Interesting. How much of it could we adapt to the arena?"

"I wouldn't know. I don't know how it works."

"Yet you participated in it today."

"I didn't know that would happen."

"How could you not?"

Clanless shrugged. "Believe me, I wish I knew."

"This is not much information."

"You didn't offer much in exchange."

"Hmm." Chuluun nodded and turned to go.

"What about Swift Claw?" Clanless demanded.

"You will see him soon." Chuluun paused. "I hope this beastman magic serves you well. Next week, you will be fighting much more."

"More opponents or more matches?"

Chuluun waited a few moments before answering. "Yes." His cane clacked against the floor as he left.

Clanless smacked his palm against the bars in frustration. Next week? He had no idea how long the trip to and from Et-Baylak would take Qara nor how much time she would need at either end. She'd been gone about a week and a half, if he were counting right. Could she make it back in one more week?

"The curiosity is killing him, even if he doesn't show it," Yul said within him.

"How can you keep talking to me?" Clanless demanded. "Zektel needed me to taint blood before she could talk."

"It's blood-wraith magic. They have their own, you know."

"Are you trying to sound like me?"

"It's hard to impersonate a voice without using a voice, I suppose."

Clanless left the bars and tried to find a relatively clean spot to sit. "If you won't tell me that, can you tell me anything else about what happened in the arena?"

"Unfortunately, no. But it's wonderful. The two of you together will create a lot of mayhem in that arena next time. If this man is truly going to put you to the test, it should be a fantastic spectacle. I'm looking forward to it."

Clanless sat on the floor. "Looking forward to it. You enjoy this?"

"Blood-wraith." Yul emphasized the first part of the word. "It's what I live for."

"I thought you wanted a body of your own."

"It would be nice. Some, like Zektel, think it will happen here. But I'm in no rush. Not when I can enjoy such lovely devastation while riding around inside you." Yul's voice faded with each word. Apparently, there was a limit to his ability to speak.

"You… you're a twisted one."

"We all have our desires and pleasures."

Clanless didn't answer, and Yul said no more after that. About an hour later, a dozen guards escorted Swift Claw to the cell next to Clanless. But the meal that followed a few minutes later did not contain any flatbread.

((((●))))

Almost two weeks went by, driving Kekeen crazy with the inactivity. During a normal High Winter, she would spend her time reading whatever books she could find and working on new songs. But she found it difficult to concentrate on almost anything when so much remained unresolved.

Koland kept close tabs on the goings-on at the palace, mainly through Sonkogh. While the priests appeared to be preparing for this big trip of theirs, they showed no signs of the urgency the Ghamba Lam had implied. Koland suspected he was stalling to find a way to prevent Daviland from joining the journey.

"We could steal one of the Hawk King's winter carriages and make the trip ourselves!" Kekeen proposed one afternoon.

Koland looked up from a scrawl of notes containing the beginnings of his latest story. "There are three of us, Kekeen. How would we pull that off?"

"I don't know. We have to try something!"

Koland set down his pen. "I have actually considered that idea. But every plan I came up with resulted in disaster."

"We can get help. We have lots of friends in the city!"

"Who?" Koland held out his hands. "They all still trust Daviland and see him as the great deliverer. Do you really think we could convince them he's been suddenly possessed by an evil force?"

"He murdered Hagh! That isn't strong enough evidence?"

"It's all just our word. Most people would rather believe the slayer of the Hawk King than the two of us."

"We could still get help," she persisted. She stalked around his table then threw up a hand. "Badaar! There's one!"

"That makes four," Sugh said from his seat nearby. He put his feet up on the table. "Who is this Badaar?"

"A Hero of the Empire," Kekeen said.

"An old soldier with one hand," Koland said.

She spun at him. "You don't have to say it that way!"

The door let in a burst of wind and snow as an early customer arrived.

"I'm sorry, dear, but it's true," Koland said quieter. "He was a great help before, but not for something like this."

"You should see the way the palace guards defer to him! He could get us in, and, and…"

"Have I come at a bad time?"

Kekeen turned to see the customer pulling a heavy scarf from around her face. She knew that face. It was…

"Qara!" Sugh exploded from his seat. He grabbed the newcomer around the waist and spun her around in the air, almost smacking her head against the ceiling. "You're alive!"

"Whoa, whoa, big guy. Let me down!"

Sugh set her down, but not before giving her a massive hug. "I am so happy to see you!"

"And I you. I didn't expect to see you here, but I'm glad." She turned to Kekeen. "I came to find you right away. Aldan is in trouble."

"Clanless lives too!" Sugh waved his arms in the air. "What a glorious day!"

Kekeen thought she might pass out. She leaned against a table for support. "Where is he?"

"He's in Ulken, but he's been taken prisoner in their arena. They're going to make him fight again."

Aldan. Alive. The details didn't matter so much. They could go to him now. They could ignore Daviland and the Ghamba Lam and everything else. Only Aldan mattered.

"What of Bain?" Sugh asked. "Do not tell me he is dead. That would not be glorious."

"I really don't know." Qara took off her outer coat and sat down. "He abandoned us to go down that big hole with all the blood."

"Bain went down the Throat?" Koland asked.

"You heard that name? Yes, he did. Very weird. Anyway, we need a rescue plan. How many soldiers can your Daviland send with us?"

"Ah, that's… problematic." Koland looked at Kekeen. "Daughter, are you all right?"

"I will be." She took a seat as well. Sugh moved behind her.

"What's the problem?" Qara wanted to know. "We put together a few squads and go take that arena down!"

"Daviland is… no longer who he once was. We are not allied with him any more."

"Oh." Qara glanced around. "You would not believe how much persuasion I had to use to get here, and you're telling me it was pointless?"

"No!" Kekeen looked up. "We'll rescue him. We'll do whatever it takes."

Qara gave her a half-smile. "No offense, dear, but you're no more a fighter than I am." She paused. "Although I did stab that beastman in the head…"

"Beastman?" Sugh exclaimed.

"We have allies," Kekeen said. "We'll get the right people together and put together a plan." She looked at Koland. "My father can plan anything."

He smiled back. "This is a challenge, but one I'm willing to try. The four of us, plus your friend the Hero, against an entire arena structure. I like it."

"Four?" Qara looked around. "What about Hagh? Is he here?"

(((●)))

Over the following week, Clanless's anxiety rose with each day. Various arena workers and guards kept speaking of the upcoming arena day as an incredibly special occasion. Duurald also seemed to enjoy describing what he'd heard about the event.

"Word has it Chuluun is going to throw everything at you for as long as he can," the big warrior said. "Until you can't handle any more."

"So he means to kill us, but hopes it will take a long time." Clanless sighed from his seat in the cell. "I can't say I'm surprised."

"You could put a stop to this," Duurald said. "Chuluun does have an offer for you."

"Another one? What does he want now?"

"Give him your bloodbond. Agree to be a regular here. Then you'd have all the privileges that I have. You could go on living and fighting, just like we've always done."

Clanless glared at him. "I am a free man. I will not be a slave again!"

"You'll be a dead man! What is freedom compared to that?"

"What is life without freedom?" Clanless shook his head. "I'm not going back to that. Tell Chuluun I reject his offer."

"What more could you want?" Duurald asked, taking hold of one of the bars himself. "I fight once a week during the mild seasons. I enjoy luxury food and living. I have my choice of women at the brothels. How could life be better?"

"Can you leave the arena if you want?" Clanless got to his feet. "Can you love one woman? Truly love? Can you marry her? Start a family?"

"Who would want those things?"

"I do." Clanless stepped up to face him. "Real life, Duurald. Not this half-life of the arena. Making my own choices."

"You're moonbent."

"Am I? To want what ordinary people have?"

"We're not ordinary." Duurald shook his head. "We're above all that other stuff. And as much as I hate to admit it, you're even higher above. You could have so much here. We could even fight together, instead of against each other."

"I don't want it. I want freedom."

Duurald kept shaking his head as he pulled away. "Moonbent. One woman. Crazy." Clanless let him go without further argument.

"You could have taken it, to gain more time," Swift Claw said from the adjacent cell. He didn't talk when Duurald was around. The first time he had, the fighter accused Clanless of speaking through him with magic.

"Notice how you weren't included in the deal," Clanless told him. "Even if I agreed, he would have made sure you died in the arena. You're too dangerous to keep around. I won't sacrifice my freedom and your life."

"You are good man. I was right to covenant with you."

"I wish you'd explain that better."

"When threat comes, we fight as one."

"You've said that, but I still don't get it. How does it work?"

"Our blood works together. When it moves, it flows together."

"So if we're facing an enemy, we fight the same way? Who is in control? Who decides the movement?"

"No decision. When blood moves, we move."

"That doesn't make sense," Clanless complained. "There has to be a mind behind the movements. And it didn't start right away. Not until... huh." The bloodrush. When it kicked in, that's when the mirrored movements began. "When the blood moves," he repeated.

"Yes." He could almost hear Swift Claw nodding. "You understand this."

"A little bit." Clanless leaned his head against the bars. "I'm sorry again. For getting you into this."

"We are covenanted. We fight as one."

"I've been thinking about that too," said Yul's voice a few minutes later.

Clanless grunted. He didn't want to explain to Swift Claw about a voice in his head.

"Relax. The beastman is asleep. Do you know how I know?" When Clanless didn't answer, Yul kept going with a triumphant tone: "Because your blood is actually linked!"

"Yes, I figured that much out."

"But you don't understand how deep it is. It's amazing! I've never seen anything like it. And that link is what's made it easier for me to talk with you, I think. Normally, it takes a lot of effort, like when I told you to use the Taint in the snow."

Clanless paused. "That was you?"

"Yes. Me. I saved Qara's life. Maybe I'm not so horrible after all, huh?"

Clanless rubbed his hands together to warm them. "Prove it. Answer any of my questions honestly, without hesitation."

"Fine. Ask."

"Um… why did Daviland's Taint not cast you and Zektel out?" He had been wondering about that since Yul mentioned it. If he could use the Taint to free people from blood-wraiths, it would be a great help. But it hadn't worked that time.

"First, Zektel is one of the elite."

"What does that mean?"

"I mean, she's more powerful than me. Or most blood-wraiths. We're not all the same, you know. If you ever meet her again, you might not be able to drive her out." He paused. "Or maybe you would. The second reason it didn't work is longevity. The longer we're inside someone, the more solid our… connection."

That made sense. So he could use the Taint to cast most blood-wraiths out, unless they'd been there a long time. Or they were extra powerful. Maybe.

"See? No hesitation. Straight answers. Anything else?"

"Why did you stay when Zektel left?"

"I told you I needed a break. I'm tired." A sound filled Clanless's mind. Had the blood-wraith sighed? "You have no idea how old I am. I don't think I can even express it in terms you would understand."

"Are you older than the Sar Empire?" Clanless found himself curious despite not trusting the wraith.

"I am older than the empire that came before the Sar Empire… or anything else you humans have done on this ball of mud."

"Ball?"

"Never mind. The point is I'm ancient. And I'm tired. And I don't want to do this any more. I don't want to scheme. I don't want to control people. I just…" He paused for a long moment. When he spoke again, Clanless almost couldn't hear him: "I want it to all be over."

❨ ❨ ❨ ❨ ● ❩ ❩ ❩ ❩

Kekeen smiled at the group gathered around the table. They might not be many, but they were enough. Together, they would rescue Aldan. After that, nothing else mattered. And the plan she and her father had put together would work. As long as everyone else thought so…

"Gogeku," Koland said. "You're the key to all of this. If you don't agree, the whole plan falls apart."

"I don't see it," the tailor protested. "Goddess knows I'd love to help Clanless, but you're asking me to lie to potential customers. It's simply not done! And my cousin would be furious!"

"I'll write the letter to your cousin," Koland explained. "I'll tell him I represent Chuluun of Ulken, and I need a tailor with arena experience to provide a new wardrobe for all of my fighters."

"It might work," Gogeku allowed, "but only if you include the arena workers as well. It has to be more than the fighters."

"I will rely on your expertise to assist me in the letter." Koland looked at the others. "Once Gogeku's cousin is appeased, we equip a carriage that will hold all of us, and we go together."

"Six of us," Qara observed. "It's going to be just as crowded as Ghouk's carriage." She sighed. "I suppose we can make it work."

Sugh grinned. "We did all right. And this is for Clanless."

Gogeku pointed at Qara. "You have her, and she just came from Ulken. Why do you need me?"

"Because once we're there, you're our way into the arena," Koland said. "Badaar, you say you know your way around there?"

The weapons master nodded. "I've been to that arena before. I know the general layout at least. And I know a few people."

"Excellent. So you can help us work out what we'll do once we're inside."

"You haven't answered my question yet," Gogeku complained.

Koland smiled. "We'll use the same excuse we're using for your cousin. You've arrived, sent by Lord Ezen, to design new costumes for the arena fighters."

"Why Lord Ezen?"

"Everyone knows Clan Torov diversifies their power. They're always looking for new things. So now they're simply expanding their reach by sending some of Et-Baylak's finest to other cities." Koland chuckled. "Also, we have some of Lord Ezen's personal stationary, already signed by him."

"You should have said that from the beginning," Gogeku sniffed.

"How did you manage that?" Badaar asked.

"Lord Ezen is… not as much against us as you might think," Kekeen said. "He shielded me at the arena when the Hawk King died. He won't speak out publicly, but he helps when we ask nicely."

"At any rate," Koland said, "that gets Gogeku inside, along with a couple of us as your assistants."

Gogeku's eyes darted around the table, expressing his dubiousness at everyone's fitness for such a task. His gaze settled on Kekeen. "Perhaps if you wore the dress I made…"

"I can get inside separately," Qara put in. "I've done it once already. I can bring one person with me."

"That gets five of us inside," Koland said. "With one person waiting outside for emergency backup. That will probably be you, Sugh. Your appearance as a fighter is far too obvious."

Sugh feigned shock. "I am an innocent little man."

"We might have a way to get you inside too," Kekeen put in. "I have an idea, but we're still arguing about it."

"Working on it," Koland corrected.

"Why must we have all this subterfuge at all?" Gogeku wanted to know. "They have imprisoned Clanless illegally, yes? Why can we not appeal to the authorities and have him released?"

"It would be hard to prove he's a free man without the help of Daviland or his people," Koland said. "And then there's the problem of his, uh, new companion."

"Clanless will not abandon Swift Claw," Qara said.

"A beastman. Fascinating," Badaar murmured.

"We don't have enough power to full-on assault the place," Koland continued.

"Says you." Sugh flexed his arms.

"So that leaves subterfuge."

"All right, so we get inside," Gogeku said. "What next?"

Kekeen grinned. "That's where it gets fun. All of this hinges on Chuluun, the arena owner. He's the one who's imprisoned Aldan, and he's the one who can release him. With Gogeku's help, we get to him and persuade him to do the right thing. We have some ideas on how to do that."

"Based on what little I saw, I don't see him doing that," Qara said. "He did not sound like a reasonable man."

"Which is why you'll go straight to where Aldan is being held," Kekeen answered. "With your blood magic, we're counting on you being able to free him if necessary. And the beastman."

"And we'll let Sugh inside if we need more power," Koland added.

"The basics are sound, but there are a thousand things that could go wrong," Badaar said. "We need to think this through some more."

"We can do that on the way." Koland chuckled. "We'll all be crowded together in a small space for days, so we'll have plenty of time to talk."

"And sitting right here talking isn't going to get it done," Kekeen said. "Let's get moving."

A COLD DAY IN THE ARENA

The crowded carriage bumped its way down the road. Kekeen, sandwiched between Koland and Qara, struggled with warring emotions of excitement and nervousness. The anticipation of seeing Aldan again was tempered by her worries over Zektel's revelations.

"This is not so bad," Sugh observed. "Was more crowded and colder on the way to the mines."

"Colder than this?" Gogeku shivered. "Goddess preserve us."

"A chaos moon winter," Koland said. "I'm too young to remember much about the last one. Badaar? Do you remember it?"

The weapons master stirred, pulled out of his own thoughts. "Last time? Oh yes. It was… cold. Very cold. We didn't think we would survive." He turned to look at the carriage door past Sugh.. "What was that?"

"I didn't say anything," Sugh answered.

"Not you. Durken was talking about being a child. I didn't think he was that old."

"Durken?" Qara wrinkled her brow.

"One of his former students," Koland explained. "Died in the barbarian fight."

"Died?"

"He wasn't that old." Badaar chuckled a few times. "I thought not."

"Wonderful," Qara said. "We're depending on a moonbent old man. Was there no one else available to help us?"

"You don't know him," Gogeku said with sudden vehemence. "There's a reason he's been named Hero of the Empire twice!"

"I don't—" Qara broke off. "Never mind. I won't say anything else." She pulled her coat tighter around herself.

Kekeen leaned a little closer. "He comes and goes," she whispered. "When he's all here, he's everything we need."

"But what if he isn't all here when we do need him?"

"I guess we just have to trust."

Qara shook her head. "Trust what? Trust only works when you're trusting in something dependable."

Around them, the men had resumed a discussion on the weather. Kekeen had grown tired of that topic three months ago. She whispered again to Qara: "You said you lived in the beastmen caves with Aldan, but you haven't told us a lot about it. Is he… how is he, really?"

Qara hesitated. "I… I haven't wanted to talk about it."

"Was it that bad?"

"Oh, no, no, no. I just… I don't know how to say this." She bit her lip before meeting Kekeen's gaze. "I don't know you, Kekeen. Not at all. But I've known Clanless—Aldan—for over two years. And now I lived with him for over a month…"

Kekeen swallowed. First Zektel, and now this? "What do you mean by 'lived with him,' exactly?"

"The beastmen thought we were a couple, so they gave us one room to share. One small cave. One bed."

"Oh." Kekeen's heart plummeted.

Qara's shoulder's slumped, and she rolled her head to the side. "Ugh. I can't lie to you. He'd hate me for it." She let out an exasperated breath. "He slept on the floor, girl. Every night."

Kekeen closed her eyes and tried not to let her sigh of relief be heard by everyone.

"But it's…" Qara looked down. "You can't spend that much time with someone and not get close to him."

"I think I understand," Kekeen said, though she really didn't.

"He's… he's a good man, Kekeen. And you're very lucky."

Kekeen smiled. She'd thought that herself for some time, but then Zektel… Had anything Aldan said to her ever been his own voice? Maybe Qara knew the real Aldan far more than she ever had.

The carriage bounced on its way. She'd have answers, one way or another, in a few days.

Chuluun's big arena event day arrived. With so little contact with others, Clanless didn't know entirely what to expect. The arena would be packed, of course. Chuluun probably charged extra on the seats for this one even though High Winter still hadn't released its grip. Snow and wind wouldn't keep it from happening unless they were unbearable. Duurald even said something about extra barriers to protect from the weather. It would be the biggest event this city had ever seen.

And Qara had not returned.

Clanless knelt in the sand inside the doors while he waited for the opening fights to conclude. The last time he'd been this nervous about a fight had been his first at Et-Baylak… against a beastman. Today, he fought with one. But the entire purpose of this day's fights would be to kill them both.

"Whatever happens, this will be glorious," Yul said.

"Oh, you're back again. Great."

"You seem discouraged. Come on. It's not that bad."

"I'm going to die today. I think that's bad."

"You don't have to. Don't play by their rules. Find a way."

Swift Claw took a step closer. "Do you speak with your moon goddess?"

"No, but I probably should," Clanless answered.

"She won't answer you like I do," Yul said.

"You're not a god."

"What?" Swift Claw asked.

"I was once," Yul said.

Clanless got to his feet. "Never mind. Whatever happens, Swift Claw, never stop. We will leave them in awe."

"This day will be legend," Swift Claw agreed.

Duurald jogged in from the arena floor while the crowd cheered. He grinned at Clanless with a face covered in blood. "You're next, taichin. I'm going to enjoy watching this."

"It's not too late, Duurald. Fight with us. That would give Chuluun a shock."

"I'm not going to die today."

One of the guards stepped closer. "It's time."

"Where are our weapons?" Clanless asked. "I don't see them out there."

"Get going," the guard said. "You'll have to retrieve them in the fight."

Clanless and Swift Claw walked out to a thunderous cacophony from the crowd, drowning out whatever the presenter might be trying to say.

"Do they mean for us to die unarmed?" Swift Claw asked.

"I don't think so. It must be some kind of game…"

The opposing doors opened and two fighters entered. Clanless understood even as the presenter explained it to the crowd: "Look at this, citizens! Our first challengers have stolen Clanless and the beastman's weapons! How will they deal with this complication?"

"Mmh. I scratch, and you burn?" Swift Claw asked.

"Maybe… ugh." The two fighters were close enough now that Clanless could tell everything else about them. "They're not going to make it easy for us. They're both wearing full leather armor." Bain had once used that tactic against him. For a brief moment, he wondered what Bain had found in the Throat of the Goddess.

"Split?"

"Split," Clanless confirmed. As he and Swift Claw circled in opposite directions, he tried to think of the best strategy, preferably one that kept the bloodrush under control. He wasn't ready to duplicate Swift Claw's moves, at least not until he had the moonblade in his hands.

"Goddess," he whispered, "I don't know if you listen or not, but… I really don't want to die today. I want to see Kekeen again."

Both of the opposing fighters pivoted toward Swift Claw. With his natural weapons, he was clearly the biggest threat. One of them glanced over his shoulder at Clanless, but immediately turned his focus back to the beastman. Their mistake. Clanless had learned from beastman tactics even as he taught them. He picked up speed, raced straight at the enemy and leaped, feet first.

The enemy holding the moonblade would be the most logical target, so he aimed for the other one. His feet struck the fighter in the dead center of his back. He pitched forward, but didn't lose his grip on the sword. Clanless paused long enough to rip off the leather helmet, then dove into the sand himself to escape the swinging moonblade.

Swift Claw leaped over the same sweep of the moonblade and raked his claws across the back of the head of the fighter trying to get back up. Clanless activated the Taint, and the fighter collapsed. Clanless seized the scimitar and faced off with the second fighter.

"That's my sword," he couldn't help saying. So far, he'd been calm and relaxed. No bloodrush.

The last fighter moved like a skilled warrior, but he had no experience with a weapon like the moonblade. Swift Claw tackled him from the side, tearing off pieces of armor. Clanless stepped in, stabbed the scimitar, and it was over. He retrieved the moonblade and tossed Swift Claw his own weapon.

"Catch your breath. More coming."

Swift Claw looked over the fallen fighters. "Is any of this usable for you?"

Huh. Good thought. Clanless picked up one of the leather helms and pulled it down over his own head. A tight fit, but it worked.

The crowd's roar alerted him to the new opponents before he saw them. A large group of rag-tag fighters—criminals probably—charged across the snow and sand toward them. Clanless didn't have time to count them. "No hesitation now," he told Swift Claw. "Let's take them down." Together, the two charged to meet the enemy.

((◖ ◖ ● ◗ ◗))

"I don't like this," Gogeku said.

Kekeen climbed out of the carriage behind him, taking care not to get the fringes of her red dress in the snow. Her father had been right. The dress was perfect for situations like this. "What do you not like now?"

The tailor gestured around them. "The streets are empty. With the weather getting milder, there should be a lot of activity."

"You're right," Koland said, pulling his coat tighter around his neck. "I'll ask one of the guards." He trotted back toward the city gates they had just entered.

Qara looked out but didn't descend. "It wasn't this quiet when I left. Something's going on."

Koland returned almost immediately, running as fast as he could. "The arena!" he shouted before he reached them. "We have to get to the arena!"

At that moment, Kekeen heard the distinct sound of a distant crowd roaring with excitement. "Aldan!" She and Gogeku climbed back inside, followed by Koland. Sugh started the carriage moving again, directed by Qara.

"This changes the plan," Koland said. "I doubt we can persuade Chuluun to see a tailor in the middle of an arena event. How do we get to him now?"

"We may have to wait until the event is over," Gogeku said.

"We can't," Qara said. "This whole event might be set up just to get Clanless killed."

"Ha!" Sugh said. "That will take many fighters. Clanless is the best."

"Based on the guard's disappointment at missing it, Qara's probably right," Koland agreed. "But how do we get in?"

"I can still get into the lower levels with the same method I used before," Qara said. "But if he's already fighting, I can't get to him."

"There's one person Chuluun would welcome into his box," Kekeen said. She turned to the only person in the carriage who hadn't said anything. Badaar stared down at his lap. "A Hero of the Empire."

"Him?" Qara asked in a skeptical tone.

Badaar stirred and looked up at her. "If we're too late already, then… I can't help you."

"Nonsense!" Gogeku pushed past Qara and seized Badaar's good hand. "You listen to me, weapons master! I've seen you at your worst, and I've seen you at your best. And you decide which one we see today. We need the best Badaar. We need the Hero of the Empire twice over."

"Geku, I—"

"No, we need something more," Kekeen interrupted. "We need you to be a hero again, but not for the Empire. We need you to be a hero for the man you trained, the man I love."

"It's for Clanless, Badaar," Gogeku emphasized. "Clanless. That worthless little brat with the brand on his shoulder and that oddly delightful wolf pelt. The young warrior with the one-of-a-kind moonblade. The leader of warriors who stood side-by-side with you against the barbarians. This is all… about… him. The last one. And only you can save him."

Badaar's eyes smoldered by the time Gogeku finished. "You made your point, Geku. I'll get us inside." He straightened up. "And if he refuses to let me in, I'll remind his assistants of exactly who I am."

"Goddess. I actually believe him," Qara muttered. "All right, Kekeen. Here's what you'll need." She sorted through a bag of blood vials, selected one, and handed it to her. "This is Clan Torov blood. I've told you how to use it. You'll also need this." She handed her a smaller vial with only a drop or two inside.

"What blood is this?"

"Aldan's," Qara said with a smile. "It'll catalyze the other blood and activate the magic. Without it, you could still do it, but it would take longer. Sugh, this one is for you. Clan Berge."

"But I am strong enough already," Sugh protested. "I need no magic."

"This time you will. Once Koland and I are inside, we'll get you in too." Qara took a deep breath. "Clanless may be the greatest arena fighter of all, and Swift Claw is impressive too. But they might need some help if Kekeen's part of the plan doesn't work fast enough."

Sugh nodded, taking the blood. "Where is the thinnest wall of the arena?"

☾☾☾☾●☽☽☽☽

Kekeen tried to feign wide-eyed excitement as she followed Badaar and Gogeku into the arena. The last and only time she'd been at an arena fight, she'd been a prisoner of the Hawk King, forced to sing while Aldan and Daviland fought. All of them had nearly died. She hoped this day's results weren't as traumatic.

Badaar wore a fashionable black coat with both of his medals hung around his neck. He strode with confident steps up toward a pair of guards. "You two! I am Badaar, Hero of the Empire. Escort me to this arena's owner at once."

The guards eyes widened at his claim. "We—I can announce you," one of them said. "But the fights have already begun. I don't know if he even has room in the box…"

"Did you not hear me?" Badaar leaned forward to make sure they got a good look at the ribbons and medals. "Hero of the Empire. Twice. Tell your master I am here to honor his arena today." He lowered his voice. "And if he does not wish to see me, then the dishonor will be his alone."

"Yes, sir." One of the guards ran ahead, while the other motioned for them to follow. He glanced at Gogeku. "And these two?"

"They're with me. If you need more of an explanation than that, I'll recommend to your master that you be thrown in with the next fight. Naked."

The guard nodded and didn't say anything more. He led them up several flights of stairs to a large set of doors. The crowd noise grew louder with every step. Kekeen knew she heard some of them shouting "Clanless!" He was fighting right now!

The first guard emerged from the doors with some kind of chamberlain. Before he could even ask, Badaar launched into his intimidation tactics again. The chamberlain listened to his words, but his eyes darted to Gogeku and Kekeen.

"You traveled during High Winter to be here?" the chamberlain asked. "And who are these two?"

"This is Gogeku, an eminent tailor of Et-Baylak, sent here by… who was it, tailor?" Badaar waved his stump.

"I have a letter from Lord Ezen instructing me to design all new clothing for your arena fighters and workers," Gogeku explained. "He and the other Lords are planning new promotions for the arenas throughout the Empire and are working towards—"

"Yes, yes," the chamberlain interrupted. "And the girl?"

The tailor snorted. "She's my slave, of course."

Kekeen kept her face placid. The story had been assistant, not slave. What kind of slave wore a dress like this? With a smile, she held up the bolt of purple she carried, as if to demonstrate her purpose.

"I traveled with them on the way," Badaar said. "Hearing of their plans, I decided it was a good time for me to tour the arenas. I worked in one for years, you know. Ghoyor." He turned toward the door. "Will you be good enough to announce me before the fights end? It's quite frustrating to be missing out here."

The chamberlain hesitated a moment longer before nodding. He opened the box door and led them inside.

Kekeen swallowed as they entered. Though nowhere near as elaborate as the Hawk King's box, the similarities unnerved her. The enclosed box was built in four levels stepping down. Luxury chairs were scattered around, some next to tables piled high with food and drink. Around a dozen people, the richest of Ulken, lounged about watching (or not watching) the arena. In an elevated area attached to the right side of the box, the presenter stared intently at the sands below and bellowed his commentary with magic-enhanced volume.

To her surprise, Chuluun wasn't seated. The chamberlain led them to a thin man leaning on a cane right at the edge of the box overlooking the arena floor. He turned as they approached, casting a critical eye across all three of them.

"My lord Chuluun, may I present Badaar, Hero of the Empire, and a, uh, tailor from Et-Baylak."

"Badaar. Yes, your exploits are well known here in the north," Chuluun said in a level tone. "And you worked with Orgina, did you not?"

Kekeen sidestepped and looked down into the arena, ignoring the conversation. Her heart skipped a beat. Aldan and a beastman fought side-by-side against at least a dozen raging opponents. The presenter's comments melded with the cheers of the crowd, drowning out anything from down below. Swords and blood flew in a symphony of madness. She wanted to tear her eyes away, but couldn't.

Watching Aldan fight Daviland had been terrifying enough, especially while being forced to sing. Here, he fought against so many… and he appeared unstoppable. The dead and wounded littered the sand around him along with gore and severed body parts. She shuddered, but kept watching.

"I must say, I am surprised to see Clanless here," Badaar said. "I last saw him in Et-Baylak a few months ago."

"Yes. It is… a peculiar story," Chuluun answered, turning back to watch. "It appears he ran away from his master, the Hawk King. I've received full authority to treat him as such."

"A shame," Badaar said. "He may have been… the greatest of this age."

Hearing a catch in his voice, Kekeen looked anxiously at Badaar. His face showed only a fascination with the battle below, but the fingers on his good hand were twitching.

"Sir, Lord Ezen sent me—" Gogeku broke in.

"Yes, yes, good tailor. I will hear all you have to say after the fights are over. Please enjoy yourself." He summoned the chamberlain back with a finger.

"I believe this is the earliest in the year I've seen arena fights," Badaar observed.

"Yes, the goddess and Suirel were kind enough to moderate High Winter's fury this week, so we decided to celebrate." Chuluun bent toward the chamberlain. Kekeen sidestepped to overhear him: "When this batch is done, release the cat."

THE CAT

Clanless leaned over, trying to calm his heart rate. The bloodrush and his link to Swift Claw had come in very useful during that fight, but he needed his head clear for whatever came next. He took in deep breaths of the frigid air. Blood oozed from a dozen or so cuts. His right hip ached from a mace blow he'd barely deflected. He'd used the Taint again and again through the fight, reminding him of another day he tried not to think about.

Swift Claw crouched on his haunches a few feet away, bleeding at least as much, including from a nasty-looking gash on his forehead. "Some of these were not your people," he observed, looking around at the bodies.

"Some were barbarians," Clanless said. "Captured and forced to fight. Like us."

"Barbarian is a good word." Swift Claw looked up at the crowd. "But not for these fallen."

Clanless couldn't argue the point. He looked toward the opposite gate, waiting for the next fight. What would it be now?

He didn't have long to wait. "What's this, citizens?" the presenter cried. "It looks like Clanless and his pet will have to deal with something a bit larger this time… larger and not human, that is!"

A cat ran into the arena and came to an abrupt stop. Clanless kept his deep breaths coming. He'd never seen anything like it. The cat was larger and more powerfully built than any creature he'd seen, except for the giant wolf. It stretched at least seven or eight feet long, its tight frame displaying strong muscles. Its front legs were longer and more powerful than the back. It lifted its head toward the crowd and hissed, showing two massive fangs that curved down from its upper jaw like scimitars.

"Ever see anything like that?" Clanless asked.

"Once. Far, far to the north." Swift Claw stood up. "I think your people call them leopards. They are not pleasant creatures."

Clanless didn't think that needed saying. He straightened up, pushing past the pain. The big fight had taken a lot more out of him than he wanted to admit.

"This has been glorious," Yul's voice said inside his head. "Thank you for such stupendous mayhem."

Clanless didn't waste his breath in responding.

The cat spotted the two fighters and advanced with deliberate steps. As it drew closer, Clanless could make out a few black spots on its tan coat. He also saw a pair of long scars on its shoulders. This creature was no stranger to battle. It paused at the first body and sniffed at it. The man, taken down by the Taint, moaned and started to move. With barely a flinch of its huge head, the cat tore his throat out. The crowd erupted.

"Plan three?" Swift Claw asked.

"We can start that way," Clanless said. "I don't know that any plan will work with this thing." The Taint might work or it might not. It hadn't worked on other creatures, but they had been like lizards. He'd never tried it against something like this.

Swift Claw scrambled off to the right. Clanless adjusted his grip on the moonblade and watched the cat advance. With the shorter back legs, it wouldn't be capable of enormous leaps. But like all felines, it could surely pounce forward at great speed.

"Don't play by their rules," Yul had said. But in a situation like this, there were no rules. Kill or be killed. He couldn't see any other options.

Clanless waved his moonblade back and forth to keep the cat's attention focused on him. Swift Claw continued moving in a wide circuit, still far from the center of the fight. The cat took no notice of him and took careful steps toward Clanless.

Clanless lunged forward and pulled back just as quick. The cat froze for an instant, then lunged forward as well, bounding across the sand toward him. Too soon. Swift Claw wasn't in position yet. Clanless braced himself, but the cat came to an abrupt halt only a couple of feet away. It snarled and swiped with one paw, trying to hit the moonblade.

"You want to play? We can play," Clanless muttered. He kept moving the sword, tempting the cat with short thrusts and swipes of his own.

Wholly occupied with this game of sorts, the cat didn't notice Swift Claw's return until it was too late. The beastman leaped from ten feet away. The cat swerved, but Swift Claw landed on its back and brought his sword down onto its spine. The sword cut through the thick fur but drew only a trickle of blood.

The cat jerked violently, shaking Swift Claw loose. The beastman fell and rolled. The cat spun toward him. "No!" Clanless shouted and intervened, swinging the moonblade. He smacked a glancing blow off its shoulder. The cat's paw retaliated, swinging up with surprising speed and striking him in the head. The claws ripped the borrowed leather helmet off and left shallow cuts from the base of his chin, across his left ear and up the side of his head. Clanless staggered and rolled as well.

Swift Claw regained his feet in time to see the cat barreling toward him. From the ground, Clanless activated the Taint. The cat let out a "yeowl!" and flexed its shoulders. The distraction was enough to allow Swift Claw to dodge to one side and create some distance.

The Taint worked, but not effectively. Maybe because the cat wasn't bleeding much? Or the thick skin? Or some other factor entirely…

Clanless wanted to charge after the beast and hit it from behind, but the fatigue from the previous fight and his lingering wounds slowed him down. The bloodrush, so strong in the previous group fight, had not returned. Just as well; moving together might not be the best strategy against a single creature like this.

"If it's any help, I do believe your Taint will work once you get it bleeding enough," Yul said.

Making it bleed was the only strategy they had. Clanless clenched his teeth and tried to pick up his pace.

The cat, sensing his presence, spun from Swift Claw toward him. Unable to get a good angle on the sudden move, Clanless smacked it across the face with the moonblade. The cat snapped at him with those horrible teeth, narrowly missing Clanless's exposed arm.

Clanless took a step back. And stumbled over one of the bodies. Quick as a flash, the cat pounced, slamming both paws down on either side of him. Clanless desperately held up the moonblade to hold back the descending scimitar-fangs.

Swift Claw leaped on top of the beast again, hacking down with his own sword and digging in with the claws on his other hand. He struck the cat again and again. It reared up and shook from side to side.

One enormous paw landed on Clanless's chest, cracking something inside and knocking the air out of him. He rolled away, gasping frantically for air.

As Swift Claw kept up his attack, the cat reared and twisted. It caught hold of Swift Claw's left hand with its teeth and yanked him off its back. The scimitar flew off somewhere. When the beastman hit the ground, the cat slashed at him with its claws. The first strike cut deep furrows across his side. The second one caught in his hair, lifted him, and tossed him rolling across the ground near Clanless. Swift Claw pushed up on his right hand, then collapsed.

Still fighting for air, Clanless got to his feet. He pushed past the pain and stood over Swift Claw, moonblade at ready. Something inside hurt more than ever. He struggled to inhale, but kept his eyes fixed on the monster.

The cat watched him. It lowered itself, preparing to pounce.

☾☾☾☾●☽☽☽☽

Kekeen gasped at the ferocity of the giant cat. She looked to Badaar. They needed to intervene soon! He glanced at her and nodded. She stepped closer to him.

"I'm afraid this may be the end of the mighty Clanless," Chuluun observed, his attention occupied by the fight below.

Badaar reached into the bolt of purple Kekeen carried. He whipped out a short sword and brought it around to Chuluun's neck. The arena master didn't move. "Ah, how dishonorable. But of course, you know Clanless better than I, don't you, Badaar?" Chuluun turned his head enough to aim one eye at the weapons master. "After all, you trained him in his dishonorable fighting methods."

"It ends now," Badaar said. "You won't kill anyone else."

"This is your plan, is it? Threaten me in the middle of the fight? I can't stop it now, even if I wanted to."

"He's not threatening you," Kekeen said. She dropped the rest of the cloth and pulled out the blood vials. "He's preventing you from stopping me."

Chuluun eyed her. "And what will you do, girl?"

She turned to see Gogeku tap the presenter on the shoulder. He pointed to Chuluun. "Another word from you, and your master loses his neck. We have a new presenter now."

Kekeen stepped to the very edge of the box. Aldan stood over Swift Claw, waiting for the cat to attack. Kekeen took a deep breath and pulled the stoppers loose from both vials. She poured them into her palm together and slapped the blood on her throat. The low neckline on the dress came in handy here. A familiar vibration shook her vocal cords.

"People of Ulken," she began. She paused at the strange sensation of her voice reverberating around the arena. She wanted to focus on Aldan, but if she did, she would forget what she wanted to say. "All of you, especially the slaves, hear my words."

Many in the crowd turned to look toward the luxury box, but most continued to watch the drama unfolding below. Several in the luxury box itself scrambled out the door.

"I have come here from Et-Baylak with news. The Hawk King is dead!" A confusing noise of various reactions rolled through the crowd. "Daviland has taken control. Slavery is hereby outlawed throughout the Sar Empire!

"Do you hear me, slaves? You no longer owe anything to those who have kept you under their thumb. Arena fighters, that means you too!"

A roar echoed through the arena. Kekeen risked a quick glance down to see Aldan still standing. She couldn't keep watching. They needed to hear her.

"Slave masters, you may be tempted to keep your slaves under control with the bloodbonds. Know this: your control is temporary! Once the Empire's soldiers arrive, they will enforce the new law, and if you have abused your slaves, you will pay the penalty.

"Everyone should be free. Everyone is free! Rise up, former slaves! Take your rightful place as free men and women!"

Kekeen paused as the crowd erupted in arguments, cheers, and confusion.

"A clever ploy," Chuluun observed. "And a delightful speech. But ultimately useless today. You may cause a short uprising, but the masters will put it down." He gestured down toward the arena floor. "Should they survive the cat, I've already given orders to unleash the next stage. Those slaves wouldn't have even heard you, so they'll fight for me." He tapped his cane, and his eyes darted up toward the door. "And then there's him."

Kekeen spun and saw an enormous arena fighter standing in the door. He carried a huge flanged mace and wore a unique set of armor consisting of shaped metal plates guarding both shoulders, his chest, and thighs.

"Duurald," Chuluun said calmly. "Do me a favor and rid my box of these three vermin."

Clanless froze and almost forgot his struggle for air. Kekeen! It was her voice! The change in voice and the tone of the crowd attracted the attention of the big cat. It straightened up from its crouch and glanced around.

Kekeen was here! She spoke of the Hawk King and freedom. She sounded passionate and, and beautiful.

But the cat had lost interest. It took a step forward and lowered itself with a growl.

One of the arena walls exploded inward off to the left. Clanless and the cat both whipped their heads to see Sugh stumble a few feet before he came to a stop. The huge warrior lifted his axe, an enormous grin on his face. "Clanless! We are here to rescue you!"

The cat yowled and crouched again at this new intruder. Spotting it, Sugh charged across the sand. The cat rotated to face him, prepared to pounce. Clanless finally caught a full breath and activated the Taint. Just before Sugh arrived, the cat cried out and jerked, arcing its front paws into the air. Swift Claw had done enough damage to make it bleed.

Sugh swung his axe with more force than Clanless could remember ever seeing. The blade cut deep into the cat's chest and hurled it across the arena. Its paws waved in the air as it struggled. Sugh caught up to it and brought the axe down again, severing the cat's head.

"Aldan!" Clanless turned his head and saw Qara and Koland peeking in through the hole left by Sugh's entrance.

Kekeen's voice continued to ring out, calling for the slaves to rise up and claim their freedom.

Clanless stabbed the moonblade down into the sand. He knelt by Swift Claw. The beastman still lived, but his breath came in ragged gasps. His left hand was a mangled mess. Blood ran freely from the deep gashes in his side and chest. Clanless didn't feel much better himself.

Sugh trotted up, carrying the cat's head with one hand. "The plan is working!" He waved at the other two to join them. "Worry not, Clanless."

Clanless lifted his eyes past Sugh and toward the luxury box. He could just make out Kekeen leaning over the railing as she spoke. She was so incredible.

"I brought plenty of healing blood," Qara cried, running up beside him. Koland came more slowly, looking around at the horrific carnage on the ground.

Qara knelt beside him. "What do you need first?" She opened a vial of blood.

"Him. Heal him." Clanless pointed at Swift Claw.

Qara hesitated. "I don't know if it will work on him. The beastmen don't use—or like—blood-magic."

Kekeen's speech stopped. The crowd's noise grew.

"We have to save him. We're…" Clanless trailed off.

"The covenant," Yul said in his head at the same time Clanless thought of it himself.

"All right, heal me. But not yet." He held up a hand and closed his eyes. He had to get the bloodrush going somehow.

"There are more fighters coming," Sugh said. "I will deal with them. I am stronger than anyone right now!"

"Something is happening in the luxury box," Koland said. "Kekeen and the others might be in danger!" He started running back toward the hole Sugh had created.

"That should do it," Yul said.

He wasn't wrong. Clanless's own rage over his treatment for the past few weeks overflowed. Combined with the desperation of Kekeen's danger and his own inability to intervene, the emotions triggered the bloodrush. His heartbeat pounded in his ears. "Now!" he shouted.

Qara poured the Clan Kurav blood over his wounds. As always, the pain erupted from them, as if he were experiencing the original injury all over again. Except this time, he felt more, much more. He experienced Swift Claw's injuries as well, pushing him to the edge of consciousness and death itself. He screamed his throat ragged, felt it heal as well, and screamed some more. In the process, the bloodrush vanished again. Did it work?

As the pain subsided, he rolled to the side onto his hands and knees. Something still hurt in his gut. That old wound still causing problems. He coughed and spat out a huge chunk of dried blood, vomiting a little with it. "Swift Claw!" he gasped.

"I live," the beastman responded. "We… heal as one."

"Qara… what's happening?" Clanless asked, trying to recover himself.

"Sugh is tearing through some more fighters, thanks to the Clan Berge blood-magic. But I can't see what's happening in the box. Badaar is fighting someone. It doesn't look good."

Badaar was here too? Clanless wanted to ask about everything and everyone, but he had no time. He reached out and took hold of the moonblade. "Swift Claw. Can you fight again?"

"I will do what I must." The beastman staggered to his feet. He looked at Qara. "You have done well, Wolf Chosen's woman."

Clanless pulled himself up. "Don't play by their rules," he reminded himself.

Sugh had defeated the four fighters who had charged in. Another group was entering with trepidation from the doors. Clanless couldn't tell how many it might be.

"Qara, get out of here. Sugh! I need you!" He half-ran, half-walked to meet the big warrior. "How strong are you right now?"

"I feel like I can do anything!" Sugh exclaimed.

"Good." Clanless pointed at the luxury box. "I need you to throw me up there."

☾☾☽☾ ● ☾☽☽☽☽

Duurald jumped onto a table, scattering the food, and leaped down toward Badaar. The remaining residents of the luxury box screamed and raced for the exit. Badaar spun out of the way as Duurald's mace smashed into the railing where he'd been standing.

Kekeen scrambled back, almost stumbling over Gogeku. "This wasn't part of the plan!" he whined, clambering over the railing into the presenter's box.

Badaar spun back the other direction. His short sword ricocheted off Duurald's shoulder armor. The arena fighter backhanded him, knocking Badaar back against one of the tables. Duurald swung his mace back around. Badaar rolled the other way off the table, flipping it into the air. The mace smashed through the table, sending wood shards flying in every direction.

Kekeen shielded her face from the debris. When she turned back, Chuluun had crossed the box and stepped in her way. "I know who you are, as well, my dear. Do you think I haven't heard the details of the Hawk King's fall already?" He pointed his cane at her. "Or about the singer whose love for Clanless inspired the battle?"

Badaar and Duurald crashed through some chairs. Badaar punched Duurald in the face with his stump.

A thin blade snapped out of the end of Chuluun's cane, pointed at Kekeen's face. She gasped, her inhalation reverberating through the arena. The vocal magic still worked.

"Now that I have you, I have Clanless," Chuluun declared, his voice still maddeningly calm. "The guards will be seizing him down below, and more will join us soon."

"How could you have known?" Kekeen asked, stalling for time. The weapons-master and the arena fighter continued their back-and-forth, seeming intent on smashing through every bit of furniture in the luxury box.

"I didn't, until you entered here." Chuluun moved the blade closer to her face. "But I always have the bloodbond of my mightiest fighter with me. A simple touch summoned him. For all your words of freedom, the magic still rules."

Duurald roared, heaving his mace in a two-handed swipe. Badaar tried to dodge back, but tripped on one of the stairs. The mace struck his sword, knocking it from his hand. It bounced across the floor near Chuluun.

"Finish him," Chuluun ordered. "Then find Clanless. Tell him—"

Aldan flew into the luxury box, moonblade held high. It tore through the canopy above the box, cutting an eight-foot-long gash. The loose ends flapped in a sudden gust of winter wind. Aldan came to a sudden stop, landing hard on his feet in the middle of the box.

He lifted his face toward Chuluun. Kekeen swore smoke came from his eyes, eyes that glowed blood-red.

☾☾☾☽●☾☾☽☾

Chuluun stood before Kekeen, holding a cane-blade aimed at her face. Blood covered her throat, but she wore an incredible red dress that would have taken his breath away in any other circumstances. Badaar was on his hands and knees nearby. Duurald growled from a higher point in the box.

"Step away from her!" Clanless roared.

"I think not," Chuluun answered. "I am in control here. You will surrender yourself and—"

Duurald bellowed a guttural yell and launched himself at Clanless. Unable to dodge in the close quarters, he threw up the moonblade to block the attack. The force of it drove him back almost to the railing. The loose ends of the canopy snapped in the wind. A flurry of snow swept through the box.

"No, you fool!" Chuluun cried. "What are you doing?"

Clanless wrenched the moonblade to the side, shoving Duurald's mace with it. Qara's healing had removed his injuries, but the trauma of them and Swift Claw's healing still lingered in his mind and body. Every movement was an agony. He needed time to recover, but he didn't have any. Breaking free, he swung the moonblade back in a weak uppercut easily dodged by Duurald.

The last time he'd fought Duurald, during their training so many years ago, the larger boy had always relied on his brute force to dominate. While it worked against the smaller boys in the class, it left him behind those like Clanless or Bain who paid attention to Kan and learned tactics.

Since then, Duurald had grown into a much larger man and might have learned something along the way. Clanless couldn't believe that brute force alone had allowed him to live and thrive in the arena system for eight years. Duurald proved it a moment later by disengaging long enough to jump onto the next level of the box. High ground.

Clanless wanted to talk to Duurald, try to reason with him. But he still fought for every breath. The bloodrush had faded, but he could feel Swift Claw fighting down below.

Duurald made a sweeping blow at him. Clanless had just enough room to lean back out of the way. Duurald used to overcommit on strikes like that, leaving him open for a swift counterattack. But not any more. He was ready when Clanless tried a quick swipe at his legs.

Clanless shifted to the right, but Duurald matched him, denying him the chance to join him on the higher level. A feint and another quick step back to the left accomplished no more.

He thrust the moonblade forward, as if to stab at Duurald's ankle. Duurald tried to slam his mace down onto the blade, but Clanless expected it. He swept the moonblade to the right with one hand, but grabbed Duurald's wrist with the other. He yanked as hard as he could, throwing the bigger man off balance. Clanless continued his swing all the way around, bringing his left hand back to the handle to deliver a two-handed blow. The moonblade crashed into Duurald's right thigh armor plate and ripped it free. The impact buckled his leg. Clanless rolled to his left onto the second level and vaulted himself back to his feet.

Part of the canopy fluttered down in between them. Clanless took advantage of the temporary loss of sight to attack, swinging through it to get at Duurald. But Duurald had the same idea. The moonblade hit Duurald's right side at the same time the mace hit Clanless's right side. Both combatants fell.

In any other fight, both strikes would be incapacitating. The pain from multiple shattered ribs almost overwhelmed Clanless, but he activated the Taint to be sure. Duurald screamed and rolled down to the lower level, leaving a trail of blood. He came to a stop, moaned, and lay still.

Through a haze of agony, Clanless turned toward Chuluun. He stared at Clanless, his normally impassive face now twisted with rage. He spun to Kekeen and pulled back his cane to strike.

Koland slammed into Chuluun, knocking him down a level and through the hole in the railing. Badaar caught Koland just in time to stop him from going over with the arena master. Chuluun tumbled over and down into the arena below.

Clanless looked up at Kekeen's face moving toward him, and then darkness overtook him.

REUNITED

The repeated pain of healing yanked Clanless awake. Qara stood over him, emptying a blood vial. "You've got to stop this," she said. "I don't have much more left. And it's still taking longer than usual."

He dragged himself upright as familiar voices chatted all around him, still in the ruins of the luxury box. All these friends. He stared as he tried to catch his breath. Koland chatted with Swift Claw. Badaar and Sugh discussed something. Gogeku stood awkwardly alone.

And Kekeen. In that dress. She stood there, watching him, wringing her hands together. He couldn't read her expression, but did it matter? She was here. He started to get to his feet.

"Can I have a few moments alone with Aldan?" Kekeen asked loudly.

As if nothing more needed to be said, the others filed out. Swift Claw looked confused, but he followed Koland.

Clanless regained his breath. He took a step toward her. "Kekeen, I—"

"Stop." She held out a palm toward him, her hand shaking. "I want nothing more than to run into your arms, but I can't."

"Wh-why? What's wrong?"

Kekeen picked up a fallen coat and wrapped it around herself, covering that amazing neckline. "Tell me about Zektel."

Clanless froze. That was absolutely the last topic he wanted to discuss with her.

"Where did you hear that name?" he blurted.

"What does that matter? Tell me about her."

A few snowflakes drifted down through the torn canopy. "Can we talk somewhere warmer, maybe?"

"Stop stalling!" Kekeen stamped her foot and folded her arms. "We worked hard to arrange all of this, to rescue you and your new friend. The least you could do is tell me the truth!"

"All right." He held out his hands and sat back down. "Zektel was… a blood-wraith." He looked down. "That's what we usually call them, anyway. She lived inside my blood for most of my life, I think. She's gone now."

"Because she's in Daviland."

Clanless looked up in surprise. "Yes, I think so. You know that?"

"She's controlling him, making him into a different person. It's…" She unfolded her arms and looked away. "It's not good."

"Controlling him? So she's in charge of the Sar Empire right now?"

"This is not about Daviland!" she snapped, her eyes blazing. "Or the Empire or anything else. It's about you. And me."

"I'm… sorry?"

"For what, Aldan? What are you sorry for?"

"I'm not even sure." Even in Chuluun's dungeon, he hadn't felt this miserable. He wanted to shrink in to himself.

"Who… who did I fall in love with?" Kekeen asked. "Was it Aldan or was it Zektel?"

Eyes wide, Clanless almost jumped to his feet. "Zektel never controlled me!"

"Never? How can I believe that, when, when that thing is completely controlling Daviland now?"

"Th-the wraiths can't always control people. Zektel talked to me sometimes, but she didn't control me!" He reached up and took a handful of wolf fur. "Qara and I met this wolf. He said the fur protected me. It's why she couldn't take control."

Kekeen wrinkled her forehead. "The wolf?"

"Yes, it saved us in the snow. Ask Qara."

"You were never controlled?"

"No!"

"She never spoke through you? Said things for you?"

"No!"

"Are you sure about that?"

He hesitated. Of course there had been times when words came to him, seemingly out of nowhere. But didn't everyone experience that? "I don't know," he admitted, slumping. "I don't know."

"Then…" Kekeen's voice cracked. "Then how can I know what you really feel? How can I know—"

Clanless jumped to his feet. "Zektel had nothing to do with how I feel about you! She didn't like you from the very beginning! She tried to talk me into staying away from you!" He took a step closer. "Everything I've said to you came from me. Everything I feel about you came from me." He put his hand to his chest. "I love you, Kekeen. Just me. Only me."

"Aldan, I… I want to believe you."

"Then believe me!" He stepped closer again. "This is all me. Why would I lie to you about this? If it was Zektel controlling me and saying things to you back then, why would I continue with it?"

"I just—" She broke down and charged into him. The feeling of her body hitting him, of his arms wrapping around her and holding her close… it was the greatest thing in the world.

"I needed to hear you say it," she whispered. "I needed to know."

"I love you, Kekeen. You're everything to me."

"I love you too." She tilted her head up toward his and kissed him. Her tears were salt on his lips. It took several moments before they could speak again. "It really is cold out here," she admitted with a giggle.

"We should go inside, wherever the others are." He started to separate from her.

Kekeen pulled him back. "You're not in the clear yet, you know. You have other things to answer for."

"Whatever you want."

"We'll talk more later. You can tell me about Pasque House, for one thing."

Clanless winced and nodded. "I will tell you whatever you ask."

He took her hand and led her up toward the exit.

"As long as she doesn't ask about me," said a voice in his head. Clanless winced again.

Outside the luxury box, Gogeku waited to escort them to a meeting room, where the others had gathered.

"Geku, I… thank you," Clanless said. "Thank you for being here."

The tailor sniffed. "Still wearing the same thing, I see. And smell. When did you last have those clothes cleaned?"

He laughed. "It's been weeks since the last time Qara cleaned them in the beastman caves. I haven't had much control over that."

"Sounds like something else I need to hear about," Kekeen murmured.

"Did-did she tell you about the past couple of months?" Clanless asked as they followed Gogeku.

"I think I heard enough," Kekeen answered. "For now, anyway."

Clanless wondered how many "talks" were waiting for him. This wasn't turning into the kind of reunion he'd been dreaming about. Then Kekeen smiled and bumped into him with her hip. Maybe it wasn't so bad.

In the meeting room, the others rose as they entered.

"All settled for now?" Koland asked. "Good. We have things to deal with."

"Wait," Clanless said. He looked around the room. "Thank you, all of you. I didn't know what Qara might find when she escaped, so I didn't know what to expect… but I didn't expect this." He took a ragged breath. "I… I don't know what else to say."

"We're all happy to be here," Koland said. "Everyone here cares about you, or they wouldn't have come. Now, let's figure out what's going on here."

"The slaves are running the arena!" Sugh declared with a big grin. Until that moment, Clanless hadn't even thought through the implications of his presence. He'd survived the mines. What about Hagh? Or Bain? There were many stories here he needed to hear. And Badaar! Where had he come from? His questions faded as Kekeen snuggled up against him when they sat down together. Swift Claw looked at him with his head cocked to the side. Oops. He would have some explaining to do to the beastman as well.

"For the moment, this is true," Badaar said, "but it is a tentative position. Already, there are representatives from some of the city Lords searching for the arena owner and answers about what is happening here."

"I'll speak with them," Koland said. "I'll do what I can to explain everything, invoke Daviland's name, and so on."

"Are we going to try to free the entire city?" Kekeen asked. "Can we even do that?"

"I don't think so." Koland toyed with Chuluun's cane. "None of us are esteemed high enough to influence things on that scale, not even Badaar."

The weapons-master nodded.

"Does Chuluun live?" Clanless asked.

"He does," Sugh said. "Very tough for such a skinny man. We let the arena healer take care of him."

"But we locked him in the same place he kept you," Qara added.

"What about Duurald?"

"In the cell next to his master," Koland said. "He's an angry one."

"I want to talk to him again," Clanless said. "I think he can come around."

"You're welcome to it. But for now, as I see it, we have two choices."

Koland looked around at everyone. "We can fortify our position here with all of the arena slaves and try to work things out with the city. Or we can run."

"Back to Et-Baylak, yes?" Gogeku chimed in. "My cousin will already be upset if I return without any new business. The sooner I'm back to pacify him, the better."

"My first inclination is to agree with you," Koland said. "But we now know Daviland is on his way to the mines. And if the Ghamba Lam is to be believed, that could be catastrophic."

"What?" Clanless tried to grasp the words. "I'm missing a lot, I think."

"Blood-wraiths," Sugh said before anyone else could answer. "Lots of them."

"The Ghamba Lam says Daviland could interfere with, um, something involving the blood," Kekeen said. "And great evil could be unleashed."

"That's bad, but..." Clanless hesitated, looking around the room. "Why is that our problem? Why do we have to do anything?" He was free again. All he wanted to do was take Kekeen and leave. But all these other friends were important to him also. They didn't need to go into danger. Did they?

Koland sighed. "We put Daviland in power, and he's now controlled by a wraith. We can't sit back while he destroys the Empire."

"Blood-wraiths," Sugh repeated. "He will release them, and they will enslave us all."

"How do you know it's wraiths?" Qara asked. "Ghouk didn't say anything about that."

Sugh shrugged. "The goddess said so. Also Suirel, I think."

"Apparently, the goddess talks to Sugh sometimes," Kekeen whispered.

"He told me that once, but I forgot," Clanless answered. He groaned and sat back. War in the heavens. And he was a part of it. "Four days of freedom," he muttered.

"What's that?" she asked.

"I've only had four total days of freedom since I became a man. Tomorrow will be day five. Can't I just enjoy it? For once in my life?"

Kekeen looked up into his eyes. "If you want to be with me, that's where I'm going. I can't sit back and let others suffer and, and be captured by the wraiths. Not when I can do something about it. Can you?"

Clanless looked over her head, and his eyes met Koland's. "If you love Kekeen, you have to love all of her, not just part of her," Koland had said in the dark streets of Et-Baylak. "Her belief in the value of each individual is what led her to you."

Like individuals captured by wraiths. No, not captured. Controlled. Enslaved. The blood-wraiths enslaved people. If not for his wolf pelt, Yul would enslave him too. As much as he wanted to run away, he couldn't. "We should go to the mines," he said at last.

"Does no one care that it's my cousin's carriage?" Gogeku complained.

"Assuming we can find a way to leave," Koland said. "We can't just roll out of here. We'd never even make it to the city gates. We're going to have to do some kind of negotiating with the city Lords."

"That's above me," Clanless said. "I can talk to arena fighters and slaves, if you need it, but Lords aren't going to listen to me."

"Or most of us," Koland admitted. "Badaar, it appears it will be up to you and me. And Qara?"

"I know some people," she said.

"All right then. Let's see what we can do. Sugh, if you would check on the slaves again? And Clanless, you're welcome to talk to that fighter." Koland stood up, followed by everyone else.

Kekeen went to speak with her father, while Swift Claw approached Clanless. "There are many things I don't understand," the beastman said.

"You and me both."

"Wolf Chosen has two women?"

"Oh, ah, no…" Clanless glanced at Qara, who only smirked at him. "I have one…" He tried to explain why he and Qara had lied.

Swift Claw struggled with the concept. "You deceived us, to protect the woman?"

"Yes. That's it exactly."

"Why did she not want a man of her own? There were strong ones willing."

"She wants a, uh, human man. One that she loves."

"But you are not that man."

"No, I'm not." He frowned at Qara for not assisting him, but her expression this time confused him. She looked… sad?

"I'm ruined," Gogeku moaned. "My cousin will be furious. Where is the profit?"

Sugh patted him on the back. "Cheer up. I am a free man now. I will have need of new clothing!" He headed toward the door. "Clanless, do you know your way around?"

"Not a bit. I've been in a cell for most of my time here."

"I will show you then. Come!"

Clanless motioned for Swift Claw to join them. "Kekeen?"

"Coming," she said, stepping away from her father.

"I think I'll keep this," Koland said, holding Chuluun's cane up and looking down its length.

"You don't need a cane," Kekeen told him.

"Need? Who said anything about 'need'?"

Gogeku looked up. "If you're keeping that, you'll need a new outfit to match, you know..."

Sugh led the way down through the arena structure. Along the way, he greeting a couple of slaves, reassuring them that Chuluun was locked up and that they'd figure out a way to deal with the rest of the city.

"I have so many questions," Clanless said to Kekeen. "How did Sugh get back? Where's Hagh? How did you even meet Badaar? How did all of this happen?"

"There's a lot to tell." She took his hand as they entered a wider hallway. "Do you want to hear it all now or after you talk with this guy?"

Clanless came to a stop. "I recognize this area. Sugh, I can find my way from here."

"Then I will let you do so." The cheerful fighter turned left down a different hall and kept going.

"All right. Let's take a break and catch up," Clanless said. "I feel like we're just running from one thing to the next." He gestured to the beastman. "Have you even met Swift Claw?"

"Not officially," Kekeen said. "But I am very glad to meet you, Swift Claw."

The beastman bowed. "I am pleased to meet Wolf Chosen's true woman."

"Wolf Chosen?"

"It's what the beastmen call me." Clanless pointed to his wolf pelt. "Swift Claw is the reason I'm alive and here. If not for him, I don't know what would have happened to Qara and me."

Kekeen took Swift Claw's hand and held it with both of hers. "Thank you for bringing him back to me."

For the first time since he'd known him, it seemed Swift Claw didn't know what to say. Clanless chuckled. He considered telling her about the covenant but decided to wait on that one. "So... what's been happening in Et-Baylak?"

While Clanless listened to Kekeen's tale, his emotions roiled. Zektel had done more damage than he'd expected. When Kekeen told about Hagh's death, he had to sit down.

"He had... three or four weeks of freedom." Life without Hagh. It hit almost as hard as Zaluu's death.

Kekeen moved behind the chair and put her arms around his neck. "How old was he when he became an arena fighter?"

Clanless cocked his head. "He once said he'd been fighting for ten years, so he must have been much older."

"Then he had some years of freedom before that, right?"

"I suppose." Clanless looked down. Again he'd been reminded how little he knew about the people around him, those he considered friends. Had that been part of Zektel's influence? Keeping him from forming bonds with anyone other than her? Or had it been his own self-centeredness? Either way, he needed to change, to be better.

"Goddess, take him to your side," he whispered. "Hagh always believed in you."

Swift Claw crossed both arms across his chest and bowed almost to the floor. "We honor the fallen."

Clanless almost smiled at the display. He took a deep breath and got to his feet.

"All right, let's talk to Duurald."

The three of them entered the prison. Clanless stopped at his former cell at first, shaking his head at Chuluun, who stood right at the bars watching them.

"I suppose you see this as some form of irony," the arena owner said calmly.

"Not really." Clanless touched the bars. "I see it as some form of justice."

Chuluun might have chuckled. "Whose justice would that be? There is no judge or Lord in the Empire that would even consider any of my actions as criminal."

"There's a morality beyond just the law!" Kekeen snapped.

"Ah, the abolitionist. You're the one who should be facing justice. Inciting slaves against their master is a crime in Ulken, and anywhere else in the Empire."

"Not any more."

"I look forward to your execution. Perhaps I can persuade the court to allow you to die in the arena. The only problem will be deciding the method. I'm leaning toward wild dogs at the moment."

Clanless slammed his fist against a bar. "That's enough!"

A long, low chuckle came from the next cell, followed by a few hand claps. Clanless left Chuluun and looked in on Duurald. The fighter sat in a disheveled, dirty mess against the wall. He laughed again at the sight of Clanless.

"Who would have guessed the mighty Clanless would lose his temper over a woman? No, not just his temper… everything! You're losing everything!"

"Are you confused about who's behind the bars here, Duurald?"

The prisoner gestured around him. "This? You've led the slaves in taking over, but you can't possibly keep things like this. What will you do when the city guards arrive?"

"Fight if we have to." Clanless stepped closer. "You could join us, you know."

"You really are crazy. Have you already forgotten how we just fought? Or how you used your taichin magic against me?"

"Chuluun held your bloodbond. I don't hold that against you. Come on, Duurald. You can be a free man."

Duurald got to his feet. "No. I can't. We've been over this." He pointed to the other cell. "You may have taken the bloodbond from him at the moment, but it's still his. I still belong to him until he dies or frees me himself."

"Kindly leave my slave alone," Chuluun called. "Duurald, would you like to execute these two when the time comes?"

Clanless leaned on the bars. "We'll get the bloodbond and force him to free you, if you want it! All you have to do is ask. Join us, Duurald. There are bigger things going on, bigger causes to fight for."

Duurald raised an eyebrow. "What do you mean? Bigger causes?"

"A great evil is about to be unleashed. We're going to stop it. Come with us. You'll have plenty of chances to fight, but this time, you'd be fighting for something important. Something more than a cheering crowd. You can be a hero."

"A hero?" Duurald snorted. "I wasn't born in a clanhold. Like you."

"Pardon," Swift Claw said, stepping out of the shadows near Chuluun's cell. "I am trying to understand this."

"Oh, the beast speaks," Chuluun said. "I heard they could be taught basic words, but this is impressive."

Swift Claw pointed to Duurald. "He could fight with us, but cannot because of this man." He pointed back to Chuluun.

"Mostly," Clanless said. "That man has made him a slave, like he tried to do with us. But it's the blood-magic that holds it. He has to release it."

"Or die," Duurald added, watching the beastman.

"That is what I thought." Swift Claw reached through the bars and seized Chuluun by the neck. Before Clanless or Kekeen could say anything, his claws ripped the arena master's throat apart.

"No!" Clanless lunged to Swift Claw's side as Chuluun collapsed. "Kekeen, get a healer! Maybe we can—"

"He is dead, Wolf Chosen. My claws do not miss their mark." Swift Claw stepped back, blood dripping from his hands.

Kekeen stood frozen, both hands over her mouth.

Duurald laughed. "You were right, Clanless! I'm a free man now!" He pointed to Swift Claw. "I like you, beastman. You know what needs to be done and do it. No wasted time with all of this talk, talk, talk."

Clanless stared down at Chuluun's lifeless body. "He didn't have to die. We could have…"

"Why not?" Swift Claw asked. "He made slaves of us. He hurt us. He made a slave of this man and others. He deserved to die."

"But you don't kill people when they're helpless and locked up!" Kekeen burst out.

Swift Claw cocked his head and looked at her. "Why not?"

"There are laws… rules… you can't do that! It's not right!"

Swift Claw lowered his head. "I must apologize then. I am not familiar with your people's laws. Perhaps I have erred."

"So." Duurald bounced on his heels. "Are you going to let me out?"

Clanless leaned his head against the bars and took a deep breath. This was not how he'd wanted this to play out. For one thing, Koland and Badaar would have a much tougher time with the city Lords now that Chuluun was dead. It would look like a slave uprising now, instead of… whatever it was. Too much. He took another deep breath. Move on.

"Can I trust you, Duurald?"

"Trust me to do what? Fight this evil stuff? Become a hero? Sure. Why not? Sounds like fun."

Clanless looked him in the eyes. "How much do you know about blood-wraiths?"

◖◖◖●◗◗◗

Kekeen slipped away with a whispered excuse of needing to relieve herself. In truth, she wanted to get away from Chuluun's dead body and the darkness of the cells. She sat down next to a small table in what must have been a guard room.

She couldn't blame Swift Claw too much. He didn't know human laws and customs. In his eyes, he'd done something completely logical and necessary. His appearance was… somewhat terrifying, but he'd saved Aldan. They'd formed some kind of bond. He'd be going with them wherever they went now, if she understood correctly.

But that Duurald… she didn't understand why Aldan wanted him to join them. Between himself, the beastman, and Sugh, didn't they have enough warriors now? Why recruit this man who'd shared none of their trials, who'd never supported their cause? It made no sense. How could they trust him?

She glanced back at the door to the cells. Aldan had spent close to three weeks here, most of it inside one of those cells. And before that, he'd spent weeks in a cave. And his first encounter with her, she'd demanded answers about a blood-wraith. Maybe that explained why he was trying to recruit an old friend. Everyone needed friends. After a life on the road, she knew that better than most.

In some ways, she envied Aldan. He had such an easygoing camaraderie with the other fighters, like Sugh. She'd never experienced anything like that. She had any number of casual friends throughout the Empire, but nothing that she could call solid.

"Oh good, there you are." Qara came down the stairs into the guard room. "They want you back up there."

Kekeen stood up. "What's happening?"

"It seems the Lords of the city are sending a delegation right now. Koland and Badaar want you to be in the meeting."

"Why me? I thought they were handling it."

Qara shrugged. "Oh, I don't know. Maybe because you helped plan this entire thing, or because you gave the big speech to all the slaves that everyone heard. Maybe they just want a pretty face to make up for theirs." She gestured toward the stairs. "They're arriving right this minute. You might want to hurry."

Kekeen headed for the stairs. "Tell Aldan where I've gone!"

"Bain used to tell stories about blood-wraiths," Duurald said. "I remember that." His mocking grin vanished once Kekeen left them alone.

Clanless looked down, recalling something. "You… you had a strong reaction to them, didn't you?"

Duurald didn't answer.

"One of them now possesses Daviland, the rebel leader who defeated the Hawk King," Clanless explained. "We believe he plans to release many more of them."

"How many?"

"All of them. Whatever that means. And Bain's in trouble."

"Bain? What does he have to do with all of this?"

Clanless told the story of what happened at the Throat of the Goddess. Swift Claw moved nearer to listen.

Duurald said nothing for a few minutes. Then: "I'll go with you."

"I'm… glad to hear it. We could use your help."

Duurald glanced at Swift Claw, then beckoned for Clanless to come closer. The beastman, recognizing the motion, moved further away.

"I know you think I'm an idiot, Clanless."

"Duurald, I—"

"Shut up and listen. I'll go with you, because if there's anything this world doesn't need, it's more blood-wraiths."

"I agree."

Duurald stared at him with the most intense look Clanless had ever seen on his face. "They're evil. Pure evil."

"I know."

"Do you? Do you know why I was sold as a slave in the first place?"

"Your family had debts? I think that was almost everyone's reason…"

Duurald smacked his fist against the cell wall. "My own mother sold me. Except it wasn't her. It hadn't been her for months. I didn't figure it out until I heard Bain's stories. A blood-wraith took her. Made her do the most horrible things. I still have nightmares, Clanless."

"I, I'm sorry, Duurald. I didn't know."

"Of course you didn't. I never told anyone." He stepped back. "And I didn't tell you either. You got that?"

Clanless nodded. "I think so. Let me find the keys and get you out of there."

SOCIETAL CHANGES

At the top of the stairs, Kekeen met Gogeku, who directed her to the meeting location. The room, furnished with a fine table and a dozen chairs, must have been used by Chuluun for important meetings. It certainly looked the part.

Koland and Badaar were welcoming two men when she arrived. A bearded man, dressed in fine clothing and carrying a crystal-topped cane, took a seat at the end of the table as if he owned it. The second man stood by his side. He appeared much younger and wore simpler clothing. Kekeen guessed he must be a soldier, though he hadn't been allowed to bring any weapons inside.

"Ah, Kekeen. Gentlemen, this is my daughter, who has been an invaluable part of this day's events," Koland said. "Kekeen, this is Lord Daban and Lieutenant Adrigray."

"Lieutenant? I would think we rated a captain, at least," she replied.

"You're lucky we're talking to you at all!" the soldier snapped. "A slave uprising should be dealt with firmly and at once!"

"Now, now, Lieutenant," Lord Daban said, settling back into his chair. "We have come to hear these people out. Am I right in assuming this attractive woman is the one who gave the oh-so-inspiring speech a few hours ago?"

Attractive woman? The dress really did make a difference. No member of the nobility had ever referred to her in such pleasant terms.

"She is." Koland took a seat two chairs away from the Lord. "But I would like to start by immediately countering the good lieutenant's misguided description of today's events. This is not a slave uprising in any way."

"What would you call it, then?" Lord Daban asked with a bemused smile.

"Justice," Kekeen said. She stood behind her father. Badaar took one of the other chairs. "The Empire is changing. It's time for Ulken to catch up to it. Both slavery and the arena system are abolished."

"Hm. So you say. Rumor has reached us of events in Et-Baylak. But until we receive official confirmation, we cannot accept any such… changes."

Badaar stirred. "Am I not official enough for you?"

Lord Daban gave him a respectful nod. "I will be honest with you all. It is only because of the presence of Badaar here that this meeting is even taking place. As the good lieutenant said, occurrences like this would normally be put down with a show of force." He paused. "A show of force that is currently waiting for the opportunity to storm this facility and deal with anyone inside. Only my word holds them back right now."

"We appreciate that," Koland said. "We would all much prefer that this be resolved without any further blood being wastefully spilled."

"I'm sure you would. The priests would appreciate it too. You must realize that regardless of how many of the arena fighters you have persuaded to join you, the rest of the slaves have no training."

"We would crush them in a matter of minutes," Lieutenant Adrigray declared.

"You see my dilemma." Lord Daban focused his attention toward Badaar. "You're the only one here we recognize, and we're frankly confused by your presence."

"That's not true!" Kekeen exclaimed. "You recognize Clanless! Otherwise, this whole arena event wouldn't even be happening."

"Yes, well, when Chuluun announced that Clanless would be fighting for him, it did create quite a stir," the Lord agreed. "But I fail to see what that has to do with any of this."

"It's the entire reason we're here," Koland said. "Clanless came here as a free man, and Chuluun took him prisoner. He was forced to fight against his will. We came to rescue him." He tapped his new cane on the floor. "And to do that, we had to free the rest of Chuluun's slaves, something that would have happened anyway, once more 'official' word arrived from the capital."

"Hm. I will need to hear this from Clanless, of course. And where is Chuluun, might I ask?"

"He is down below."

"He's dead," Kekeen interrupted. "He succumbed to injuries he received when he tried to kill me." She could see Koland stiffen at her words. It would have been helpful to be able to tell him about Chuluun before this.

"That's all we need to know," the lieutenant said. "There's no one left here to rescue, then."

"Except us, if you are insistent on insulting our hosts," Lord Daban said, his affable look vanishing.

"Regardless of what happens here, we will not detain you," Koland said.

"Then let's go." Adrigray took a couple of steps toward the door.

Lord Daban tapped him with his cane. "Don't be a fool. There are factors here we must consider."

"What factors?" Adrigray spread his hands. "Chuluun is dead. His slaves have killed him and taken over the arena. That's all we need to know. The only proof of anything different is one old man wearing a pair of medals."

Badaar rose to his feet. "Would you like to test your mettle against that old man?"

Lord Daban rapped the table with his cane and stomped his foot. "This is ridiculous." He pointed at Adrigray. "The name of Badaar is well known and respected. If you weren't so young, you'd know this. Now come back here and let's finish this."

The lieutenant glared around the room but returned to his place behind Lord Daban's chair. He folded his arms and didn't speak again.

"How can we come to a peaceful resolution?" Koland asked as Badaar sat back down.

Lord Daban sighed. "Regrettably, I don't see a clear way forward. The best I can probably offer is that you three may leave with whoever accompanied you here. There is no way the other Lords will agree to allowing the slaves to go free."

"Is there... no way to convince you otherwise?"

"Nothing comes to mind."

Koland paused a very long time. "Well then."

Lord Daban shook his head. "I suggest you take my offer. Otherwise, we shall leave and allow the attack to commence."

"There is... one other factor you should consider," Koland said. Kekeen tried not to let her face show her confusion. She couldn't remember her father ever speaking so slow.

Someone knocked at the door. Koland let out a huge breath. "Ah, finally. Kekeen, would you see to that?"

She stepped over to the door and opened it. An irritated Gogeku stood to one side. "My job isn't to escort people around," he grumbled. To Kekeen's shock, a Daghilch stood beside him, a furious expression on his face.

"Um, please come in." Kekeen stood to one side as the red-robed priest swept in.

"Who summoned me?" he demanded. "What is the meaning of all this?"

Koland got to his feet. "You see, Lord Daban, the priesthood also has a voice in all of this."

"In all of what?" the Daghilch demanded. "The slave uprising? It should be ended at once!"

Koland reached inside his coat and withdrew an envelope. He handed it to the Daghilch. "I believe you recognize the seal?"

The Daghilch's eyes widened. He tore the envelope open. His eyes darted over the words of the letter inside. He licked his lips and grimaced. Taking a deep breath, he turned to the end of the table. "Lord Daban, I have received instructions from the Ghamba Lam himself. It is my duty to insist that your soldiers withdraw from the arena and leave the freed slaves to become their own people."

Kekeen tried to control her own shock. When had Koland been able to pull that off?

Lord Daban stood. "Why didn't you begin with that, sir? It would have rendered all of the rest of this discussion moot!"

Koland smiled. "I had to wait for the Daghilch to arrive. He's the only one who could verify the document. You would have assumed a forgery, of course."

"Of course, of course." The Lord shook his head. "Most irregular. This will change everything. Lieutenant? I believe we will be leaving now."

Lieutenant Adrigray unfolded his arms. "You mean you're going to let them all go?"

Lord Daban pointed at the Daghilch. "Never fight against blood, young man. There all the power lies."

The soldier looked from the Lord to the Daghilch. His shoulders slumped, and he moved toward the door.

"We'll select a negotiator to work with the freed slaves," Lord Daban said. "Will you be representing them as they start new lives?"

"I'm afraid not," Koland answered. "They'll need to choose their own leader. We have to be leaving as soon as possible."

Daban's eyebrows rose. "Going to free another city, are you?"

"No, not yet. But we might be saving the world."

Lord Daban chuckled and followed the lieutenant out the door.

Once the guests were gone, Kekeen whirled on her father. "How did you do that? When did you do that?"

Koland grinned. "When you were busy with Gogeku arranging our trip, I made a quick visit to the Ghamba Lam. I persuaded him to provide his help in exchange for the promise that we would bring Clanless to the mines as soon as we were done here."

"Aldan? Why does he want him there?"

"I'm not sure. I suppose he thinks he needs someone who can physically match Daviland, if needed." Koland spun his new cane in a circle.

"I don't trust him," Badaar said. "I've never trusted the priests."

"I don't blame you." Koland tapped the cane on the floor a few times. "That's why I wrote the letter myself. I only needed his signature and seal to make it official."

"Why didn't we just show up with that?" Kekeen demanded. "Why go through all these other plans?"

"I intended it as a backup," Koland explained. "I left the wording a little bit vague about 'freed slaves.' When I wrote it, I intended it to refer only to Aldan and any other arena fighters that might be in the same situation as him." He shrugged. "Of course, it would have been nice to solve it all without any violence. But we had no proof that Clanless was a free man. Now, it applies to him and all the other former slaves. It worked out better than I expected. Having the Daghilch open it here in front of the Lord was the best outcome, I think."

He sighed. "Now, I know we've only been here a single day, but we have to be ready to leave in the morning. Daviland will already be on his way to the mines. We're closer now, but we'll be lucky if we get there on the same day." He opened the door. "I only hope it won't be too late."

CAST DOWN

"Salkhi? Really? Salkhi?" Kekeen shook her head. "I never would have guessed she worked at Pasque House. She even called me cute." She wrinkled her brow. "I don't know what to think of that now."

"Have you seen her since… since I left?" Clanless hesitate to ask, but his curiosity took over.

"Why? Did you want to visit her again?"

"No! I was just… wanting to know if she was all right… after being freed."

"I'm teasing. Mostly." Kekeen smiled at him. "It's High Winter. Even though we're traveling all over the place, most people aren't, you know."

"Right…"

They kept talking for hours. When Koland finally made them separate and get some sleep, much of the night had worn away. In an unused room that once belonged to an arena fighter, Clanless slept in a bed for the first time since leaving Et-Baylak, almost three months ago. He felt more relaxed and at peace than ever. With his fifth day of freedom, he hoped to make it last.

Duurald laughed when he saw the assembled team preparing to depart the next morning. "This is it? This is the great team that will take down the new emperor?"

"We're not going to war," Clanless tried to explain.

"We might be," Sugh put in as he loaded a box of supplies into one of the two carriages. "Who knows how many guards Daviland will have."

"And only the three of us to fight them?" Duurald laughed again. "Oh, I'm sorry. The beastman too."

"Don't forget Badaar," Sugh said cheerfully. "Hero of the Empire."

Duurald shook his head. "This is a joke."

"Then why are you coming?" Kekeen asked from the carriage door.

Duurald spread his arms. "I am a free man. Apparently, I can do whatever I like. Clanless here asked me to join you." He patted Clanless on the shoulder. "And I have nothing better to do."

Kekeen gave a disgusted grunt before ducking back inside.

"At least we have two beautiful women along," Duurald observed.

"If you lay a hand on either of them, you will answer to me." Clanless narrowed his eyes.

"Come now, you can't keep both of them for yourself."

Sugh swung his axe through the air in a nonchalant manner. "And if Clanless is not around, I will defend the women. They are not for you."

Duurald wrinkled his brow. "I know this one is Clanless's girl, but the other—"

"Is not for you," Sugh repeated.

"Why am I going on this trip?" Duurald asked the moon.

"She is not sure either," Sugh said, heading back into the arena.

Duurald looked at Clanless, but he didn't bother to explain. Swift Claw joined them. "We are going to the place of blood, yes?"

"I guess you could call it that," Clanless answered. "We need to stop the blood-wraiths. A man who is possessed by one wants to release them all." Swift Claw had heard his explanation to Duurald, but it wouldn't hurt to repeat it.

"It would not be good." The beastman looked at the sky. "The wind of the Death Lord has been quiet. It is strange."

"Strange how?" Clanless had assumed High Winter was fading.

"The time is too short. It should be seeking still." Swift Claw ran his hands through his hair. "Perhaps it has found a place to rest."

"I don't understand, but, uh, let me know if you notice anything else strange." Clanless still didn't quite grasp the beastman beliefs, but they correlated closely enough that he didn't want to ignore anything Swift Claw might observe.

Koland approached. "Is everyone about ready?"

"I think so." Clanless surveyed the two carriages and the teams of oxen. At least it wouldn't be as crowded as his first trip to the mines. Pleasanter company too.

"I'll be driving the first carriage with Badaar, Qara, and Sugh," the storyteller said. "Can I trust my daughter with you overnight in the other carriage?"

"Swift Claw and Duurald will be with us," Clanless pointed out. When Koland only stared at him, he added, "Yes. You can trust me."

"Glad to hear it. All right, people, let's move! The end of the world isn't going to wait for us!" He clapped his hands and headed toward the first carriage.

"Does he really believe that?" Duurald asked, following Clanless to the second. "The end of the world?"

Clanless nodded. "If everyone is telling the truth about all this, then the priests have been trying to stop this for generations." He pulled himself into the carriage. "That's why they've collected so much blood all these years."

Duurald climbed in after him. "That part is still over my head."

"You still haven't given a good reason for coming," Kekeen said from where she sat, arms folded.

"Clanless, I don't think your girl likes me. I'm hurt." Duurald smiled at her.

"It would help if you told her what you told me," Clanless suggested.

Duurald lost his smile. "That was in confidence."

Clanless nodded and sat down next to Kekeen. "It's your choice."

"Yes." Duurald sat down opposite him and watched Swift Claw clamber in. "Yes, it is."

((((●))))

Two days travel from Ulken took them a little over halfway to the mines. The sun began its sluggish pursuit as though it had lost motivation. Sugh was spending longer than usual preparing the oxen for the day's travels.

"Swift Claw is right." Kekeen pulled the carriage door closed behind her. "It's cold, dreadfully cold out there, but there's almost no wind. I've never seen it like this in High Winter."

"It's the chaos moon," Duurald said. "It causes… chaos."

"The chaos moon is Suirel," Clanless said, "and the beastmen talk about a Lord of the Dead who controls these winds."

"It is his wind!" Swift Claw interjected.

"So Suirel is the Lord of the Dead?" Kekeen asked.

"Mmh. I do not know this name."

Clanless pointed up. "The chaos moon. The second moon in the sky right now. It's only there every thirty years. That's Suirel."

"This moon comes at the same time as the Lord of the Dead's Wind, yes. But the moon is not the Lord of the Dead." Swift Claw cocked his head.

"Not the moon itself." Clanless gestured weakly. "We don't believe the regular moon is actually the goddess either. It's like… where they live."

"They are beings of Wind. Why do they need a place to live?"

"Talking with you is really frustrating sometimes."

"I find it fascinating," Kekeen said. "Tell me more about the winds, Swift Claw."

"I'm going to check on Sugh." Duurald left the carriage, leaving the door open far too long for Clanless's liking. It let in too much cold air.

He settled back and half-listened while the beastman and Kekeen talked. Despite Swift Claw's confusion, it made sense that Suirel and their Lord of the Dead were one and the same. The coincidences were too great. And yet, the beastmen's True Wind and the Empire's goddess had almost nothing in common. It was confusing. For a brief moment, he wondered what the Ghamba Lam would say about all this. He still found it strange that Koland and the others were working with the priests.

Two days of traveling with Kekeen, after not seeing her for months, had been glorious. They sat close together and talked a great deal, but the presence of Duurald and Swift Claw prevented any serious relationship discussion… or action. Many times, Clanless reconsidered his decision to join this mission. He and Kekeen could have gone with Gogeku back to Et-Baylak, and then from there set out to anywhere else in the Empire.

Realistically, he knew he couldn't run away, unless it was somewhere very far. His experience in Ulken had taught him that much, at least. He was too recognizable. He was a free man now, but where could he find peace?

Duurald yanked the door back open. "You need to see this!"

"What is it?" Kekeen asked.

"The biggest wolf in the world! Gotta be."

Clanless and Swift Claw exchanged quick looks before jumping to their feet and clambering out of the carriage. Outside, all of the passengers of the second carriage stood together looking toward the north. Clanless and the others joined them. His eyes meet Qara's briefly. He hadn't said more than a few words to her since the rescue. A twinge of guilt pushed its way into his thoughts. They'd grown so close throughout the winter, but now… He tried to ignore the thoughts and looked out across the winter desert.

Seeing nothing, he almost asked Duurald if he'd been making it up. Then the wolf stepped out from behind a rock around a hundred yards away. It stood still, looking back at them.

Kekeen clutched Clanless's arm. "Is it him? The same wolf?"

"It has to be." His hand reached up to touch the fur pelt on his shoulder. Though the wolf stood much further away than the last time, he recognized its gray fur and the scars, not to mention its unusual size.

"It has come to see its chosen one," Swift Claw said. He knelt in the snow and lowered his head.

"It's just standing there," Koland said after a few moments passed.

"It spoke to us last time," Qara said. "In our heads."

Another half a minute passed.

"I don't hear anything," Duurald said.

"The Wolf Chosen must go nearer," Swift Claw said, his voice muffled from its proximity to the ground.

Clanless didn't argue. He released Kekeen's hand and took several steps toward the wolf. It remained unmoving, watching him. A gentle breeze stirred its fur.

"Do you have something to say to me?" he called. He took a few more steps and tried to remember all that the wolf had said the first time. "Are we still in the dark time?"

"The winter of winters nears its end." Clanless almost jumped when the voice spoke in his head again. It was nothing like Zektel or Yul. There was power behind this voice, power of a different kind than he'd experienced before.

"Isn't that good?" he asked.

"The dark time will continue unless the dark one is cast down."

"What does that mean? Who is the dark one?"

The wolf turned its head to look toward the northwest. "He comes even now. You must hurry."

"You are the most frustrating… person I've ever talked with," Clanless said. "Why can't you answer a simple question?"

"You would do well to listen to me." The wolf looked back at him, piercing him through with its golden eyes.

Clanless took a step back. "I'm listening! But I don't understand. What do you want me to do?"

"Cast down the dark one. Protect those who follow you."

"All right. I… want to protect them." He gestured back. "Swift Claw says you chose me. Is this what he meant?"

"You were chosen, but not by me."

"Do you… do you mean the goddess?"

The wolf's head swung away again. "He comes. You must hurry."

Before Clanless could ask anything else, the wolf bounded away. It loped across the snow at a pace faster than any beast Clanless knew.

Kekeen caught up to him and grabbed his arm again. "What did it say to you?"

Clanless watched the wolf leave. "We need to hurry."

((((●)))))

The gates to the mine complex were closed when they arrived. Nothing appeared much different from the last time they'd been here. But Sugh pointed at the ground. "Someone else has been here recently," he said.

Koland examined the road and the area around the gates. "Very recently. A number of wagons or carriages have gone through here." He looked up. "And then they closed the gates behind them."

"A lot of trouble would have been avoided if we'd done the same," Clanless said. He took a look around, hoping not to spot any of the lizard beasts again.

"So Daviland is already here?" Qara asked.

"Looks that way." Koland rapped on the gates with his cane.

"The rope ladder is missing," Sugh said, walking along the front of the twenty-foot-tall wall. "How are we to get inside?"

"There's a mountain and high hills, but I can't see much of anything," Kekeen complained. "What a desolate place."

Swift Claw touched the wall. "What is on the other side?" he asked.

"There is a bar holding the gate closed," Sugh said. "It is very heavy. But if the rope ladder were here, we could climb up—" He broke off as Swift Claw dug his claws into the surface of the wall and clambered up it without any difficulty.

"That'll work," Duurald said.

A moment later, Swift Claw threw the rope ladder down. The three arena fighters climbed up and over. Together, they lifted the bar and opened the gates. Only then did Clanless turn to see much more than he'd expected.

At the foot of the hills in the inner yard waited a caravan of wagons and carriages. Four wagons carried massive crystal containers full of blood, much like those he'd seen beneath the temple in Et-Baylak. A fifth one, the closest to the inclined road, also held one of the containers, but it had been shattered by an avalanche of falling rock. A pool of blood larger than the baths of the arena sank slowly into the ground around it. The same avalanche had destroyed part of the road after the first switchback, making it inaccessible to anything with wheels.

Several dozen red-robed priests gathered around the wagons. A few of them lay face-down on the ground near the spilled blood. Were they dead or praying? They had no doubt seen the newcomers entering, but no one came to greet them.

"We helped the priests clear out the rockslide from before," Sugh said. "But this is much worse. It will take many men to fix this."

Their two carriages entered through the gates. "Let's get this closed again," Clanless said. "I'd rather not repeat the mistakes of last time."

"By all means," Duurald said, helping him, "let's make new mistakes."

Once the gates were shut and barred, Koland led the group toward the priests. "Hello!" he called. "Is the Ghamba Lam available, by any chance?"

A Daghilch approached them, eyes darting from one party member to the other. His gaze lingered on Clanless. "The Ghamba Lam is… occupied," he declared in a solemn tone.

Koland rolled his eyes. "Listen, we know he came here with Daviland. We're here to help. Where are they?"

"They're up there," Clanless said, pointing toward the mines. "I'm guessing they went up before the rocks fell."

The Daghilch glared at him. "I do not answer to abominations."

"We're here to help your master," Koland said. "Daviland is not himself. He needs to be stopped."

"You're a little late for that!" another priest broke in. "Aren't you one of those who put him in power?"

Clanless stepped forward. "Regardless of anything that's come before, or whatever you may think of me, I am here to stop what's happening up there. Let us through. Unless you want a swarm of blood-wraiths claiming the lot of you!" He waved the moonblade for good measure.

The priests stepped back, talking and grumbling amongst themselves. The ones who had been lying on the ground got up out of curiosity.

Clanless and company walked between two lines of red robes. They made their way around the spilled blood and came to the base of the inclining road. Together, they stared up at the destruction of the avalanche.

"He certainly made sure they can't get the blood up there," Qara observed. "What do we do now?"

"Who's up there with him?" Koland asked the priests.

"The Ghamba Lam and Daviland were accompanied by that heretic, Demujin," one of them spat.

"No guards or anything?"

"Two guards. And two Daghilches to accompany the Ghamba Lam."

"Why do I have to drag everything out of you people? Can no one in my life give a straight answer?" Clanless wanted to throw something.

Sugh examined the rocks. "I think we can climb over it," he said. "But we must be careful."

"I'm not climbing that," Qara declared.

"We can do it," Duurald said, hefting his mace. "The arena fighters. And the beastman, of course."

Kekeen took hold of Clanless's arm. "Don't leave me again."

"Kekeen… I…" He swallowed. "I have to go. Zektel is in Daviland because of me. And I think I can get her out." Not to mention what the wolf said.

"Daughter." Koland stood nearby. "You have to let him go." He glanced toward the gate. "And we might be needed down here."

"Whatever for?" Qara asked.

Koland looked up as a small flurry of snow swept over their heads. "The weather has been too nice. We won't be the only ones traveling."

Clanless set the moonblade down and took Kekeen in his arms. "I will come back to you," he promised. "I will always come back to you."

"So you say. I had to come get you this time."

He kissed her then. No other words mattered.

"The blood-wraiths aren't going to wait for us," Duurald said. He slung his mace onto his back where it slipped into a holder. Sugh and Swift Claw joined him on the road.

Clanless looked at the moonblade. "I, uh…"

"Oh goddess." Qara ran to one of the wagons. "This is exactly what the beastmen were talking about!" She pulled out her dagger and cut off pieces of the reins, much to one of the priest's displeasure. Together, she and Kekeen rigged a quick strap to hold the moonblade on his back.

Once equipped, he gave Kekeen one last kiss and chased after the others. They passed the first switchback and came to the debris of the avalanche. The rocks had torn through the road, carrying most of it down the hill. To cross it now, they would have to cling to the rocks and dirt as they moved sideways.

Sugh scratched his head. "If we had time and some big trees, we could build a bridge here."

"We have neither," Clanless said, reaching toward the nearest protruding rock.

"I will go first," Swift Claw said. He moved past Clanless and scrambled onto the rocks. He moved across with ease, arriving on the other side in a few moments.

"Great," Duurald said. "Does anyone else have claws on their hands and feet?"

"We can do it." Clanless pulled himself on to the rock and sought out another handhold. Step by step, he made his way across.

"Very close," Swift Claw encouraged.

At that moment, the rock he'd grasped with his right hand tore out of the dirt. Clanless lost his balance and wavered. Swift Claw seized his wrist and yanked him the rest of the way across.

"Thanks." Clanless caught his breath while watching the other two cross without incident.

"Should have let us go first and show you how it's done," Duurald said.

Clanless took a quick look down at Kekeen before facing the road. "Let's finish this."

Step by step, they trudged up the road. They passed by the mine entrances, dark and snow-trimmed, and beneath the two "eyes." Though he couldn't see anyone, Clanless felt sure Daviland or someone else watched their ascent from one of those vantage points.

At last they reached the main entrance. A single guard stood waiting and watching them, holding a torch. "You are expected," he called as they drew near.

"Of course we are," Sugh said. "Are you here to fight us, or escort us to your master?" He unleashed his axe and took a practice swing.

The guard laughed. "I would be moonbent indeed to try to fight the four of you!" He turned and gestured for them to follow.

"We know the way," Clanless mumbled. He struggled to remove the straps holding his moonblade, then moved to join the others. At the same moment, it hit him again: the overwhelming sensations of the smell, taste, and presence of blood. So much blood. He'd somehow forgotten about how it affected him. He bent over, crouching with the moonblade between his knees.

"Wolf Chosen. Are you all right?" Swift Claw stood before him.

"It's the blood," he whispered. "Give me a moment to adjust."

Swift Claw raised his snout and sniffed. "Yes, there is much blood here."

Clanless almost laughed. "You don't know the half of it."

"What's the problem?" Duurald asked.

"It is the blood," Swift Claw answered. "It calls to him."

"Sands." Duurald shook his head. "Even if you're not a taichin, you're still strange, Clanless."

"I won't argue with that." He straightened up, struggling to keep the sensations under control. "Let's go."

The tunnel sloped upward. Somehow, it seemed longer than the first time. It didn't matter. He had to do this. Zektel was his responsibility. He would cast her out. That had to be what the great wolf had been hinting. At last, they entered the huge chamber containing the Throat of the Goddess.

Weak sunlight filtered up through the "eyes," but the current inhabitants of the chamber had mounted torches all around, filling it with flickering light. In the presence of the Throat, though, all of his determination and willpower fled. He dropped to one knee, gasping. The sensations were stronger than before. He couldn't breathe. Something radiated from that bizarre hole in the floor. The blood, yes, but something more. Different from the last time. Malice. Evil.

"You can feel it, can't you?" asked a familiar voice.

Clanless lifted his eyes to see Daviland watching him. The rebel leader stood near the entrance of the Throat, flanked by the Ghamba Lam and another man he took to be Demujin. Two Daghilches stood nearby, shifting nervously and looking around. The guard who escorted them joined a second guard and stood watching the four newcomers, hands on their maces.

Daviland licked his lips. "The sheer power of the blood… and so much more. Clanless, you can feel it, just as I do."

"Are we going to fight then?" Duurald asked.

The Ghamba Lam laughed, almost hysterical. "It's too late for fighting! I warned you all! Without the blood down below, there's nothing to hold back the evil!"

Sugh pointed down to the wagons. "We will bring the blood up here. How long do we have?"

"Even if you could, it's too late," Daviland said. "But you won't. Demujin here made sure of that."

Clanless looked at the cult leader. He appeared completely ordinary. How?

"I wouldn't get near him," Daviland went on. "Clan Berge blood-magic gave him the strength to tear those rocks apart… but he took a lot, and it hasn't worn off yet."

Swift Claw leaned close to Clanless. "Share with me, Wolf Chosen. We fight as one."

"Not that… kind of fight," he answered.

"It matters not." Swift Claw clenched his fists, lifted his snout and let out an ear-splitting howl.

"Is that supposed to intimidate us?" Daviland asked.

"It intimidated me," Sugh said.

At once, the blood sensations and the malice faded, and Clanless straightened with a gasp. Swift Claw wavered, but stood next to him. "We fight as one," he repeated.

Clanless couldn't believe it. "You're taking half my struggles. That's amazing."

"I have no idea what's going on here, but—" Daviland broke off. "Oh."

"He's coming," the Ghamba Lam murmured. He backed away with his two priests before falling to his knees. "We've failed. All these centuries... and we've failed."

Clanless felt it too. The source of the malignancy drew closer.

"Who's coming?" Duurald asked. "None of this makes any sense!" He started toward Daviland, but Demujin stepped in the way. Duurald swung his mace at the smaller man. With utter calm, the cult leader caught the mace in mid-air. He yanked it, pulling Duurald toward him. A palm heel strike to Duurald's chest sent him flying across the chamber. He hit the wall and slid down. Clanless couldn't tell if he were conscious or even alive.

But the sensations grew. A fearsome presence of hate, malice and anger. Even with Swift Claw sharing the feelings, Clanless staggered back.

A cold wind swept through the chamber. Swift Claw dropped into a crouch, baring his teeth, claws at ready. "His wind..."

The eyes of everyone in the chamber turned to the open passage on the opposite side. Somehow, Clanless knew what he would see before it happened. He'd seen it in his nightmares. The whole world seemed to shake.

"Great Lord," Yul whispered inside his head.

A one-eyed, blood-soaked god strode into the chamber.

BAIN

Kekeen watched until Aldan and the others disappeared from view into the mine entrance far above. She closed her eyes and whispered a prayer. If anyone could stop Daviland now, Aldan could. She had to believe it.

A thump came from the gates.

"I knew it," Koland said. "But too soon!" He raced up the inclined road toward the first switchback. Kekeen and Qara chased after him.

"What is it? Who is it?"

Koland stood still, staring out past the gates. The women joined him. From this height, they could see over the wall. What Kekeen saw chilled her beyond the cold air that surrounded them.

"Goddess," Qara whispered.

Another loud series of thumps came from the gates. Beyond it stood hundreds, maybe even thousands of soldiers of the Sar Empire. Kekeen couldn't count them all. Beasts of burden, war mounts, and wagons carrying supplies were interspersed among the orderly formations of soldiers.

"The weather has been too good," Koland groaned. "So many more than I expected." He hurried back down the road.

"Is it… General Ghan?" Kekeen asked.

"Yes, yes. We have only one chance now."

Several of the priests met them at the bottom of the road. "Storyteller, who is it? Should we open the gates?" they asked.

"It's the army. And you may as well open the gates. They'll break them down if you don't, and they'll probably be in a bad mood if they have to do that."

Several priests hastened toward the gates while others continued to ask questions. Koland pushed his way past them and hurried to the carriage where a solitary figure stood patting one of the oxen.

"Badaar! We need you!" Koland grasped the man's shoulder and turned him to face them.

"How?" Qara muttered. "He's been worthless since the arena."

Badaar looked toward the gates without seeing them. "What is it?" he asked without any energy.

Koland pointed. "General Ghan is here. You know him. 'The Leopard King,' you called him."

Badaar's eyes flickered. "Leopard. Yes. Very fierce."

A group of priests struggled to lift the mighty crossbar.

"Out of all of us here, you're the only one who can speak to him." Koland pointed to himself and the priests. "He doesn't know me, or any of the rest of us, and he has little respect for religion. He's a soldier. We need you, weapons master. We need the Hero of the Empire."

"I don't know… if I can."

Kekeen stepped up. "Badaar, we need you. I need you." She pointed up the hill. "Aldan—Clanless—may be in the fight of his life, and he needs you! Your last fighter!"

The gate opened. A group of soldiers immediately rushed in, pushing the priests aside. Three other soldiers walked in through the center of them, heading toward the blood wagons and the road.

Badaar straightened up. "I will do it. For Clanless." He looked at Qara. "Will you come with me?"

She blinked. "Me?"

"I listened to you in the carriage. You worked with arena fighters for years too."

"I, I didn't know you heard any of that."

"Many voices speak to me, but I hear them all. Now, let us greet the Leopard." Badaar held out his handless arm, and Qara took it. Together, they marched to meet the approaching General.

"We're not going to hang back, are we?" Kekeen asked.

"Of course not." Koland offered her his arm. She chuckled and took it. They trailed behind the other two but stayed close enough to hear.

Kekeen hadn't known what to expect with General Ghan, but he didn't disappoint. His immaculate gold and red uniform didn't look as though he'd been traveling across the frozen wilderness. He stood a few inches taller than the two soldiers escorting him and walked with a firm and deliberate stride, almost inhuman in a way. His face, decorated with a short goatee, appeared locked in a perpetual frown.

His eyebrows rose when he recognized the weapons master. "Badaar? You're the last person I would have expected to meet here today. What is all this?"

Badaar snapped his heels together and gave a short bow. Qara, not expecting it, almost stumbled before she turned it into a curtsy of her own. "General Ghan, sir. I would be delighted to explain exactly what is happening here, if you don't mind."

The General turned to one of his escorts. "Have the troops start moving in. Move those blood wagons out of the way. Tell the engineers to get me across that rockslide." He turned back to Badaar. "Now, I will hear from you, Hero of the Empire."

"Twice," Qara said just loud enough to be heard.

"As you may have heard by now, the Hawk King is dead," Badaar said. Without waiting for a reaction, he kept going: "Daviland, who overthrew him, has been ruling the Empire during High Winter. Unfortunately, based on testimony of those I trust, he has been possessed by a blood-wraith and now seeks to disrupt the religious ceremony here."

"I see." The General stroked his beard.

A Daghilch gained the courage to speak out. "Noble General, if we are not able to deliver this blood to the Throat of the Goddess, it will be a disaster!"

Ghan's eyes darted to Koland and Kekeen. "Are these some of those you trust?"

"Yes, sir. And my best fighters, led by Clanless himself, have ascended to stop Daviland. Perhaps, with your help, we can aid them."

"We'll have to see what we can find up there." He turned back to the his second aide. "Tell those engineers I want to walk across the rockslide in the next five minutes. The situation is more dire than I suspected."

Kekeen wrinkled her forehead. More dire? What could he have known or suspected? The army had been trapped in the north by High Winter. How would he have any clue about what was happening here at the mines? She started to open her mouth to ask when the General swung back again.

"You will, of course, accompany me," he said to Badaar. "Bring whoever you like. Without the Hawk King, it is up to us to determine the destiny of the Sar Empire. Come!"

"Bain!" Sugh shouted. "You live!"

"It's not Bain," Clanless said.

Outwardly, the newcomer appeared to be Bain. He looked exactly as he had on the day over two months ago when he slid down into the Throat… except, of course, that he was covered in blood. And yet he couldn't be Bain. The horrifying hate and malice radiated from him. His very presence felt like a violation of the natural order, an upright abomination in shades of red.

"Oh, Bain is here," the thing said in Bain's voice. "We're together. He came, seeking power for himself. And he found… me." He looked around the room. Aside from Swift Claw's combat pose, everyone else stood still, staring. "Do I need to introduce myself, perhaps?"

"Suirel," Demujin said in a low voice. He dropped to his knees and put his face to the floor.

"Yessss… that is what most of you call me." He turned to Daviland. "Zektel, my dear. How delightful. You have done well. Once you stopped wasting your time with that one, of course." He gestured with his thumb at Clanless. Daviland, with a smile, knelt beside Demujin, but kept his face up.

"Clanless?" Sugh stepped near him. "What should we do?"

"I don't know."

"Do?" Suirel/Bain chuckled. "You will do whatever I want you to do. I am lord of this world." He swept his hands in a circle, and a gust of wind swirled around him. "I am the ruler of the power of the air. You will worship me."

"Never!" the Ghamba Lam shouted. "We worship the goddess alone!"

Suirel rolled his eye. "Your goddess is weak. She couldn't stop me. And now there is no one to oppose me. I will have dominion over all life on this pathetic planet. And my children will rule beside me."

Clanless stepped forward, fighting against the blood sensations and Suirel's aura. "We will oppose you."

Suirel regarded him. "Who is this 'we'? You alone are immune to my children's control, and only so long as you wear that fur. As for everyone else…" He swept one hand through the air as though gathering something, then flicked his open palm toward Sugh. A gust of wind rushed across the chamber and embraced him. Sugh stiffened.

"No, no, no." Clanless spun to face his friend, just in time. Sugh swung his axe with what would have been a devastating stroke. Clanless caught and deflected it with the moonblade. "Sugh!"

"His wind is not his own!" Swift Claw launched himself at the big fighter.

At the same moment, Suirel repeated his wind gesture. Across the chamber, Duurald's body shook. His eyes opened, and he reached for his mace.

Sugh caught Swift Claw with the back side of his axe, shoving the beastman away. Clanless tried to swing the moonblade, hoping to cut Sugh just enough. But his strike moved too slow, hampered by the churning turmoil within him.

Duurald pulled himself to his feet.

"You are utterly alone, Clanless. You and this pet of yours," Suirel taunted. "As my children claim more and more of your friends, what will you do?"

Clanless barely sidestepped another strike from Sugh.

"Will you kill as many as you can before they defeat you?"

Duurald took a halting step forward.

Swift Claw leaped and swung his scimitar. Sugh ducked to avoid it, but as Swift Claw passed him, the beastman kicked out. The claws on his left foot scratched Sugh's shoulder.

"Or will you submit to me, as all will, in time?"

"He bleeds," Swift Claw shouted.

Clanless reached for the Taint. When they'd been here before, he'd been unable to access it. The blood had been too overwhelming. But with Swift Claw sharing the burden now, he could feel it. But it didn't want to activate. Something stood in his way, pushing against his will. He recognized it, like the one time Zektel had almost controlled him.

"Yul. Get out of my way."

"I am sorry, Aldan. There is one will I must obey above all others."

Duurald appeared to gather himself and started forward, mace at ready.

"Why do you wait?" Swift Claw shouted. He dodged another swing of Sugh's axe.

Clanless fought a battle Swift Claw couldn't see. He pushed against Yul, trying to activate the Taint. If Suirel won here, nothing would stop him from possessing everyone with blood-wraiths. No one would be safe, not even Kekeen. Her face filled his mind. For her.

Duurald broke into a jog, lifting his mace. He would join the fight in seconds.

"Fight as one!" Swift Claw's voice penetrated his internal fight. The beastman stopped and closed his eyes, concentrating. Sugh lifted his axe to take the easy strike.

Clanless felt a sudden surge of will, melding with his own, pushing back against Yul's control. The Taint was there. Like twisting a knife, he activated it.

Sugh froze, shaking. Two steps away, Duurald did the same, his mace only inches from Clanless.

"Stop him!" Suirel yelled.

Sugh and Duurald's faces blurred with red. A thin mist of the color, like blood itself, ripped free from them and rushed toward Suirel. Both wavered, dropped their weapons and collapsed, writhing in pain.

Clanless straightened, sweat pouring from his brow, despite the cold. "I will not kill them," he said between gasps for air. He glared at Bain's body, possessed by the chaos god. "I will free them from your slavery."

Suirel looked back, without anger or frustration. He looked… amused. "You took down two and think that makes you the winner here?" He gestured with both hands and released gusts of wind in opposite directions. "How about four?" From one side, the two guards dropped their torches, drew their maces, and started forward. From the other side, the two priests pushed aside the horrified Ghamba Lam and ran toward Clanless. "Or six? Demujin. Daviland. If you please?" The cult leader bounded to his feet and spun around. Daviland drew a short sword.

"You really can't win," Yul said.

"How many of you are there?" Clanless asked before whirling to meet the charge of the guards.

"Thousands," Yul answered without hesitation. "He can keep bringing more through as long as he keeps his connection to our world."

Swift Claw took down the two priests without assistance. Clanless experienced the urge to move in sync with the beastman, but the bloodrush hadn't taken over yet. He could still fight his own way. He shoved one of the guards aside and swung the moonblade just wide enough to catch the second one on the thigh. One quick use of the Taint, and he fell.

Suirel was the real target, but what could he do against a god? Could he free Bain from its control like he did with the blood-wraiths? He had to make the attempt. Maybe it could disrupt this connection Yul mentioned.

"Cast down the dark one," the wolf had said.

Swift Claw engaged Daviland. The second guard understood the potential of the Taint and stayed out of range of the moonblade, feinting and trying to draw Clanless away from the rest of the fight.

Not for the first time, Clanless missed Zaluu and his throwing knives.

Something huge flew past Clanless's head, almost tearing the wolf pelt from his shoulder. He turned in time to see a chunk of rock bigger than his head smash against the wall. He spun to see Demujin casually snapping off a stalagmite from the corner of the room. The cult leader hurled this one at Clanless as well. He dodged and almost ran into the mace of the remaining guard.

"Come, Clanless," Suirel called. "I can find a place for you. Surrender yourself to me. Bain is convinced you can see reason."

Clanless took a step back from the guard, who didn't advance. "Then he's forgotten how stubborn I can be," he answered.

"Wolf Chosen!"

Clanless turned to see Swift Claw land on Daviland's back, reach around with his left hand, and tear deep scratches across his face. Clanless activated the Taint without hesitation. Nothing happened. He activated it again, pushing it harder.

Daviland's face blurred with red even as blood flowed from the scratches. "Aldannnnn!" he screamed… in Zektel's voice. The now-familiar mist of red tore from his face and rushed toward Suirel. Daviland fell senseless.

Suirel shook his head. "That was not wise. After all she's done for you." He held out his hand. A swirl of blood and wind surrounded it. "Now I'll have to put her back… or maybe find a better home for her. Ah, here comes the perfect candidate now!"

A deep and sudden fear pierced Clanless. Keeping his guard up against the two remaining foes, he stepped back and shifted to see the main entrance to the chamber. A tall man in uniform led a squad of soldiers and four other people with them.

"Aldan!" Kekeen exclaimed.

DOWN THE THROAT

Kekeen didn't know what to make of the scene before her. Aldan didn't appear injured or anything as he faced one of the royal guards. But Sugh and Duurald lay unmoving, along with two or three other bodies. Her eyes widened and her hands shook. Their fallen forms merged in her mind with that of Hagh. Not again! Swift Claw stood over Daviland, blood dripping from his hand. Demujin stood alone off to one side, arms folded and a smirk on his face. The Ghamba Lam cowered alone on the other side.

And in the center, standing near that gaping hole: could that blood-soaked figure be Bain? Even as she thought it, a sudden wave of emotions struck her. Anger, hate, malignancy, all radiating outward from the bloody figure. He held out his hand and a red wind swirled around it. Kekeen shook from the pure evil of it.

And yet... aside from that, it looked as though Aldan and Swift Claw had conquered.

"No!" Aldan shouted. "Stay back!"

"What is going on here?" the General demanded.

"Ah, General Gahn, I presume," Bain said. "I will speak to you momentarily. First, I—"

"It's Suirel!" Aldan interrupted. "Don't listen to him. Get out of here!"

"That is all I needed to hear," the General answered. He strode forward without hesitation.

Suirel watched with an amused expression as the General came within a few feet of him, but he said nothing.

To the utter shock of almost everyone in the room, General Ghan dropped to one knee and bent his head. "All hail to the Lord of Chaos. I and my army are at your service."

The Ghamba Lam let out a low moan.

Koland caught hold of Kekeen's arm and pulled. "I don't think we should be here," he said in a low voice. "This is much worse than I thought."

Suirel. The chaos moon. Here. How?

Several of Ghan's soldiers formed up behind them, preventing any exit. The odds had turned against them.

"I had not expected this so soon," Suirel/Bain said. "Welcome, General." He turned back toward Aldan. "Well, Clanless? What now?"

Aldan stood trembling. He didn't answer.

Suirel held up the hand with the red wind. "The friend you confided in for all those years. The woman you love. What a combination they would form! I can't think of anything better."

"No!" Aldan held up a palm. "I-I'll do what you say."

"Aldan?" Kekeen put her hands to her mouth. He couldn't surrender for her. Not again!

"Wolf Chosen!" Swift Claw exclaimed. "You cannot!"

Aldan stared hard at Swift Claw, then pointed at Kekeen. The beastman cocked his head at first, then lowered it and nodded.

At a touch from Suirel, General Ghan stood and stepped to the side.

The Ghamba Lam sank to the floor, holding his head.

Demujin laughed.

"What is happening?" Badaar asked.

"The worst thing that could happen," Qara whispered.

Aldan stared at Kekeen. He mouthed, "I love you."

"I love you!" she responded. "Don't do this for me!"

"I'm doing this for all of us," he said. "Please remember that."

"Enough sentiment," Suirel said. "Kneel. And remove that fur."

Aldan set the moonblade on the floor. Sugh stirred and lifted his head, brow furrowed.

"I've been hearing all about you for months," Aldan said, starting toward Suirel. "Everyone seems to have a different name or title for you."

"When you've been around for millennia, you pick up a few names."

"I understand. I have three names so far myself." He pulled aside his shirt, exposing the brand. "The priests and the arena call me Clanless, and it's usually how I think of myself. But my parents named me Aldan."

"Yes, yes. I know. Kneel."

Aldan stopped in front of him. "But I have a third name now. The beastmen gave it to me. Maybe you heard Swift Claw calling me by it. They named me Wolf Chosen."

Suirel's eye narrowed.

Aldan started to kneel. "The wolf, you know? I suspect you know who I'm talking about. He told me something about you."

General Ghan took a step forward.

"He told me to cast you down."

Aldan surged up and wrapped his arms around Suirel. Caught by surprise, the blood-soaked figure staggered back and slipped. Aldan's legs drove forward, propelling them down and back.

Both men disappeared into the Throat of the Goddess.

(((●))))

In only a few seconds, Clanless and Suirel plunged into utter darkness. The Throat passage took a sudden turn, cutting off the meager light from above. Clanless couldn't tell what direction they'd turned, save that they continued down, down, down.

The walls of the Throat were smooth and slick, a byproduct of centuries of blood pouring through it. Some kind of soft and wet moss grew in patches along the surface of the rock. While the plant life helped speed their descent, it did little to shield them from bumps and bruises. Each time the passage shifted, Clanless slammed against the side, usually bouncing off to hit the opposite side as well. At this rate, he would be one big bruise by the time he reached the bottom. At least there were no sharp edges. He didn't like the idea of adding to the collection of blood, although that might be inevitable now.

There must be a bottom. Bain had been there and returned. But he'd been gone for weeks. Had it taken that long to journey back up? Not that it mattered. Clanless knew he'd done the right thing.

The sensations of falling so far and so fast were new to him. Most of his life had been spent in places where he had nowhere to fall. He held tight to Suirel, determined that whatever happened, their fate would be the same.

"Such an unexpected move." Somehow, Suirel could speak while they fell. Clanless didn't think he could even open his mouth. "I didn't think you had it in you."

"Neither did I," Yul said.

"Zektel, of course, left me the moment you struck. I wonder who she's claimed by now?"

Clanless gritted his teeth. That was the only thing he couldn't control.

He hoped Swift Claw would understand and be enough to protect Kekeen and the others.

"Do you feel bursts of wind passing you by?" Suirel asked. "Each one of them is another of my children, rising toward the surface to claim their own bodies…"

One awareness now eclipsed all the others, even drowning out Suirel's taunting voice. The blood. The overwhelming power of the blood. The strength of it had been so powerful up top that he'd needed Swift Claw's help to get past it. But the further they descended, the stronger it grew, until Clanless could see nothing but blood, smell nothing but blood, taste nothing but blood, feel nothing but blood, and hear only the sound of his own heart beating in coordinated rhythm with something beyond what he could fathom.

He tried to form words, but even coherent thoughts eluded him. Pressure grew on his chest, and he struggled to breathe. At last, one word escaped the chaos within his mind: "Help."

A moment—or five minutes; he couldn't tell—later, the sensation lessened. He gasped for air. The sudden change loosened his grip on Suirel, and they broke free of each other. He could still smell and taste blood like nothing else, but it faded to the level he'd been experiencing at the top.

"What was that?" Yul murmured.

Clanless found he could see… a little. A dim light suffused the tunnel, though he couldn't identify the source. Even as he noticed it, the passage opened up into a wide and flat slide. Flailing, the two bodies sped apart from each other. No longer descending, their speed slowed, though they still skimmed along the moss-covered surface at a tremendous rate. The light grew ever so slightly, coming from somewhere in the direction they now slid. Clanless had no idea if the light itself was red or if he couldn't see any other colors now.

If he'd kept the moonblade, maybe he could slam it into this rock and slow his movement. But with nothing to catch hold, the momentum the two men had accumulated carried them on to the very end.

Clanless spun out into open air. He flew on, unhindered, for a great distance, flipping over and spinning around. He caught glimpses of an enormous chamber, crystals, and a vast reservoir of red that rushed up to meet him. He smacked into its surface, bounced once, and plunged into the unfathomed depths of a lake of blood.

For a few long moments, no one moved. Everyone in the cave stared at the Throat in disbelief.

General Ghan recovered first. "He'll be back," he declared, turning away. "Nothing can stop the coming of the Chaos Lord."

He surveyed the stunned crowd. Daviland sat up, shaking his head. The General pointed at him. "Seize him." Two of his soldiers rushed to obey.

"As for the rest of you…" He looked over the group, frowning.

Sugh pulled himself up, bringing Aldan's weapon with him. He looked even more impressive than usual, holding his axe in one hand and the moonblade in the other. Both he and Swift Claw moved to shield Kekeen and the others with her.

Badaar shook his head. "General, what are you doing? I don't understand."

Ghan sighed. "As I said, my friend, your presence here was an enormous surprise. Much has changed in the Empire since you and I fought together." He looked toward the Ghamba Lam and shook his head. "Trust me. This is all for the best."

Demujin stepped forward. "There is the matter of command here," he said. "With our lord now gone, however temporarily, I believe I hold seniority. I am Demujin, head of Suirel's followers in the Sar Empire."

The General folded his arms and leveled a severe look at the cult leader. "I have been serving the Chaos Lord since before you left your mother's breast. I am not turning over command of my soldiers to you, of all people."

"I need you to trust me," Koland whispered in Kekeen's ear. He took her hand and stepped up, gently pushing past Sugh.

"I realize I look like no one to be respected, but the mind of this human is exactly what I needed right now," Koland announced. "If anyone is to lead here, it's me."

General Ghan's eyes narrowed further. "I don't even know who you are."

"The body belongs to a storyteller who helped that one"—he pointed at Daviland—"succeed in his rebellion." Koland tapped his head. "But he's not in control here now. I am Zektel, older than this world, let alone this Empire. You would do well to listen to me."

Kekeen gasped and tried to pull free. Koland held her hand a little tighter. Swift Claw cocked his head.

"Nonsense!" Demujin exclaimed. "Koland is a clever one, General. Don't listen to him."

Koland glared at the cult leader. "What evidence do you need? I spent the last eight years within Clanless before transferring to Daviland. Should I tell you of that time? Or the time before? What about the time before your world, when we traversed the endless night among the stars? What would you hear, you who have ever sought our wisdom?"

Demujin didn't answer.

"What do you suggest then?" General Ghan asked.

Koland pulled on Kekeen's hand. "This one is beloved by Clanless. Should he somehow return, we will need her for leverage." He gestured to Sugh with his other hand and pointed past the Throat. "You, take her over there. The other girl too. She might be an added incentive."

Swift Claw sniffed at Koland. "Your wind—"

"Let's do as he says," Sugh interrupted. "Come, you women. Over here."

Released by her father, Kekeen followed Sugh, Qara and Swift Claw out of the way. Qara flicked her eyes toward an opening in the wall, indicating something. Maybe a way out?

The Ghamba Lam slunk over beside them. "I know where I want to be," he mumbled, looking at Sugh's weapons.

Kekeen looked back at the rest of the cavern. Koland stood beside Badaar, arms folded, with a sneer on his face. She'd seen him adopt similar mannerisms and personalities in his story-telling. Was he doing the same now, or had he truly been possessed?

"Now," Koland said. "What is your plan regarding the blood in the yard, General?"

"By now, all of that blood is ruined," Ghan answered. "Why? What other use could it have?"

"Pity," Koland said. "We could have—"

A zephyr teased Demujin's hair. He jerked, and a smile spread over his face. "That's enough, human. You aren't Zektel."

General Ghan tilted his head to look at him. "I suppose you are?"

"No. I am Turdai, firstborn of Suirel. In his stead, I speak and lead." He pointed at Koland. "And I know my sister Zektel. This human is free of her or any other influence."

"Why would one of them take him instead of the General?" Qara wondered. "I'd think they would go for the most powerful."

"Who can understand the mind of a blood-wraith?" Kekeen said, watching the other men argue.

Qara leaned closer. "We can get out through this side passage. I know the way."

Kekeen nodded. "Be ready. But we also need my father and Badaar, if possible."

"What about Duurald?" Sugh asked.

Kekeen had forgotten him. She turned and saw the arena fighter pulling himself up onto his hands and knees, shaking his head. He'd been thrown across the room by Demujin, possessed by a blood-wraith, and had the wraith ripped from him by Aldan's Taint. It was hard to believe he could move at all. Badaar stepped over next to him and offered his hand. Duurald took it and allowed himself to be pulled upright.

So much was happening with so many people so rapidly... Kekeen hadn't even had time to process Aldan's actions. She couldn't even be sure how much time had passed since he went down that horrible hole.

Sugh caught her eye. "He still fights," he said in a low voice. "Clanless still fights for us."

She wanted to ask how he knew, whether the goddess had told him, or he merely guessed. But her attention was drawn back to the argument around her father.

"More of my siblings join us," Turdai/Demujin said. "In short order, all here will belong to us." He lifted his hand as Suirel had done, and a visible breeze swirled around it. "I shall send them where they need to be."

"I am immune to such things," General Ghan said. "It was part of my deal with the Chaos Lord. But you are welcome to take anyone else here."

He glanced toward Kekeen and her protectors before looking toward Duurald. "I'm inclined to add some brute force to my side." He made a quick motion with his hand. Duurald stiffened.

"Resist it!" Badaar cried. He pulled Duurald toward himself. "You are an elite arena fighter! So fight!"

"I don't believe that's possible, old man," Duurald said in a monotone. He picked up his mace and examined it with a smile.

"Don't fear, weapons master," Turdai said. "I have one for you as well." He gestured and the flutter of a breeze swept across the chamber again.

Koland took a couple of steps backward, inching toward the others. Kekeen mentally begged him to hurry, but kept her eyes on Badaar.

The old warrior swept up his right arm with its stump, pointing it at Turdai. He bowed his head and closed his eyes.

"Not him too," Kekeen whispered. "Please."

"You do not understand," Badaar said without opening his eyes. "You cannot threaten me this way." He lifted his head and turned with a smile. "My head is already full of voices. There isn't room for another." He flicked his stump, and a burst of air rushed back across the chamber toward one of Ghan's soldiers.

"Impossible." Turdai stared. "Who is this man, General?"

Badaar retrieved his own mace. "Storyteller, join the others. The Hero of the Empire will hold the line."

Koland turned and bolted for Kekeen. Qara made a frantic wave and ducked into the side passage. The Ghamba Lam ran after her.

"Stop them," General Ghan ordered. A squad of his soldiers moved forward. Sugh, Swift Claw, and Badaar stood waiting for them.

Koland grabbed Kekeen's hand and pulled her into the side passage. "We can't leave them," she protested.

"We are right behind you!" Sugh called.

"Go! Protect them!" Badaar shouted. "I said I will hold the line!" He looked to either side of him. "I have all the help I need."

Swift Claw stumbled, then bounded into the passage behind Kekeen. Sugh followed, cursing Bain's name.

Qara produced some kind of light and hurried down the passage. "Follow me!"

Kekeen took one last look at Badaar standing in the doorway, facing down an entire squad of soldiers. She whispered a quick prayer to the goddess and turned away, her heart tearing itself apart.

🌘🌗🌖🌕🌔🌓🌒

Clanless flailed, trying to push himself out of the liquid, seeking air. His bruised and battered body broke the surface, and he sucked in a desperate breath. Almost at once, his head slipped below the surface again. He churned his arms and legs, having no idea what to do. The deepest water he'd ever encountered had been the arena baths. He'd never learned to move through liquid in any way. His heavy winter clothing, including the wolf pelt, now soaked through, dragged him down.

He surfaced again, gasping for air, then sank. His toes caught the edge of something. He propelled himself forward and found a floor. He kicked off from it, emerging yet again. After another gulp of air, he slipped down and kicked off the floor again and again until it sloped up enough for him to stand with his head above the surface.

He stood still for a moment, eyes closed, letting his heart and breathing slow down. He was alive. His body, beneath the soaked clothing, ached all over. His chest hurt with each breath. None of his major bones appeared to be broken, but he couldn't be sure of his ribs. When he lifted his arms to push back his hair, pain erupted on the lower right of his chest.

He moved his foot forward tentatively. When the surface continued to slope up, he pushed forward until he reached a spot where the blood only came to his knees. Relieved, he turned to look at his surroundings.

He stood near the wall of an enormous cavern whose every surface and wall appeared to be made of the almaz crystal, the same used to make the vials for blood used throughout the Empire. In many places, the crystal jutted out from the walls in enormous spikes. Clanless shuddered when he realized he could have struck one of those when he arrived.

The shudder revealed something else that surprised him: he was warm. In fact, he felt almost too warm. Somehow, heat permeated this cavern, perhaps radiating from somewhere deeper in the earth. He pulled off his outer coat and tossed it to a small area nearby where the blood didn't cover a crystal floor.

The blood. He stood knee-deep in a lake of blood which filled almost the entire cavern. He couldn't guess how deep the center might be, but the width of the lake exceeded—no doubled—the entire arena, stands and all, of Et-Baylak. The light Bain mentioned cast a soft red glow across everything

A chuckle alerted him to the other occupant of the cavern. Bain—Suirel—crawled out of the blood onto another dry spot around thirty feet away along the same wall. He'd survived too, of course. But what now?

"That was… exhilarating, wouldn't you say?" Suirel wiped blood from his face. "I should thank you for the experience."

Clanless peered at him, trying to discern whether the other man had been cut in the process. He could use the Taint, maybe, and—

"Wait." Suirel lifted one hand, palm up, toward him. "You might not want to use your Taint in here… unless you wish to remove all the barriers to my power."

"He's right," Yul whispered. "It would hurt him terribly, maybe more than he could abide, but… everyone else would come."

"Who's everyone else?"

"Everyone," Yul repeated.

Suirel got to his feet and gestured around him. "Behold the blood of your ancestors. This… this is how your accursed priesthood has kept us at bay for centuries."

Clanless tried to wipe more blood from his face. "How?" he asked. He needed time to think, to decide a new course of action. Could he get across the blood to Suirel? How deep was the blood between them? What could he do once he got there?

Suirel gestured and threw something into the air. A light exploded above his hands and arced into the space above the blood lake. "Behold the gateway of the gods!"

With the added light, Clanless could now see much more of the cavern. The crystal formations he'd taken for random explosions of points were something else. His eyes traced them up and up and across the lake. It formed a complete arch before descending into the blood on either side, possibly creating a full circle. Large outcroppings marked the highest points on either side, and one gigantic gathering of crystals marked the dead center at the peak of the cavern. One enormous crystal stalactite protruded straight down, like a tetragonal tooth. A similar formation rose from the blood below, nearly meeting it.

"In ancient times lost to the memories of all but a few of us, the precursors to your people discovered this place somehow. At first, it meant nothing to them." Suirel stared up at the "gateway" as the light he'd created slowly faded into the red glow. He seemed ecstatic with his own story. "But then our world came within the grasp of this planet. Even as the planet itself seized hold of our world, this place… this place seized hold of us. We discovered we could traverse the firmament and enter this world here. The first of us shaped it to our liking."

He turned to look at Clanless. "In time, the guardians of your world realized what had happened and taught the people the only certain way to stop us." He dipped a hand in the lake and let the blood flow out between his fingers. "The blood. Your blood. Somehow, enough of it blocks our ability to traverse. Over the centuries, your priesthood developed its regular method of bringing blood here." He chuckled. "I suppose in your eyes, it's more civilized than what the earliest adherents had to do: sacrificing themselves in this very room, spilling their lifeblood across its floor. If it weren't detrimental to my designs, I would consider it a beautiful thing. Such wanton death."

Another stronger reddish glow lit up the cavern. Suirel pointed. "There. See. Another one has made it through."

The huge stalactite in the center of the ceiling radiated with the glow. It pulsed and then faded. A whisper of wind rushed past Clanless.

"But… there's still plenty of blood here. How do they get through now? How did you get through?"

"This strange crystal you people use so much"—Suirel patted the wall behind him—"preserves the blood to a remarkable extent. But even so, it does degrade over time. And some leaks out or evaporates. That's why the priests are always adding more. When it gets low enough, some of my children slip through. I had to wait for just the right circumstances. I've been planning for this day for so long."

"So… it's still blocking some of you?"

"Some? Thousands. Tens of thousands." He pointed to the crystal gateway. "Now that I'm here, I can find a way to clear this space and release them all."

"Why?" Clanless clenched his fists and waded a step toward him. "Why come here at all? Why enslave humans?"

"Enslave. You don't like that word." Suirel ran a hand across his head, doing little to remove the blood. "Ah, Clanless. Aldan, if I may. I feel I know you so well, from Bain and Zektel. What you don't understand is that humans need to be enslaved. They're inherently barbaric. What was it your trainer said when you were boys? Something about how deep down, everyone wants to be the villain?" He shook his head. "The evil of humanity is always there. You hide it under a veneer of civilization. But give people the right excuse, the right justification, and phrase it in a way that gives them some kind of 'moral' cover… and they'll happily cheer on the most barbaric practices."

He pointed a bloody finger at Clanless. "Your arena system is a perfect illustration. They come to see blood and death, confident in their own morality, because they've relegated such practices to a somewhat controlled system, not at all like those evil barbarians outside the walls. They even have priests telling them how the blood obtained from the arenas is morally helpful to the Empire and important to the worship of their goddess." He glanced in the direction of the moon and sneered.

"But you still haven't grasped it all. Your people call my world the 'chaos moon.' Some call me the Lord of Chaos." His bloody face broke open in a disturbing grin. "And that's what it's really about. Do I enjoy ruling? Of course. Am I happy that my children can find new bodies? Absolutely. But chaos… now that's where I find true pleasure. And there's so much potential for it here, thanks to your human nature seeking out violence and evil while excusing it away.

"All I had to do to create utter chaos in your Empire, for example, was send one of my children in the guise of a prophet, choosing a charismatic young man to lead an uprising. Instant chaos! And all of his followers— like your beloved Kekeen—convinced that whatever they do as freedom fighters is justifiable in the name of stopping the great evils of the arena and slavery. And the fact that you got pulled into it only made it better, by the way.

"But that wasn't enough." He took wet footsteps across the ledge. "I need more. I need to see humanity's full barbaric potential. And what better realm for that than… war.”

The warmth vanished, and a cool prickling ran over Clanless's skin. "What have you done?”

"I sent another prophet. Daviland wasn't enough. You see… there's another land full of humans north of here who consider themselves morally superior to your Empire. They worship a different god, one who, I might add, is more inclined to my way of thinking. A few pushes here, a few prophetic utterances there… and they're ready for war.” He spread his hands. "And all in the name of rescuing your people from themselves. They will kill. They will slaughter. They will rape and pillage, all while assuring themselves they are morally right for doing it to a group of oppressors.”

Clanless pointed up the tunnel. "But… the General. You have the Empire's army at your command!”

Suirel only smiled. "Chaos.”

"I don't understand. The blood-wraiths. They'll be controlling people in this war you're starting. They'll lose the bodies they've claimed. How does that help you?” Clanless took another step through the blood.

Suirel shrugged. "There are always more humans. And the goals of my children do not… always line up with my goals.”

"That much is true,” Yul said with what sounded like a sigh.

"Oh, Yul. You disappoint me.” Suirel curled his fingers in a summoning gesture.

"Wait… what…?”

Clanless heard and felt the tearing as Yul left him, the same sudden wrenching he'd felt with Zektel, as if all the blood in his body were being yanked forward. He stumbled another couple of steps toward Suirel.

Suirel held up his hand and watched the red zephyr swirl around it. "You had such an opportunity after Zektel left. Poor Aldan was still ignorant about the fur. You could have used that. You're lazy. Go do something more productive.” With a flick of his wrist, he sent the blood-wraith off into the air somewhere.

"Bain,” Clanless said. "Can I talk to Bain?”

Suirel looked back to him. "Bain is a part of me now.”

"But can I talk to him instead of you? Like you just talked to Yul instead of me.”

"Why would you want to do that?” Suirel laughed.

"He's my friend.”

"He says he's your friend. But you and I both know everything Bain ever did was for himself.” Suirel patted himself on the chest. "A completely self-serving, power-driven human. Exactly what I needed.”

"I still want to talk to him."

"No. No, you don't. Haven't you been wondering how Bain got his freedom from the Hawk King?" Suirel took a step into the blood. "He betrayed you, Aldan."

Clanless pushed that aside. He'd managed to get somewhat closer to the dark god, but several feet of deep blood still separated them. He couldn't wade through it. Any further movement would be an obvious attack. And even if he could get close enough, could he win? He believed he had the strength to beat Bain in a straight-up fight. But with Suirel in control? What kind of power did he command?

Suirel stretched. "As exhilarating as all of this has been, I suppose I should kill you and get back to the chaos."

"Wait! I'll make you a deal!"

Suirel paused mid-stretch. "What could you possibly offer me?"

Clanless grabbed hold of the blood-soaked wolf fur. "This. Me. I'll take it off."

"To what end?"

"First, you agree to leave my friends alone. All of them up there. They go away free and with no blood-wraiths in them."

"And I get you in return? Why? What good does that do me? The Taint? I have Daviland, you know."

Clanless pointed at him. "Do you really think Bain's is the best body for you to have? He only has one eye! You know I can beat him. So why not take me instead?" He spread his arms out. "In return for my friends. Take me."

33

A SEA OF BLOOD, A SEA OF POWER

Suirel burst out laughing. "Oh, Aldan. You do entertain. You're almost… chaotic. I like it." He shook his head. "But no. Bain may not be the greatest specimen of human potential, but he has what I need. You do not. And besides, I'll soon have as many arena fighters and soldiers as I want. There was a time when you would have been my primary choice, when Zektel worked so hard to prepare you… but that time is passed. I don't need you." He clapped his hands, blood slinging. "So. Now it's time to kill you."

A sudden rush of wind slammed into Clanless. He fought against it, trying to step forward. Instead, the wind increased and shifted around him, like a living thing. It lifted him up off his feet, hovering over the blood. He pushed against it, trying to find any kind of leeway. Nothing worked. He hung helpless in the air.

"Now… how to do it?" Suirel waved, and Clanless spun in a slow circle. "I could slam you against the crystal, maybe impaling you with one of them. That would be entertaining. Or I could simply lower your face down under the blood until you drown. I know you'd really hate that one. Or maybe—"

This could not be happening. He'd fought so long and so hard, all these years. And this was how he would die? Helpless at the hands of a mad god? It couldn't be right. But there was nothing he could do. He'd only had eight days of freedom. Eight days. There had to be more than that. There had to be a way out of this.

"Goddess…" he whispered. "Is this what you wanted? Help me. Do something!"

A soft light flooded through his mind. Suirel's voice stopped. Warmth enveloped him, removing the chill of Suirel's wind.

"Aldan… I am sorry."

"Why? What is going on?"

"My connection to your world is weaker than ever. I cannot interfere in your current situation. Suirel planned this well. I am… engaged elsewhere."

"But the wolf told me to do this!"

Clanless thought he heard a sigh from the goddess. "The wolf does not belong to me. There are other powers at work, some far above me."

"Then… can you help Kekeen? Can you help my friends? I can die if they'll be all right."

"Again, I am unable to directly interfere in your world now. Even this brief communication is a strain."

"You talk to Sugh, don't you? Tell him what he needs to know! Get them out of here!"

There was a long pause. "I will do what I can."

"Thank you." Clanless waited a moment before another thought occurred to him. "You said there are other powers above you. If you can't interfere, why can't they? I mean, if they're more powerful, they can stop Suirel, right?"

"I do not speak with… them. Not in a very long time."

"So what? Why not do it now?"

"You don't understand." The goddess sounded exasperated. "I may not even be heard."

Clanless struggled to move, but the wind still held him. Or something else did. He had no idea if Suirel were frozen as well, or still talking. All he could perceive was the light. "You said you were put in charge of our people, to take care of them! If you can't do it, then ask someone who can! Isn't it worth it?"

"It's a matter of pride, Aldan. Among other things. I—"

"I surrendered to Daviland to save the Empire from the Hawk King," he interrupted. "I gave up everything to bring Bain down here. Can't you lay aside your pride long enough to help us?"

For another long moment, he thought the goddess had left, but the light lingered. Then: "I will do what I can."

The light and warmth faded. He still hung helpless in the air above the lake. Suirel stood on his ledge, gesturing with one finger in a circle. "It's hard to decide, you know. Do you have a preference, perhaps?"

Something itched in Clanless's nose. Such a strange thing to be concerned about, but it annoyed him. He tried to wiggle it, to relieve the itch. He snorted, breathed in and out. Nothing worked.

"I think we'll go with the drowning," Suirel said. "It seems the most apropos. Farewell, Aldan."

"Here is their answer," the voice of the goddess whispered in his ear.

A wind, not Suirel's, gusted through the cavern.

The chaos lord frowned.

Something broke loose in Clanless's nose. Liquid welled up inside.

Suirel lifted one hand, preparing to lower him into the lake.

The wind swept past Clanless again.

A single drop of blood fell from his nose.

☾ ☾ ☽ ☾ ● ☽ ☽ ☽ ☽

"It's the catalyst, you see," Daviland's voice said in his head.

"I just need a drop of your blood for catalyst," said Qara.

"The blood of the clanless one," Ghouk's mocking voice said. "You don't even know."

Clanless had been battered and bruised from the journey down the tunnel.

But he hadn't bled. Until now.

The single drop from his nose fell toward the lake in slow motion.

"No!" Suirel's shout echoed throughout the crystal cavern.

The drop plunked into the vast lake of blood. Blood collected over the centuries from everyone in the Sar Empire. Blood from all twelve clans, each of which could manifest a different type of blood-magic. Blood-magic that required a priest with the knowledge of how to activate it.

Or a single drop of the blood of a clanless individual who possessed what the priests called the Taint.

Suirel's wind power dispersed in a blaze of light and heat. Clanless dropped into the activated blood.

He burst back up, mind racing at a tremendous rate, helping him calculate his next moves. The power of Clan Shasin blood.

Heat pushed out from him, and light filled the entire chamber. Clan Dendsu blood.

Pain erupted in his chest as the broken ribs reformed, fully healed. Clan Kurav blood.

He laughed, and the force of his laughter shook the room, forming ripples across the lake. Clan Torov blood.

Any hint of fatigue or tiredness vanished. Clan Dalbai blood.

He could see and hear everything in the cavern with perfect clarity. Clan Dariachin blood.

He rushed across the shallow part of the lake toward Suirel, moving faster than he'd ever moved in his life. Clan Zavi blood.

A wave of blood moved with him, forming up at his mental command. Clan Ghamkiin blood.

He punched Suirel in the torso with tremendous strength, slamming him several feet back against the crystal wall. Clan Berge blood.

In a single step, Clanless caught up to Suirel and swung at his face with the other fist.

Suirel caught it.

He stared at Clanless through Bain's singular eye, malice radiating through his glare. "You think you're the only one who can use the blood-magic?" He side-kicked Clanless, throwing him out over the lake.

His injuries healed before he surfaced.

"Bain is from Clan Ghutalta!" Suirel snarled. "Like all of their misbegotten clan, he tried to keep their blood-magic a secret, didn't he?"

Clanless gestured and the blood parted, leaving a crystal floor between him and the dark god.

"Clan Ghutalta magic duplicates any others in use around them!" Suirel launched himself at him.

In a crystal cavern, surrounded by a lake of blood, Clanless fought a desperate battle against an embodied god. The blood formed a red whirlwind around them. Their fists flew, smashing into each other's bodies with devastating impact. Each injury, no matter how traumatic, healed almost instantly.

No more taunts. No more words at all. Only the fight.

Clanless's mind raced with the help of the Clan Shasin blood. He had to keep up the attack without pause. As long as he kept Suirel engaged in this fight, the chaos lord couldn't bring his wind power to bear, something Clanless couldn't match with blood-magic. He couldn't let up for a single second.

And he didn't need to. His movements, enhanced by all the various magics, kept going, smooth and powerful and fast. With a vicious elbow strike, he shattered Suirel's forearm. A split-second later, Suirel's other fist snapped his jaw, sending teeth flying. Both injuries vanished within seconds. Even the teeth regrew.

With Clan Dalbai blood providing endurance, and Clan Shukan blood potentially extending their lives, this fight could last as long as the blood lasted. And in that moment, Clanless realized the truth about his own clan's blood. Clan Tokuur was thought to create weakness… but it only did that because it was transferring energy back into the blood around him, revitalizing it! In a place like this, it created a loop of continually restoring magic. The fight could literally last for eternity.

Maybe that's what he would have to do. If it kept Kekeen and the other safe, he could fight on. And on. And on.

If he could cause an injury that healing magic couldn't restore, it could make a difference. But the only such injuries he could think of were a loss of limb or eye. After a couple of early strikes, both he and Suirel had shifted to protecting their faces. Getting to Bain's remaining eye would not be easy. All of the other debilitating injuries he could think of would require grappling of some kind, practically impossible when both combatants were slick with blood.

One of his blows crushed Suirel's hip. In response, Suirel splintered his knee.

The force of their combat sent them further out into the lake. The blood swirled higher and higher above them even as they kept their feet on dry ground.

Suirel shouted something. The enhanced volume at close range exploded ear drums. As they healed, Clanless shoved Suirel away, hoping to gain room for a different attack. Suirel charged back just as fast.

The time he'd spent with the beastmen had given him more experience with hand-to-hand fighting, but Suirel matched his every move. He wondered if all of the moves came from Bain, or if the chaos god had memories of other fighting in the distant past. So far, Clanless hadn't seen anything unusual. If all the fighting came from Bain, maybe he was closer to being in control somehow.

"Bain," he said before remembering that his voice would be amplified. A moment later, he tried whispering: "Bain. Fight him. Help me out here."

Suirel dodged one of his punches and flipped backward. He somersaulted in reverse and came to his feet half a dozen yards away. Clanless paused and did not immediately pursue him.

"I told you: you can't talk to him!" Suirel whispered, but his voice echoed throughout the cavern.

"You're afraid of that, aren't you?" Clanless shifted his stance, watching his opponent and calculating multiple lines of attack. If only he had the moonblade.

"I fear nothing."

Over Bain's shoulder, Clanless saw the top crystal light up again, signaling the arrival of another blood-wraith. As long as that kept happening, it wouldn't matter if he kept Suirel down here. The wraiths would take over everyone, given enough time. In that moment, he decided on a course of action.

He took two steps and launched himself through the air, feet first like a beastman. It wasn't a move Bain would have known and caught Suirel by surprise. He still managed to dodge the leap but left himself a little unbalanced. It was all Clanless needed.

He caught hold of Suirel's arm, making sure one hand caught above the elbow, and pulled with all his Clan Berge-enhanced might. Suirel had two choices. He could pull back with equal strength, which would yank his arm out of its socket, at the very least. Or he could let himself be pulled to save his arm and prepare for his own attack. He opted to save the arm.

Clanless spun in a complete circle, lifting Suirel off the ground. With Clan Ghamkiin power, he used an enormous burst of blood to help him throw his enemy's body high into the air… directly at the hanging crystal stalactite.

Suirel smashed into it, probably breaking half the bones in his body. A loud crack resounded through the cavern. The crystal trembled, but did not fall. Suirel plunged back down into the lake, using the blood to break his fall.

It was Clanless's first real opening. He could try to get to Suirel before he healed completely. Or he could finish the job. He crouched and leaped into the air, again using a surge of blood to push himself higher than he would have been able to jump, even with the enhanced strength.

He slammed into the crystal as if tackling an enemy in the arena. This time, it cracked the rest of the way through. The tooth-shaped stalactite plunged down with Clanless riding it. He managed to leap aside as it crashed into the lower outcropping, shattering into thousands of shards.

Suirel's fist struck his face before he could recover, splintering his eye socket, nose, and jaw. He managed to shift so that the follow-up punch struck under his right armpit, breaking ribs and driving their fragments into his internal organs. The pain of the injuries and the equal pain of their healing almost knocked him out. For the next few moments, Suirel had the upper hand. But since he couldn't deliver a death blow either, Clanless regained parity in their struggle.

Only then did he realize why the fight could not last forever. The mental strain of the repeated injuries and healing was already beginning to wear on him. Clan Shasin blood-magic kept his mind moving at a fearsome rate, but the sheer stress of everything would eventually tax his brain too much. Would such a thing even matter to a god? Or would Bain's mind give out first?

Suirel grunted. "If breaking a few crystals was all it took to stop us, don't you think your priests would have figured that out long ago?"

"You tell me."

Both combatants shoved each other at the same time, throwing them apart. As Clanless fell, he used a quick burst of blood with Clan Ghamkiin magic to cushion himself. He still struck the ground a little harder than he liked and bounced backward into the shards of the broken crystal. The sharp edges opened new cuts and gashes across his body, all of which were immediately healed with equal pain. He kept his eyes on Suirel, but fumbled about with his right hand. His fingers closed around a broken piece of crystal: a weapon at last.

"Clanless? Aldan?"

He froze. It was still Bain's voice, but something was different. He didn't hear Suirel's arrogance and anger. "Bain?"

"I, I wanted this, Aldan."

Clanless got to his feet, keeping the crystal shard behind his back. Bain crouched in shallow blood a few yards away. He stared at his own hands. "I wanted to be your friend. I really did. But I… I always came first. I had to do what helped me."

"It's not too late, Bain. Fight him. Cast him out." He put his left hand on his blood-soaked wolf pelt. "You can take this. It'll help you—"

"No. It's too late for me." Bain shook his head. "I wanted this power. I asked for it, and now I have it. I just didn't know…" He winced suddenly as if struck.

Clanless took a few steps forward. "No. It can't be too late."

"He's only letting me talk, because he insists I tell you one thing."

"What do you mean?"

Bain looked up at him, his one eye boring into Clanless's. "I've told you not to trust me. But you did. You gave me too much. You let me know too much. And I couldn't resist."

Clanless felt a chill on his blood-soaked skin. "What are you talking about?"

"The Hawk King was willing to give anything, even my freedom. I couldn't pass that up. I couldn't."

"You…"

"I gave him you, Aldan. I gave him Kekeen."

Everything fell into place. Incredulity battled with rage. Clanless knew the Hawk King had informants. How else could he have known about Kekeen and kidnapped her for that final arena fight? But Bain… Bain was the one. And the Hawk King had been willing to give up one of his elite Dohor for the sole purpose of keeping Clanless under control.

"I wanted to be your friend, Aldan," Bain repeated. "Even if I—" His expression shifted into a grin. "And I think that's enough of him for now." Suirel.

The speed granted by Clan Zavi propelled Clanless forward faster than humanly possible. At the same time, he used the Clan Ghamkiin blood control to throw a burst into Suirel's face, combined with heat from Clan Dendsu. The momentary distraction allowed him to close the gap and throw his left arm around Suirel's neck.

"Leave him!" he shouted, accepting the blown eardrums again.

"You don't get it," Suirel hissed as their ears healed. He grabbed Clanless's arm and pushed to free himself. "He's mine until this body wastes away into nothing. And with all this wonderful, magical blood, that won't happen for hundreds of years. You thought the Hawk King reigned a long time? It will be an eye blink compared to my rule!"

Clanless whipped the crystal shard around and stabbed it into Bain's eye. "Try blinking without any eyes!"

Suirel roared, an unearthly sound that should not have been possible for a human voice. Wind erupted out from him, throwing Clanless into the air. He smashed against another wall that broke bones and stabbed him with more crystal formations, catastrophic injuries that should have killed him. He plunged down into the blood as his body knit back together.

"I'm sorry, Bain," he whispered.

He struggled to lift his head. Suirel had somehow crossed the entire cavern and now stumbled away into a passage that appeared to lead up. Clanless gathered himself, preparing to charge across the lake of blood after him… but his mind refused to focus on the idea.

Instead, he fell back and lay still, floating on the bloody sea, as the light dwindled and faded into an all-consuming red glow.

His gut ached. Even after all that healing, something down there still hadn't recovered. Maybe it never would. Though the rest of his body had been healed by the magic, his mind demanded rest, at least for now. Energy coursed through his body, urged on by all of the various blood-magics, fighting against his relaxation. But now that he wasn't actively using the magic, its effects began to fade. The light and warmth from Clan Dendsu blood decreased with each passing moment.

Somewhere far above, he could sense Swift Claw. It comforted him.

The beastman would defend Kekeen. If he still lived, then so did she.

And yet, they were separated again. All he'd wanted, all he'd fought for… was her. And now they were apart. At least this time, he knew he could get to her. Bain made it back up from here, so he could too. He would find her.

And then what? Suirel still walked the planet, blind or not, and in control of the Sar Empire and its armies. And he wanted a war—no, he'd already started a war! Thousands could die, and the lord of chaos would love every minute of it.

Where could they go to escape it? He'd considered taking Kekeen to the Melkute Kingdom, but that plan wouldn't work now. There were other lands out there, other places. He'd read about some of them long ago. And he'd fought people from some of them. Maybe they could go there.

Eight days. He'd had eight days of freedom. And… he was still free. More free than he'd been since his thirteenth birthday so many years ago.

He bumped against the floor, having floated into a shallow area. Clanless sat up and pulled his knees toward his chest with a sigh. Kekeen would not be happy with running away, not when people were in danger. It was part of her. She couldn't stand watching evil triumph. That sense of… rightness. He had to love it to love her.

He would have to keep fighting. There was no way around it. The violent memories Zektel had repressed were a part of him, just as the rightness was a part of Kekeen. He could let them haunt him, or accept it and channel his abilities in the direction Kekeen pointed.

Somehow, he had to follow Bain—Suirel—and stop him.

But not alone. Kekeen would have ideas. And Koland. The storyteller might be the smartest person he'd ever met. And with the help of Swift Claw, Sugh, and Duurald… and maybe others they could find… maybe, maybe they could find a way.

Or maybe they couldn't. Maybe they would all die trying. And how different was that from every week of his life in the arena? At least this time, he would be fighting as a free man, fighting for something that mattered.

They could expect no help from the goddess, apparently. And the mysterious power above her had intervened only enough to give him a fighting chance against Suirel. Maybe that was all he needed. A fighting chance.

Clanless stood up, blood pouring from his body. He'd take that chance.

For now, he needed to start moving. The scent and taste of blood was starting to overwhelm him again.

Somewhere, in the tunnels above, a blind god stumbled onward.

Clanless strode after him, ready to continue the fight.

EPILOGUE

Koland snapped a stick in half and tossed the pieces on the tiny fire. Swift Claw assured him none of Ghan's soldiers were near enough to see any smoke, but he kept the blaze small, just in case. He glanced up at the beastman who crouched on a large outcropping, exposed to the night's falling temperature. Koland had a feeling Swift Claw wouldn't sleep until Aldan returned.

After Qara led them through the passage and past the pagoda, they'd traveled at least a mile along the plateau before finding a sheltered place to make camp for the night. They needed to be away from the General and his forces but still close enough in case Aldan—or Badaar, should he have somehow survived—came looking for them.

Sugh returned with a much larger armful of wood than he'd expected. The pickings were slim in this frozen wasteland. Koland had traveled through here, as he had almost everywhere in the Empire, but never during High Winter. It was an altogether different place at this time of year.

"Is this enough, do you think?" Sugh dumped the wood into the pile he and Koland had already accumulated.

"If we keep the fire small, it should last the night." Koland used one of the sticks to stir the blaze.

Sugh stretched. "If you do not mind, I think I will get a little sleep myself."

Koland nodded. "I'll stay up for now." He pointed up. "And Swift Claw is there."

Sugh chuckled. "I do not think anything will get past his eyesight. Very amazing, these beastmen."

"Yes." Koland watched as Sugh made a place for himself on the ground, separate from where the two girls lay already asleep. They were close to the fire and to each other, getting every bit of warmth they could find.

Kekeen had fallen asleep almost right away. And that troubled Koland. She'd been through a lot in the past few hours, especially emotionally; exhaustion would be natural. He felt that himself. But something bothered him. Something, or rather someone, was missing.

Zektel.

The chaos lord had been about to send the blood-wraith into Kekeen before Aldan took him into the Throat. But what happened to the wraith after that? Other wraiths had emerged, such as the one that took Duurald. So where had Zektel gone? He recalled every word spoken in the cave, but nothing gave evidence to her location.

Koland was reasonably certain he remained wraith-free. He still controlled himself and detected no other presence… though he supposed a wraith could lie dormant. It seemed Zektel had done so with Aldan for years. But with their master released, the wraiths no longer had reason to be subtle. They were seizing control of everyone.

He watched Sugh close his eyes. The big man came with them. If he were under Zektel's control, he could have stopped or killed them all. Koland couldn't think of any reason why he wouldn't have.

The same applied to Swift Claw, though perhaps even more so. The beastman claimed he could feel Aldan's presence down below somewhere. And Koland wasn't even sure beastmen could be possessed.

He stared glanced to his right at the most unlikely member of their group: the Ghamba Lam. The priest stared into the fire without blinking. He had the haunted look of a man who'd lost everything. He could have been possessed, but then why come with them? His only value lay in his leadership over the blood-priests. It made no sense to take control of him and then run away from his power.

That left the two girls. He looked across the fire at their sleeping forms. Qara and Kekeen. It could be either of them.

But Qara had led them through the tunnel and opened the hidden door for their escape. Would Zektel do that?

Koland's eyes settled on his daughter. A chill swept through him that didn't come from the air around them.

Suirel's last command. Had Zektel followed it?

For more information on Clanless & his world,
upcoming books and more,
visit timfrankovich.com

(Sign up for the newsletter and
you'll get access to free short stories)

If you enjoyed this book, please post a review on Amazon,
Goodreads, B&N, or wherever you find books!
There's no better way to spread the word.

On the Day the Sun Surrendered

Lyrics & theme by Tim Frankovich. Musical notation by Bradford Eide.

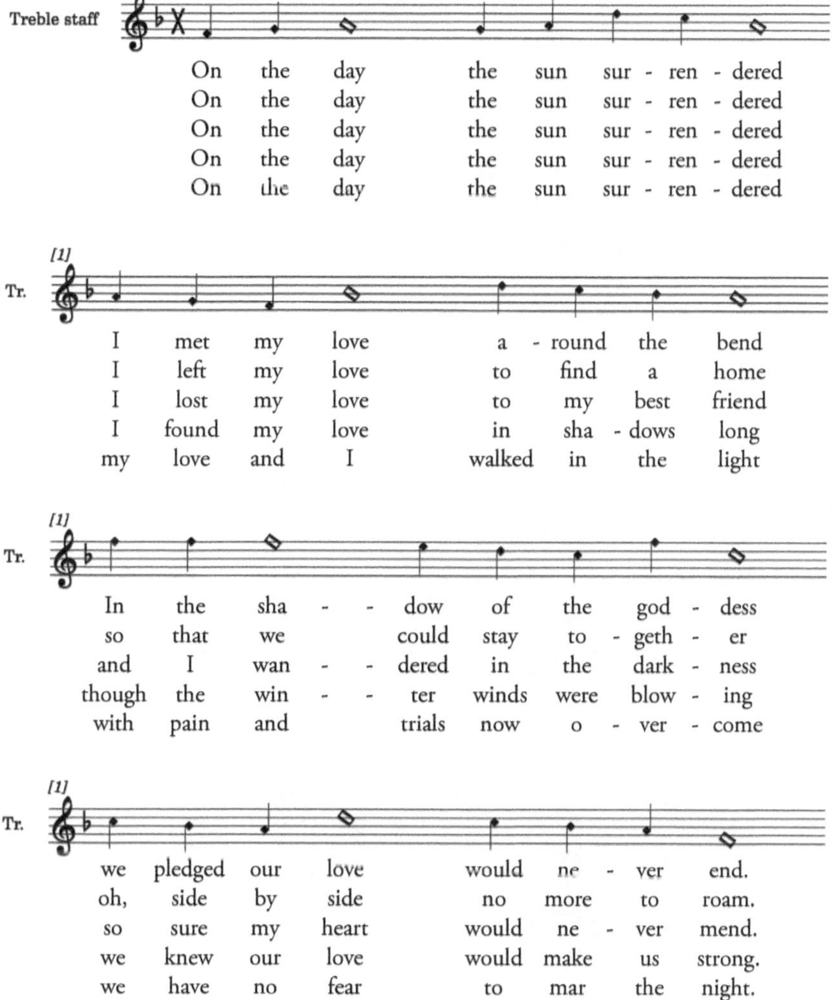

Clans of the Sar Empire
(This includes spoilers for the end of *Wolf Chosen*.)

The Sar Empire consists of twelve clans of various levels of power and influence.

Clan Shukan - One of the four most powerful clans, vying for power within the capital. The Hawk King comes from this clan, which gives them the greatest prestige. They also have a great deal of influence over the priesthood. Owns a large portion of the city.
Blood-magic: Life extension

Clan Ghutalta - Second of the most powerful clans. Controls most of the banking system within the capital, and has significant influence over the priesthood.
Blood-magic: Duplicates other blood-magics

Clan Kurav - Third of the most powerful clans. Has arrangements with many smaller clans to bring in their goods, thus controls much of the market within the capital.
Blood-magic: Healing

Clan Torov - Fourth of the most powerful clans. Owns the largest portion of the city, and has bits of control throughout everything. Diversifies their influence, but is always scheming to increase it.
Blood-magic: Voice

Clan Zavi - Their richest family owns a mansion in the capital, but their primary influence is over the harbor city and the shipping industry.
Blood-magic: Speed

Clan Shasin - While they only have small influence over the priesthood in the capital, this clan virtually controls religion in most of the other cities and quite a few clanholds.
Blood-magic: Accelerates thought

Clan Dendsu - Richest members own a couple of large homes in the capital and another city. But they control the largest amount of farmland in the country, via several clanholds.
Blood-magic: Heat (and light)

Clan Dalbai - Operates the arenas in all of the cities. (Shares capital city arena management with Clan Torov.) Has some influence within the priesthood to help them find new gladiators.
Blood-magic: Endurance

Clan Berge - Military-focused. Highest officers are all from this clan. Also maintains a very large blacksmith guild throughout the land.
Blood-magic: Strength

Clan Tokuur - The low clans, agricultural, mostly live in clanholds.
Blood-magic: Drains strength, but revitalizes blood

Clan Dariachin - The low clans, agricultural, mostly live in clanholds.
Blood-magic: Enhances hearing and vision

Clan Ghamkiin - The low clans, agricultural, mostly live in clanholds.
Blood-magic: Controls the movement of blood

Acknowledgements

I spent more time worldbuilding, plotting, consulting experts, and otherwise preparing for *The Certainty of Blood* than I had any book so far. So when I started work on the sequel, I felt a bit trepidatious. Had my preparation for the first book been enough for the second as well, or would I have to spend a ton of time just getting ready to write?

Thankfully, my preparations were enough… mostly. But even with that, I think I struggled over this book more than any others. Even as I wrote the first few chapters, I didn't know how it would end. I knew what the third book of this trilogy (yes, I said trilogy) would involve, but not how I would get there. I struggled. A lot.

Part of the challenge was that I believed *The Certainty of Blood* was the best thing I'd ever written, so a sequel had to be worthy of it. More than that, I knew it needed to be a solid story in itself, not just another day in the life of Clanless. More of *The Empire Strikes Back*, less of *Indiana Jones and the Temple of Doom*.

I agonized way too much over obvious things. Was it okay to start telling some of the story from Kekeen's point of view? I had to. It would be stupid to just have her tell Clanless everything that happened so that I could keep it only from his viewpoint. Plus, she needed to grow as a character herself. Would it feel cheap to have Clanless back in the arena for a while? No, it's a vital and logical part of the story. And so on.

What do I do with Bain? And how do I introduce the "dark lord" style character that I've been hinting at from page one of the first book? Oh. By now, you know the answer to that.

I still owe a lot to the people who helped with the first book. Dr. Sonny White of the Limitless Space Institute and NASA Flight Engineer Kjell Lindgren provided the basis for the science of this world, and their words continue to resonate throughout every location and seasonal change. Anything that doesn't fit with the science is my own wacky imagination intruding. They didn't suggest prehistoric animals, for example.

Dinosaurs are just cool, and I can include them in my books if I want to.

Thanks as always to the beta readers: Allen Perkins, Stephen Tallman, and Ben Stringer ("I'm a beta reader than you!"). Thanks to all the writers in the Apex Writing Group, who continue to motivate me to keep going.

The story of Clanless and his supporting cast is becoming exactly what I envisioned in the beginning… no, it's becoming more than that. I'm grateful for all those who are on this journey with him, and I'm excited to start work on the conclusion. It will be epic.

About the Author

Tim Frankovich has been exploring fantastic worlds since third grade, when he cut up a grocery sack and drew a Godzilla-meets-superheroes story. Since then, he's gotten a little bit better at the writing part (not so much with the drawing).

His goal as a writer is to transport readers to another world, make them care deeply about characters in dire situations, and guide them deeply into life itself.

At the moment, he is suitably conscious somewhere in Texas with his beloved wife, awesome kids, and a fool of a pup named Pippin.

9 798990 454002